PLUM TEA
CRAZY

PLUM TEA CRAZY

Tea Shop Mystery #19

LAURA CHILDS

BERKLEY PRIME CRIME
New York

BERKLEY PRIME CRIME
Published by Berkley
An imprint of Penguin Random House LLC
375 Hudson Street, New York, New York 10014

Library of Congress Cataloging-in-Publication Data

Names: Childs, Laura, author.
Title: Plum tea crazy / Laura Childs.
Description: First edition. | New York : Berkley Prime Crime, 2018. | Series:
A tea shop mystery ; 19
Identifiers: LCCN 2017042055| ISBN 9780451489609 (hardcover) |
ISBN 9780451489623 (ebook)
Subjects: LCSH: Browning, Theodosia (Fictitious character)—Fiction. | Women
detectives—South Carolina—Charleston—Fiction. |
Murder—Investigation—Fiction. | BISAC: FICTION / Mystery & Detective /
Women Sleuths. | GSAFD: Mystery fiction.
Classification: LCC PS3603.H56 P58 2018 | DDC 813/.6—dc23
LC record available at https://lccn.loc.gov/2017042055

First Edition: March 2018

Printed in the United States of America
1   3   5   7   9   10   8   6   4   2

Cover art by Stephanie Henderson
Cover design by Annette DeFex

ACKNOWLEDGMENTS

A special thank-you to Sam, Tom, Grace, Roxanne, Bob, Jennie, and all the amazing people at Berkley Prime Crime and Penguin Random House who handle editing, design, publicity, copywriting, social media, bookstore sales, gift sales, production, and shipping. Heartfelt thanks as well to all the tea lovers, tea shop owners, bookshop folks, librarians, reviewers, magazine editors and writers, websites, broadcasters, and bloggers who have enjoyed the Tea Shop Mysteries and helped spread the word. You make this all possible!

And I am forever grateful to you, my dear readers, who have embraced Theodosia, Drayton, Haley, Earl Grey, and the rest of the tea shop gang (even crusty Timothy and a slightly addled Delaine) as family. Thank you so much and I pledge to bring you many more Tea Shop Mysteries!

1

Tall sailing ships, their masts and sails outlined with glowing white lights, ghosted across Charleston Harbor in a glittering parade. Canvas snapped, wooden hulls creaked and rocked, and an enormous crowd of onlookers, completely galvanized by this amazing spectacle, let loose shrieks of joy.

"This is fantastic," Theodosia Browning said as she lifted a hand to her face to block out a sliver of ambient light. "I've never seen anything like it."

"Magnificent," Drayton Conneley declared. "There hasn't been this much razzle-dazzle since the Union shelled Fort Sumter back in 1861."

It was the night of the Gaslights and Galleons Parade. Two dozen tall ships had sailed here from all points of the globe—Britain, France, South America, even Singapore—to dazzle the thousands of people who had gathered in White Point Garden on the shell-strewn banks of Charleston's famed Battery. Of course, Theodosia and Drayton, as invited guests of Timothy

Neville, were thrilled with their perch high up on the third floor widow's walk that graced their friend's Archdale Street mansion.

"Wouldn't you love to be sailing on one of those ships right now?" Theodosia asked Drayton in a dreamy voice. Running the Indigo Tea Shop was her number one passion, but sailing wasn't far behind. She was in heaven when she was out on the water, the wind snapping her riot of auburn hair into long streamers and the salt air making her blue eyes sparkle and lending her fair complexion a soft glow as if lit by a saint's candle.

But Drayton looked absolutely horrified as he answered. "Me? On a sailing ship? Absolutely not. Don't you know by now that I'm a confirmed landlubber?"

"What if you were magically transported to a clipper ship?" Theodosia favored him with a wry grin. "One of the early ships tasked with transporting bales of wonderful black tea from China to England?"

"Say, now," Drayton said, taking a step back from the railing. "That's not quite playing fair. You're appealing to my weakness for tea and history."

Drayton was sixty-something, the portrait of a proper Southern gentleman with his tweeds, bow ties, grayed hair, and regal bearing. He was also the best tea sommelier Theodosia had ever encountered. Drayton was so well schooled in the art of tea and tea blending that she considered herself fortunate to have wooed him away from his teaching post at Johnson & Wales culinary school to work side-by-side with her at the Indigo Tea Shop. They'd been together for a half dozen years now, always refining their tea menu, upgrading the décor of the charming Church Street tea shop, and catering countless tea parties.

Tonight was one of those parties. Well, sort of.

A recent spate of warm spring weather had caused native plum trees to explode in a riot of purple glory all over the Historic District. In a nod to this auspicious occasion, Theodosia had brought along a wicker hamper heaped with plum and black currant scones. Drayton's contribution was a special plum-flavored Ceylonese black tea that he'd custom blended. These offerings were in addition to the elegant light supper buffet that Timothy had laid out in the downstairs dining room for his two dozen guests.

"Getting chilly," Theodosia said, pulling her pink cashmere wrap tight around her shoulders. She was outdoorsy and loved to jog, sail, and hike. Delighted in breezing around the low country with the hardtop off her Jeep, but tonight had turned downright cold.

"But nobody's leaving," Drayton pointed out. They were standing at one end of the widow's walk, a long, narrow wooden walkway that ran the length of the home's roofline. All along the walkway, people were spread out, conversing quietly in small groups, eagerly watching the ships as they bobbed and wheeled in the harbor. It was difficult to see who these other guests were up here, since the night sky was so black and moonless and Theodosia and Drayton had arrived a little late to the party. Too late to be properly introduced. In any case, all the folks up top had to concentrate on watching their step, since the decorative wrought-iron railing that bordered the widow's walk was barely three feet high.

"Perhaps we should go in," Drayton suggested. "Warm up and enjoy some light supper along with Timothy's hospitality." He glanced at his watch, an antique Piaget, and frowned. "It's gotten so dark I can't quite make out the time."

Theodosia glanced sideways at St. Sebastian's, the nearest neighborhood church in a city so filled with churches it had been dubbed the Holy City. A lighted clock in a red brick steeple shone the current time. "It's just nine o'clock," she said.

"Still, tomorrow is a workday," Drayton said. "You know how I like to get a jump on Mondays."

"I hear you," Theodosia said. "Plus, we've got . . ."

BOOM!

A thunderous roar pierced the night, frightening onlookers and rattling windows in homes up and down the block.

Theodosia clapped a hand to her chest. "What was that?"

"Cannon volleys," Drayton said. "From two of the ships in the harbor, I'd guess."

Theodosia peered through the still mostly bare treetops. "Let's hope they don't do it—"

BA-BOOM!

"—again," she finished.

But this time the cannons' roar was followed by a high-pitched scream.

"Help!" came a woman's cry from the far end of the widow's walk. "He's been shot!"

"What?" Drayton said, startled.

A second scream rose up, a terrified yelp that quickly morphed into an anguished and frantic shriek, like steel wheels grinding against hot metal rails.

Then came a terrifically loud thumping, like the sound a flat tire makes when it *whap whap whap*s against pavement. Except this was no flat tire. This was . . .

"Someone's fallen!" a man's voice bellowed. This was followed by a dozen voices rising in a collective, jangled outcry.

Theodosia spun quickly and peered down over the edge of the roof. Off to her right, twirling head over teakettle, a man was hurtling down the sloped slate roof of Timothy's house as if he were zipping down a child's slide.

"Help!" the falling man cried as he flailed and fought for handholds. His pleading, anguished note pierced the darkness. Pierced Theodosia's heart as well.

"Dear Lord!" Theodosia cried. She hoped the poor man would find something, anything, to break his fall.

"This is dreadful," Drayton said with a sharp intake of breath.

They watched helplessly as the man flopped and tumbled, then landed in a deep V that formed one of the eaves in the expansive roof. His arms flew out, beating wildly, as his fingers scrabbled desperately to find something to grasp. But he was moving too fast to completely arrest his fall and immediately catapulted down another few feet, heading for a decorative balcony. The man floundered again, making a grab for a balustrade to halt his terrible descent. His fingers grazed it by a mere inch. Then his body torqued grotesquely as he banged his forehead against the top of a stone window pediment and a thin mist sprayed out in slow motion. Blood.

Theodosia was in shock. It was as if the poor man had been caught in a hellish pinball machine, helplessly spinning and bouncing his way downward.

Theodosia felt Drayton's hand grab her shoulder in a death grip as they watched the man take a final, sharp tumble and then disappear into darkness.

"Was he really shot?" Drayton asked, his voice hoarse and shaking. "By the cannon? Or did he fall?"

But Theodosia had already bolted past Drayton and was dashing for the doorway.

"Does anybody have a phone?" she cried out. "Someone call an ambulance right now! Please!"

And then Theodosia was running, practically stumbling, down a flight of steps, the thick Oriental carpet whisper soft under her fast-moving feet. She hit the second floor landing, spun past a man and woman who stared at her with quizzical expressions, and then rushed down a wider stairway to hit the first floor landing. From there she was pounding down a long hallway past a parade of Timothy Neville's Huguenot ancestors, all memorialized in gleaming oil portraits and staring down at her with faintly disapproving looks.

Out the front door she ran, across the broad piazza, down the front steps, and around the side of the house into Timothy's garden. It was an elaborate Asian garden replete with reflecting pool, thickets of bamboo, statuary, and pattering fountains.

Maybe the poor man hadn't been fatally wounded at all, Theodosia reasoned. Maybe he'd simply lost his footing, tumbled down, and somehow landed in Timothy's reflecting pool. That was her one hopeful thought. That he was spitting water right now, shaking his head, moaning over a broken arm or smashed collarbone. He'd need an ambulance, of course. And a wild-lights-and-siren trip to the emergency room. But perhaps there was still hope. There was always hope . . . wasn't there?

But when Theodosia reached the backyard, she slid to a stop and gasped in shock. The poor man had landed directly on top of the antique wrought-iron fence that encircled Timothy's property. Reeling from such a frightful sight, Theodosia put a hand to her mouth and stifled a groan. Like a carefully collected insect held in place by a pin, the man was grotesquely impaled upon the sharply pointed fleur-de-lis spikes that topped the old fence.

Tiptoeing closer, drawn almost hypnotically to this gruesome tableau, Theodosia stared at the hapless man. His eyes were open wide in surprise and his white shirt was splattered with blood. Worst of all, one of the razor-sharp points of the fence had been driven clean through his neck.

2

"An accident," a gruff voice behind Theodosia said.

"You think live ammunition from a cannon could reach this far?" another voice asked.

"No, no, he clearly fell," another man cried.

Theodosia drew a deep breath and spun around. A dozen people were bunched up right behind her, staring at the body in collective wide-eyed shock. She supposed these people must have followed her out of the house, maybe even stampeding along behind her. She hadn't heard them, so intent had she been, so hopeful that the poor man might have landed on something soft and bouncy. But here they were, the proverbial gang of gawkers drawn to the scene of this terrible accident.

"Is he breathing?" a woman asked. She sounded slightly more curious than stunned.

The question startled Theodosia. Was it possible to fall three stories, sustain a piercing neck injury, and still be alive?

She didn't think so. Still . . . somebody should check the poor man's pulse and respiration.

"Let me through, let me through!" Timothy Neville's querulous voice rose up through the crowd. Then the onlookers slowly parted as their host elbowed his way through, looking both miserable and terrified.

Theodosia turned toward Timothy and said, "I don't think there's any hope."

Timothy Neville was the octogenarian director of the Heritage Society, a multimillionaire, and old guard Charlestonite. He lived the life of a plutocrat and was known to be dictatorial and terse. Under his crusty outer shell, however, Timothy possessed a kind heart. Right now, he looked devastated by the words Theodosia had just uttered. But he was bound and determined to see for himself.

With trepidation, Timothy approached the body that lay tangled upon his fence. "Carson," he said, his voice an anguished note.

"That's Carson Lanier, the banker," somebody in the crowd said in a hushed whisper.

Timothy reached a tentative hand out and lightly touched the fallen man on the side of his neck. At his pulse point.

Theodosia was aware of Timothy's distress and somber expression, caught as he was in the yellow light that spilled from a nearby parlor window. She thought Timothy looked old— older and sadder than she'd ever seen him.

"Anything?" she asked.

Timothy drew his hand back as he shook his head in sorrow. "I'm afraid he's gone."

One look told her it was all over for Lanier. The lights had winked out, there was nobody home. Permanently.

"He's gone?" Drayton called out, as he, too, pushed his way through the crowd.

"Just bled out too fast, I guess," Timothy said. "Look there." He pointed to a dark splotch on the grass, directly below the body.

Theodosia leaned forward to look. "If that's blood, I don't think it came from this man's neck."

"What?" Timothy said a little too loudly.

"Maybe he really was shot," Theodosia said. She didn't think the cannons had been firing live ammunition; then again, you never know. She reached down and touched an index finger to the wetness that had dripped onto the grass below him. "This is blood, all right," she said. It was hot and sticky. Fresh. "But I don't think it came from . . ." She was suddenly, dangerously curious. "Here . . . can someone help lift him up a notch? I think he must have sustained a far more mortal wound somewhere else."

"Should you be moving him?" a man asked.

"I'm not leaving Carson like *this*," Timothy said. "Like a turkey on a spit."

Timothy, Drayton, and two other pairs of hands reached out and gently lifted Carson Lanier up about four inches. Theodosia leaned sideways and peered at the man's chest.

"Holy crap," was all she said.

Timothy blanched white. "Is there a more serious wound?" Then his voice faltered and he began shaking, suddenly looking as if he was about to collapse. "Oh my goodness," he groaned. "This . . . this is all my fault." He touched a trembling hand to his narrow chest. "If I hadn't invited guests over . . . let them go up top." He gasped. "That cannon fire. Who knew it was *live?*"

"No, no," Theodosia said hastily, her voice rising in alarm. "There's something else going on with him. Try to raise him up again, will you? This time, see if you can turn him ever so slightly so we can get a better look." She glanced into the crowd. "Does anyone have a flashlight I could use? Or a cell phone with a flash?"

"Here," a woman said, punching on her flash and handing over her phone to Theodosia.

The men struggled and strained with Lanier's body again, lifting it higher and turning it at an awkward angle so Theodosia could run the wavering light up and down the front of him. When she got to the area just above Lanier's belt buckle, she literally gasped out loud.

"Please hurry," Drayton barked. "We can't hold him forever."

"You can let him down," Theodosia said.

"What's wrong?" Timothy asked. His voice was high and thready, as if he was having difficulty breathing. "What did you see?"

Theodosia pushed a hank of curly hair away from her face. "There's something stuck in him."

"What do you mean *stuck* in him?" Timothy asked.

"I don't know for sure." Now it was Theodosia's turn to sound agitated. "But I think . . . I think he's been shot with some kind of arrow."

The four men who'd held up the dead man jumped back collectively.

"Impossible," Drayton said. "What you saw must be a part of the fence. A piece that broke off."

"What are you trying to tell us?" Timothy asked in an old man's squawky voice.

"It looked more like a metal arrow," Theodosia said. "Smaller and shorter than a regular hunting arrow. Like what you might call . . . a quarrel?" Her mind was spinning like a runaway centrifuge. "I think Lanier's been shot, all right, but not by any cannon fire."

Timothy's eyes went wild. "Someone *shot* Carson Lanier with an arrow? Up there on the widow's walk?" His mouth gaped open. Then, in an almost whisper, "Who would do that?"

"How about his wife?" someone muttered from far back in the crowd.

Timothy focused intently on Theodosia. "He didn't just lose his balance? Someone *shot* him?"

"I think maybe . . ." Theodosia hesitated. The reality of the situation was almost too much for her to accept. And yet . . . here it was. A dead man stretched out in front of her. Blinking and swallowing hard, she tipped her head back to stare up at the widow's walk. A turret stood out against the purple night sky; an ornate balustrade loomed in profile. She wasn't exactly sure what she was looking for. All she could see was the slightly sinister silhouette of Timothy's Italianate mansion.

And then, as if slowly connecting the dots, Theodosia turned her gaze to the oversized building that was directly next door. The Stagwood Inn, one of several B and Bs that had proliferated in the Historic District over the past few years.

Way up on the third floor, a filmy curtain wavered in an open window. A shadow flitted almost imperceptibly from left to right across it and then disappeared.

"There," Theodosia yelped. "Someone's up there."

"Up in the attic?" Drayton asked.

"This was no accident!" Theodosia cried. And with her words still hanging in the air, she spun and took off running again.

3

This time Drayton was right behind her, his feet slapping the pavement, his breath coming in short gasps.

"Someone shot Lanier," Theodosia cried over her shoulder as they dashed up the front walk leading to the Stagwood Inn. "Maybe from a third floor window. The curtain was fluttering in the wind and I think someone was up there."

"That doesn't mean it was the shooter," Drayton said as they pounded up the stairs and across the wide front porch, its fanciful posts curling with ivy. "It could have been anyone peering down. A guest, perhaps."

"Got to check it out," Theodosia panted. She pushed open the front door with so much force that it banged hard against the wall, rattling the pictures and making such a terrible racket that it startled the young woman who was standing behind the reception desk.

"Um . . . checking in?" the woman asked with a nervous

smile. She was young, early twenties, with long brown hair and trendy wood-frame glasses.

"Not quite," Theodosia said in a sharp voice. She glanced around the Stagwood Inn's lobby, trying to see past the leather sofas, antler lamps, and potted banana plants, until she finally spotted a staircase that led upstairs. "C'mon, Drayton, it's this way!"

Theodosia and Drayton pounded across the lobby and up the wooden staircase like a stampede of wild buffalo, clattering loudly, not worrying whom they might disturb. When they reached the second floor landing, they slid to a stop. The staircase continued on up to the third floor, as did a back staircase that stood at the far end of a long carpeted hallway.

"Which one?" Drayton asked.

Theodosia hesitated. She could hear footsteps moving overhead, so she had to make a quick decision. "Back stairway," she said.

Theodosia and Drayton raced down a hallway, all brass sconces and dark floral wallpaper, past a number of suites with designated names on the doors. The Honeymoon Suite, the Velvet Victorian Suite, the Hideaway Suite. When they reached the end of the hallway, they hurried up the narrow back stairway, hooked a right at a tiny landing, and continued on up. They hesitated when they reached the third floor. The lighting was extremely dim up here, the ceiling low and slightly claustrophobic. There appeared to be only two suites occupying this floor. Each suite had a door that was painted dark green and rounded at the top, looking as if it might lead to a hobbit hole.

Theodosia tried to concentrate and get her bearings. If Timothy's home was on her left, then the shadow in the window had to be . . .

"You can't just barge into these rooms," Drayton cautioned.

His words slowed Theodosia for all of two seconds. Then she grasped the doorknob on her left and pushed her way into the room marked TREETOP SUITE.

The room was black as pitch.

Theodosia moved slowly, taking two, then three steps, allowing her eyes to become accustomed to the gloom.

If there's someone hiding in here . . . well, that could be very bad, she thought to herself. *I've got no weapon and there's only Drayton as my backup.*

Still, Theodosia continued to tiptoe forward. In the low light she could see a sleigh bed on her right, a dresser and small club chair just to her left.

"Theodosia," came Drayton's voice from behind her. He sounded frightened. "Do you see anything?"

"There's a balcony just ahead," she whispered. What she'd initially thought was a window with a filmy curtain appeared to be a sliding glass door. So anyone could have been standing out there. "I want to—"

"Don't!" Drayton hissed. "Somebody could still be out there. If they're armed and they came bursting in at us, what am I supposed to do? Assault them with my pocket watch?"

Theodosia reached a hand out and grasped a glass cat statue off the dresser. It wasn't exactly a MAC-10, but it might do in a pinch.

"I'm just going to take a tiny peek," she said. Her breathing was hyped from all her running, and her heart fluttered inside her chest like a wounded bird. But she was determined to see if someone was hiding on that balcony. After all, she was pretty sure it looked directly out at Timothy's house. If a shooter, or whom she thought of as the archer, had been standing there . . .

WHAM!

Theodosia's shoulders jerked up to her ears and she whirled around suddenly. "What was that?"

"Somebody just slammed the door on us!" Drayton cried.

Together, Theodosia and Drayton raced to the door, stumbling over each other in the dark, arms in a tangle as their hands struggled to pull open the door.

When the door flew open they popped out into the hallway.

"Nobody here," Drayton said. He looked relieved.

Loud footfalls sounded on the front stairs. Somebody was pounding down the steps as if their very life depended on it!

"But there was!" Theodosia cried. "C'mon, this way." She took off like a shot, still grasping the cat statue as she raced down the stairs. But every time she whipped around a tight corner, the person she was chasing was just that much ahead of her. It felt like she could catch his shadow but not his actual person!

Gotta go faster, she told herself.

Theodosia hit the second floor landing, glanced quickly down the long hallway, and saw someone slide around a corner and disappear.

"Stop!" Theodosia yelled out. But of course they didn't.

She raced the length of the hallway, spun left, and found herself rushing down a set of linoleum-covered stairs.

Frantic footfalls just ahead of her clattered like a horse's hooves against cobblestones.

This must lead down to the kitchen or one of the breakfast parlors, Theodosia decided. *So maybe there's a chance I can corner them!*

Head down, jaw tensed, placing every foot just so, Theodosia spun around a final turn. But the narrow pie-shaped stairs created a crooked angle here, causing her right foot to catch on the sharp edge of a step. She stumbled, dipped down onto one knee, and grasped wildly for the wooden banister. Her hand found purchase just in time to save herself from a nasty, bone-rattling fall.

Drawing a shaky breath, Theodosia pulled herself to her feet, only to have a large, dark shadow loom up in front of her.

"No!" she cried. She raised the cat statue high above her head, prepared to defend herself. The dark figure wavered slightly, but didn't budge an inch.

"Don't," the figure growled. He was backlit, whoever he was, which meant Theodosia was unable to make out his face. But she wasn't about to take any chances.

Theodosia's arm fairly twitched, ready to smash the glass cat against the man's head if it came to that, if he made a threatening move. But this man, whoever he was, had the reflexes of a ninja warrior! Before she could do anything, his hand shot out to grab her arm, pinching it hard. Wincing from the pain, Theodosia watched helplessly as the cat statue slipped from her grasp, tumbled to the floor, and exploded like a live grenade.

"Aggh!" she cried out, half in anger, half in fear.

The figure wavered again. "Theodosia?"

What? Theodosia gasped. There was something deeply familiar about that low, rumbling voice. And then her instincts kicked in big-time and she said, "Tidwell? Detective Tidwell, is that you?" And then his face finally swam into focus for her.

It was him, of course. Looking disgruntled, angry, and slightly confused.

"What are you doing here?" Theodosia blurted out.

Tidwell stared at her with beady, bright eyes. "The question is, what are *you* doing here?" Burt Tidwell was a burly bear of a man, the head of Charleston Police Department's Robbery-Homicide Division. Brilliant, shrewd, and driven, he was not one to suffer fools lightly.

"I was chasing . . . someone," Theodosia said.

Tidwell moved back a step and looked around. "I see no one."

"There was someone here. Running down these steps. I think that . . ."

"Yes, I've just come from there," Tidwell said. He cocked his strange bullet-shaped head at her. "It seems you moved the body. Instigated it, in fact."

"We had to see if the man was still alive," Theodosia said. "Still breathing." That wasn't exactly true and, from the look on Tidwell's face, he knew it wasn't exactly true.

But all Tidwell said was, "Come."

Detective Tidwell, Theodosia, and Drayton walked back toward Timothy Neville's home.

"How did you know we were at the Stagwood Inn?" Theodosia asked Tidwell.

Tidwell gave a perfunctory smile. "When I arrived, Timothy informed me that you so helpfully ran over to investigate." The words *helpfully* and *investigate* rolled off his tongue as if he were talking about camel dung.

"That's because we saw something," Theodosia protested. "Up in the third floor window. Just like I told you." She'd already explained her efforts to him and was frustrated that he wasn't taking her seriously. Now, as they approached Timothy's backyard, she could see two police cruisers and an ambulance parked in the alley. The crowd was still there, too, but they'd been pushed back and some black-and-yellow crime scene tape had been strung in an effort to keep the gawkers in check.

Tidwell gazed at the body, still hung up on the fence, and murmured a single word. "Strange."

"He fell," someone in the crowd said.

Tidwell descended on the man like an avenging angel. "Did you see him fall?" he asked.

Cowed, the man shook his head. "No," he said in a small voice.

"Then perhaps Mr. Lanier was pushed." Tidwell's words hung in the air like a cartoon word bubble. "Or, better yet, perhaps you should stay out of it."

The crowd around them fell silent. Now the ball was clearly in Theodosia's court. "He wasn't pushed, he was shot," she said.

Tidwell's furry eyebrows arched up. "Excuse me?"

"With an arrow," Theodosia said. "Well . . . you can clearly see that he bled profusely and that the puddle is not from the finial that ripped through his neck."

"Do we know who this poor soul is?" Tidwell asked. "Does he have a name? Do we have identification on him?"

"He's one of my guests," Timothy said, stepping forward. "Carson Lanier. He is . . . he was . . . a friend." Timothy looked suddenly faint at having to speak of Lanier in the past tense.

"Here, now," Drayton said, ever mindful that Timothy was fairly advanced in age. "Perhaps you should go inside and sit down."

Timothy waved a hand. "I'm fine right here," he shot back in a cranky tone. "Well, not fine. But . . . you know."

Five minutes later, the crime scene team arrived in a shiny black van. They jumped out and set to work. Technicians set up light stanchions, took photos, then bagged Lanier's head and hands. Theodosia was thankful she no longer had to stare at the man's shocked expression.

When they'd taken enough evidence, they lifted him down off the fence.

"There's some kind of arrow in him," one of the techs mumbled.

"I've never seen an arrow like that," a second one responded.

Tidwell stepped closer and watched as they slid Lanier's body into a black plastic bag that lay atop a metal gurney.

"My guess was a quarrel," Theodosia said, trying to edge closer.

"Possibly," Tidwell said, squinting. "From a pistol crossbow."

"What's that?" she asked.

"A smaller-type crossbow that looks as if it's mounted on a pistol grip," Tidwell said.

"Who makes that kind of weapon?"

"More important is who shot it," Tidwell said, glancing up, for the first time, at the third floor window of the Stagwood Inn. "And where it was shot from."

Theodosia's eyes searched the crowd of lookie-loos who continued to press forward. It was an interesting study in human nature. People are terrified of death, yet they're fascinated by it, too. "What are you going to do now?" Theodosia asked Tidwell.

"Get the names and addresses of everyone involved here," Tidwell said. "From up on Mr. Neville's roof as well as in the neighborhood."

"And then what?" Theodosia asked.

There was a distinct zipping sound as one of the techs closed the body bag.

Tidwell's upper lip curled. "Then I shall find the killer."

4

❦

Kettles steamed, candles flickered, and the aroma of sweet Moroccan mint tea and malty Assam tea permeated the Indigo Tea Shop. It was Monday morning and Drayton and Theodosia were standing at the front counter brewing tea as they whispered and strategized on how best to tell Haley about the terrible accident last night.

"We must break it to her gently," Drayton said, plucking at an invisible piece of lint on his tweed jacket. "You know what a sensitive soul Haley is."

"She can be a tough enough cookie when she wants to be," Theodosia said. Haley Parker was their chef, baker, and the third leg in their tea shop troika. Though she was still in her early twenties, Haley ran the kitchen like a marine drill sergeant. Thus, suppliers delivered orders on time, vegetables were always just-picked fresh, and nobody (nobody!) ever got away with passing off mushy strawberries or peaches.

"You're the boss," Drayton said to Theodosia. "So it falls upon your capable shoulders to break the awful news to her."

"Break the news?" Haley said. She strolled out of the kitchen rattling the main section of the Charleston *Post and Courier.* "You're too late. I already know what happened at Timothy's place last night." She shook her head and her long blond hair swished around her shoulders like a golden curtain while her pert nose pulled into a wrinkle. "And from the gist of this lead story, it wasn't exactly an accident. It was murder."

"You don't have to make it sound so salacious," Drayton said.

"But wasn't it?" Haley replied. "I mean, a rich fat-cat banker shot right through the heart?"

"It wasn't his heart," Theodosia said.

"Oh," Haley said. "I guess bankers don't have hearts, then."

"This is nothing to joke about," Drayton said. "It was really quite horrible."

Haley nodded. "The paper mentioned the part about landing on the fence, too. And even named the man who constructed the fence."

"Philip Simmons," Drayton said. "Who was a very famous artisan around these parts."

"You two are making a name for yourselves as well," Haley said. "You're forever getting tangled up in these unsavory crimes."

"We certainly are not," Drayton said. He glanced at Theodosia, who was giving him a questioning look, and abruptly changed direction. "Well, we're not involved in *this* one, that's for sure."

Theodosia rolled her eyes. They'd been plenty involved last night when they were charging through the Stagwood Inn, looking for the shooter.

"Good to know," Haley said. "Because I get worried when you two crime stoppers chase all over Charleston trying to solve the latest murder."

"Haley, we don't do that," Theodosia said. "And we certainly won't get tangled up in this one." She gave Haley her warmest smile, all the while thinking, *Then again, you never know.*

Twenty minutes later, the tables were draped with white linen tablecloths, Drayton had set out their Royal Doulton teacups and saucers in the Arcadia pattern, the silver gleamed, and a fire crackled in the small stone fireplace in the corner. The walls were festooned with Theodosia's handmade grapevine wreaths decorated with teacups, and antique plates were propped on wooden shelves along with collectible cup and saucer sets. Haley had brought out a tray of fresh-baked cinnamon scones and banana muffins, and now those tasty treats were displayed in the glass pie saver that sat on the front counter.

"In case you hadn't noticed," Theodosia said to Drayton, "we've got a fairly busy week ahead of us."

Drayton reached up and grabbed a tin of silver tips tea from his floor-to-ceiling shelf of teas. "Not so bad," he said. "We've got . . . what? Delaine's Silk Road Fashion Show luncheon on Wednesday, the Tea Trolley stopping by Thursday, and then our Plum Blossom Tea on Friday."

"If the plum blossoms last that long," Theodosia said.

"That could be an issue," Drayton said. "Most of the Japanese plum trees are in full bloom right now, so we may have to pinch-hit with silk flowers."

"Then we should order from Floradora. They could get some in, no problem."

"Or," Drayton said, "the plum trees at the Featherbed House

might not have blossomed yet, so Angie would probably let us take some cuttings."

BAM. BAM. BAM.

Drayton glanced toward the front door. "Sounds as if someone is overly anxious for their morning cuppa."

Theodosia hurried to the door, peered through a wavering glass pane and said, "It's Delaine." Delaine Dish was the colorful, quixotic owner of Cotton Duck, one of Charleston's most elite boutiques.

"Uh oh," Drayton said. He generally found Delaine to be both a trial and a tribulation. She was one of those women that most men—and some women, too—considered *difficult*. Which, of course, was code for crazy as a loon.

"Come in, Delaine," Theodosia said, turning the lock and pulling open the door.

Delaine came barreling in as if a group of angry villagers were nipping at her heels, shaking torches and wielding pitchforks.

"I can't tell you how *glad* I was to miss all that horrid *excitement* last night!" she blurted out.

"Heavens," Drayton said, wiping out the interior of one of his prize blue-and-white teapots. "Does everyone know about the accident at Timothy's place?"

"Huh," Delaine snorted. "That was no accident. According to the *Post and Courier*, CNN, *Good Morning Charleston*, my Facebook news feed, and my Twitter feed, it was murder. Bloody blue murder." For some reason she looked rather pleased with herself. Then she turned and pointed a finger at Drayton. "And you were there." Her finger wavered until it refocused on Theodosia. "And so were you."

Drayton sighed. "And I suppose you want to hear all about it."

"Oh my, no," Delaine said. She was wearing a bright purple

skirt suit with an enormous jeweled bumblebee pin. "I intend to get my information from another source."

"Excuse me?" Theodosia said.

Delaine dropped her voice to a conspiratorial whisper. "I happen to be *very* well acquainted with the murdered man's wife."

"Carson Lanier's wife?" Theodosia said. "Someone mentioned her last night. After poor Mr. Lanier had fallen, someone in the crowd muttered something about her." Theodosia's brows pinched together. "As I recall, there was an accusation of her being the killer."

"Probably because the Laniers are . . . well, they *were* . . . in the throes of a really nasty divorce," Delaine said.

Drayton looked suddenly interested. "A divorce? Are you sure?"

"My dear Drayton," Delaine said. "Sissy Lanier happens to be one of my very best customers. The woman is head over heels in love with my long, flowy skirts, and quite gaga for my French lingerie." Delaine's jewel box of a boutique sold elegant cashmeres and silks and supple leather bags, as well as imported sandals, French perfumes, and over-the-top costume jewelry.

"Wait . . . her name is Sissy?" Theodosia asked.

"Well, her given name is Susan, but Sissy was her sorority name. Which she prefers to use and so do I."

"Have you talked to your friend Sissy this morning?" Drayton asked. "She must be upset. I mean, if she was *married* to Carson, you'd think there'd still be some sort of bond."

"I haven't talked to her yet," Delaine said. "But I know there *isn't* any bond left between them, and I doubt she's been hanging crepe on her mirrors. She and Carson have been living apart for several months now and were this close to having their divorce finalized." She held her thumb and forefinger a quarter inch apart to demonstrate.

"But Sissy is still technically his wife," Theodosia said.

"Well, yes," Delaine said, bobbing her head. "I suppose she is."

"Legally she is," Theodosia said. A dark thought bubbled up in her brain. A woman in the throes of a nasty divorce . . . hoping she wouldn't have to settle for half? Or maybe less than half if Carson Lanier had engaged a really cutthroat lawyer? Could Sissy have had a hand in last night's murder? Could she have been the shooter? Or hired the shooter? Theodosia frowned and shook her head. Gracious, she was really letting her imagination run wild today. She tried to focus on what Delaine was chattering about now. Namely her Silk Road Fashion Show.

"Are you folks going to be ready to cater my luncheon on Wednesday?" Delaine asked. "Last time we talked, the menu was still somewhat iffy."

"Right," Theodosia said. "The menu."

"I have it," Drayton said. He pulled a card from the pocket of his apron and handed it to Theodosia, where it was immediately snatched away by Delaine.

"Let's see, now," Delaine said, squinting at the index card. "Oh yes, this all sounds quite lovely. Shrimp toast, egg rolls, blah blah blah." She looked up and said, "So the fashion show is slated to begin at eleven thirty and should run for about thirty minutes. Afterward, my salesladies and I need time to take orders from our guests and allow them to shop for a while. Which means you have to have the buffet table set up and ready to go no later than one o'clock."

"Not a problem," Theodosia said.

"It should be a fabulous event," Delaine said. "I'm bringing in professional models to show off my silk dresses to perfection. Plus, my event planner is working on some wonderful décor. We're going to make the shop and runway look very Chinese. You know, á la the Silk Road?"

"If you want to add a touch of Asia, you should talk to the woman who opened that new gallery just down the street from us," Drayton said.

Delaine's brows arched into twin question marks. "What new gallery would that be? And why haven't I heard of it?" Delaine considered herself the arbiter of all things fashionable and artistic in Charleston.

"The gallery's called Haiku Gallery," Drayton told her. "You know, after the type of Japanese poetry. Although now that I think about it, a name like that pretty much indicates their art and antiques are Japanese rather than Chinese."

Delaine fluttered a hand. "Doesn't matter. They grow those squiggly little silkworms in both China and Japan, don't they? Yes, I'm quite positive they do."

"Haiku Gallery is actually having their grand opening party tonight," Theodosia said. She was back behind the counter now, setting up a half dozen teapots for Drayton. "The owner, Alexis something, sent us an invitation last week."

Delaine did a double take followed by an exaggerated head bob. "A gallery opening? Of Asian art? Theo, I simply *must* attend."

"It's probably just a small party," Drayton said. "A few shop owners from the neighborhood. Brooke from Heart's Desire, Leigh from Cabbage Patch . . ."

But Delaine wasn't about to take no for an answer. If there were a League of Pushy Women, Delaine would be a designated chapter head. "Drayton, you don't seem to understand," she said. "I *have* to go. You know how much I adore Asian art."

"Fine," Theodosia shrugged. "Tag along with us, then." She figured one more guest at the party wouldn't make or break the evening.

Delaine pulled a bright red lipstick from her Chanel bag, smeared the tip across her enhanced and plumped lips, and said, "You know what? I believe I'll meet you there."

"Five minutes," Drayton said as he smoothed his long apron and adjusted his bow tie. "We have to open our door in five minutes."

Theodosia glanced around the tea room. Everything looked lovely and serene and she could hear Haley singing in the kitchen as she rattled pans, prepping for lunch already. Well, good.

"So, you think you can handle Delaine's tea by yourself?" Drayton asked.

"The tea isn't the problem," Theodosia said, giving him a slow wink. "Delaine's the tricky one."

"She is that."

"But if Haley has all the appetizers packed and ready to go and you pick out the perfect teas, then I think I can manage solo."

"So all we have to worry about is our Plum Blossom Tea on Friday," Drayton said.

Along with our day-to-day operations and the ugly murder that's hanging over our heads, Theodosia thought.

"I'm still thinking about décor for Friday," Drayton said slowly. Then, "You know, depending on how friendly the gallery people are tonight, perhaps we could borrow a few Japanese artifacts to give our tea shop a nice, authentic feel."

Theodosia smiled at him. "I think that's a lovely idea. I'll leave it to you to ingratiate yourself."

Business was brisk this Monday morning. Local shopkeepers dashed in and out, grabbing cups of tea to go, along with scones and muffins. A gang of tourists who had been poking around the supposedly haunted graveyard behind St. Phillip's Church came tumbling in for tea, and so did a dozen other folks. Theodosia moved efficiently among the tables, distributing small pots of tea, explaining brewing times, talking with her regulars, and delivering baked treats. Once Haley pulled a loaf of apple bread from the oven, that was also served piping hot with homemade honey butter.

In the midst of all these fine aromas and conversational buzz, Timothy Neville came strolling in. He was dressed in a navy jacket with splendid gold buttons, dove gray slacks, and a yellow Hermès tie that featured miniature keys. And though his outfit may have looked spiffy, his face betrayed deep sadness. His skin, stretched tight across his aging face, made every bone look like a knife blade.

"Timothy," Drayton said, glancing up from behind the counter.

Theodosia hurried to greet Timothy as well. "Would you like a table?" she asked. "Do you have a guest joining you?"

Timothy waved a hand. "No, no. No time for that. But it's most important I speak with both you and Drayton."

"Okaaaay," Theodosia said. They were right in the middle of morning tea, but Timothy looked awfully upset. Not as bad as last night, but still hovering on the edge of frayed nerves.

"What is it?" Drayton asked as Timothy leaned his elbows heavily on the wooden counter and Theodosia crowded in close.

"Concerning last night," Timothy said. "I sorely need your help." Now he was staring directly at Theodosia.

"You already have Detective Tidwell hot on the case," Theodosia said. She sensed a request in the making and wanted to cut it off. "He's tenacious and as good as it gets. For heaven's sake, the man heads the entire Robbery-Homicide Division at Charleston PD, he's ex-FBI . . . what more could you ask for?"

"But you were the one who spotted that open window last night," Timothy said. "You were the one who chased after Carson's assassin."

Theodosia shook her head. "I don't know if I did or not. I chased after *some*body, but it might not have been Mr. Lanier's attacker. It could have been a goofball guest playing a stupid trick on us. Or someone who was hanging around where they shouldn't be."

"But you saw someone," Timothy insisted.

"I thought I did." Theodosia glanced over at Drayton. "We thought we did."

"It almost had to be the killer," Timothy insisted. "And you were the only ones to catch a whiff of him."

"Please don't say that," Theodosia said. If it *had* been the assassin, the man might have seen her charging after him. And now he could have a wary eye out. Theodosia didn't relish the idea of a silent archer keeping tabs on her every move.

"You realize, don't you, that Carson Lanier was one of our board members at the Heritage Society?" Timothy said. "He's the one who donated most of his antique firearms collection to us. Several pieces from his collection will be featured at our Rare Weapons Show that opens this Saturday night."

"I didn't know that," Theodosia said. "That Lanier had been a weapons collector, I mean."

"Antique weapons," Drayton said.

"You think there's some sort of connection?" Theodosia asked. She glanced out at the tables in the tea room. Everyone seemed to be doing just fine. Her services weren't needed quite yet.

Drayton shrugged.

"You know, Timothy, the killer could have been one of your guests," Theodosia said.

"That would be my worst nightmare," Timothy said.

Theodosia continued. "Because we don't know for *sure* that the offending arrow came from the Stagwood Inn."

Timothy shifted from one elegant Church's shoe to the other. "You really think one of my guests could be the killer?"

"It's not out of the realm of possibility," Theodosia said.

Timothy gave them both a long, searching look, then reached into his jacket pocket. "The thought had occurred to me, too. Which is why I brought along my guest list."

"Oh no," Theodosia said, practically backing away from him. "You need to turn that list over to Detective Tidwell immediately."

"I already have," Timothy said as he set the list on the counter and smoothed it out. "I assured Tidwell that he'd have my complete cooperation."

"Of course you'll cooperate," Drayton murmured.

Timothy took a deep breath and continued. "But I'd like Theodosia to go over this list, too."

"Why on earth?" Drayton asked.

Timothy leaned forward across the counter again. "Because she's clever. Because she brings a different perspective to things."

"Oh, not really," Theodosia said.

Now Timothy studied her carefully. "You're also resourceful and skilled at drawing information out of people."

"You want me to talk to the people on your list?" Theodosia asked. "Try to browbeat information out of them?" No, she couldn't do that. Timothy was asking too much of her.

"Nothing that obvious," Timothy said smoothly. "I want you to do what you do best. Charm them and disarm them."

Theodosia's brows pinched together. "I see."

"Holy cats," Drayton said. "You really do want us involved."

"Of course," Timothy said. He pursed his lips. "There's more. Information, I mean. I happen to know someone who vehemently disliked Carson Lanier. Someone who's not on this guest list."

"Who's that?" Theodosia asked. She was taken aback by Timothy's request, but had to admit she was intrigued. A random murder, a chase through an old inn . . . it all added up to pretty heady stuff.

"Have you ever heard of Jud Harker?" Timothy asked.

Theodosia shook her head. "No. Who is he, please?"

Timothy pulled his face into a grimace. "I've never met him personally, but he's a busybody who's been lobbying my board of directors to kill the Rare Weapons Show."

"Ah," Drayton said. "I do remember Harker, our lone protester. He's been sending us angry messages and threats."

"This Harker person," Theodosia said. "Do you think he's dangerous?"

"He's been trying to kill the weapons show," Timothy said. His eyes were pinpricks of intensity. "So why wouldn't he want to kill a well-known gun collector like Carson Lanier?"

5

"What did Timothy want?" Haley asked. She was standing at her stove, adding a half stick of butter to her simmering pot of tomato bisque. Haley always added butter to a soup or sauce at the very last minute to help pull all the flavors together.

"He just wanted Drayton and me to go over his guest list," Theodosia said. She was placing slivers of ham and Cheddar cheese onto slices of buttered bread. Once the sandwiches were cut and quartered, and their crusts sliced off, they'd join Haley's luncheon menu of soup, chicken salad on croissants, and citrus salad.

"So you *are* getting involved."

"Not necessarily."

"Hah," Haley said. "Don't try to pull the wool over my eyes. I know you, Theo. You're the proverbial curious cat."

Theodosia positioned a final slice of cheese. "I should go check on Drayton. See which teas he's going to offer for lunch. And the shop is starting to fill up. Is it okay if I start taking luncheon orders?"

"Don't try to change the subject," Haley said. She grabbed a large soupspoon, tapped it on the counter, and then shook it at Theodosia. "You. I want you to be careful."

"I'm always careful," Theodosia said, trying to feign casual.

"No, you're not. You're the poster child for rushing in where angels fear to tread."

"Haley, I really don't."

"You do!"

Theodosia made her escape into the tea room, where Drayton had just placed three steaming pots of tea on the counter.

"You're just in time," Drayton said. "The silver tips in the Brown Betty teapot goes to table two, the Lapsang souchong in the Chinese blue and white goes to table five, and . . . let's see . . . oh yes, the Formosan oolong in the small white teapot should go to table seven."

Theodosia did her tea room ballet then. Delivering pots of tea, whirling back around to greet guests and lead them to a table, taking luncheon orders, and then spinning into the kitchen to deliver them to Haley.

It all worked like clockwork because they'd done it so many times before. Drayton brewed tea and handled takeout orders, Haley kept the luncheon entrées coming, and Theodosia . . . well, she simply immersed herself in the goings-on. The Indigo Tea Shop was her baby, after all. And, aside from her dog, Earl Grey, her Aunt Libby, and her dear cohorts Drayton and Haley, this was the thing she cared most about in all the world. Even when she'd been working as a marketing executive, she'd dreamed about creating this sort of tea room. A cozy little shop, a bit English, a modicum of Victorian, with a pegged wooden floor, beamed ceiling, fireplace, leaded pane windows, chintz curtains, and sturdy tables and chairs. Oh, and add in a couple of antique wooden highboys stacked with tea tins, jars of honey, tea strainers, cups and saucers, tea cozies, teapots, and sweet-grass baskets.

And glory be, she'd somehow made it happen. Her dream had come true.

"Theodosia. Theodosia . . ."

Drayton was saying something to her.

"Yes?" Theodosia said, shaking her head to clear it and then hurrying over to the counter.

"Be a sweetheart and grab me a handful of blue bags from your office, will you? The Library Society down the street just called in an order for scones. I guess they're having an im-promptu afternoon soiree."

"Did they ask for tea as well?"

"Yes, a tin of citron-flavored green tea. They're going to brew their own."

"Good for them."

Drayton did a semi—eye roll. "But I'm going to write out proper instructions. No sense having them oversteep it and in-terfere with that tea's delicate flavor."

"You tell 'em, Drayton."

An hour later, Theodosia paused to take a breath. Actually, a couple of breaths. She was sitting in her back office, sipping a cup of gunpowder green and nibbling a cream scone. Besides paging through her vendor catalogs, writing up orders for tea and tea accoutrements, she was perusing Timothy Neville's guest list. It was a short list, just two dozen people, but it held the names of more than a few heavy hitters. That is, people with old names, founding fathers' names, who lived in the

BIG HOMES in the Historic District. Names like Aiken, Manigault, and Rutledge, with addresses on Meeting, Church, and East Bay streets.

I'm going to go knocking on the doors of these folks? Hardly. Their staff would send me around to the service entrance and then not bother to answer the bell.

"How are you doing?" Drayton asked. He was posed in the doorway of Theodosia's office, posture ramrod stiff, eyebrows raised, looking like some sort of etiquette instructor.

"Just going over Timothy's list right now," Theodosia said.

Drayton left his post in the doorway and moved closer to her desk. "May I see?"

She slid the paper around. "Be my guest."

Drayton scanned the list. "This is a veritable who's who."

"Which is going to make any kind of inquiry or investigation on our part a whole lot tougher."

"Not tougher," Drayton said. "Nigh on impossible."

"Okay, I'm glad we agree on that." Theodosia took a breath. "If Timothy wants us to look into things, and I'm not saying we should . . . but if we do, then we need a more focused way of going about it."

"In other words, we need actual suspects to investigate," Drayton said.

Theodosia nodded. "We need to figure out exactly who in Carson Lanier's circle of acquaintances might have wanted him dead."

"That could be a big circle."

"Then we'll tighten the noose."

"Delaine said Lanier was in the throes of a nasty divorce," Drayton said. "And Timothy seemed to think that man, Jud Harker, hated Lanier because of his interest in weapons."

"So maybe that's where we start," Theodosia said. "And go from there, if that's what we want to do." She studied Drayton carefully. "Is that what we want to do?"

"I for one certainly want to give an assist to Timothy," Drayton said. "But we don't want to step on Detective Tidwell's toes, either."

"Drayton, we don't want to venture anywhere near his magnetic field nor breathe a word of this to Tidwell."

"I hear you."

"Knock knock," Haley called out. Then, "Hey, guys?"

Theodosia and Drayton glanced at the doorway. Haley was standing there, a quizzical look on her normally sweet and placid face.

"Who's minding the store?" Drayton asked.

Haley flapped a hand. "I was. But don't worry, everything's cool. I made the rounds, pouring tea and serving up a few more scones. Listen, this won't take but a minute."

"What won't take but a minute?" Drayton asked.

"Here's the thing," Haley said, nervously stuffing her hands into the pockets of her blue checkered apron. "My cousin Jamie Weston was coming to visit my Aunt LaBelle over in Goose Creek, but now Aunt LaBelle has to go into the hospital to have her feet scraped." She let out a long breath and stared at them.

"Um . . . that's a medical thing?" Drayton asked. "Feet scraping?"

Haley shrugged. "I don't know. I guess it is."

Drayton winced. "Sounds painful."

"Excuse me, Haley," Theodosia said. "What are you trying to say, here?"

"Since Jamie's going to be staying with me now . . . upstairs," Haley said, "I wondered if we could put him to work for a couple of days. You know, as a kind of busboy, helping out around the tea shop."

"Wait a minute," Drayton said, a look of suspicion creasing his face. "This is all coming back to me like one of the bad dreams you have after ingesting too many ghost peppers. We're talking about your *cousin* Jamie?"

"That's the one," Haley said.

"The young man who saunters around without a care in the world and his nose in the air?"

"The one Drayton took to calling Little Lord Fauntleroy?" Theodosia asked, looking slightly amused. "The last time he visited us?"

"Jamie can be somewhat aloof," Haley admitted. "But it's probably because of all those years spent in private boarding schools."

"And we know he's been booted from some of the best," Drayton said. "Exeter, Choate . . . I could go on."

"Jamie's a whole lot calmer now," Haley said. "He's been studying art and taking his meds."

"Aren't we lucky," Drayton said. "And you say he'll be staying upstairs in your apartment? Theo's old apartment?"

"Well, yeah," Haley said. "That's the plan. But I know Jamie would love to help out around here. In fact, I think he'd be good at it."

"That would be just fine, Haley," Theodosia said. "Jamie's more than welcome to help out in the tea shop." She figured that Haley, always a martinet in the kitchen, would ride herd on Jamie. At least she hoped Haley would.

"When will Little Lord Fauntleroy be gracing us with his presence?" Drayton asked.

"Jamie's coming in tonight, so I could put him to work first thing tomorrow," Haley said.

"Drat, Haley," Drayton said. "You really know how to put a crimp in my workweek, don't you?"

"I *promise* he won't be any trouble."

Drayton held up an index finger as he spun on the heels of his highly polished brogues. "We shall wait and see."

6

But still Theodosia didn't get around to writing up her orders. Five minutes later, Detective Tidwell sauntered into her office, clutching a half-eaten scone in one hand, gripping a cup of tea in the other. Obviously he'd stopped by the front counter for some much-needed fortification.

"May I come in?" Tidwell asked. "Or are you in the throes of something extraordinary?"

"Come in," Theodosia said, indicating the stuffed chair across from her desk.

Tidwell sat down heavily and Theodosia could mentally hear the springs creak and groan.

"I see Drayton's already arranged your afternoon tea," she said.

Tidwell took a bite out of his scone and nodded happily as crumbs cascaded down the front of his too-tight jacket. "Delicious," he said. Only it came out *dulishush* because his mouth was full.

"How can I help you?" Theodosia asked pleasantly. All the while telling herself, *Be careful, be careful of this man. He's so very clever.*

Tidwell chewed noisily, swallowed hard, and said, "What's that you're looking at?"

Theodosia moved a magazine to cover Timothy's list. "Nothing."

"I don't know where I'd get such a silly idea," Tidwell said in a sour tone. "Perhaps I've suddenly gone to a higher plane and developed mind-reading skills, but something tells me you're poking your pert little nose into my investigation."

"Not really," she hedged.

"Then why exactly were you creeping around the Stagwood Inn last night?"

"I explained that to you already. Besides, I wasn't creeping, I was running like a frightened rabbit."

Tidwell tilted his head toward her. "You were meddling. Something you're inclined to do."

"Is there something important you wanted to tell me?" Theodosia asked. "Aside from delivering your rather cryptic warning?" She leaned back in her chair. "Perhaps you'd like to share your list of suspects?"

"You probably know that Timothy Neville has already pointed a finger at someone."

"Yes, a man named Harker, Timothy mentioned that. I take it you've spoken to this Harker? Interviewed him?"

"We will when we locate him, yes," Tidwell said.

"You haven't found him?"

"It's only a matter of time."

"What's going on with the third floor of the Stagwood Inn? Have your crime scene guys been over it?"

"With a fine-tooth comb."

"Did they find anything?" Theodosia asked.

"You mean in the evidentiary realm? We'll have to wait and see, won't we?"

Theodosia tried not to let herself get frustrated by Tidwell's dips and dodges. It was just the nature of the beast. "What about the guests that were staying in those third floor suites?"

Tidwell gave a half smirk. "Mitchel Cooper, the manager, informs me those two rooms were unoccupied last night."

"That may be so, but *somebody* was up there."

"So you say."

"No, there was someone," Theodosia said with certainty. "I wasn't chasing up and down staircases for the fun of it. There's no reason I'd indulge in a real-life game of Chutes and Ladders."

"We're still in the initial stages of the investigation," Tidwell said. "And we have any number of avenues to pursue."

"That sounds awfully vague."

Tidwell's beady eyes sparkled. "Purposefully so."

"You know I'm going to keep looking into things."

He pursed his lips and his jowls shook. "Why on earth would you do that?"

"Because I have a stake in this," Theodosia said. "Because I witnessed Lanier's terrible fall, because I found him impaled on that dreadful wrought-iron fence." She drew a quick breath and continued. "And because I'm positive I saw someone's shadow moving across that curtain."

Tidwell made a motion with his mouth that was somewhere between a smile and a grimace. "And because Detective Riley is involved?"

"He has nothing to do with my interest in this case," Theodosia said.

"You realize that Riley is one of my finest detectives, don't you?"

"Yes."

"And that you've thoroughly bewitched him."

"Excuse me?" *Did he really just say bewitched? Really?* Theodosia wasn't sure if she should be flattered or insulted.

"Please don't be coy. I know you've been dating Detective Riley. And since he will be working this case with me, I'd appreciate it if you didn't interfere." Tidwell hoisted himself to his feet, moving quickly for such a large man. "Do consider my words fair warning." And with that he disappeared out the door.

Tidwell's fair warning had a shelf life of about ten minutes.

By three o'clock, business in the tea shop had begun to wind down, so Theodosia slipped out the back door and hurried down the alley with one thing in mind—pay a daytime visit to the Stagwood Inn. She figured that the crime scene team would be finished by now, so she could poke around freely and have a careful look. What she was looking for, she wasn't sure. Maybe just reassurance that *something* had occurred there?

Mitchel Cooper, the inn's manager, was tall, bespectacled, and slightly stoop-shouldered. Though he was probably midforties, he seemed older than his years and had a desultory air about him, as though every issue he dealt with was burdensome. Which was a strange attitude for an innkeeper to have, especially since he worked in one of Charleston's most popular tourist neighborhoods.

After introducing herself and explaining her small part in last night's drama, Theodosia asked Cooper if she could go upstairs and look around.

"I don't see why not," Cooper said. His eyes and mouth drooped like the figure in the famous Munch painting as he sat behind his desk in his small office tucked beneath the main staircase. "The police and their *CSI*-type people finished several hours ago." He shook his head. "Terrible thing. That man falling from Mr. Neville's widow's walk."

"Did the police explain to you that Mr. Lanier had probably been shot with an arrow? That that's what caused him to fall?"

"Yes, one police officer mentioned it. But I still don't believe anyone at the Stagwood Inn could have been his killer. The police didn't seem all that convinced, either."

"I couldn't help but notice that the Stagwood Inn has a sort of hunting lodge theme," Theodosia said. "Do you have any weapons on display? Antique guns? Dueling pistols? Crossbows of any kind?"

"No, we don't. We used to have a dueling pistol hung in the breakfast room, but someone stole it a few years ago."

"Mr. Cooper, I'm guessing that you weren't here last night?" Theodosia asked.

"I most certainly was on the premises," Cooper said in a slightly petulant tone. "I have a small apartment near the garage."

"But you weren't aware of the activity that was going on?"

Cooper shook his head. "Well . . . no. Not until an officer knocked on my door around nine o'clock. I had the TV turned up loud, you see." He tapped his right ear. "Hard of hearing. Got this awful ringing in my inner ear. Tinnitus, they call it. Drives me crazy sometimes."

"So there was just the young lady working the front desk last night? No other staff on duty?"

"Could have been a couple people from housekeeping still here. But please understand, Sunday nights are never particularly busy. Most all our guests have checked out by then. We don't start gearing up again until Wednesday."

"I see," Theodosia said. "So it's okay if I go upstairs? The doors to the third floor suites are unlocked?"

"Nobody's been up there since the police left," Cooper said. "I suppose I'll have to send housekeeping up to tidy the rooms. Lord knows what state the police left them in."

Both third floor suites had black-and-yellow crime scene tape strung across the doorways. No matter; Theodosia just ducked underneath. She was most interested in the room that faced Timothy Neville's mansion. The room she'd crept into last night when it had been shrouded in darkness.

Now, with shafts of afternoon sun streaming in, the suite looked a lot less threatening. There was a claret-colored duvet on the bed with three poufy faux fur pillows. The bedroom set and bureau weren't Charleston-quality antiques—no Hepplewhite or Sheraton here—but it was nice, the kind of stuff you might find in an antique shop in nearby Mount Pleasant or Summerville. The walls were covered in a dark floral wallpaper and hung with horse and hound prints and two oil paintings that depicted European hunting lodges. The only evidence that the police had been poking around here were smudges of fingerprint powder left on the bureau and small wooden nightstands.

Theodosia looked around the room, but wasn't struck by any major revelations.

But, of course, there was the curtained window.

Walking over to the window, Theodosia slowly pushed aside the filmy curtain. Then she slid open the window and stepped out onto the small balcony. Sunlight filtered down; a damp, salty breeze wafted in from Charleston Harbor and stirred the air as Theodosia gazed across the alley to the roof of Timothy's house.

With its widow's walk, assortment of balustrades, and fancy finials jabbing the air, this dizzying, slightly out-of-whack view almost stopped Theodosia's heart. It reminded her of a black-and-white cinema verité shot straight out of a Hitchcock film.

Back downstairs, Theodosia leaned into Cooper's office to thank him.

Cooper barely looked up. "What?" he said. Then, "No problem. I hope you were able to satisfy your curiosity."

Theodosia was halfway across the lobby when another thought popped into her head. She went back and poked her head into Cooper's office again.

"I know this is kind of a strange question," she said. "But did any of the officers ask you about a man named Harker?"

Cooper set down his pen and frowned at his paperwork. "Harker? Jud Harker?"

Theodosia took a step into his office and gripped the back of a side chair. "You *know* him?"

Cooper looked up at her. "Of course I know him. He works as a handyman around the neighborhood."

"And the police didn't mention his name to you?"

"I'm sure I'd remember if they did."

"And you say Harker's a handyman. Does he ever work here?" Theodosia asked.

"When we need him, yes," Cooper said. "Say there's a plumbing problem or we need tree pruning. Or something needs fixing in one of the suites." He shook his head. "You have no idea how destructive some guests can be. They have a few drinks, start to get rowdy, pretty soon they're ripping down the curtain rods. Or worse. One couple even tore the front off a set of drawers."

Theodosia's heart was beating a little faster now. "So Harker would basically have the run of this place?"

"I suppose you could call it that."

"Is Harker here now?" She wondered if Tidwell knew that Harker worked here.

"I don't know," Cooper said. "I haven't seen him today."

Maybe he's laying low.

"Was Harker here last night?"

"I'm not sure. We'd have to ask Jennifer. She was the one minding the front desk." Cooper was chewing the end of a yellow pencil and giving Theodosia a very strange look. "Why . . . why are you asking these questions about Jud? Is there a problem?"

"I hope not," Theodosia said. "I really hope not."

"I don't think Tidwell knows," Theodosia said to Drayton. He was hanging his apron on a peg behind the counter when she came flying into the empty tea shop. The air was still fragrant with tea, a few dying embers glowed red in the fireplace.

"Doesn't know what?" Drayton turned to ask.

"That Jud Harker, the man Timothy pointed a finger at, is the neighborhood handyman. That he helps out at the Stagwood Inn."

Drayton did a kind of double take. "He *works* there? The same Jud Harker who was pressuring Timothy to shut down the Rare Weapons Show?"

"That's the guy."

"How on earth did you come by this tasty nugget?"

"I talked to Mitchel Cooper, the manager."

Drayton touched a hand to his bow tie. "So Timothy's instincts might have been correct. Harker could be our killer, after all."

"He could be."

"Are you going to inform Tidwell?" Drayton asked. "I mean, this is a real hot potato."

Theodosia considered Drayton's question. Knowing that Harker might have been close by last night certainly put her in the catbird seat when it came to looking into things for Timothy. So . . . should she reveal her information to Tidwell? Or was it better to play it close to the vest for as long as she could? That way she could conduct her own shadow investigation.

"Well?" Drayton asked. He was staring at her with great curiosity. "Are you going to tell him?"

Theodosia met his gaze evenly. "I don't know," she said. "I'm still deciding."

7

For Theodosia, Haiku Gallery was almost a dream come true. Besides being packed wall-to-wall with party guests, it carried the most elegant Japanese art and antiquities she had ever set eyes on. There were Japanese prints, colorful Oribe ceramics, baskets and lacquerware, gorgeous painted screens, and sensuous Japanese kimonos that reminded her of butterfly wings. Branches of plum blossoms were arranged everywhere, creatively displayed in large antique Tamba jugs, their sweet fragrance permeating the air and creating an almost dream-like effect. There was even a sushi bar, complete with sushi chef!

But while Theodosia was taking in all the fabulous antiques, Drayton was at her elbow, pressuring her for more information about Jud Harker.

"You say the man works as a handyman in our *neighborhood*,"

Drayton said. "That makes Timothy's accusation slightly more ominous."

"I know," Theodosia said. "It also means Harker could have had access to that third floor suite."

"Was he working at the Stagwood Inn last night?"

"That's the thing of it," Theodosia said. "Apparently this Harker guy comes and goes of his own accord. Mr. Cooper said he's never sure when Harker's going to pop up."

"So Harker works according to his own schedule and at his own pace?" Drayton touched a hand to his polka-dot bow tie. "Goodness, that doesn't sound like a very efficient work situation."

"Not everyone is as buttoned-up as you are, Drayton," Theodosia said, a faint smile on her face.

"Well, they should be. Keeping regular hours is good discipline."

"Hello, hello!" Delaine suddenly screeched. She was waving excitedly as she steamrollered through the crowd, looking glamorous in a black off-the-shoulder cocktail dress, her hair pinned up into a messy topknot.

"Hi Delaine," Theodosia said as Delaine skidded to a stop in front of them, accompanied by a pretty, dark-haired woman who wore a simple black silk dress and a string of creamy pearls.

"Have you met Alexis James yet?" Delaine asked.

"Oh my goodness," Theodosia said, reaching out to grab the woman's hand. "You're the owner of this fabulous shop."

"This is Theodosia," said Delaine, quickly taking charge. "And Drayton Conneley. These are the people I was just telling you about? From the Indigo Tea Shop down the street?"

"Your tea shop is definitely on my to-do list," Alexis said. Then she erupted in warm, rich laughter and threw up her hands. "But as you can see, I've been more than a little busy."

"I was also telling Alexis about that nasty business at Timothy's last night," Delaine said in hushed tones. She seemed to relish injecting bad news into a nice, normal conversation.

"Luckily it didn't stop anyone from coming to your grand opening," Theodosia said, trying to steer the subject away from Carson Lanier's murder. "You seem to have drawn quite a good-sized crowd."

"Your shop is lovely," Drayton said, jumping in as well. "And your inventory is very impressive."

"Thank you," Alexis said. "How very kind of you. I must say, it's been a labor of love putting all this together." Alexis was midthirties with short, dark hair. She was attractive, with a direct, open manner. She seemed flattered by Drayton's words as well as slightly amused.

"Was that a bowl by Hamada that I saw sitting on your lovely Japanese kitchen cabinet?" Drayton asked.

Alexis fairly beamed at him. "You have a very good eye."

Drayton ducked his head. "I have a passion for beautiful art objects."

"Then we really must talk," Alexis said. "Because I've got several more exquisite pieces that are still in storage."

"Alexis and I are fast friends already," Delaine sang out suddenly. "Even though we've just met."

"Tell me," Drayton said to Alexis, ignoring Delaine's outburst. "Is there a particular reason you named your shop Haiku Gallery? Other than the obvious reference to Japanese poetry?"

"This is probably a bit obscure for most people," Alexis said, "but I'm a huge fan of the Japanese poet Bashō. So I named it in tribute to him."

Drayton cocked his head and recited:

Temple bells die out.
The fragrant blossoms remain.
A perfect evening!

"Oh my goodness," Alexis said, clapping her hands together. "A man who can recite Bashō." She moved closer to him. "Tell me, are you a fan of Japanese sake as well?"

"I've been known to imbibe," Drayton said.

"Well, come with me. I have a bottle of Otokoyama sake sitting behind the bar that I've been dying to crack open."

"Huh," Delaine said, narrowing her eyes and pouting as she stared after the retreating Alexis and Drayton. "What am I, chopped liver? Nobody's offering me a cup of premium sake, even though I just invited Alexis to sit front row at my fashion show."

"I don't think Alexis gets a chance to talk to people who know a bit about art," Theodosia said in an attempt to soothe Delaine's ruffled feathers.

"*I* know about art," Delaine said. "I love art. "Why, I . . . I even have an Andy Warhol print in my bathroom."

Theodosia eased herself away from Delaine and mingled. Grabbed a few pieces of sushi and talked to Leigh Carroll from the Cabbage Patch Gift Shop and Brooke Carter Crockett who owned Heart's Desire Fine Jewelry.

As she moved about the shop, chatting with folks from the neighborhood, she noticed there was one unwelcome guest at the party.

Bill Glass, the publisher and editor of *Shooting Star*, a glossy local gossip rag, swaggered in Theodosia's direction. He was dressed in baggy cargo pants, a khaki photojournalist jacket, and had a blue scarf along with several Nikon cameras slung casually around his neck. He looked like he'd just returned from war-torn Afghanistan, though the closest he'd ever come to that was watching CNN.

"Hey," Glass said when he caught sight of Theodosia. "I need to talk to you."

Theodosia bit her lip. Glass always spelled trouble.

"What do you want?" she asked. She didn't want to be unkind, but she didn't want to engage him, either.

"I heard you were at that fancy-schmancy party last night where the guy from Capital Bank took a nosedive."

"He didn't take a nosedive, as you so inelegantly put it. He was—" Theodosia stopped abruptly. She'd probably said too much already.

"Yeah?" Glass said, leaning in to her, a smarmy, questioning look on his face. "You were saying?"

Theodosia shook her head. "Never mind."

"Hey, you're the one who popped the lid off this can of worms," Glass said. He dropped his voice to a conspiratorial tone. "Carson Lanier was shot, right? But his fatal wound wasn't from any stray cannon fire, like was first reported. The cannons were shooting blanks. It was some kind of arrow, is what I heard."

"How would you know about that?"

"I'm press. It's my business to know."

"You're not press, you publish a trashy gossip rag that's printed on grade Z paper and comes out once a week for a few hundred subscribers. If you're lucky."

"Don't rub it in," Glass said with a sigh. "The sad fact is . . . even a lousy blogger or Instagrammer can qualify as press these days." Glass paused, looking keenly unhappy. As if his vaunted position in the community had been recklessly usurped by tech-crazed millennials. "So, tell me what happened. What really happened."

"Leave me alone, Bill. You shouldn't even be at this party. I doubt you were invited."

"What are you gonna do? Make a big fat scene and have me kicked out?" He lifted one of his Nikons. "Come on, strike a pose, will you? You're a cute gal, you could do with some press in my paper."

"No thank you." Theodosia ducked away from Glass, threaded her way past a Coromandel screen, and met up with Drayton. "How was the sake?"

"Excellent," Drayton said. "Smooth, yet bracing."

"Alexis seems nice. She's a good addition to our block, don't you think?"

"Absolutely," Drayton said. "And she's so knowledgeable. She was really bending my ear about prints by Hokusai and Utamaro, which I confess I know very little about."

"But you know other things. Your expertise is in Early American furniture and tea ware and sterling silver. And oil paintings."

Drayton nodded. "Yes, I suppose I do know a bit about those things."

"Look at this woodblock print," Theodosia said. She'd just spotted a Hiroshige that would certainly merit a place of honor over her mantel. Mount Fuji in the moonlight done in pinks and blues. Then she peeked at the price tag. Six thousand dollars. Well, yes, she supposed that's exactly what a genuine Hiroshige cost these days.

"I'd have to say Haiku Gallery is off to a rousing start," Drayton said. "Considering this is only their first day."

"You think people are buying?"

"Alexis already rang up several sales."

"That's great, then."

"Oh. And I saw a lovely antique ceramic teapot." Drayton paused and looked back over his shoulder. "I really should go check the price tag. It could make a fine addition to my collection."

"Something to consider," Theodosia said. "Since you only have about a hundred teapots."

"You should talk," Drayton shot back.

Theodosia wandered toward the front of the shop, admiring a bright red kimono that was displayed on a rosewood kimono stand. In the right contemporary home, hanging on a wall . . . it would make a stunning piece of modern art.

"Theodosia," said a familiar voice.

She glanced up to meet the cool blue eyes of Detective Pete Riley. He was tall, with an almost languid posture, and what she thought of as an aristocratic nose and cheekbones. If she didn't know he was a detective, he might've passed for a Southern lawyer from a deep-rooted family.

"You," Theodosia said, sounding pleased. "What are you doing here?" This was a complete surprise. They'd been dating for the past couple of months, but they hadn't made a date for tonight. Or had they? Did she screw up?

Riley held up his hands in a gesture of appeal. "I'm afraid I wasn't issued an official invitation. Which I guess makes me the quintessential party crasher."

"I wouldn't worry about the technicalities," Theodosia said. "Since there are more than a few guests of guests here tonight. But how on earth did you know where to find me?" She wasn't a bit unhappy that Riley had shown up. Truth be told, she was delighted.

"I'm a detective," Riley said, tapping an index finger against the side of his head. "Which means I detected."

Theodosia offered an amused, slightly tolerant smile. "Come on, how did you *really* track me down?"

"Ah, I made a pest of myself," Riley said. "I banged on the

back door of your tea shop until your young chef came bounding downstairs to shush me. Then I turned on my charm and smooth-talked her until she told me where you were at."

Theodosia smiled. "Haley always was a pushover for a smooth-talking guy."

"Actually, I told her I was seriously addicted to her artisan scones."

"*Artisan* scones?" Theodosia nodded. "That would win her heart even more." She hesitated. Tell Riley about Harker? Not tell him? She reached out, snagged his sleeve, and pulled him behind a bamboo screen.

"Ah, a secret?" Riley leaned in to kiss her.

Theodosia let him kiss her and then put both hands on his shoulders and gently pushed him back a couple of inches.

One of his eyebrows arched up. "Problem?"

"Kind of."

"Us?"

"No, no, nothing like that. It's about the murder last night."

Riley stared at her as if he was waiting for the other shoe to drop. "Yes?" Then, "I heard you were there."

"Detective Tidwell tells me you've been assigned to work that case."

"Yes. Wait, this is strange. It feels like we're playing twenty questions. Are we?"

"No," Theodosia said. "But here's the thing. I just discovered some very . . . um, let's call it pertinent information."

"How pertinent?" Riley looked uncertain now. "Doggone, this back-and-forth questioning makes me crazy. Just spit it out, Theo. Tell me what's got you all wound up."

"It seems that Carson Lanier had a couple of nasty run-ins with a man named Jud Harker," Theodosia said. Riley continued to stare at her expectantly, so she went on. "And I just found out, from the manager at the Stagwood Inn, that Jud Harker is their part-time handyman."

Riley took a step back. "What?"

"I just found out that—"

He held up a hand. "No, I heard you just fine. What I meant was . . . well, I'm not sure what I meant." His jaw tensed. "Harker *works* there?"

"Yes," Theodosia said. "You think that's important? Because I sure think it might be."

"Of course it is," Riley said. "I may not be one hundred percent up to speed on the Lanier case yet, but I know that Timothy Neville named Harker as a person of interest."

"So that means you'll investigate Harker?" She figured Riley would be great backup. He'd do all the legwork and then share his information with her. Hopefully.

"I'll jump on this first thing tomorrow. I'd do it tonight if I knew where to find the guy."

Theodosia rubbed a finger against his lapel and smiled. "Um, maybe not tonight."

Harker smiled back. "You make a good point."

"Ooh, look what the proverbial cat dragged in!" Delaine cooed. She was suddenly standing before them, beaming happily, as if she'd just discovered the lost treasure of the Sierra Madre. "Detective Riley. What a pleasant surprise. And might I inquire what you two lovebirds are up to?"

"Delaine," Theodosia said, a cautionary note coloring her voice.

Delaine waved a hand in front of her face as if she were erasing words from a chalkboard. "Oh, don't mind me, I'm just happy and excited over all sorts of things."

"You must have had a glass or two of the good sake," Theodosia said.

"Indeed I did," Delaine said. "And before I forget . . ." She thrust a pink postcard into Theodosia's hand. "Remember that sample sale I told you about a few weeks ago?"

Theodosia shook her head no.

"Well, it's happening tomorrow."

"Wait . . . *you're* having a sale?" Theodosia asked.

"Oh, no no." Delaine chuckled. "Not me. My friend Tania Blakely is holding a ginormous sample sale over at the Lady Goodwood Inn. Tania picked up a *ton* of designer clothes when she attended Market Week in New York last month. Of course they're all teensy-weensy sizes. Zero, two, four . . ." Delaine eyed Theodosia carefully. "Think you can squeeze in, sweetie? I know how you adore your carbs."

"Theodosia looks just great the way she is," Riley said. "Nice and toned, with a strong runner's body."

"Before you two start putting my various body parts up for auction on the international market," Theodosia said, "I think I'm going to help myself to another piece of sushi." Anything to get away from Delaine.

"Attagirl," Riley said. "I'll join you."

But Delaine, not to be outmaneuvered, followed them to the hors d'oeuvres table.

While Theodosia and Pete Riley helped themselves to a couple pieces of salmon sushi, Delaine selected a California roll and then proceeded to pick out the rice. Carbs, of course.

"The other thing I need to remind you two about," Delaine said, nibbling at a piece of seaweed, "is that the Carolina Cat Show begins this Friday night."

"A cat show?" Riley said. He sounded almost amused.

"A very *prestigious* cat show," Delaine said, suddenly getting serious, since cats were definitely her thing. "It's a fund-raiser for Cat's Paw Shelter with a silent auction and then a formal ball to follow." She dug into her purse and pulled out a fancy invitation. It was printed on crisp cream-colored paper and edged in purple and gold. "Detective Riley, perhaps we can persuade you to attend our formal ball?" Delaine nodded in Theodosia's direction. "With a certain date?"

"That sounds like it might be fun," Riley said. "I've never actually been to a black-tie affair. Especially one that benefits homeless cats." His eyes scanned the invitation. "Holy smokes. You're calling it the Hair Ball?"

Delaine gave a wicked grin. "Seriously, can you think of a better name?"

8

"Did your cute little detective find you last night?" Haley asked. She was hustling around the tea room, wielding a broom and making short work of any stray crumbs that might be lurking under the tables. It was Tuesday morning at the Indigo Tea Shop, and Theodosia and Drayton were in a tizzy as well, getting ready to open for morning tea.

"Yes, he did," Theodosia said. She'd just whipped white linen tablecloths onto all the tables and was debating whether to use the Shelley Chintz or the Coalport china.

"Riley sure is a handsome devil," Haley said. "Seems to me the two of you have something serious going on."

"I'll tell you what should be going on, Haley," Drayton called from behind the counter. "You need to set out the tea warmers, light the candles, and then scoot back into the kitchen and pull your scones out of the oven before they turn into a charred mess."

Haley studied Drayton from beneath half-lidded eyes. "Have

you ever known me to burn my scones, Drayton? Hah, that's a good one, that is."

"So everything's under control in the kitchen?" Theodosia asked, taking the broom from Haley. "Here, let me finish up."

"The scones are fine," Haley said. "The banana bread is fine. But what I really want to know about is the grand opening at Haiku Gallery last night." She put her hands on her hips. "Is anybody gonna clue me in?"

"It was a lovely party," Drayton said. "The gallery carries a spectacular inventory of rare Japanese prints, ceramics, and furniture, and the food was first-rate. A delicious selection of sushi and fried tempura." He glanced in Theodosia's direction. "Oh, Theo, I spoke to Alexis last night and she said she'd be delighted to lend us a few pieces for our Plum Blossom Tea on Friday."

"Perfect," Theodosia said. "Now I'm looking forward to that event even more."

"Did you, um, mention the Jud Harker thing to your friend, Detective Riley?" Drayton asked her.

"I told him," Theodosia said. "He promised to jump right on it."

"Good," Drayton said. "Which means you can steer clear of that whole mess." He suddenly brightened. "Yes, I'm definitely feeling relaxed and ready to face the day. Looking forward to the week, especially our Plum Blossom Tea."

"Now I just have to come up with a killer menu," Haley said.

"I have complete faith in you, Haley," Theodosia said. "You've never let us down yet when it comes to our event teas."

"And I never will," Haley said. "In fact, I was— Oh." She stopped abruptly as a young man crept slowly into the tea room from the back hallway. He looked sleepy and disheveled, like he'd just rolled out of bed.

"I see you're finally up," Haley said. There was a distinct edge to her voice.

"Jamie?" Theodosia said. Though she hadn't seen him in a few years, she was pretty sure this was Jamie Weston, Haley's cousin and houseguest who was staying upstairs. The one Drayton referred to as Little Lord Fauntleroy. Although in his jeans and Fetty Wap T-shirt he looked awfully dressed down.

Jamie waved a hand in the general direction of the tea room. "Howdy," he said. Then his eyes focused on Theodosia. "You're Theodosia, right? The owner?"

"Yes, and it's lovely to see you again, Jamie," Theodosia said. "Welcome to the Indigo Tea Shop. I'm sure you remember Drayton? He's the gentleman standing there like a statue on a pedestal, back behind the front counter?"

Jamie yawned broadly and waved a hand in Drayton's general direction. "Dude," he said. Jamie was twenty years old, six feet tall, string bean thin, with a thick mane of blond hair and a saucy, preppy demeanor that made him look as if he'd just sauntered off the pages of a Ralph Lauren ad.

Drayton looked so startled at being called "dude" that Theodosia was forced to stifle a laugh.

"Is it safe to say you're reporting for work?" Theodosia asked Jamie.

"Do I have a choice?" Jamie asked, shifting his gaze to Haley. Then he leaned forward and shook his blond hair vigorously, in the manner of a Labrador retriever who'd just bounded out of a lake.

"Here, now," Drayton said, his posture going even more rigid. "I think we need to get you looking a tad more presentable, Mr. Jamie. I suggest you go back upstairs, slick down your mop of hair, and put on a clean white shirt. When you return we'll find you a nice black Parisian waiter's apron to wear."

Jamie looked curious. "I gotta dress up just to serve tea?"

"Not quite," Drayton said in slightly iced tones. "Because you're not going to be serving tea; you're going to be clearing tables."

"That seems awfully menial."

"We must all start somewhere," Drayton said.

Five minutes later, customers began to trickle into the tea shop. Drayton was in his element, greeting people and brewing pots of Chinese Ying Feng green tea and Lapsang souchong smoky black tea, while Theodosia filled tiny glass bowls with strawberry jam and fluffy dabs of Devonshire cream.

But when Jamie came sidling up to the counter, practically invading Drayton's territory, Drayton's mood suddenly shifted.

"If you're going to be working here," Drayton said, "I'd say a quick lesson is in order."

"You got it, dude," Jamie said.

"Lesson number one, I am not a dude. You may call me Mr. Conneley, sir, or even Drayton. But kindly do not refer to me as 'dude.'"

Jamie gave Drayton a thumbs-up. "Got it."

"Now please observe carefully," Drayton said. He picked up a tin of Harney & Sons Vietnamese Black OP and tilted it toward Jamie. "This particular tea is steeping right here in my Brown Betty teapot. Smell that aroma? It's a smooth, full-bodied tea with a hint of sweetness. Really excellent for breakfast." He grabbed another tin of tea and indicated a second teapot. "Here's a breakfast black tea with a more distinctive flavor, some lovely hazelnut and orange undertones. Now I'm going to pour you a small cup of each tea and I want you to sample them so you can clearly taste the difference."

Drayton poured and Jamie tasted both teas.

"Now do you see what I mean?" Drayton asked.

Jamie shook his head.

"No?" Drayton said.

"No."

"It's going to be a long day," Drayton muttered.

"I'm here for the week."

"Then perhaps it's best if you just . . . cleared tables and washed dishes."

But the mood in the tea shop improved immensely when, a few minutes later, Alexis James popped in. She was smiling and bubbling over, obviously still riding a high from the success of her big party last night.

"Miss James," Drayton enthused when he spotted her. "May I formally welcome you to the Indigo Tea Shop?"

"Please, call me Alexis," she said. "Since we've already bonded over teapots and Tamba ware, I feel like we're kindred spirits."

"Indeed we are," Drayton said.

Alexis waved a hand in Theodosia's direction. "Hey there, Miss Theodosia, long time no see."

"Good morning," Theodosia said, coming over to join Alexis and Drayton at the counter. "I hope you'll be dropping by on a regular basis now, since your fabulous gallery is just down the street from us."

Alexis's eyes lit up as they roved about the tea shop. "Are you kidding me? This tea shop is so lovely and cozy I can hardly believe it. And yes I intend to become a regular customer. I mean, holy smokes, it looks as if your tea shop was magically transported from the English countryside and plopped down right here in the middle of Charleston."

"We pride ourselves on our authenticity and charm," Drayton said modestly.

"Again, congratulations on your grand opening," Theodosia said. "We really enjoyed your party."

"Not as much as I did," Alexis said. She lowered her voice. "Can you believe I sold almost forty-five thousand dollars' worth of objects already? And that I've got holds on two Utamaro prints as well as a lacquer box?"

"You've sold that much already?" Drayton said. "Amazing."

"Good for you," Theodosia said. She was thrilled when a local small business thrived. Their prosperity was often contagious for other shops in the neighborhood.

"I knew Charleston was populated by art lovers and collectors," Alexis said, "but I had no idea they were such capable spenders."

"I think you'll find there's a good deal of wealth here," Drayton said.

"Would you like to be seated at a table?" Theodosia asked Alexis. "So you can enjoy a proper cup of tea? Or did you just pop by for a cuppa to go?"

"Regretfully, I do have to get back to my shop," Alexis said. "But a take-out cup of green tea would be wonderful."

"And perhaps an apple cinnamon scone?" Theodosia asked.

"You talked me into it."

Drayton busied himself with brewing a pot of Japanese sencha while Theodosia placed a scone in one of her indigo-blue take-out bags.

Alexis knit her brows together and focused on Theodosia. "So, I picked up a bit of strange gossip at last night's party. Was there really a murder here two nights ago? I don't mean *here* here, but a couple of blocks over?"

"I'm afraid so," Theodosia said. "At Timothy Neville's home."

Alexis tapped a manicured finger against the counter. "I've been so busy with the grand opening that I haven't bothered reading any news. But . . . did it occur during a robbery?"

"No," Theodosia said. "It wasn't that." She could see that Alexis was concerned about her shop being held up by armed robbers. After all, robberies had occurred on Church Street before. "This murder actually happened at a private party. The victim was a banker, so we think there might have been bad blood over a business deal."

Alexis still looked nervous.

"But the police are investigating," Theodosia said, trying to sound reassuring even as her mind wandered to Detective Riley. "And we have complete faith in their detectives."

Drayton glanced up. "There's nothing to concern yourself with, dear lady," he said. "It will probably all be over in a day or two." Snapping a lid on a take-out cup, he handed it to Alexis. "Here you are—tea that's been custom blended just for you."

"I love this," Alexis said, her mood suddenly upbeat again. "I'm going to make coming here my morning ritual."

"You're welcome anytime," Theodosia said. "And I've been meaning to ask. How on earth did you amass such a spectacular inventory of Japanese collectibles? It looks as if you've been tromping all over the globe for years, gathering priceless treasures."

"I completely lucked out," Alexis said. "A shop over near Walterboro came up for sale a few months ago and I jumped right on it. The owner, a fellow named Riddle, who was old as Methuselah, passed away, and his nephew put most of his inventory up for sale. I was at the right place at the right time and was able to sort of cherry-pick the better pieces."

"Riddle," Theodosia said. "I recognize that name. There was

a man named George Riddle who owned a large plantation out by my Aunt Libby's place on Rutledge Road."

Alexis nodded. "Probably the same family. I think there have been Riddles living in and around Charleston for ages."

"What's on the menu for lunch today, Haley?" Theodosia stood in the doorway of their postage stamp–sized kitchen, watching Haley bob and weave as she spun from the stove to the sink and over to the counter.

"Since the days are finally getting warmer, I'm lightening up on our entrées," Haley said.

"Okay."

"So . . . smoked gouda and mushroom tartlets, my apple-yogurt chicken bake, and wild mushroom soup."

"Fabulous," Theodosia said. "And for dessert?"

"I got a good deal on a case of blood oranges, so I'm in the throes of whipping up a parfait. And then, let's see . . . I've got a pan of brownie bites baking in the oven, and—"

WHAP. WHAM. SLAM.

Haley straightened up like a gopher popping out of its hole. "Holy butter beans, what was that?"

"Sounds like the football team from The Citadel just trampled down our front door," Theodosia said. She spun around, flew through the celadon-green velvet curtain that separated the tea room from the back of the shop, and slid to a stop midway into the tea room. "What on earth?" she cried.

A man in work clothes—olive green slacks and a light green shirt—stood near the front counter. He had a leather tool belt slung low around his hips and was holding up a handful of pamphlets. Waving them around, actually, as he yelled at Drayton!

"I've asked you people nicely," the man shouted. "And you still won't listen to me. Very well, I've written out all my reasons—good reasons, I might add—right here. And I demand that you read them." He pulled a pamphlet from his stack and slapped it down hard on the counter.

"Excuse me," Drayton began, but the man ignored him as he continued his tirade.

"This isn't just an idle whim on my part," the man continued. "It's a huge concern, which is why I feel the need to enlighten you." His voice rose higher, causing customers to turn in their chairs to see what was going on.

"Stop it!" Theodosia said. "If you don't stop shouting this instant I'm going to call the police." She stepped closer to the man and put a hand on his arm to restrain him. "Just who do you think you are?"

The man turned around to face her. He had a long, thin face, a mottled gray beard, and slightly protruding brown eyes that had the gleam of a crazy, zealous true believer. With his hair pulled back in a scruffy ponytail, he gave the impression of an old stoner.

"Go ahead and call the police," the man said. "But I still have a right to free speech."

Theodosia shook her head even as she stood her ground. "Not in my tea shop, you don't. Not when you come barging in here and disturb my customers."

Startled now, the man looked around, saw a half dozen faces staring at him with genuine curiosity, and made a quick decision to take his rant down a notch. "I just wanted to pass out my—"

"*Who* are you, anyway?" Theodosia demanded.

"I'm Jud Harker," the man said. He raised a fist and gestured at Drayton again. "I'm the one who's trying to—"

"Shut down the Rare Weapons Show," Theodosia finished for him, somewhat breathlessly. Then her heart did an extra blip inside her chest. This was the man who'd been threatening many of the Heritage Society board members. Now he was standing right here, in her tea shop, chattering like a rabid chipmunk. It was no wonder Timothy had pointed a finger at this man as a possible suspect in Carson Lanier's murder. Harker was brash, angry, and obviously had no impulse control.

"We need to shut down that show," Harker shouted again, thrusting a pamphlet into Theodosia's hands.

Theodosia grabbed the pamphlet without looking at it and stuffed it into the pocket of her slacks. "I'm afraid you'll have to leave," she said in an even voice. No way was she backing down. She just wasn't engineered that way.

"Leave?" Harker said, shuffling a step closer so he could loom over her. "I don't think so."

"You're creating a disturbance."

Harker's eyes gleamed. "I haven't even started—"

"Hey man," said a quiet voice at Harker's elbow. "Crank it down a notch, will you?"

Theodosia blinked. Jamie was suddenly right there, talking to Harker. But he was doing it in a low-key, nonthreatening manner. Now, wasn't this interesting? Was Jamie mature enough to take care of this? Or would she have to get tough and run this jerk off?

"Don't just come in here and start yammering at everyone," Jamie said. "That's no way to make your point."

"What?" Harker was staring at Jamie, as if he were just emerging from a trance.

"There are some nice ladies in here who are trying to enjoy their lunch," Jamie said, a boyish grin lighting his face. "So be a gentleman and leave quietly, okay?"

Harker looked as if the wind had been taken out of his sails. "Can I give you one of my pamphlets?" he asked.

"I guess so," Jamie said. He had a good four inches of height on Harker, and now his hand was on Harker's upper arm, steering him toward the front door, giving him a friendly but firm bum's rush. Seconds later, Harker was outside on the sidewalk with Jamie nodding a polite good-bye. And when Jamie stepped back inside the tea shop, he made a big point of closing the door and locking it.

For a few seconds, nobody uttered a word. In fact, you could've heard a pin drop until Drayton said, "I'd say you just earned a few brownie points, young man."

Jamie nodded solemnly at Drayton. "Mr. D."

Five minutes later, Theodosia was busy greeting a dozen new customers, taking their orders, serving luncheon plates, and ferrying steaming pots of tea to various tables. Behind the counter, teakettles whistled and chirped their merry birdsongs as Drayton eased back into the swing of things. (Yes, his precise and somewhat controlling nature had taken a slight hit, but he did seem to be recovering.)

As Theodosia bustled about, Jud Harker's pop-up appearance was still very much top of mind. Had Detective Riley had a conversation with Harker, just as he'd promised he would? Had it turned into a confrontation that set Harker off on this tangent? Or had Tidwell gotten hold of Harker and threatened him? Tidwell could be confrontational bordering on outright intimidating. Whatever had happened with the police must have gotten Harker all wound up. Theodosia decided that, as soon as she had a free moment, she'd call Pete Riley and get the full story.

And, all the while, Theodosia pondered the fact that Harker had seemed more than a little unstable. If he was a rabid anti-gun crusader—and it sure looked like he was—could he have murdered Lanier the banker? Maybe he hadn't wanted to *kill* him, exactly; maybe he just meant to fire a warning shot and it all went horribly wrong.

Theodosia furrowed her brow, thinking. Or maybe Harker was just the neighborhood fruitcake. A guy who was lonely, disenfranchised, not fully employed, and had found a cause to wrap his mind and arms around. Maybe Harker was simply a nuisance—a disconcerting presence, to be sure, but nothing more than that.

"Theo?" Drayton said.

Theodosia looked up from the counter where she was cutting a lemon into thin, almost translucent slices. "Yes?"

"Would you accompany me to the Heritage Society's board meeting tonight?"

"Why would you want me to do that?" Theodosia asked. This was an unusual request that had come shooting out of the blue. "If I remember correctly, I'm not on the board, *you're* on the board."

"Here's the thing," Drayton said. "First off, Timothy asked if I might persuade you to attend."

"Okay, that alone sounds fairly mysterious. Does Timothy have a reason for wanting me there?"

"I'm sure he does."

"But you don't know what it is?"

Drayton shook his head. "Not exactly."

"So what's the second thing?" Theodosia asked. "Wait—*is* there a second thing?"

"Yes. Apparently there's a prospective new board member who's ready to step in and take Carson Lanier's place."

"So soon? Just like that?" She was surprised by Timothy's haste in filling the vacant slot. "Isn't that somewhat unorthodox? Don't potential board members have to be vetted?"

"It's unusual, yes," Drayton said. "But Lanier was a man who liked everything signed, sealed, notarized, and wrapped up in a nice tight bundle. So I'm guessing this successor is probably a like-minded chap. And Timothy is willing to meet with this potential successor in light of what's transpired. Obviously I'm referring to the, uh . . ."

"Murder," Theodosia said.

"Yes." Drayton licked his lips nervously. "Anyway, in light of the circumstances, Timothy feels voting in a colleague of Lanier's might be a nice way to honor him for his years of service to the Heritage Society. Which obviously means this new potential board member will be attending tonight's meeting."

"And what's my role in all this?" Theodosia asked. "You want me to do a psychic reading? Deal out the tarot cards and see if this new guy is the King of Wands and destined to be an effective board member?"

"No supernatural trickery is needed," Drayton said with a chuckle. "Timothy and I just want you to come and be your usual charming self."

"That's it?"

"And be an excellent judge of character as well." Drayton paused. "Can you help us? Will you help us?"

"Yes, Drayton, I'll come with you tonight." *Because now you've got me more than a little curious.*

9

Once lunch was over and afternoon teatime well under way, Theodosia ran into her office and called Pete Riley. But he wasn't in his office and, for whatever reason, wasn't answering his cell phone.

So, okay. When his voice mail came on, she said, "Hey, it's me. Jud Harker came bombing into my tea shop this morning, ranting and raving his head off like a gibbering capuchin monkey. What I want to know is—what on earth did you guys do or say that sent him spinning into my orbit? So call me, okay?"

Theodosia hung up her phone and thought for a few moments. Hurrying into the tea shop, she whispered a few words to Drayton, and waited for his approving nod. Then she slipped out the back door and drove the few blocks to the Lady Goodwood Inn.

Theodosia hadn't planned on going to the sample sale, but then she thought about the charity ball this Friday night. The one Delaine had slyly christened the Fur Ball. If she was going to attend—and she knew Pete Riley was already on board with it—there was the question of a ball gown. Or, at the very least, a long skirt she could pair with a sparkly top.

So the die was cast.

As Theodosia strode through the lobby with its overstuffed chairs and potted palms, it looked as though the sample sale were being held right here. Tables were set up everywhere, smiling young faces looked to greet her. But no. When she approached one of the tables, she was told that this was registration for a pharmaceutical trade show. The sample sale was being held down the hall in the Magnolia Room.

Two skinny teenage girls sat at a table, essentially blocking the entrance to the Magnolia Room. One was blond, the other dark-haired. Both were studying their cell phones intently, their fingers poking furiously at the screens. Texting.

"This is the sample sale?" Theodosia asked politely. She figured they must be gatekeepers. Or gatekeepers-in-training.

The skinny blonde's fingers continued to work her keyboard until finally she looked up. "You're here for the sample sale?" She couldn't have sounded more bored.

"No, I thought the G7 summit was being held here," Theodosia said.

"What?" the blonde said.

"We're the official greeters," the dark-haired girl said. She was chewing gum and snapping it every few seconds.

"Mindy's cousins," the blonde said.

The dark-haired girl went back to studying her phone. "From Savannah."

"Well, bless your little hearts," Theodosia said as she pushed her way past them and entered a room that had been turned into fashion mayhem, or what some might call Dante's First Circle of Retail Hell. Giant metal racks, stuffed with colorful clothing, were parked everywhere, creating a zigzag maze that didn't seem to have any rhyme or reason. There were no tidy rows with sizes clearly marked, no racks set judiciously around the perimeter. In fact, it looked as if worker bees had just shoved a couple dozen racks into the Magnolia Room and then run for their lives.

Theodosia decided she had to start somewhere, so she dug into the first rack she saw.

Skirts. She could definitely go for a long, fancy skirt. But no, this rack was all wool dresses. Theodosia moved on. Nobody in their right mind wanted a wool dress just as Charleston was heading into a summer of industrial-strength heat and humidity. Yes, that heat helped keep your skin soft and hydrated, but on the flip side, it frizzed your hair so bad that, by July, it looked like frayed tufts of twine.

Glancing around the room, Theodosia noticed dozens of teensy, tiny women, all poring through the racks. They were wasp-waisted, slim-hipped women who must have barely weighed a hundred pounds soaking wet. She knew this event was billed as a sample sale, which meant it featured smaller sizes. But, dear Lord, what on earth did these women exist on? Rarefied air? A new kind of hybrid low-cal kale? Bibb lettuce shooters? Somehow they'd become miniaturized with hardly any figures at all.

Just as Theodosia decided to turn tail and leave Munchkinland, Delaine popped out from behind a rack of clothes, looking like a stylish jack-in-the-box. "Theo!" she cried. "*Here* you are!" Delaine grabbed her by the arm and dug in her bloodred nails. "I've been looking for you *everywhere*. Did you find anything that fits?"

Theodosia shook her head and pulled her arm back. "I just got here."

Delaine grimaced. "Hopefully the really nice things aren't gone already."

"Gone? There have to be thirty racks of clothes here."

"But so many pieces are from last season," Delaine whispered.

"That's bad?"

Delaine managed to grip her arm again and pull her along. "It's not good. Come over here. You mentioned you needed a long skirt?"

"I guess." Somehow, Theodosia wasn't feeling the moment. Actually, she was feeling a little sick.

Delaine began ripping through a rack of clothing, pulling out skirts, muttering to herself in some kind of crazy fashion lingo. "Black silk, too McQueen. Panne velvet . . . winter collection. Maybe this chiffon?" She held it up to herself, then shook her head. "No, it's too Antigua. We can do better."

"Delaine," Theodosia said, "I'm perfectly capable of picking something out by myself."

Delaine looked pained, as if she'd suddenly developed a chronic case of indigestion. "No, honey, you should let me do what I do best."

"And what would that be?"

"Function as your stylist, of course. Someone has to make a measured, tasteful decision here."

"Excuse me, are you saying I have no personal style? No taste?" It wasn't often Theodosia got an opportunity to needle Delaine right back. She was enjoying it immensely.

"Not at all," Delaine purred. "It's just that I'm a retail professional and you're basically a civilian." She threw an impassioned look at Theodosia. "Theo, if you could *see* the women, the poor little lambs, who stumble into my shop. Most are in dire need of a total fashion makeover." Delaine's eyes took on a slightly evangelical look as her hands gracefully carved the air. "They need a carefully nipped and tailored jacket. Blouses that show off what the good Lord gave them. And accessories . . ." At this Delaine threw up her hands in despair. "Don't get me started on accessories."

"I won't," Theodosia said.

"Handbags," Delaine blurted out. She was jacked up and ready to rhapsodize about accessories no matter what. "Absolutely essential to every outfit." She shook an index finger at Theodosia. "Yet *nobody* seems to understand the appropriateness of carrying a frame bag as opposed to a more casual shoulder bag."

"Sounds like there's a bag crisis brewing."

"And there isn't a woman alive who couldn't benefit from a strand of pearls, a colorful silk scarf, and a great pair of sunglasses." Delaine took a reverent pause. "Those are the key pieces that make or break an outfit."

"I never realized you were so passionate about accessories," Theodosia said. She was keenly aware that she'd been carrying the same Fendi shoulder bag for two years now—maybe she was due for a change? Or, considering the price of designer bags these days, maybe not.

Delaine picked out three different skirts, led Theodosia to a dressing room, and pushed her inside. When Theodosia emerged, wearing a silver crepe skirt, Delaine said, "I love it. That fabric really helps camouflage the hips."

Theodosia peered hesitantly into the three-way mirror. "You mean *my* hips?"

"Anybody's hips. I'm a big believer in camouflage no matter what size the body part."

"If we're into camouflage, maybe I should just throw on an army jacket."

Delaine tittered. "The military look was popular *last* year, dear." She turned to grab another skirt, then her hand shot into the air and she yelled, "Sissy!" at the top of her lungs. At which point a tall, flamboyant-looking blonde in a bright red leather jacket came crashing toward them.

"Delaine!" the woman yelped back.

"Theo," Delaine said, as Sissy practically smashed up against them, "this is my dear friend Sissy Lanier."

"Pleased to meet you, pleased to meet you," Sissy chortled. She stuck out her hand and shook Theodosia's hand as she managed a lopsided, manic grin.

As Sissy continued to pump her arm in greeting, Theodosia realized that this lady was the soon-to-be ex-wife of Carson Lanier. Also known as the wife of the dead guy.

"Nice to meet you," Theodosia said as she gave Sissy an appraising glance. Besides her leather jacket, Sissy was wearing black leather slacks and carrying a black handbag covered in silver studs. Sissy also wore tons of makeup, had medically enhanced trout-pout lips and an enormous swirl of hair. Seriously, her cloud of hair was so massive it could probably generate its own atmospheric conditions.

When Theodosia finally pulled her hand back from Sissy's grasp, she said, in what she hoped was a serious voice, "I'm very sorry for your loss."

"Don't be," Sissy drawled. She shrugged and pushed at her hair to give it an extra plumping. "Turns out my loss is also my gain."

"That's for sure," Delaine said.

"Excuse me?" Theodosia wasn't sure she'd heard Sissy quite right. What was she referring to?

"Carson and I never finalized our divorce papers," Sissy said in a tone that was a boisterous half whisper. "The poor jerk kept putting it off. He was *so* busy being the important, high-powered Capital Bank executive that he never could find time to drop by my lawyer's office and sign the papers."

"Men can be so self-absorbed," Delaine said, studying her lipstick in the mirror.

"Now look where it got him," Sissy said, her voice growing louder. "Carson ran plumb out of time. In fact, he's dead! Now *I'm* the bereaved wife who inherits *everything.*" She let loose a sharp, high-pitched chortle. "And you know what the best thing is?"

"Is there a best thing?" Theodosia asked. She thought Sissy seemed bizarrely jubilant about her situation.

"Of course there is," Sissy said. "Best of all, Carson's dopey girlfriend—the one he was probably planning to marry—gets *nothing* from his estate. Zip, zero, zilch."

Delaine's eyes lit up and she leaned forward expectantly. "Your husband had a *girl*friend?"

Sissy curled a lip. "Absolutely, he did. Although I suppose the technical term would be mistress."

"Goodness," Theodosia said. She had a feeling the plot had just gotten a whole lot more complicated.

"Or maybe badness," Delaine said. Her eyes were wide and searching. "Do you know who the girlfriend was? Is?"

"I most certainly do," Sissy said. "Charleston isn't that big a town. You can't hide a torrid affair like they had when you're enjoying flirty lunches at the Peninsula Grill or all-day golf outings at Coosaw Creek Country Club."

"Then who is it?" Delaine asked. She was dying to discover the woman's name, practically choking on her words.

Sissy waved a hand. "It was a woman who worked with Carson at the bank."

"Probably one of the tellers," Delaine said.

"Carson didn't think I knew what was going on," Sissy continued. "But I wasn't the dumb-bunny little wife he thought I was. I knew darned well that he was carrying on with Betty Bates."

That name meant nothing to Theodosia. But she filed it away in her memory. Just in case.

You didn't buy anything at the sample sale?" Haley asked, as Theodosia let herself in the back door of the tea shop.

"No, things kind of went off the rails."

"You mean Delaine was there?"

"And being a bit disruptive."

"Yup, she's like that," Haley said. "Mad as a hatter."

"Did I miss anything important?" Theodosia asked. She dropped her bag on her desk and pulled off her suede jacket.

"Lover boy dropped by."

"Pete Riley was here?" Theodosia was suddenly hyperalert. And wondering why Riley hadn't called her on her cell phone. Or maybe he had and she'd just been too distracted to notice.

"I'm not sure whether he came to see you or partake of my scones," Haley said. She fluttered her lashes and twisted a hank of long blond hair. "Probably both."

"So what's up?" Theodosia asked. "What did he say?"

"You'd better go talk to Drayton," Haley said. "He's the man with all the answers."

But when Theodosia asked Drayton about Riley's visit, he made an unhappy face.

"Detective Riley told me that he interviewed Jud Harker, all right," Drayton said. "But it wasn't until *after* Harker paid us a visit."

"Okay." Theodosia had a feeling something strange was brewing, and it wasn't a new blend of tea.

"It seems that Harker fed your Detective Riley a completely different story than what actually went on here."

"What are you talking about?" Theodosia asked.

"Harker told Riley that you upset him terribly."

Theodosia reared back in surprise. "*I* upset him?"

"Apparently Harker gave Riley some tearful song and dance number about how you yelled at him, hurt his feelings, and then shoved him out the door."

"Wait a minute." Theodosia flapped a hand in disbelief. "I hope you set the record straight, here. Did you tell Detective Riley that Harker came in chattering like a demented ferret? That he was out of control and pretty much upset our customers?"

"I told him that, yes," Drayton said.

"And what did Riley say?"

Drayton thought for a moment. "Riley said that Harker probably concocted his whitewashed version of the story as a way to assert his innocence."

"But Harker may not be innocent," Theodosia sputtered. "In fact, he might be guilty as sin!"

Drayton gazed at her calmly. "You'll get no argument from me."

"Jeez." Theodosia shook her head, put both elbows on the counter, and leaned forward. "What a crazy day. First Sissy Lanier and now this."

"Excuse me?" Drayton said. "Did you just say . . . ?"

"Sissy Lanier, yes," Theodosia said. "Delaine introduced us at the sample sale, which launched Sissy into a bizarre rant."

"About her dead husband?" Drayton had a sympathetic look on his face. "Perhaps the woman just needed some kind words."

"I think Sissy needs an exorcism. She was cackling away

about the fact that her husband never got around to signing the divorce papers, so now she inherits everything."

"Gracious."

"She isn't one bit gracious," Theodosia said. She was about to tell Drayton about Carson Lanier's affair, too, and then decided that might be a little too gossipy and inappropriate. Besides, maybe Carson Lanier *hadn't* had an affair after all. Perhaps the affair was all conjecture—or smoke screen—on Sissy Lanier's part. Maybe Sissy had been trying to assert her innocence as well.

Theodosia watched Drayton as he went back to brewing a pot of lemon gunpowder tea. And decided that Sissy, with her devil-may-care attitude, suddenly felt like the perfect suspect.

10

❧

I told you before that we couldn't go for a run tonight," Theodosia said. She was sitting in the living room of her small cottage a few blocks from the Indigo Tea Shop. And she was having a conversation with her dog, Earl Grey.

"This meeting at the Heritage Society came up unexpectedly."

Earl Grey looked at her with limpid brown eyes and slowly cocked his head.

"Come on, don't give me that accusing look. Show me some mercy, will you? I really don't want to go to this stupid board meeting. I'm only doing it as a favor to Drayton."

This time Earl Grey sighed visibly.

"How about if we negotiate a make-good? What if we take an extralong run tomorrow night?"

"Rowwr?" Earl Grey's tail thumped a couple of beats.

"You want to go when I get back tonight? I don't know—it could be pretty late. Well, I guess we'll just have to play it by ear."

That seemed to do it for Earl Grey. He bobbed his head and strolled over to the fireplace, where he curled up on his favorite Aubusson rug.

Theodosia let loose a long breath from her perch on the chintz-covered sofa. It was good to be home. Cozied up in her small cottage in the Historic District. And no matter her promise to Drayton, she would've preferred to stay home and enjoy Earl Grey's sweet companionship. He was, after all, a terrific dog who had changed dramatically from the terrified, half-starved puppy she'd found huddled in the alley behind the Indigo Tea Shop some years ago. Earl Grey had since grown into a magnificent animal with his dappled coat (which is why Theodosia considered him a Dalbrador); expressive eyes; and fine, aristocratic muzzle.

Theodosia leaned back and gazed about her living room. She loved the beamed ceiling, parquet floor, and brick fireplace with built-ins on each side. When she'd moved here a couple of years ago, she'd been thrilled that her chintz and damask furniture, antique highboy, and elegant oil paintings from her old apartment had fit right in. As if they'd always belonged here. As if it had been destiny.

Theodosia glanced at her watch. It was twenty to seven.

Okay, gotta get going. But first I'm going to try Pete Riley again.

His phone rang and rang, finally going to voice mail.

Where is he? Pulled into some new aspect of the investigation?

The notion made her fairly vibrate with energy. But this was no time to start spinning a web of what-ifs. Right now she had to grab her basket of scones and go pick up Drayton.

Drayton was waiting on the curb outside his house a few blocks away. When Theodosia pulled over and Drayton clambered into the passenger seat, she said, "I could barely see you out there."

"Dark of the moon," Drayton said.

"You make it sound so ominous," Theodosia said as she pulled away.

"That's because everything that's happened lately verges on the strange and unusual."

Theodosia hung a left down Tradd Street. "I brought our leftover scones along for the meeting tonight."

"Good," Drayton said. "We can throw them at anyone who tries to block the vote for Lanier's replacement."

"Is there going to be opposition?" Theodosia asked.

Drayton looked out the window as they sped along. "There's always opposition, no matter what we're voting on or talking about. A few years ago, we didn't seem to have such a contentious board. But now . . ."

"Do you think it has to do with the Heritage Society's recent financial troubles?" Theodosia asked. She knew that donations hadn't been rolling in like they used to. Unfortunately, some of their wealthier donors had passed away recently, and now the place was being run on a shoestring budget. No wonder Timothy Neville was pumping out all sorts of different events, hoping to attract a raft of new patrons.

"Could be because of tight money," Drayton said. "On the other hand, people seem a lot more prickly these days. I don't know what it is. Politics in this country, world problems . . . the Internet."

Theodosia made another left turn. "The Internet?" She sounded amused. "You're blaming technology for rude behavior?"

"People are way too connected," Drayton said.

Theodosia chuckled. "You're not. You're not on the Internet. You didn't even want the simple e-mail account I set up for you at the tea shop and then tried to stuff down your throat."

"That's because I'm a Luddite, pure and simple. I can get

along just fine without texting, tweeting, and chirping. I came into this world without the benefit of technology; that's how I'll probably go out."

"Please don't talk old," Theodosia said as she changed lanes. They were almost at the front door of the Heritage Society.

"I am getting old."

She pulled over to the curb and put her car in park. Stared at Drayton across the dark interior of her Jeep. "You're not old, you're seasoned."

He gave a faint smile. "Ah, I suppose that does sound better."

As they walked down the main hall of the Heritage Society, Theodosia was once again reminded of why she adored the place. The building was an enormous pile of gray stones, assembled to look almost castlelike, and hung with tapestries, oil paintings, and the most fantastical chandeliers. There was an enormous library filled with leather-bound books and leather chairs, and meeting rooms that featured candelabras and stained glass windows. Then there were the various galleries, all stuffed with art and antiquities. Even better were the enormous basement storage rooms. Theodosia loved wandering through storage, imagining that she was in a labyrinth beneath the streets of Rome or Paris, never knowing when she'd stumble upon some priceless treasure—or even something spooky!

They caught Timothy Neville just as he was exiting his office.

"Wonderful," Timothy said when he spotted Theodosia. "You came after all. Appreciate it."

"Only because Drayton twisted my arm," Theodosia said.

"And we come bearing gifts," Drayton said, holding up the basket full of scones.

"Thank you," Timothy said as they walked along. "They'll

pair nicely with the tea that Sylvia, my admin assistant, just brewed. Nice of you to send a tin of your special Palmetto State blend over to us."

"No problem," Drayton said. "Um . . . is our new board member here yet?"

"They're on the way," Timothy said. "So hopefully all will go well."

They paused in the hallway outside the main conference room, and Theodosia decided this was as good a time as any to speak up.

"Before we go in there," Theodosia said, "I have to tell you about a strange incident that happened this morning."

"At the tea shop," Drayton said.

Timothy shuffled papers as his sparse eyebrows crawled up his smooth forehead. "Yes? What is that?"

"That man who's been so vehemently opposed to your Rare Weapons Show—" Theodosia began.

"Jud Harker." Timothy pounced on the name like he was swatting an insect.

"It turns out Harker works as a handyman at the Stagwood Inn," Theodosia said. "You know, the B and B right next door to you."

Timothy's mouth dropped open and he blinked in surprise. "Are you serious?" When they both nodded, he said, "That's utterly bizarre . . . I had no idea." Then his expression hardened as it took him all of two seconds to forge a connection. "So Harker *could* have been lurking in the area Sunday night. He could have fired that deadly arrow from the third floor."

"That possibility exists, yes," Theodosia said. "The police have already questioned Harker, and he's categorically denied everything. But they're not about to let this go. They'll keep after him, maybe even put a watch on him."

"Don't be surprised when the police circle back to talk to you again," Drayton said. "Looking for more information."

"You know, all I've ever received from this Harker person are angry letters and phone calls," Timothy said, his hand settling on the doorknob. "I don't believe I could identify the man if he walked into this room."

"Well . . . you probably *should* find out what Harker looks like," Theodosia said. "Just in case he ever tries to accost you in person. Really, the man struck me as being positively unhinged."

The board members, six men and four women, sat around a mahogany table the size of a yacht's main deck as Timothy called the meeting to order. The secretary read through the minutes of last month's meeting, and they went over a few matters that were easily settled with verbal ayes or nays.

Then Timothy pushed back his chair and stood up, ready to address the real reason they were all there.

"You're all aware," Timothy began, "that one of our board members met with a terrible fate." Feet shuffled and papers rustled all around him in the uncomfortable silence that spun out. Still, everyone remained focused on Timothy. "Carson Lanier was fatally shot with an arrow," he continued. His voice remained strong, but his shoulders began to sag. "And this unholy deed happened while he was a guest in my home."

A board member, a man named Nicholas Clayton, cleared his throat. "So Mr. Lanier's death wasn't an accident?" He glanced around the table. "I think we were all hoping that the press reports were wrong."

"It appears to have been cold-blooded murder," Timothy said. "Which is why the police are in the middle of a full-scale investigation."

"So they'll be talking to all of us?" another of the board members asked.

"That I don't know," Timothy said. "Perhaps the police will want to interview all of you; perhaps they'll confine their questions to the people who were present at my home that night."

"What can we do to help?" one of the female board members asked. Theodosia recognized her as Louella Rayburn, a well-heeled social doyenne.

Timothy opened his mouth to talk, but was suddenly so distressed by the circumstances that nothing came out.

"You can pray," Theodosia spoke up in a soft voice. "And keep a good thought that this matter is resolved as quickly as possible."

"Amen," Drayton said.

Timothy cleared his throat. "There's no hesitation on my part when I tell you I feel responsible." He seemed to have recovered his bearings somewhat. "And that I'd like to help set things straight."

"What exactly are you saying?" Clayton asked him.

"I know this is going to sound slightly unorthodox," Timothy said. "But a possible successor has stepped forward. Someone who was quite close to Carson Lanier and feels they could adequately take his place here on the board."

Timothy picked up a stack of papers and passed them around the table. When the papers got to Theodosia, she passed them on without taking one.

"What you see here is a résumé. A curriculum vitae, as it were," Timothy said.

"And you're recommending that we accept this new candidate?" Louella Rayburn asked. "To vote on them?" She wasn't challenging Timothy, she was just clarifying his intentions.

"Absolutely, I want you to consider them," Timothy said.

"When do we get to meet this new fellow?" Drayton asked.

"Right now." Timothy stepped away from the table and pulled open the door. "Hello," he said as he leaned out into the hallway. "Please come in and I'll introduce you to our board of directors."

All eyes were focused on the woman who stepped into the room. She was tall, with dark hair cut in a pageboy, a thin face, and narrow black metal glasses. She also wore a pink tweed skirt suit that looked both serious and expensive.

"Oh," Drayton said under his breath. "Not a fellow at all."

"People," Timothy said, "I'd like you all to meet Ms. Betty Bates."

11

❧

For Theodosia, the name suddenly hung in the air like a sharp, discordant note.

"Ms. Bates is also an executive at Capital Bank," Timothy said. "And, as you can see by her rather impressive résumé, she was a trusted colleague of Carson Lanier's."

"A colleague?" Theodosia said under her breath. Her elbow shot out and connected firmly with Drayton's ribs. She had to tell him!

Drayton bent forward from the impact and twisted toward her, a puzzled look on his face. "What?" he whispered.

Theodosia ducked her head down and cupped a hand to her mouth. It took her barely sixty seconds to inform Drayton that Carson Lanier and Betty Bates were rumored to have had an affair. As she whispered, and as Timothy's introduction continued, Drayton's eyes grew bigger and bigger. Finally, he nodded. He understood.

Drayton's hand shot up, interrupting a pleasant conversation

Betty Bates was having with Louella Rayburn. "May I make a suggestion, please?" he asked.

Timothy smiled amiably at him. "Yes, Drayton?"

"I make a motion that we table any sort of vote for now. That we give ourselves ample time to get acquainted with our candidate."

Timothy's face fell. "Here I thought we might—"

But Louella Rayburn jumped in. "I second Drayton," she said. "I think we do need adequate time for us to meet Ms. Bates and go over what looks like a very fine curriculum vitae. And, of course, she'll want to familiarize herself with us and our workings."

"Very well," Timothy said. "The motion has been put forth and seconded. All in favor of allowing us a grace period of—shall we say two weeks?—to get better acquainted with Ms. Bates, kindly say aye."

There were seven ayes.

"Opposed?"

There were only three nays as Betty Bates glared across the table at Drayton.

"The ayes have it," Timothy said. "And might I suggest we organize a small cocktail party for Ms. Bates and the board members this Saturday night, right before the opening of the Rare Weapons Show? That might be a good first step in us getting to know one another."

"A fine idea," Drayton said.

And with that, Timothy adjourned the meeting.

But just because the meeting was over didn't mean the issue was put to rest.

As Timothy and the other board members began to file out

of the room, Betty Bates practically flew across the table to accost Theodosia and Drayton.

"You were the one who stopped the vote," Betty snarled at Theodosia. Her professional demeanor had cracked wide open to reveal a woman who was furious, just this side of rabid.

Theodosia shook her head. "Not me—I have no vote. I'm not even on the board of directors. I'm just an observer tonight."

"Just an observer," Bates mimicked. "But your friend here, Drayton . . ." She glared hotly at him. "Is that your name?" Betty turned back to Theodosia. "You whispered something to him and then the vote was delayed. Tabled."

"Excuse me," Drayton said. "But it was the board's prerogative to do so."

Bates set her mouth in a hard line and her dark eyes gleamed. "But *why* did you want the vote delayed? I submitted a résumé that details my past board experience as well as all the critical business requirements." She shifted her gaze to Theodosia. "Something's going on, I can smell it."

"Like Drayton told you," Theodosia said. "It's a mere formality, a time period that will allow everyone to get better acquainted."

But Bates wouldn't let it go. "This is not only suspicious, it's humiliating." She narrowed her eyes and seemed to search Theodosia's face for an answer. "Why do I have a feeling you've been listening to that witch Sissy Lanier?"

Theodosia flinched. And Betty Bates caught it. She pointed an accusing finger at Theodosia and pounced. "I was right. You *have* been listening to her dirty, filthy lies."

Theodosia shook her head. "Anytime there's a high-profile murder, there's bound to be all sorts of wild rumors flying around. That's not to say we're going to believe them." Theodosia felt exposed for being caught and guilty for buying in to

Sissy's nasty rumor. Perhaps it wasn't true? But how could she be sure?

But it didn't matter what Theodosia said or did; Betty Bates had launched into full-blown confrontational mode.

"Wait a minute," Betty said. "Do you think *I* had something to do with Carson Lanier's murder?"

Theodosia just stared at her. The idea had begun to percolate in her brain.

"You people are out of your minds!" Betty shouted. "Do you think I was the one who was stalking Lanier? Do you think I was the one who shot an arrow at him?" She gulped a breath and swallowed hard. "The two of us worked together, for cripes' sake."

"I take it you were friends?" Theodosia asked.

Betty raised a shoulder. "I suppose we were friendly enough."

But her lukewarm answer made Theodosia wonder just how close they'd really been.

"We've not put any stock in idle rumors," Drayton protested, although he pretty much had. Touching a hand to his bow tie, he threw Theodosia a helpless look, practically begging her to slide back into the conversation.

But before Theodosia could get another two cents in, Betty said, "If you people are snooping around for suspects, you know who you should take a look at?" Her cheeks flared red and she practically bared her teeth. "You should be investigating Bob Garver!"

Theodosia, who was getting more and more annoyed by Betty's histrionics, decided the woman could easily fit the profile of suspect. Anyone who harbored that much anger and rancor probably had a serious problem. If Betty had professional jealousies or issues at the bank, she certainly *could* have killed Lanier. The other thing that made Theodosia suspicious was Betty's attempt at misdirection. She'd immediately started throwing shade on this Garver person.

"Who is Bob Garver?" Theodosia asked.

"Garver was Lanier's business partner," Bates cried. She took a step back and threw up her hands. "Holy buckets, don't you people know anything?"

"Do the police know about Bob Garver?" Theodosia asked.

"They should," Betty said. "They ought to. But from the bumbling efforts I've seen so far, maybe not." She pulled her mouth into a smug smile. "The investigators don't seem particularly smart."

"Exactly what business were Lanier and Garver partners in?" Theodosia asked. She knew Lanier had been an executive VP at Capital Bank. But she hadn't heard word one about any other business he'd been involved with. Obviously, neither had Drayton. And maybe not the police.

Betty Bates hissed at them like an ornery cat. "Bob Garver is a garden-variety crook that Lanier hooked up with a few months ago. They were going to rehab a bunch of Charleston single houses over on Beaufain Street." She smirked. "Go ahead, I dare you to track down Bob Garver and ask him about the low-interest loans he conned from the City Redevelopment Fund. See if you think he's putting that money to good use or just lining his own pockets!"

"Are you telling us that Lanier was in on this scam?" Theodosia asked.

"Maybe, maybe not," Betty said. "But think about it. A dispute over three point nine million dollars could definitely lead to murder!" She waggled an index finger in their faces to reinforce her point, then fled out the door.

"Oh my," Drayton said. He looked like he was ready to faint. "That was so unpleasant."

"I'm sorry," Theodosia said. "I know how much you hate confrontation, but we need to talk to Timothy right away." She grabbed Drayton's sleeve and pulled him along. "We've got to make him understand what a liability Betty Bates would be to the board."

"Will you please explain to me why you were so adamant about delaying the vote tonight?" Timothy barked as soon as Theodosia and Drayton pushed their way into his office. He rapped his knuckles angrily against his desk. He'd obviously been waiting to grill them. "And why we were mousetrapped into *insulting* our new board candidate?" Timothy was sitting in a high leather chair behind his ping-pong-table-sized desk, looking perturbed and a little worn-out.

Drayton immediately flapped a hand at Theodosia. "You tell him, Theo."

"Tell me what?" Timothy rasped. "Whatever it is, it better be good."

"You asked me here tonight because you believe I'm a good judge of character," Theodosia began. "Correct?"

Timothy inclined his head toward her. "Yes."

"Well, I heard an ugly rumor today," Theodosia said. "Unproven, but still very troubling."

"Who was the source of this rumor?"

"Sissy Lanier," Theodosia said.

Timothy's eyebrows pinched together. "Carson's estranged wife."

"Yes. Sissy told me that her husband had been having an affair with Betty Bates," Theodosia said.

Timothy froze. "What?" Some of the color drained from his face. "That is . . . most troubling indeed." He leaned back in his desk chair and let his head drop forward, as if this news were almost too much to fathom. "You're positive about this?"

"Like I said, I heard it from Sissy. And she was quite adamant that they were carrying on an affair."

"This is a shock," Timothy said. "Clearly we'll need to question Ms. Bates about what appears to be a rather indelicate situation. We certainly don't want a hint of impropriety among our board members. Especially when we've just come through a rough patch financially and are starting to regain our footing."

"I agree," Theodosia said. "You need to get Ms. Bates's side of the story."

"I'll do that," Timothy said.

"There's something else," Theodosia said.

Timothy sighed. "There always is."

"Betty Bates could also be the killer."

"What!"

"Besides pooh-poohing our suspicions of a love affair, Betty Bates tried to impress upon us the fact that she *wasn't* the killer," Theodosia said. "Seeing her as a suspect hadn't seriously crossed our minds until she started vehemently denying her involvement."

"Dear Lord," Timothy said. "Do you think Betty Bates could have killed Lanier? If she wasn't his paramour, then was there professional rivalry at the bank?"

"That's always a possibility," Theodosia said. "But, get this, Betty came right out and accused a man named Bob Garver of murdering Carson Lanier."

"Sissy Lanier points a finger at Betty, and then Betty points it at someone else?" Timothy muttered. "How many suspects can there be?" He seemed to collapse inward. "And who is Bob Garver? I'm not familiar with that name at all."

"Neither are we," Drayton said.

"I don't know," Theodosia said. "But we need to ask Detectives Tidwell and Riley about this Betty Bates rumor. And look into her accusation about Bob Garver."

Timothy reached across his desk and fiddled with an old Cartier pen that was stuck in a marble stand. "You'll notify the police about this? And keep me in the loop?"

"Of course," Theodosia said.

Ten minutes later, Theodosia pulled up in front of Drayton's home. The night was full-on dark, the only hint of light coming from globes of antique streetlamps that were strung down the narrow street like so many glowing rosary beads. Sweet hints of jessamine rode currents of air.

"Do you want to come in for a cup of chamomile tea?" Drayton asked. "Mull over the night's turn of events?"

Theodosia shook her head. "No thanks."

"What if I offered you something stronger? Sherry?"

"I think I just want to go home." What Theodosia really wanted was to get in touch with Pete Riley. Burn up the phone lines and ask him the million unanswered questions that were buzzing inside her brain. About Jud Harker, Betty Bates, and now this guy Bob Garver, whoever he was. Maybe, hopefully, Riley could shed some light on what was turning into a frightful mess.

A few minutes later, Theodosia was back in her own neighborhood, gliding past her cozy little home that had come with the endearing name of Hazelhurst. It was a Queen Anne–style cottage, complete with wooden gables, a slightly asymmetrical design, rough cedar tiles that replicated a thatched roof, and the blip of a two-story turret. Curls of ivy meandered up the home's brick and stucco walls.

At the end of the block, she made a sharp right-hand turn and bumped down the cobblestone alley behind some slightly larger homes and pulled into her car park. Once she slipped through the wooden gate into her backyard, she was able to breathe a sigh of relief.

Home at last.

With tiny shards of light from a streetlamp slanting through a tangle of greenery, her backyard looked like an enchanted garden. A small patio surrounded by shrubs and magnolia trees and a tiny fountain that pattered and splashed, adding a musical note to the stir of wind through the trees.

When Theodosia opened the back door and stepped into the kitchen, Earl Grey was right there, Johnny-on-the-spot to meet her. Tail wagging, ears pricked forward, eyes shiny bright as oil spots.

"You want to go outside for a while?" she asked him. "Make sure the raccoons haven't been staging brash raids on our fishpond?" Five small goldfish swam around and basically enjoyed life in the tiny backyard pond. They also brought Earl Grey hours of gazing pleasure.

"Woof!"

"Okay then, I'll see you in a bit. I'm just going to brew a cup of rooibos tea and make a phone call."

Theodosia closed the door, kicked off her shoes, and brewed a quick pot of tea. Then she called Pete Riley. When he answered, she started right in without benefit of preamble.

"I tried to call you before, several times—where were you?" Then, "I heard a very troubling rumor tonight. About a man named Bob Garver."

"Hello to you, too," Riley said. "Because I'm home now. And

why are you asking me about some guy I've never heard of? Also, why should I care about some random dude when I'm stretched out in my easy chair listening to a RiverDogs baseball game on the radio and drinking a Holy City Pilsner?"

"A what?"

"Craft beer."

"Okay."

Theodosia calmed down and spent several minutes bringing Riley up to speed. She told him about Sissy Lanier's accusation that her husband and Betty Bates had been carrying on a torrid affair. Then she segued into Betty Bates itching to take Lanier's place on the Heritage Society's board. And finished with an instant replay of Betty Bates screaming about how she wasn't guilty of killing Lanier, but some guy named Bob Garver had cheated the city out of low-interest loans and had probably murdered Lanier.

When Theodosia was finally done, Riley remained silent.

"Well?" Theodosia said. "What do you think?" She could hear the faint voice of the play-by-play announcer in the background, calling the game. Every once in a while there was the roar of the crowd. A big play, she guessed, though she wasn't much of a baseball fan.

"I'm thinking about how you get pulled into the strangest things," Riley said. "I mean, silly me. I've been stumbling around all day like a model detective, questioning witnesses, trying to pry a shred of information out of them, diligently taking notes, and writing police reports in triplicate. And in one fell swoop you come up with two viable suspects."

"You really think they're both viable?" Theodosia asked. "Betty Bates and Garver?" A thrill ran through her that Riley was taking this seriously. Or was he simply humoring her?

"I don't know, tell me more," he said.

Okay, he wasn't humoring her. Good.

Theodosia attempted to fill in some more of the blanks. Elaborating on her meet-up with Sissy Lanier, the tone and temper of the Heritage Society board meeting, and Betty Bates's verbal assault on her and Drayton.

"Lady," Riley said. "You pack a lot of living into one day."

"Do you think Betty Bates could have killed Lanier?"

"I don't know, but I'd like to hear her alibi for Sunday night."

"Does that mean you're going to interview her?" Theodosia wondered if Betty would go postal with Detective Riley like she had with her and Drayton.

"Couldn't hurt."

"What about this Bob Garver fellow?"

"What about him?"

"If Garver really did cheat the City of Charleston out of three point nine million dollars in low-interest loans . . . well, a man that crooked could easily murder his partner in crime, don't you think?"

"Maybe. Though white-collar crooks generally aren't killers. They tend to be narcissistic and manipulative, but prefer not to get their hands dirty."

"This guy could be different," Theodosia said.

"He could be."

"So you'll look into this city home loan thing?" Theodosia asked, just as a loud BANG sounded at the back door. It was Earl Grey smacking the door with his paw, asking to be let in. She put her hand over the mouthpiece and listened to Riley.

"I'll make a couple of calls first thing tomorrow," Riley said. "I know a few people who work in city government, so it shouldn't be difficult to get a read on this."

"I need to ask you about Sissy Lanier, too," Theodosia said.

She paused, knowing she might or might not get an answer. "Is Sissy a suspect in her husband's murder?"

"Now, why would you ask that?"

"Like I told you, I met Sissy today," Theodosia said, as Earl Grey banged again, getting more impatient. "And she seemed . . . well, awfully blasé, more than a little unconcerned, about her husband's rather grisly demise."

"Uh-huh."

"And then Sissy mentioned the fact that Lanier had never bothered to sign the divorce papers, so now she stands to inherit everything." Theodosia paused. "You've probably investigated her already, huh? Don't the police always look at the spouse first?"

"That's only in TV crime dramas."

"Really?" Theodosia could hear a combination of cheering and static rising in the background that blended in with Earl Grey's insistent banging. It was starting to drive her crazy.

"Kidding. I'm kidding," Riley said. "Of course we look at the spouse first. Because twenty-five percent of the time they're the ones who did it."

"Okay, thank you," Theodosia said. "The other thing I wanted to know about is . . . the autopsy? On Carson Lanier?"

"Good Lord, Theo, why do you want to know about that?"

"Because it's important."

"That information is confidential."

"Come on, there's just you and me here. And I've already seen Lanier at his worst."

"Well, it wasn't the arrow that killed him," Riley said.

"I didn't think so," Theodosia said. "There was so much blood at the scene. So his heart was still pumping when he landed on that spike."

"I think so, yes."

"Grisly. What else was in the autopsy report?"

"Lanier sustained several fractures and multiple lacerations," Riley said.

"Anything else?"

"That's about— Oh, wow!"

"What?" Theodosia asked.

"Jeez, I think Kaczmarski just hit a home run!"

"What. Is. Wrong?" Theodosia asked as she opened the back door and let Earl Grey in. "Don't you know I was on the phone?"

"Rowr." Earl Grey fixed her with a baleful gaze.

"Now? You want to go for a run now?"

He continued to look at her.

"It's pretty late, but . . . oh, I suppose we could. Why not?"

Run was the magic word that rang the bells and spun the lemons and cherries. Theodosia changed into a hoodie and leggings, snapped a leash on Earl Grey's collar, and they headed out.

Ten o'clock at night and the neighborhood was quiet as a graveyard. A few lights burned in the second stories of the Georgian, Victorian, and Italianate homes that surrounded her. But there was no one on the street. No cars, no walkers, not even a stray cat.

"You sure this was a good idea?" Theodosia asked. But Earl Grey surged ahead, pulling her down the alley like a sled dog muscling through a snowdrift. They ran for a couple of blocks down Chalmers Street, warming up, feeling good, blowing out the carbon. Then they cut over to Church Street, where they drifted past the Indigo Tea Shop, the Cabbage Patch Gift Shop, Antiquarian Bookshop, and a few other small neighborhood shops that were battened down tight for the night. Just past St. Phillip's, they turned in to Philadelphia Alley.

PLUM TEA CRAZY   103

Originally called "Cow Alley" because it had mostly been used to corral livestock more than a hundred years ago, this narrow passageway was also referred to as Dueler's Alley by locals who knew its history. Paved with cobblestones that had come from the ballast of Colonial ships, this narrow alley ran between several large, fancy homes and boasted high walls and limited points of access. In days of yore, when dueling (swords, pistols, or choose your weapon) was popular in Charleston, this was the designated spot to defend your honor or settle an argument for good.

Theodosia had slowed to a walk and was halfway down Dueler's Alley when she decided this probably wasn't the smartest route to take. Fog had crept in from the harbor, turning the minute bits of lamplight that filtered in from the street into yellow smudges. And the darker and foggier it became, the more Theodosia was reminded of the alley's strange legends and lore.

As in numerous ghost stories that concerned a jaunty whistling doctor who haunted this particular alley.

"But we don't believe in ghosts, do we?" Theodosia said to Earl Grey, even though most of the stories were regarded as gospel truth.

As if in answer, the dog dropped his tail and hunched his shoulders.

"As soon as we pop out of here, we'll make a dash for home," Theodosia said. "Get warmed up." A damp chill had seeped in and she knew her speaking out loud was a form of bravado to help ward off any unwanted phenomena.

Didn't work.

Halfway down the dark alley, Theodosia heard the scrape of shoe leather against cobblestone.

What? There's somebody behind me?

Theodosia's heart suddenly blipped faster, her breath rasped in the back of her throat.

And I don't think it's ectoplasm or ghostly phenomena. This is real!

Theodosia didn't turn around. Instead, she tightened Earl Grey's leash and picked up the pace. Seriously picked up the pace.

So did whoever was right behind her.

Theodosia sprinted for the end of the alley, in a sudden, all-out, gut-busting effort that would have made Usain Bolt proud. All the while, the names of Jud Harker, Sissy Lanier, and Betty Bates kept running through her brain like chase lights on a movie marquee. Was one of them coming after her because she'd stuck her nose in where it didn't belong? Had this investigation just become a lot more dangerous than she'd ever suspected?

Emerging from the alley on State Street, Theodosia and Earl Grey kicked their sprint into a gallop. And kept up their blistering pace until they were safely at home.

12

"This is going to be a busy morning," Drayton sang out as he reached up and grabbed a tin of Assam from his floor-to-ceiling collection of teas.

"They're all busy," Theodosia said. She had enlisted Jamie's aid this Wednesday morning and, together, they'd set plates, silverware, and teacups on the tables, added tea lights, and arranged everything just so. Now Jamie was placing daffodil stems into antique milk glass vases, while Theodosia was on her hands and knees, restocking one of her highboys with jars of honey, marmalade, lemon curd, and her various T-Bath products.

"How many flowers go in each vase again?" Jamie asked.

"Have you ever studied mathematics?" Drayton called to him. "Long division? Short division?"

Jamie nodded. "I guess so."

"Then take the number of vases you have sitting in front of you and divide it into your total number of flowers."

"Yeah, I suppose that could work," Jamie said.

"Private schools," Drayton muttered. "When did their standards begin to slip?"

Theodosia stood up and dusted her hands together. "Don't mind him," she told Jamie. "Drayton's always a little grumpy before he downs his first cup of English breakfast tea."

"Drayton doesn't bother me," Jamie said. "In fact, I find him fascinating."

Drayton looked startled. "Why on earth would you say that?"

"Because you're so multifaceted," Jamie said. "You grew up in South China, worked in London, create all sorts of great bonsai trees, and know everything there is to know about tea, art, and classical music."

"Please don't flatter him," Theodosia told Jamie.

Drayton held up a finger. "No, the boy makes a good point."

Five minutes before the tea shop was set to open, Detective Riley called.

"Theodosia," Drayton called to her. He held up the phone and waggled it. "For you."

She snatched it out of his hands. "Hello?"

"Okay," Riley said. "I did some checking on your guy Bob Garver."

"What did you find out?"

"Not a whole lot. Just that he's a commercial developer whose most recent project, Gateway Gables, was a mixed-use building."

"What is that, exactly?" Theodosia asked. She was pretty sure she knew what that meant, but it wouldn't hurt to get an exact definition.

Papers rattled and then Riley said, "Apparently, Gateway Gables entails retail space on the ground floor and apartment rentals on the top two floors."

"But what did you find out about Garver himself?"

"Nothing," Riley said. "Besides the fact that he collects monthly rent from his tenants."

Theodosia glanced at the front door, where Drayton was letting in the first customers of the day. "Okay, let me know when you get more."

Riley drew a sharp breath. "Theodosia, you know I can't do that."

"Whyever not?"

"I appreciate your giving me tips, but there's no way I can share proprietary police information with you."

"That's just plain silly," Theodosia said. "Especially after we've hashed out a number of things already. The autopsy . . . Sissy Lanier and Betty Bates."

"I really can't give you any more," Riley said. "My boss would kill me . . . in fact, he'd hang me by my thumbs and flog me with a push broom if he knew I'd talked to you about any of this."

"Tidwell," Theodosia said. His name came out as a long sigh.

"Yes, Tidwell. You know what a bear he can be."

Theodosia had always thought of Burt Tidwell as more of a teddy bear, but she didn't tell Riley that. "Okay then, what's the latest scoop on the arrow that Lanier was shot with? The quarrel?" She'd focused solely on suspects so far, but wondered if the actual murder weapon might be a worthwhile angle to pursue as well.

"Obviously, once the arrow was delivered from the medical examiner's office, we had our top ballistics people go over it."

"And what did they say?" Theodosia asked.

"Um . . . I don't have their full report yet."

"But they must have shared some information with you."

"Nothing I should share with you," Riley said. He sounded

anguished. He wanted to be forthcoming with her, but clearly feared he might compromise his investigation.

"You realize," Theodosia said, "that I was the first to spot it. That I made the call on it being a quarrel."

"I know that," Riley said.

"And my initial impression was that the arrow was quite old. Possibly an antique." She paused. "Is that what your people think as well?"

"Theodosia . . ." Now Riley sounded even more anxious. "Yes, the people in the ballistics lab suspected it might be antique as well. And that's all I'm going to say for now."

Theodosia was humming as she stepped up to the counter to grab two pots of tea.

"You're in a good mood," Drayton said. "Looking forward to Delaine's Silk Road Fashion Show today?"

"That and a few other things," Theodosia said. "Drayton, you know that short arrow we found stuck in Carson Lanier?"

Drayton gave a mock shudder. "The image remains seared in my brain."

"Your impression was that it was antique, am I correct?"

"I believe it was," Drayton said slowly. Then, "Yes, now that I recall, there was a hand-hewn, old-world craftsman feel to it."

"If one wanted to purchase an old-fashioned crossbow and quarrel, where would one go?"

Drayton aimed a level gaze at her. "You could be heading down a very dangerous pathway."

"It's just an innocent question," Theodosia said.

"No, it's not. But . . . let me think for a minute." Drayton poured hot water into a blue-and-white teapot, swished it around to warm the pot's interior, and then poured it out. "I suppose if I were looking for that sort of antique weapon, I might pay a visit to Chasen's Military Relics over on Bee Street."

Theodosia smiled sweetly. "What a lovely suggestion. Thank you."

"What are you two conspiring about now?" Haley asked. She was suddenly at the front counter, balancing a large tray of maple scones. Then she forgot her question and said, "I'm going to stick these in the pie saver. I have a feeling we're going to be extra busy today."

"It only stands to reason," Drayton said. "Since Theodosia will be gone over lunch."

"Do you think Jamie could give me an assist?" Theodosia asked Haley. "I mean, go along with me to Delaine's shop and help set up?"

"I think we could manage without him for a short while," Haley said.

"We've managed without him so far," Drayton mumbled.

Haley gave Drayton a sharp look. "Be nice. Jamie really does admire you." She took the top off the glass pie saver and started arranging her scones. "So, how was the board meeting last night?"

Drayton frowned. "It was your basic disaster."

"Yeah?" Haley's ears perked up. "What happened?"

Drayton nodded at Theodosia. "Care to give Haley a recap?"

"Oh," Theodosia said, "Timothy was presenting a potential board member to the existing board and it turned out to be a woman who works at Capital Bank who may or may not have been having an affair with Carson Lanier."

Haley reacted with a shocked expression. "She was canoodling with the dead guy?"

"Back when he was still alive," Drayton said. "Allegedly."

Intrigued, Haley said, "And they were carrying on at the bank?"

"Apparently so," Theodosia said. "Allegedly."

"Holy sweet potatoes," Haley said. "Who is this bank chick, anyway?"

"Please don't repeat this," Theodosia said, "but her name is Betty Bates."

Haley held up a finger and sketched the air. "You want to know what I think?"

"Not really," Drayton said.

But Haley was undeterred. "I think Lanier and Bates had a lovers' quarrel."

Drayton snorted.

Haley was stung by his reaction. "Don't be so blasé," she told him. "A lot of affairs are all hearts and flowers to begin with and then end in tragedy."

"Only if their story was written by Shakespeare or Lord Byron," Drayton said.

"But you know where that kind of conflict leads?" Haley asked, completely undeterred.

Drayton looked seriously pained. "Please enlighten us, Haley."

"To a duel. Like in days gone by, when two men would vie for the same woman's hand. Or two people would take the law into their own hands."

"You've been listening to too many legends about Dueler's Alley," Drayton said.

But Theodosia was suddenly alert. And it wasn't just because Drayton had mentioned Dueler's Alley. "Haley brings up a good point," she said. "Lanier and Betty Bates could have had a lovers' quarrel. You know the old saying—Hell hath no fury like a woman scorned."

Haley looked thoughtful. "So Lanier and Betty Bates—they both worked at Capital Bank?"

"They were VPs there," Theodosia said. "Well, I guess Betty still is."

"Huh. You know who works at that same bank?" Haley said.

"Who's that?"

"Linda Pickerel."

"I don't know her," Theodosia said.

"Sure, you do," Haley said. "Linda, the pretty red-haired girl who used to wait tables at that bistro over on East Bay Street. Um . . . Temptations, I think it's called."

"Oh, that Linda," Drayton said. "I do remember her. Nice girl."

"She works at Capital Bank now?" Theodosia asked. She was spinning the beginnings of an idea in her head.

Haley nodded. "Yeah. I ran into her at the farmers market a couple of weeks ago, and she mentioned that she'd started a new job there. I guess she's in some sort of trainee program for home mortgages."

"Do you think Linda would talk to me?" Theodosia asked. "Maybe give me an inside scoop?"

"You mean about Lanier and his chicky-poo?"

"Her correct name is Betty Bates," Drayton said.

"Whatever." Haley shrugged. She turned back to Theodosia. "But Linda may not know anything."

"That's not what Theodosia asked you," Drayton said. "She asked if your friend Linda would talk to her. On the QT. You know how employees like to talk." His lips twitched. "Dish the gossip."

Haley colored slightly. "Yeah, I guess." She gazed at Theodosia. "I suppose I could give Linda a call and ask her if she'd talk to you."

Theodosia smiled. "Do that, would you please?"

*   *   *

Theodosia seated a few more customers, delivered tea and scones, and chatted with Jamie about having him help set up the luncheon table over at Cotton Duck. He said he'd be delighted to go along and assist.

"Go grab Haley, will you?" Theodosia asked Jamie. "We need to know when she'll have everything packed up for us."

But Haley was more than ready.

She ducked out of the kitchen and said, "The food's all ready to go. You can grab it anytime. Now if you want."

"Did you talk to your friend Linda?" Theodosia asked.

Haley bobbed her head. "I did. And Linda said she'd talk to you."

"When?"

"Whenever. Today, even. You just have to call her and set up a time and place."

"Thank you, Haley," Theodosia said. "I appreciate it."

"No problem." Haley put her hands on her hips. "So. Your apps are ready whenever you want to take off. Just don't forget to load the warming trays as well."

"Apps?" Drayton said to her. "You mean like apps for your phone?"

Haley gave him a crooked grin. "How would you know about that?"

Drayton pretended to bristle. "For your information, Haley, I'm not totally ignorant. I don't exist under a rock."

"No," Haley said, "you're just a happy-go-lucky Luddite."

13

Theodosia and Jamie carried in the half dozen hampers packed with food and discovered that Cotton Duck was already a madhouse. Racks of clothes and display shelves packed with scarves, bags, and jewelry had been jammed together, one against the other, so workers could put the finishing touches on the runway. Folding chairs were being set up amid tools and sawdust. Models in various states of undress were running around everywhere. And Delaine was in a complete tizzy.

"No, no, no!" Delaine screamed at her frazzled assistant, Janine. "Our VIPs sit in the *front* row! You need to check my seating chart!" She turned, blew a hank of hair out of her face, and noticed Theodosia standing there. "You're here," she said. "With our refreshments."

"Actually, Chinese dim sum," Theodosia said. "In keeping with your Silk Road theme."

"Whatever," Delaine snapped. She pulled down the front zip tab of her cream-colored silk jumpsuit to make it slightly more revealing, then made a one-handed rolling gesture. "Bring everything over here, I've got a table for you. And for goodness' sake, don't you dare let any food aromas drift in the direction of my clothing racks."

"It's lunch, Delaine. It's supposed to smell good."

Delaine tapped a foot nervously. "I'd rather it smelled good *after* the fashion show, okay?"

"No problem," Theodosia said. She'd long since learned that it was easier to agree with Delaine than to argue with her. Besides, in two seconds Delaine would be fretting about something else. She had the concentration power of a gnat.

But Delaine hadn't budged. "Who are you?" Delaine asked, eyeing Jamie with suspicion.

Caught in her slightly manic, thousand-watt stare, he said, "I'm J-Jamie."

"Well, J-Jamie, you'd better get cracking. We haven't got all day."

"Yes, ma'am," he said.

"And don't you dare *ma'am* me," Delaine said. "Do I look old enough to be your mother?" Before Jamie could squeak out an answer, she said, "Of course not," and rushed off toward the dressing rooms.

Theodosia and Jamie carried the hampers to the table Delaine had set up for them, plugged in the food warmers, and got everything as near ready as possible. Then, as Janine and her helpers shoved the clothing racks back into place, the guests began to arrive. Theodosia thanked Jamie for his help and sent him back to the tea shop.

When the store was put together again, Janine came over, looking like she'd just staggered off a battlefield.

"Are you hanging in there, Janine?" Theodosia asked her. Janine was Delaine's long-suffering assistant, a brown-haired, brown-eyed woman who always looked as if she carried the weight of the world on her back. The only time Janine ever came alive was when she smiled. She had a fabulous smile, but it didn't come often when Delaine was barking at her.

Janine shook her head. "It's always like this, before every show. Delaine goes a little bit bonkers."

"But it looks like it's shaping up to be a wonderful show. I got a peek at your silks as I came in and they all look spectacular."

"Wait until you see all the silk dresses and gowns and outfits on the models," Janine said. She finally let a smile slip out. "Va-va-voom."

With not a lot to do until after the fashion show, Theodosia wandered through the boutique. More guests had arrived and were eagerly looking around, shopping for one-of-a-kind fashion musts before taking their seats near the runway. They tried on sunglasses, fingered long strands of shimmering pearls, and admired displays of fancy ball gowns.

"Hello there," came a voice at Theodosia's elbow. "Looking for that special piece to fill out your summer wardrobe?"

Theodosia turned to find Alexis James, the owner of Haiku Gallery, smiling at her. "Actually, I'm serving the luncheon today."

"Oh, what fun," Alexis said. "If you need any help, just let me know."

"That's very kind of you, but I happen to know you're one of Delaine's special guests. In fact, I saw your name on one of the chairs in the very front row."

Alexis waved a hand. "Oh, I've already checked out most of the clothes. You know how Delaine is . . ."

"Pushy," Theodosia said, grinning.

"Enthusiastic, anyway. But can you blame her? The spring silks she's showing really are spectacular." Alexis kept up her friendly chatter as she followed Theodosia back to the buffet table. "I'll probably pick up a couple pairs of silk slacks after all." She glanced at the silver food warmers. "But I think what you're doing right here looks like a lot more fun." She slid open the top of one of the warmers and peeped in. "Ooh, are those egg rolls?" She giggled. "They look good enough to eat!"

"Fried spring rolls, shrimp toast, and steamed pork buns. Plus, I'll be serving a nice Chinese black tea. As soon as everyone's seated and the show gets underway, I'm going to turn up these warmers and get everything ready to go."

"Heat and eat," Alexis said. "Sounds good to me."

"Alexis!" Delaine cried from across the room. "You're seated in the front row, dear. Better hurry and take your seat."

"Gotta go," Alexis said, scampering off.

Theodosia got busy then. Filled her four-gallon commercial brewer with water, turned it on, set out two large teapots. Then, just as she was unpacking several dozen small ceramic teacups, Sissy Lanier bounded up to her table. Today she was dressed in a hot pink jacket, black leggings, and jewel-encrusted stilettos.

"Hey there," Sissy said. "Delaine told me you were catering lunch today."

"Nice to see you again," Theodosia said. She debated asking Sissy about Bob Garver and decided, *What could it hurt?*

"Sissy," Theodosia said, "are you acquainted with a developer by the name of Bob Garver?"

Sissy's eyes went wild at the mere mention of Garver's name. "That pirate?" she cried as she curled a lip in disdain. "You know he was Carson's partner, don't you? In a development called Gateway Gables."

"I heard something about that. How . . . uh . . . how well do you know Garver?"

"I've never actually met the man," Sissy said. "But I've heard enough through the grapevine to know that he's a complete sleazeball."

"But I understand Garver was working on a more recent project with your ex-husband," Theodosia said. "Something about rehabbing Charleston single homes?"

Sissy tilted her head to one side in what Theodosia thought was a slightly studied manner. "He was?" she said. "I hadn't heard about that project."

Theodosia wondered what Sissy was trying to hide.

"You know nothing about them obtaining low-interest loans from the city?"

Sissy shook her head. "Nope. Not a thing."

"Three point nine million dollars in loans?" Theodosia was positive that Sissy knew something. She was acting way too chirpy and innocent.

Now Sissy gave a dismissive shrug. "Sorry. This project is news to me."

Theodosia studied her for a few more seconds. "Okay, I'm sorry I brought it up. I didn't mean to upset you."

"You didn't."

"Because you had kind of a funny look on your face."

"Probably my low blood sugar," Sissy said. "Whenever I skip breakfast I just start to crash."

"Do you want something to munch on?" Theodosia offered. "To kind of tide you over until lunch?"

"That would be nice." Now Sissy bubbled with enthusiasm again.

Theodosia grabbed two fried spring rolls, wrapped a piece of foil around them, and handed them to Sissy. "Here you go." The DJ had just started to spin the opening music and everyone had taken their seats. "You'd better go sit down and watch the show."

"Thanks," Sissy said. "I will." She turned and ducked away. And just as Sissy was about to take a bite of spring roll, she collided roughly with a woman who'd just come bombing through the front door.

"Hey!" the woman yelped as Sissy slammed up hard against her. The two fried spring rolls flew out of Sissy's hands, hit the woman's chest, and tumbled down the front of her yellow dress, leaving an enormous grease spot. Then the woman took a step backward, gaped at Sissy and shouted, "You!"

"Oh no," Theodosia said. She'd just recognized the woman Sissy had collided with. It was Betty Bates!

At that precise moment, Delaine rushed over to help sort things out, the DJ jacked up the music, and a bevy of long-limbed twenty-two-year-old models began parading down the runway.

Theodosia decided it was like watching a three-ring circus. Delaine mopped at Betty's dress with a wet wipe, Betty kept trying to shove Sissy away from her as if she carried some dreaded plague, the guests started screaming their heads off at the spectacular clothes, and the Beastie Boys song "Girls" clattered over the sound system.

The models whirled and twirled, Sissy stomped out of reach from Betty, no doubt cursing her under her breath, Betty slapped Delaine's hands away from her, and the Beastie Boys continued to wail.

And then, for the buttercream icing on the lost-your-marbles cake, Bill Glass came schlumping into the boutique, multiple cameras strung around his neck, and began shooting photos.

Theodosia stood on tiptoe, trying to see how this merry little adventure would play out. Finally, the furor did die down slightly. Sissy retreated to a seat somewhere, while Delaine led Betty Bates to a prime chair in the front row, trying all the while to smooth Betty's ruffled feathers.

Well, good luck with that.

But as the fashion show continued, Theodosia thanked her lucky stars that she never had to contend with diva behavior in her tea shop. No, she'd been lucky. Guests were generally well-mannered and tended to fall under the spell of the amazing tea aromas that permeated the air and seemed to promote relaxation. Definitely aromatherapy at its finest!

Theodosia got seriously busy then. Turning up the temperature on her warming trays, setting out the teacups, dumping the loose-leaf tea that Drayton had carefully measured out into her brewer. It wasn't quite the same as making a pot of tea to order, but it would suffice for today.

Every few minutes Theodosia looked up to catch a bit of the show. And, thankfully, Delaine's fashion show seemed to be checking all the boxes for the guests' entertainment. The show was colorful, splashy, exuberant, loud, and exciting to watch.

Good. That meant all the guests would be in an upbeat mood when it came time to enjoy some Chinese dim sum.

Theodosia watched as the runway show wound down to its conclusion. Ten models, all dressed in Chinese silk dresses, gowns, and flowing outfits, marched down the runway. They carried red Chinese lanterns on long sticks and fluttered elegant fans in front of their faces. Wonderful! Then a brass gong rang out to signify the end.

The applause from the audience was deafening. So of course the models all came out again to take a final strut down the runway. And then Delaine hopped up onto the runway and blew tearful air kisses to everyone.

With the runway show concluded, Theodosia was busier than a one-eyed cat watching two mouseholes. She served dim sum, poured tea, and chatted amiably with all the women who crowded around her buffet table.

But the good juju didn't last for long.

Betty Bates stalked up to the table and grabbed a cup of tea at the exact moment Sissy Lanier was putting a pork dumpling on her plate. And the dumpling wasn't the only thing that was steamed.

Sissy, still upset from their earlier encounter, took one disdainful look at Betty and said, "A little bird told me you might be taking my husband's place on the Heritage Society's board of directors."

"It's none of your business what I do," Betty shot back. She sounded angry, and the front of her dress still looked like she'd been squirted with hot grease. Which she kind of had been.

Sissy's eyes took on a menacing gleam. "Oh no? You realize that board seat should rightfully belong to *me*."

"Last time I looked, the Heritage Society didn't allow killers on their board!" Betty shot back.

"You can't be serious!" Sissy said, a sneer twisting her face. "When *you're* the one who had an affair with Carson and then *murdered* him. You were probably gunning for his job all along! Which means you, of all people, had the biggest reason to want him dead!"

Now people all around had quieted down and were staring at the two women in rapt and total disbelief.

Betty's face clouded with anger. "How *dare* you accuse me of murder, you lying freak."

"You *killed* him," Sissy shouted at the top of her lungs. "You killed my husband!"

"I did no such thing," Betty shouted back. She glanced down at the cup of tea she held in her hand, set her mouth in a determined line, and tossed the hot liquid directly in Sissy's face.

"Whuh!" Sissy shrieked. She reared back, stunned, her voice rising in a piteous, jangled cry that easily hit high C.

"Oh no," Theodosia murmured. "Oh no." The behavior she'd just witnessed was shocking and utterly insane. What dreadful thing could happen next?

She didn't have to wait long to find out.

Hands pulled into fists, still dripping wet, Sissy uttered a low growl and threw a right-hand punch that hit Betty square in the jaw and sent one of her pearl earrings flying. Betty, no slouch in the fine art of catfighting, hopped forward—bing, bing, bing—and put up both fists like some kind of cartoon kangaroo. Then, in a shocking, no-holds-barred fit of rage, the two women began to jab, slap, and hiss at each other. They circled one other, dodging and weaving like a pair of punch-drunk prizefighters. Bumping into guests as they hurled insults, they knocked over a rack of clothes as their ridiculous battle escalated. Now every guest in the place had circled round to watch them, eyes wide with surprise, mouths dropped open in total shock.

When Sissy and Betty stumbled in the direction of the buffet table, Theodosia gripped her teapot with both hands. She didn't want to sustain any collateral damage and spew hot tea everywhere.

"Stop!" Delaine screeched. Her shrill scream rose above the din of mass confusion as she stepped into the circle and put out a hand to try to separate the two women. "Stop fighting this instant!"

But Sissy and Betty were too far gone to heed Delaine's shouts. In fact, Betty escalated the fracas by gripping Sissy's shoulders, shaking her hard, and then giving her a mighty shove backward. Sissy staggered back, arms flailing wildly, teetering dangerously on her high heels. At the very last second, just as

Sissy tipped over backward, she managed to hook a finger in Betty's belt and pulled her down with her.

BANG!

Tumbling like a couple of circus monkeys, the two women fell against a clothes rack, sending the whole thing crashing to the ground. Now they were sprawled on the floor, kicking and batting at each other atop a pile of silk blouses and scarves.

"This can't be happening," Theodosia groaned, while Bill Glass moved in close to get a better shot. It was a train wreck of epic proportions.

"Theo!" Delaine screamed above the clucking of the shocked onlookers. "Do something!"

Theodosia turned toward Delaine, an incredulous look on her face. "You want *me* to step in there and break up the fight?"

"Please, you *have* to," Delaine implored. "Those women are crazy. They're going to *ruin* everything." Tears sparkled in Delaine's eyes. "The clothes, my potential orders . . . my beautiful fashion show." She clutched a hand to her breast as if in horrible pain. "This fight in the middle of my shop is crazy . . . plum crazy! They're ruining my show!"

Technically, Delaine's fashion show was already in shreds, but Theodosia did see her point. She glanced about, saw the stricken faces of the guests, then noticed a nearby display of ladies' golf clothing. Two sporty-looking silver mannequins were all decked out in pink-and-white golf garb and holding the necessary sports equipment. Thinking fast, Theodosia grabbed a four iron from the nearest mannequin's hand.

Wading into the fray, Theodosia flipped the club around and jabbed the splayed-out Betty in the shoulder. Hard. "Fight's over, Betty. Time to go home."

Betty cranked her head around and gaped at Theodosia. It was as if she were emerging from a dream state. As if she had no memory of throwing tea and clawing Sissy like a rabid wolverine.

Theodosia poked the golf club at Sissy, too, and mustered up her sternest voice. "Sissy, this means you, too. You've embarrassed yourself horribly and are no longer welcome here."

Sissy crawled away from Betty on all fours and then struggled to her feet. Tears streamed down her cheeks and her chin quivered. "I buh— I buh—"

"I don't want to hear it," Theodosia said.

Shaking with rage, Betty Bates slowly pulled herself to her feet. "She can't get away with—"

"No," Theodosia said in a firm voice, the kind of voice you use when potty training a puppy. "Both of you need to leave. Right now. Do not utter another word. Do not pass Go. Do not collect two hundred dollars."

"You can't talk to me like that," Betty snarled.

"I just did," Theodosia said. "Now move it, lady."

Betty and Sissy limped around for a few moments, trying to regain their bearings and their composure, smoothing down their rumpled clothes, collecting their handbags.

Delaine was suddenly overcome with gratitude that Theodosia had actually been able to stop the fight. "Oh my, oh my gosh." Delaine hopped up and down, giddy with relief. "How can I thank you, Theodosia!" She threw both arms around Theodosia and gripped her tightly.

"How about not asking me to cater any more fashion shows?" Theodosia responded.

Nervous titters sounded from the crowd.

But Delaine was all jacked up and ready to rhapsodize. "But, Theo, you literally saved the day. You were so bold and decisive. Stopping this fight—clearly coming across as the voice of reason—this is something you're good at." She shook her head. "So much better than poking your nose into all those crazy murders."

At Delaine's words, a sudden hush fell over the crowd. And then Betty and Sissy, who were almost at the front door, turned back to stare at Theodosia.

And Theodosia swore she could see inquisitive wheels turning inside each of their banged-up little heads.

14

How was the Silk Road show?" Drayton asked when Theodosia walked into the Indigo Tea Shop, dragging two wicker hampers behind her.

"Awful," Theodosia said.

Drayton looked stunned. "Oh no, was the tea not right? Let me guess, too brisk?" His brow wrinkled in deep concern. "I had a feeling I might be coming on a bit strong with that blend of Chinese Yunnan and Keemun. Oh, Theo, I am sorry."

"Don't be," Theodosia said. "Your tea selection was perfect; it was the guests who were horrible. Well, really just two guests, if you want to know the truth."

Drayton seemed to relax. "Tell me what happened."

At that exact moment, Haley came strolling out of the kitchen nibbling the top of a chocolate chip muffin. "Something happened?" she asked.

"Remember Betty Bates?" Theodosia asked. She flashed a knowing glance at Drayton. "From last night? The lady banker who crabbed at us?"

Drayton nodded. "How could I forget?"

"She showed up at Delaine's Silk Road Fashion Show."

Haley shrugged. "Didn't everybody and his brother get an invitation to that?"

"But not everybody got into a huge kerfuffle with Sissy Lanier," Theodosia said.

"Wait . . . Betty and the dead guy's ex-wife?" Haley asked. Her eyes glowed; now she was interested. Here was a choice chunk of gossip she could wrap her head around.

"Actually, it was more than a kerfuffle," Theodosia said. "It was your basic knock-down-drag-out slugfest."

"What!" Drayton said.

"Creepers," Haley said. "Like on *Jerry Springer* when people get conked on the head with folding chairs?"

"Exactly like that," Theodosia said. "Except instead of folding chairs they used racks of clothing."

"No," Drayton said.

"Yes," Theodosia said. "Betty and Sissy pretty much wrecked the place. They were clawing and yelling at each other, even throwing punches."

"What were they fighting about?" Drayton asked.

"They each accused the other of murdering Carson Lanier," Theodosia said.

"No!" Drayton cried again.

"Whoa," Haley said. "The plot thickens."

Theodosia touched a hand to her forehead and massaged it gently, trying to knock back her headache. "They hissed at each other like a couple of spitting cobras and threw so many punches that they fell on the floor and knocked over a rack of clothing in the process." She drew a deep breath. "Then Delaine freaked out and begged *me* to step in and break up the fight."

"Glory be," Drayton said. "Did you?"

Theodosia rubbed her shoulder. "Yes, and I've got the bruises to prove it."

"Nobody said refereeing a fight would be easy," Haley said.

Drayton stared at Theodosia, a look of horror on his face. "And after that, you served lunch?"

"Let me tell you, it was a balancing act of epic proportions."

"But everyone liked the spring rolls and dumplings?" Haley asked.

"I think they did. The food all disappeared, anyway." Theodosia sighed deeply.

"So it was over just like that?" Haley said.

"Not with a bang but a whimper," Theodosia said. She pushed back a few stray auburn curls that hung in her eyes. "The thing is . . . what I need to figure out now . . . are either Sissy or Betty legitimate suspects?"

"You think one of them could have killed the banker guy?" Haley asked.

"It sounds as if they both have terrible tempers," Drayton said. "So either one of them could be suspects."

Haley looked confused. "But . . . what would be their motives?"

"Sissy is salivating because now she'll inherit her soon-to-be ex-husband's money," Theodosia said. "And Betty Bates . . . I'm not exactly sure about her. Maybe Betty wanted to step into Carson Lanier's job at the bank? Or she coveted his seat on the Heritage Society's board of directors? I don't know."

"People have killed for a lot less," Drayton said.

"You just said a mouthful," Haley said. "Gangbangers and dopers knock over convenience stores all the time for, like, twenty bucks and a Slim Jim." She gave them a bug-eyed look. "I guess because they're so convenient. They're like corner ATMs, only with soda pop and chips."

"Good heavens, this has become a complete mess, hasn't it?" Drayton said.

Haley's eyes glowed. "Actually, I think it's kind of exciting. If Theodosia keeps investigating, that is."

"I don't know if I should," Theodosia said. She was starting to have serious doubts about being involved. Too much craziness had gone on already. She didn't want anything else to suck her into a nasty vortex that would put her friends or her tea shop at risk.

Jamie had been standing a few feet away, wiping teapots and listening to the conversation. Now he stepped forward to put in his two cents' worth. "There sure is a lot of fighting going on around here," he said.

Drayton lifted an eyebrow. "Did you hear that? Out of the mouths of babes . . ."

Theodosia settled back in her office chair and tucked her feet underneath her. It was three thirty in the afternoon and there were only two guests lingering in the tea shop. Pretty soon she and Drayton could swish out the teapots, turn off the lights, and go home. Live to fight another day.

Fight.

Theodosia shook her head wearily. No, that wasn't the word she wanted. Because the fight she'd witnessed today had been awful. Two perfectly respectable women rolling around on the floor and . . . well, pretty much causing her to *lose* any respect she'd ever had for them.

So what was the matter with Sissy and Betty? What weird chemicals had zapped their brains and set them off like that? Sissy seemed half-crazed about getting her mitts on her estranged husband's money. While Betty was completely full of herself and seemed to revel in accusing Sissy of murder.

Had Betty Bates been trying to put up an angry, venomous smoke screen? To deflect any accusations that might be aimed at her? It certainly seemed like a possibility.

Of course, the million-dollar question Theodosia had to reckon with now was . . . should she continue her investigation into the shooting of Carson Lanier?

Timothy had asked her for help, but the Charleston PD was quite capable of conducting a thorough investigation.

But would they be able to apprehend the killer?

Theodosia glanced down at the papers on her desk. Haley had given her a short menu for tomorrow afternoon's Tea Trolley stop. And Drayton had filled out a rather lengthy order form. He was anxious to stock up on citrus blend and rose petal–infused teas in anticipation of the upcoming spring teas they'd soon be hosting. Engagement teas, bridal shower teas, Mother's Day teas . . .

Theodosia closed her eyes to rest them. Just a few moments of peace and quiet before she got back to—

WHAP! BOOM! SMASH!

Her office window exploded with an awful crash as shards of glass flew everywhere. A split second later, a good-sized rock bounced across her desk, sending a stack of tea magazines slip-sliding all over the place. Then the rock spun around like a crazed top and bounced to the floor, where it banged hard against a nearby metal file cabinet.

What. On. Earth?

Two seconds later, her office door burst open and Drayton, wild-eyed and fearful, rushed in. "What happened?" he cried.

"I . . . I don't know," Theodosia said. She was momentarily

stunned. Then she quickly gathered her wits. "Somebody threw a rock through my window." There was a large hole in the center of the glass, the edges jagged and pointed like a bunch of shark teeth.

"What? Who?" Drayton asked. He seemed utterly gobsmacked.

But Theodosia didn't take time to answer him. She bolted suddenly from her leather chair and set it spinning. Flying across her office, she pulled open the back door and ran into the alley. She saw polished brown cobblestones, the garden apartment across the way, a line of magnolias and two scruffy palmettos, and traffic crawling by at the far end of the alley. But there was nobody there. No *culprit* she could scream at or chastise. Whoever had flung the rock, for whatever reason, was gone. Poof. Vanished into thin air like a wisp of swamp gas at her Aunt Libby's plantation.

Hasty footsteps sounded behind her. "Anything?" Drayton called out loudly. "Did you see who did it?"

He was breathing hard, and Theodosia saw that he wielded a large clay teapot in his right hand. He'd ducked around the corner to grab it. To use as a weapon, she supposed.

"Nobody here," Theodosia said.

"Who could have done this?" Drayton wondered.

Theodosia shook her head. "I don't know. A couple of mischievous kids out on a tear?"

"Maybe rode through on their bikes," Drayton offered. "Or . . ."

"Or someone intended to send me a message?" Theodosia said.

"Maybe," Drayton said in a quiet voice. Which really meant *probably*.

They continued to stare down the deserted alley for a few moments, then when nothing materialized, they went back into the shop.

Haley was waiting for them just inside, practically dancing with excitement. "What the heck was that?" she asked. "I was closing the door to the cooler and I thought I broke the hinges on the dang thing."

"Somebody tossed a rock through Theodosia's window," Drayton said.

Haley glanced at the broken window and her eyes bugged out. "No kidding. Wow. Did you see who did it?"

Theodosia shook her head no. She wished she had reacted faster. Had run outside immediately and . . . what? She didn't know what.

Haley gestured at the crockery teapot Drayton still had in his hand. "What were you going to do with that? Conk somebody on the head?"

"It's stoneware," Drayton said. "It would've made a severe dent in the vandal's noggin."

But the party wasn't complete without Jamie.

"What happened?" he asked.

The three of them pointed at the broken window. Haley said, "Some jackhole dinged a rock through Theo's window."

"Holy smokes," Jamie said. He aimed a worried glance at Theodosia. "You're lucky you didn't get hit."

"What are we going to do now?" Haley asked. She looked like she was ready to round up a posse and take off in a trail of dust.

"I'll grab some hunks of cardboard and patch things up temporarily," Jamie said. "But we should call a hardware store." When nobody moved or said anything, Jamie said, "I could make that call, if you want."

"Thank you," Theodosia said. "I appreciate your help." Then, "This is about Lanier's murder, isn't it? Almost everything that's happened since that fatal night is about the murder. Jud Harker yelling at us, Betty showing up at the board meeting, the fight between Sissy and Betty today . . ."

"What are you going to do?" Drayton asked. "How are you going to figure this out?"

"She's not," Haley said. "The best thing Theo can do is let her *boyfriend*, Detective Riley, figure it out. That's what the City of Charleston pays him for. That's the smartest thing, the safest thing, to do at this point."

When Haley retreated to her kitchen to grab a broom and a dustpan, Theodosia said, "Maybe Haley's right. Maybe I should back away from our so-called investigation."

"But you promised Timothy," Drayton said. He wasn't wheedling, but he did sound concerned.

"I know that. And it grieves me to think I'd let him down."

"Then don't."

Theodosia touched a hand to her hair. For some reason, as the day had progressed, her hair had increased in volume. Now her auburn locks were swirling about her head like a friendly Medusa. It wasn't humidity—maybe it was stress?

"Do you think the rock was a signal for me to back off?" Theodosia asked Drayton. "Is it related to the fight I just broke up? Does it have to do with a sore loser? A nasty killer? I mean, what's going on?"

"Sounds like you're still curious. Like you want to find the root cause of all these strange goings-on," Drayton said.

Theodosia thought for a few moments. "I suppose I do. Maybe I want to run with this and see where it takes me."

Drayton nodded his approval. "Attagirl."

*   *   *

Even after Haley had swept up the broken glass, and a man from the hardware store was on his way, Theodosia still felt unsettled. She hated loose ends, and it seemed like there were an awful lot of them to contend with.

Okay. Of all the names that have come up so far, who's the loosest, most frazzled end?

The answer was easy. It was Bob Garver, Lanier's real estate partner. Theodosia knew next to nothing about Garver. Could he be the puppet master in the shadows? If you followed the money, did it end up with him?

Theodosia found it was fairly simple to research Garver on the Internet. In fact, within a few minutes, she pulled up several articles as well as a grainy photo of one Robert T. Garver.

She knew it was the correct Bob Garver because he was posing in front of some slightly dilapidated row houses over on Hagood Street.

Gotcha.

Now. Did he have anything to do with antique weapons? Namely, a crossbow and quarrels?

Another couple of minutes of hunting around brought two more grainy photos of Bob Garver. One was from the Charleston *Post and Courier*'s business section that showed a square-jawed man with brush-cut hair shaking hands with some muckety-muck from the city council. Garver had apparently been awarded some sort of housing grant.

Okay, now we're cooking. This is for sure the guy.

The second photo was from a small local newspaper called the *Piedmont Piper*, and it showed Garver participating in a dove hunt. Theodosia knew that mourning doves were the second most popular quarry in South Carolina next to deer. But did anyone hunt doves with an antique weapon?

Maybe they do.

She knew that antique weapons were everywhere in Charleston. There were old muskets and squirrel guns stuck in people's attics, bows and arrows stored in garages, Civil War–era pistols that had been passed down from great-grandpappy to great-grandson, as well as the odd World War I and World War II souvenir weapon. And they were all rattling around Charleston. Some probably still in use, some brought out only for Civil War battle reenactments or memorials.

Theodosia tapped her fingers nervously on her desktop. How to find out about these old weapons? Particularly a crossbow and quarrels?

Well, Drayton had given her the name of a shop. What was it again? She let her mind wander. Oh yes, Chasen's Military Relics over on Bee Street.

And the more Theodosia thought about Chasen's Military Relics, the more intrigued she became. Until she decided it might be a smart idea to head over there and check things out for herself.

15

⁂

Chasen's Military Relics smelled like Hoppe's gun oil, brass polish, and musty military surplus left over from World War II. Or maybe it was World War I. The shop was an old-fashioned-looking place, the kind that once populated downtowns in the forties and fifties. Elaborate gold script on two front windows, a bell over the door that tinkled loudly when you stepped inside, tall counters with rounded glass tops, a wooden floor that creaked, narrow aisles. Kind of like an old hardware store, except instead of nuts and bolts and tools, this store was filled with weapons. Every type of handgun, rifle, shotgun, flintlock, sword, and dagger that you could imagine. All lovingly arranged in cases on some kind of green suede-like material.

Theodosia peered into the first case and saw a derringer, what was often referred to as a pocket pistol. It sat alongside a large, rounded pistol that had ivory handles and silver filigree trim. The type of gun that might have been used in an eighteenth-century duel. Perhaps the type of gun that Aaron Burr had shot poor Alexander Hamilton with.

Fascinated now, Theodosia moved down the case, studying the various weapons. She stopped to examine two pistols that were large and black, nasty-looking things.

"Them are Nazi items," a man's voice said. He was walking toward her now, an older gent, midsixties, who was wearing a gray shirt and camo pants tucked into old lace-up army boots. He looked like he was ready to journey back to Normandy and storm the beaches if necessary. He positioned himself behind the counter and winked at her. "There's a big demand for Lugers and other guns like this. A couple of generations go by and people think this stuff is cool."

"Well, I don't," Theodosia said somewhat stiffly.

"Then, how can I help you, ma'am? What exactly are you looking for?"

"You're the owner?" Theodosia asked.

The man bobbed his head. "Murrell Chasen, proprietor. My father started the business in the late forties, I took over when he passed a few years ago."

"I'm sorry for your loss."

"Don't be," Chasen said. "The old man lived to be ninety-two. Landed at Anzio with the First Ranger Battalion during the big one."

"Impressive." Theodosia tried to let a hint of admiration creep into her voice. After all, flattery will get you everywhere.

"Me, I was in the Marines." Chasen managed a quick fist pump. "Semper fi."

"Do you carry antique bows and arrows?" Theodosia asked.

"Sure do. We have a good selection in the cases at the back of the store. What exactly are you looking for?" Chasen turned and headed that way, and Theodosia followed.

"Maybe some information right now," Theodosia said. "I'm looking for the kind of crossbow that shoots shorter arrows. I think they're called quarrels?"

"That's exactly right," Chasen said. He slid open a glass door, reached in, and lifted out a strange-looking apparatus. "This is a pistol crossbow," he said. "Swiss made, probably from the thirties or forties. Takes that shorter-type arrow."

Theodosia studied the weapon. It looked much like an old-style pistol but had a small crossbow apparatus on top. "You put the quarrel on top and then fire by pulling the trigger?" she asked.

"Well, you have to load and engage it first, but that's how it works." He handed the weapon to her. "Here, you can hold it. Nothing to be afraid of."

Theodosia accepted the pistol crossbow. It was heavy but felt balanced at the same time. As if the maker had been keenly aware that this weapon would be held in the hand much the same way any pistol would, yet had the added objective of firing an arrow.

"What was this used for?" Theodosia asked.

"The usual," Chasen said. "Hunting or target practice."

"Hunting." Theodosia lifted the weapon and sighted it. "It's easy to fire?"

"Fairly basic. You load your arrow here." He tapped the top apparatus with his finger. "Then pick your target and pull the trigger. Not very complicated if your aim is true."

"This is from an old design?"

"Ah," Chasen said. "There's been some debate on that. But my guess is the pistol crossbow was adapted around about the turn of the century—the last century, not this century—from medieval and Chinese crossbows."

"And the advantage of this weapon is . . . ?"

"It's silent and deadly," Chasen said.

Theodosia hefted the weapon again. It felt deadly, and the mechanism was simple but ingenious. She could just imagine loading a quarrel into the crossbow apparatus, choosing your target, and then squeezing the trigger. A gentle *whoosh* would be all that your victim would hear. If he heard anything at all.

"I can offer you a good deal on this piece," Chasen said. He took the weapon back from Theodosia and looked at the price tag. "I've got it marked at seventeen hundred, but I'd be willing to let you have it for fourteen."

"Have you sold many of these?"

Chasen shook his head. "Not for a long time. This one's been in my inventory for a good five years."

"How did you come across it?" Theodosia asked.

"A military relics show."

"That's a real thing?"

"Oh yeah," Chasen said. "There are military relics shows all over the country. Minneapolis, Huntsville, Louisville, one really big one south of Chicago. You go to these shows, there's always a few dealers who have something tasty they're willing to trade."

"I have another question."

"Shoot," Chasen said, then chuckled.

"Do you know a man named Bob Garver?"

"Garver? Sure, I know Bob. He's a customer of mine. In fact, he belongs to my shooting club."

"Shooting?" Theodosia said, trying hard to contain her excitement. "What kind of shooting?"

"Guns and bows."

"And you say Garver's a member of your club?"

"Brittlebush Gun and Bow Club over on Johns Island." Chasen smiled. "Women are encouraged to join, too, you know. They even have ladies' day at the range."

"That sounds like fun," Theodosia said. Her brain was trying to quickly form her next question.

"I could come down to twelve hundred on the pistol crossbow," Chasen said. "I think you'd like this piece. Get yourself a membership at Brittlebush, plunk away at some targets. Eventually move up to birds. Lots of quail and duck hunting around here."

"Thank you, I'll think about it." Theodosia hesitated. "Will you be going to the Rare Weapons Show at the Heritage Society?"

"Oh, sure," Chasen said. "That should be fun. Lots of my customers are planning to attend as well."

"You know that the show has encountered a few problems?"

Chasen gazed at her, a questioning look on his face.

"Some guy named Jud Harker was . . ."

"That troublemaker!" Chasen burst out. He pursed his lips and shook his head with anger.

"You've had issues with him, too?" Theodosia asked.

"Harker comes around here preaching his anti-gun crap, trying to scare away all my customers. Even the ones who are just collectors."

"Do you think Harker is harmless?" Theodosia asked.

Chasen set the pistol crossbow back in the case and slid the door closed. "If Harker isn't, then he'd better watch out. A lot of us are very well armed."

Back in her car, Theodosia dialed Pete Riley's number. Once again, she was routed to voice mail. Frustrated, she hung up without leaving him a message.

Okay, be that way.

Theodosia glanced at her watch. It was just slightly past

four. She had time, if she wanted to, to head out to that gun
and bow club. Did she want to?

Yes. I think I do.

She punched in Brittlebush Gun and Bow Club on her
phone and found the address. Even though she figured nothing
would come of it, she wound her way past the medical center,
cut over to the James Island Expressway, and then took the
Maybank Highway out to Johns Island.

When Theodosia arrived at the club, she was a little surprised. The notion of a sporting club to her conjured up images
of a clubhouse, patio, adjacent restaurant, and wide-open spaces
where all manner of shooting took place.

Instead, she found a brown wooden building, about the size
of a three-bedroom ranch home, and a dusty parking lot filled
with pickup trucks and a few late-model cars. A sign that said
BRITTLEBUSH GUN AND BOW CLUB hung over the front door of
the modest clubhouse.

But when she got out of her car, there was no mistaking the
sound of gunfire. Members were out in full force, all right, and
they were firing away like crazy.

The interior of the Brittlebush clubhouse looked like the
lobby of a mom-and-pop motel in South Dakota. Knotty pine
walls, weapons displayed in glass cases, photos of guys holding
guns, a few trophies sitting on shelves, a scatter of brown
Naugahyde chairs for relaxing, an old-fashioned Coke machine.

Theodosia stepped up to a counter where a young man
leaned forward to greet her. He had red hair that stuck up
slightly and one eye that seemed to gaze off sideways.

"Help you?" he asked.

"I'm thinking about joining your club," Theodosia said.
"Would it be possible to have a look around?"

"Not a problem," said the young man. "As long as you stay

in the viewing area and don't venture out on any of the ranges."
He turned around, plucked a brochure out of a holder, and slid
it across the counter. "Here's some membership information
along with our rules. You need to know that we don't allow any
alcoholic beverages here and that everyone is required to attend
a safety class. Now. What kind of shooting are you interested in?"

Theodosia picked up the brochure. "What do you offer?"

The man ticked off the various venues on his fingertips.
"Sporting clays, trap and skeet, rifle and pistol range, bow and
arrow." He stared directly at her, though one eye wandered
slightly left.

Theodosia cocked a finger at him. "Bow and arrow." She
wondered how good his aim was.

"Got five lanes for that," the man said. He reached under
the counter and retrieved an ear protector. "Put this on, head
straight through that door, and stay in the viewing area. If you
don't, the range safety officer will be all over you."

"Thank you."

Theodosia slipped on the ear protection and stepped outside.
Even wearing the protection, there was an overwhelming ca-
cophony of sounds. *Pop. Bap. Whap.* Still, the grounds looked
fairly safe. A white wooden fence divided the viewing area from
the various gun ranges, and a man dressed head-to-toe in khaki
and wearing mirrored sunglasses seemed to be monitoring all
activity. The range safety officer, she decided.

Strolling along the fence, not venturing through the gates
that led to the ranges, Theodosia watched as a dozen men and
two women plunked away at targets. Some of them were pretty
good, hitting the targets at center or in the adjacent rings and
then letting out whoops of triumph. Other shooters were just
plain abysmal.

Theodosia wondered how she'd do. She hadn't fired a weapon since her dad had set up a small shooting range out at Cane Ridge Plantation, where he'd grown up. And that had just been target practice with a varmint gun.

She watched the shooters for a few more minutes, started to get bored, and decided this place was probably a dead end. The man inside had mentioned an archery range, but she had no idea where to find it and didn't relish doing any kind of exploring that might put her in the line of fire.

Ambling along the fence, Theodosia headed off to the right-hand side of the viewing area, still not seeing any archery lanes. She decided to abandon her mission. There was nothing here. Following a gravel path that circled around the far end of the clubhouse, she figured she could pop in the front door and return her ear protection.

That's when she heard a telltale *twang* and a *thunk*.

Theodosia stopped in her tracks and listened.

Twang. Thunk.

There it was again.

A gravel path veered off from the one Theodosia was on and wandered toward a copse of trees. Slowly, quietly, she followed it. Tree branches brushed her shoulders, gravel crunched underfoot, as she continued on. Fifteen steps later, she emerged at the archery range.

Three people were shooting. Two men and one woman. They were all geared up with leather armguards and gloves. And they were good. Very good. Two were using a traditional bow, while the man shooting in the farthest lane had a crossbow fitted with a scope. The crossbow shooter wore a chest protector, cap, and yellow sport glasses. His bow was a tricked-out black metal contraption, and his arrows were long and thin with green, spiky feathers.

Theodosia watched the crossbow shooter for a few minutes. He would bring up his bow fast, take a quick peek through his scope, and then fire. It looked like he was in the middle of an imagined battle scenario. Perhaps a horde of Visigoths was descending upon an English castle that he had been tasked with defending.

He hit the bull's-eye every time.

The crossbow shooter was firing even more rapidly now. *Thwack, thwack, thwack,* still hitting the target as if his muscle memory was helping him do half the work.

Then he stopped and nodded, as if giving himself tacit acknowledgement of his rather fine performance. He turned away from the range, slid off his cap, and glanced around.

That's when Theodosia did a double take.

Garver? Is that Bob Garver?

She was pretty sure it was. Or at least he bore a faint resemblance to the man in the grainy picture she'd found on the Internet.

As Garver gathered up his gear, preparing to head for the parking lot, Theodosia intercepted him.

"Excuse me," she said. "Are you Bob Garver?"

The man stopped in his tracks and gazed at her. "Who wants to know?" He sounded disinterested.

"I'm sorry," Theodosia said. She mustered a friendly smile as she touched a finger to her chest. "I'm Theodosia Browning. I was a friend of Carson Lanier."

This was a whopper of a white lie, but Theodosia figured that Garver probably wouldn't question her convenient ruse.

But talking to Theodosia was the last thing on Garver's mind. "I have nothing to say to you," he said as he turned his back and hurried away.

Theodosia headed down the path after him. "Excuse me. Just one quick question?"

Garver kept on walking. Correction—he picked up the pace.

"Hey!" Theodosia called to his retreating back. But Garver had already put considerable distance between the two of them and was stalking across the parking lot now.

"How rude is that?" Theodosia muttered to herself. She shrugged in dismay, then walked into the clubhouse, where she tossed the ear protectors on the counter, thanked the counter man, and came back out.

Now what? she wondered. Then answered her own question. *Now . . . nothing.*

Theodosia climbed into her Jeep, still grumbling, and pulled out onto the highway. Okay, so Bob Garver was a member at the Brittlebush Gun and Bow Club. And he was a man who favored crossbows. What did that prove? Absolutely nothing. There were probably several hundred archers—maybe even a thousand—in the Charleston area who enjoyed shooting with a crossbow.

Theodosia headed back toward Charleston, sailing across a narrow wooden bridge, the boards rumbling under her tires, and then around a sharp curve. Yes, Garver had a business connection with Lanier. And yes, Betty Bates had accused Garver of murdering Lanier, while Sissy had called him a pirate. But did that mean the man was a murderer?

No, it only meant Garver was unpopular with the ladies.

Theodosia sighed as she drove along, focusing on the road ahead. It was pretty out here. Not very developed yet, lots of stands of fine Carolina pine, scrub oak, and a few cherry laurel trees. There was the occasional farm field, too, as well as some swampy areas. In these places the standing water shimmered brilliantly, reflecting bits of sunlight like jewels. The swamps could have been old rice fields or possibly even tidal creeks that flowed in to create wetlands teeming with woodcocks and cedar waxwings.

She glanced in her rearview mirror and saw a car coming up fast behind her. Probably wanted to pass, which was always difficult on these narrow country roads.

Theodosia lifted her foot off the gas pedal and slowed down. At the same time, she veered toward the right shoulder, trying to give the speed demon a bit more room to go around her.

He came up fast behind her, a big silver SUV, and then, as if he'd changed his mind, didn't pass. Just hung right there on her back bumper. Theodosia glanced into the oncoming lane, saw nothing coming, and gave a quick wave. A signal that said it was safe to go.

The SUV stuck right on her tail.

What?

She slowed down some more.

Come on, pass me.

The SUV crept closer. The entire front end of the vehicle seemed to fill her rearview mirror. And then, in a shocking, dangerous twist, it bumped hard into her back end.

Holy crap!

This jerk in the SUV—Theodosia couldn't tell if it was a Toyota or a Range Rover—was smack-dab on her tail. Bumping her, kind of goosing her along.

Theodosia tromped down hard on the gas and took off. If this was a game of chicken, she didn't want any part of it. She hit sixty, then sixty-five miles per hour. The SUV was still behind her.

Like a bubble slowly oozing its way up from a tar pit, a thought occurred to Theodosia. *Is that Garver? Is that him right behind me?*

This was not the ideal time to find out. She glanced sideways at her hobo bag sitting on the passenger seat, then snicked a hand over and pulled out her cell phone. Her eyes darted back to the road, and she saw a large truck rumbling toward her. She dropped the phone in her lap and put both hands on the steering wheel. When the truck had passed, she grabbed her phone again and dialed 911. But just as she was about to press ENTER, she glanced in her rearview mirror.

The SUV was gone.

Theodosia's heart thudded inside her chest and her back felt hot against the car seat. She lowered her window, letting the fresh air wash over her. Theodosia hit the number for Drayton's home phone. It rang and rang, but there was no answer. No answering machine, either, thank you very much.

On a hunch she dialed the Indigo Tea Shop. And was surprised when Drayton picked up.

"You're still there," Theodosia said.

"Where else would I be?" Drayton said.

"Home?"

"Yes, well, the man from Sheeby's Hardware who came to fix our window just left a few minutes ago. And then I had a few other things to take care of."

"I need to talk to you."

"What's wrong?" Drayton asked.

"I'll be there in twenty minutes," Theodosia said. "Tell you then."

16

The minute Theodosia walked into the dimly lit tea shop, Drayton pounced on her. "What happened? You sounded so strange and tense on the phone."

"That's because I was," Theodosia said.

They sat down at a table and she gave him a quick two-minute recap of her visit to Chasen's gun shop as well as her stop at the Brittlebush Gun and Bow Club. Then she told him about running into Bob Garver and her experience with the jerk in the SUV who'd taken tailgating to a dangerous extreme.

"Do you think it was Bob Garver who was following you?" Drayton asked.

Theodosia shook her head. "I have no idea."

"I mean, if Garver was outright hostile to you at the gun club, then he could have waited for you to leave and driven after you. Gotten it in his fool head that he was going to scare you—teach you a lesson, so to speak."

"It could have been Garver," Theodosia said. "Or some other

random, crazy driver. It's possible that Garver didn't want anything to do with me."

"Why not?" Drayton asked.

"Maybe Garver's in enough trouble over the three point nine million dollars in low-interest loans. Maybe the city had second thoughts about his rehab project and asked for the money to be returned. Maybe Bob Garver is a sham and a charlatan and is trying to bilk the city."

"That seems like a difficult proposition," Drayton said. "Wouldn't the city have an oversight committee? Or a cadre of bean counters who watch the money like hawks?"

"Unless one of the bean counters is a part of Garver's con game," Theodosia said.

"Mmn, you have a very facile mind."

"Thank you."

"Was there any damage to your bumper?" Drayton asked.

"Just the tiniest of scratches. You can barely see it."

"Well, that's a break." Drayton stood up. "Would you care for a cup of tea? I just brewed a pot of black jasmine. Thought you might need a pick-me-up."

"A quick cup," Theodosia said. "Because I'm scheduled to meet Linda Pickerel from the bank in twenty minutes."

Drayton scurried behind the counter and busied himself with cups and saucers. "That's right. You're supposed to get the lowdown on Betty Bates."

"If Linda will be honest with me, yes."

"What possible reason would she have to deceive you?"

"People give very selective responses when they're worried about keeping their jobs."

Drayton carried two cups of tea out into the tea shop and set them on the table. "At the very least, we can enjoy—"

BAM, BAM, BAM!

They both stopped midsip and turned to stare at the front door. Whoever was out there had knocked so hard they'd rattled the windowpanes. And the last thing Theodosia and Drayton needed today was another broken window.

"Now what?" Drayton said. He sounded tired.

"Theodosia!" came a muffled cry from outside. "Drayton?" Now the voice was more insistent. "Are you in there?"

"That's Delaine," Theodosia said, rising hastily from her chair. "Something's wrong. She sounds practically hysterical."

"What could have happened?" Drayton asked as he jumped up and followed Theodosia to the front door. "Some other silly thing with her fashion show?"

But when Theodosia unlatched the door and tugged it open, two very unhappy faces stared in at her. One belonged to Delaine, the other to Sissy Lanier. Only, Sissy was shaking and sobbing uncontrollably.

"Delaine?" Theodosia said, a little stunned at seeing the two of them together, as if the fight in Delaine's shop had never happened. "And . . . Sissy?"

"May we come in?" Delaine asked. But before Theodosia could respond, Delaine barged in, dragging the whimpering Sissy along with her.

"What's wrong?" Drayton asked.

Delaine shoved Sissy down into a nearby captain's chair. "She's just had the most awful shock," Delaine said as Sissy began to moan and rock back and forth in her chair.

"Maybe you should explain," Theodosia said, fixing Delaine with a questioning gaze. That the two of them should suddenly show up together, after the big fight this morning, was beyond strange. It was veering into Area 51 territory.

Sissy lifted her head as tears continued to roll down her cheeks. Her once-ballooned hair had de-poufed into a messy, unflattering helmet. Her exotic eye makeup had melted into dark, greasy blobs that made her look like a panda in mourning. "My esh lesh tesh," Sissy blubbered. She made no sense whatever and seemed to have a loose tooth that produced a small, sharp whistle whenever she opened her mouth. Theodosia imagined that one of Betty's well-placed uppercuts had knocked it loose.

Delaine patted Sissy on the shoulder. "Don't try to talk, dear."

"Delaine," Theodosia said in an authoritative voice. "What *happened*?"

Delaine bit her lip. "Sissy just received her statement from Fidelity, and it looks as if the better part of three million dollars is missing from her account."

"Half of that wush mine!" Sissy managed in a high-pitched squeak. "Carson must have shpent all the money before the divorce wush finalized! Before he died!" She put a hand to her mouth and let loose a pitiful wail.

"Now, now," Delaine said. "Perhaps there was a clerical error."

"Or maybe Carsen gish the fundsh to *her*," Sissy bawled.

"Wait a minute," Theodosia said to Delaine. "Besides Sissy's rambling, something isn't tracking here. Five hours ago she was acting like a deranged banshee and we had to oust her from your shop. Now she's crying on your shoulder."

"I know, I know," Delaine said. "But the poor dear turned up on my doorstep whimpering and wailing, completely distraught. What was I supposed to do?"

"Deposit her on *our* doorstep, I guess," Drayton said.

Delaine stuck her nose in the air and sniffed loudly. "Well, pardon me for trying to be a *friend* to poor Sissy." She threw up her hands in a helpless, indignant gesture. "*I* don't have a clue how to unravel this sort of mess. *I'm* not the big pooh-bah investigator that Theodosia is."

Theodosia cocked her head at Delaine. "Why do you make that sound like an insult?"

Delaine was immediately apologetic. "I didn't mean to, Theo. I really didn't. And besides, money really *is* missing from Sissy's account. If you'd been wiped out financially, wouldn't you be completely *unhinged*? Wouldn't you want to wail and scream?"

"I suppose," Theodosia said. Though she knew she'd never allow something like that to happen to her. Never in a million trillion years.

"It looks as if Sissy's estranged husband stole *all* the money and then hid it somewhere," Delaine said. "Now he's dead." She managed an ominous look as she held up an index finger. "And dead men tell no tales."

"But maybe dead men having hiding places," Drayton said. "Or secret accounts. Because three million dollars is an awful lot of money to make disappear in a matter of weeks. Or spend in a mad rush."

"What if Lanier really did give the money to Betty Bates?" Delaine asked in a harsh whisper.

Theodosia considered that possibility. Maybe Carson Lanier *had* given the money to Betty Bates. Maybe she'd flirted with him, encouraged him in a little workplace hanky-panky, and then bilked him out of his money and killed him. Shot him with an arrow and was now living in the lap of luxury in a plantation out on Ashley River Road.

Theodosia knew there was another possibility. What if Bob Garver had gotten his sticky hands on Lanier's money? He and Carson Lanier had been real estate partners at one time. Perhaps Garver had convinced Lanier to cash out his Fidelity account in hopes of investing the money and reaping a big fat payoff.

Sissy was still crying, making sounds somewhere between pitiful moans and shoulder-shaking hiccups. Drayton was attempting to soothe Sissy and hand her a cup of hot tea, but every time Sissy tried to grasp the cup and saucer, the cup chattered and shook.

Theodosia knew there was another possible scenario to explain the missing money. Maybe the money wasn't really missing at all, and Sissy was lying about the whole thing. Maybe she was putting on a fabulous Academy Award–worthy, drama queen performance. Sissy could have murdered her husband, absconded with the money, and set up this rather brilliant defense to make herself look like the poor, bereft woman.

Narrowing her eyes, Theodosia studied Sissy. And wondered if her theatrics were genuine. *Are you crying because you truly lost all your money, or are those just crocodile tears rolling down your cheeks?*

"I'll tell you what we should do," Theodosia said slowly.

Delaine pinched her brows together. "What's that?" she asked. "Give the poor girl a makeover?" Delaine was starting to look bored, as if she was sick to death of ministering to Sissy.

Sissy wiped at her eyes, looking sadly inquisitive. "Whush?" she said.

"Sissy needs to take a meeting with my uncle," Theodosia said.

"The lawyer," Drayton said. "Jeremy Alston. What a splendid idea. Best to let a professional get involved. Have him ferret out what's happened to all that money. I'm sure Theodosia's uncle can get to the bottom of things."

Delaine was nodding along, looking like a well-groomed bobblehead. "That sounds like a fine solution." She pulled a hanky out of her bag and handed it to Sissy. "How about you, dear, does that sounds like something you could manage?"

Sissy grabbed the hanky, wiped at her nose, and nodded. "Yeth."

"Good," Theodosia said. "Then it's settled. I'll call my uncle first thing tomorrow and set up an appointment."

Sissy stared at Theodosia with red-rimmed eyes. "Thank you," she said. But between the crying, whistling tooth, and plugged nose, it sounded more like *thang shu*.

"See?" Delaine said. "I knew things would work out if we just talked to Theodosia. She's the lady with all the answers."

"I wish," Theodosia said.

"As for me," Delaine said, "I have to run off to a final meeting with my planning committee. Can you believe the Carolina Cat Show starts *this* Friday? Goodness!"

"I'm sure it's shaping up to be a wonderful event," Drayton said.

Theodosia placed a hand on Sissy's shoulder and gave her what she hoped was a reassuring smile. "Sissy, will you be attending your husband's memorial service tomorrow?" Theodosia knew that people from both Capital Bank and the Heritage Society had planned a service at the rather elegant Charleston Library Society.

Sissy swiped at her nose again and snorted, mustering up her indignation. "Ish you kidding? If Carson washn't going to be cremated, I'd wear a red dresh and dansh on hish grave!"

Theodosia ran the three blocks to Screamin' Beanies Coffee Shop, barely managing to be on time for her meeting with Linda Pickerel.

Linda Pickerel was skinny and tall, had frizzy reddish-blond hair and gorgeous green eyes. She was wearing a filmy pink top and a long paisley skirt. Very bohemian, like she'd just stepped off the pages of *Mother Earth News*. The first thing Linda said to Theodosia was, "I could lose my job for this."

"I wasn't going to ask you to spill any trade secrets," Theodosia said. "Or divulge any banking confidentialities that the FDIC holds dear."

Linda twitched her nose like a nervous rabbit and took a sip from her coffee cup. "Then what do you want? Haley said that you wanted to ask me some questions?"

"Not so much questions as I'd just like to get your general impression on a few things at the bank," Theodosia said. She wanted to tread lightly and not frighten Linda off.

"I don't understand," Linda said. "My impression of what?"

"You're aware of the situation with Carson Lanier?"

Linda stared at her. "Mr. Lanier got killed. Murdered."

"And you're acquainted with Betty Bates?"

"Sure," Linda said. "But what . . . ?"

"It's my understanding there was a relationship between Betty Bates and Carson Lanier."

Linda frowned. "What do you mean?"

Theodosia drew a deep breath. Perhaps she'd have to spell out their indiscretion a little more clearly. "It's been rumored that the two of them were close, that they were carrying on an affair together."

"Wait. What?" Linda looked surprised. "Betty and Mr. Lanier? I don't think so."

"Are you sure?"

"Pretty sure."

Theodosia decided to pursue a slightly different angle. "Okay then, do you know anything about Betty vying for the same job that Carson Lanier held?"

Linda shrugged. "Well . . . yeah. I mean, a few months ago they were both up for executive VP and wanted it pretty badly. And a lot of us women at the bank wanted Betty to get it. We thought she deserved it. You know how it is. Women start out in this training program they have at the bank, bottom of the totem pole, but they hope they might eventually be headed for the top."

Theodosia gave a commiserating nod to keep Linda talking.

"The sad reality is they end up working in clerical positions and training the men who actually *do* make it to the better jobs," Linda said.

"That doesn't sound very fair," Theodosia said. She could understand the women's frustration. And Betty Bates's probable anger.

"It *isn't* fair," Linda said. "I remember when they called this huge meeting at the bank, everybody was there in the conference room, all excited. And then the bank president, Mr. Grimley, announced that Carson Lanier was going to be the new executive vice president."

"Do you think Betty was disappointed?"

Linda took a quick sip of coffee. "Duh. You should have seen the look on Betty's face when they announced Lanier's name. Everybody started clapping politely, but she had this stone-faced, bitter look." Linda paused. "Disappointment, I suppose. Or anger. Like maybe she wanted to kill him."

It was the perfect opening for Theodosia to ask another question.

"What does everyone at Capital Bank think about Carson Lanier's murder?"

"Nobody knows what to think." Linda stuck a stir stick in her coffee and moved it about slowly. "It's kind of a mystery, huh? I know the police came to the bank and interviewed a few people, mostly the higher-ups who worked with Mr. Lanier. But we haven't heard anything since. And when you read the stories in the newspaper, it seems like the police don't have any suspects."

"Do you think there are suspects at the bank?"

Linda stared at her. "I know what you're asking. You're asking me if I think Betty could have done it."

"Could she?"

Linda shook her head. "Nah. Betty was one of us. A woman who was trying hard to make it in what's essentially a male-dominated arena."

"Couldn't that be all the more reason for Betty to have it in for Lanier?"

"I don't know," Linda said. "For her sake, I hope not."

Theodosia was just pulling up in front of her cottage when her cell phone rang. It turned out to be a panicked call from Drayton.

"I need you," he said.

"What's wrong?"

"Timothy just called. There's some sort of dire emergency at his home."

"Where are you? At your house? You want me to drive over there and pick you up?"

"No, no, I'm leaving for Timothy's place immediately. It's only a couple of blocks. You just meet me there, okay?"

"Sure, but what's the big . . ." But Theodosia was suddenly talking to dead air. Drayton had hung up.

17

Theodosia came in hot like a fighter pilot, screeching to a halt in front of Timothy's home, tires scraping hard against the curb. No matter. She jumped out of her vehicle and ran up the front steps, thundered across the wide porch, and banged on the enormous double doors.

Two seconds later, Drayton was there to let her in.

"Good," he said. "You're here." His face betrayed nothing of Timothy's situation.

"What's wrong?" Theodosia asked. "Is Timothy okay? It's not his heart, is it?" Timothy had experienced heart palpitations in the past, and there was always a concern about his advanced age.

"It's not that; Timothy's heart is fine. In fact, he'll probably outlive us all. But there's something rather strange that you need to see." Drayton crooked a finger and said, "Follow me, please."

Theodosia followed Drayton down a long hallway, glancing up at the portraits of Neville ancestors that had hung there for almost a century. Then Drayton turned and led her into an enormous Victorian parlor, what Theodosia had always thought of as the red room because of the dark red wallpaper and cherrywood paneling.

Timothy was sitting in a red brocade wing chair in front of an enormous carved white marble fireplace. A few embers glowed as if he'd been sitting there in quiet contemplation while the fire burned low. Perhaps pondering whether to crack open the last, dusty bottle of a Montrachet '62 that resided in his wine cellar.

Or was something else going on? Drayton had sounded like it was an emergency.

"You're here," Timothy said. "Good." His body was set in a fairly relaxed pose, one leg crossed over the other, but his facial muscles looked twitchy.

Theodosia pushed a hank of hair off her face. "Will someone please tell me what's going on?"

Timothy lifted a hand, like an emperor bestowing a blessing. "Show her," he said to Drayton.

"Over here," Drayton said. He was standing next to an antique gaming table that was set against a large bay window. The table was a walnut Queen Anne style, flanked by two intricately carved chairs. "Timothy received a rather cryptic note today, and we wanted you to look at it."

Theodosia moved toward the table, a feeling of dread suddenly lodging in her chest. What was going on?

A sheet of paper sat in the middle of the table atop a red leather insert. The paper was smaller than the regular eight-and-a-half-by-eleven paper you'd use in a standard printer or copy machine. This sheet was maybe six by nine inches in size, white, not particularly fine paper stock, with a message hand-printed dead center.

It read, YOU'RE NEXT.

"Where did this come from?" Theodosia asked. "Did you find it in today's mail?"

"No," Timothy said. "Someone must have slipped it through the brass mail slot at the front door. It was lying in the entry when I arrived home."

"The note must have been hand delivered," Drayton said.

"Was anyone here today?" Theodosia asked. "Cleaning lady, housekeeper, gardener? Maybe someone saw who left it."

"Nobody was scheduled to be here today," Timothy said. "Hence, no one was here."

"What about Henry?" Timothy had a trusted butler who'd been with him for decades.

"Henry is semiretired now. Mostly he just drops by on Fridays and we go over household details together."

Theodosia leaned forward to study the note. The printing was basic and slightly childish-looking, but then again, most people's printing looked a little childish. She lifted a hand to touch it, then pulled back. She let the note sit there, like some kind of strange, pulsing evil. Like Poe's tell-tale heart.

"What do you think?" Drayton asked.

Theodosia knew the question was aimed at her. "This has to be about the weapons show, right? Someone is determined that you call off the show. Or else . . ." She decided not to finish her sentence.

"Do you think this note could have been written by Jud Harker?" Drayton asked.

"Maybe," Theodosia said. "Maybe not." She turned toward Timothy. "Do you have any enemies that we should know about?"

"I don't believe I have any enemies at all," Timothy said. "Perhaps I've ruffled a few feathers here and there, but nothing to warrant a threat of this magnitude."

"This most definitely is a threat," Theodosia said. "And considering what happened on your rooftop this past Sunday evening, this note has to be taken seriously. Which means we need to contact the police."

Timothy's brows pinched together. "I hate to bother them with something as inconsequential as a childishly scrawled note."

"It's not inconsequential," Drayton said. "And Theodosia's quite correct. We must alert the police immediately."

"I'm going to make that call right now," Theodosia said. She was going to do it before Timothy had a chance to disagree or put up an argument.

But Timothy simply dropped his head forward and said, "Very well."

Much to Theodosia's relief, Detective Pete Riley showed up some thirty minutes later. And, lo and behold, he was shadowed by his boss, Detective Burt Tidwell.

"My goodness," Timothy said, once everyone had shaken hands and made polite, slightly strained introductions. "I didn't expect an entire police contingent."

Riley gave a friendly nod. "Taking into consideration the homicide the other night . . ."

"Show us the note," Tidwell said, interrupting him in solemn tones. "Where is the note?"

"Here," Drayton said. He led the detectives across the plush Aubusson carpet to the gaming table. "It's right here."

Tidwell stopped in front of the table and bent his bulk forward. He read the note, his mouth moving slightly as if he were testing the veracity of the words. Then he blinked and straightened up again. "Who touched this, please?"

"Only me," Timothy said.

"No one else was in the house?" Tidwell asked.

"Not today," Timothy said.

"And where were you most of the day?"

"At the Heritage Society," Timothy said. "We're putting the finishing touches on our new . . ."

"Yes, I'm well aware of your Rare Weapons Show," Tidwell said. "You're showcasing a wealth of weapons similar to the one that eviscerated Mr. Lanier's liver and spleen the other evening."

Theodosia blanched at Tidwell's frank description, but was determined to press him for ideas. "Do you think there's a link?" she asked. She'd remained quiet thus far; now she stepped forward to confront Tidwell. "Do you think it's the same person?"

Tidwell stared at her. "Do you believe in coincidences?"

"Truthfully, this doesn't strike me as a coincidence," Theodosia said.

"Precisely my point," Tidwell said. He made a quick hand gesture and Detective Riley stepped forward. He pulled on a pair of purple nitrile gloves and then carefully picked up the note. He handled it gingerly, as if it were a dead, infested rat, and slid it into a large evidence bag.

Tidwell turned his attention on Timothy. "Perhaps you should cancel your weapons show."

Timothy gave a disdainful look and shook his head. "Impossible. This is an important show for the Heritage Society. Prominent collectors will be attending. Important donors as well."

"Your life is important, too," Tidwell said. "I urge you to consider canceling your event."

"Never," Timothy said.

Tidwell rocked back on his heels. "Ridiculous," he muttered under his breath.

"Detective Tidwell," Theodosia said. "Jud Harker is still a suspect in Carson Lanier's murder, is he not?"

Tidwell gave a terse nod of his large, slightly egg-shaped head.

"And he's been a very vocal opponent to Timothy's show."

"Are we going somewhere with this?" Tidwell asked.

"Yes," Theodosia said. "Why wouldn't Harker be the prime suspect in this note incident as well?"

"I didn't say he wasn't," Tidwell said.

"Good," Drayton said. "Then the man should be questioned."

"I say we confront the man right now," Riley said. "Strike while the iron is hot."

"No," Tidwell said. "Detective Riley, you'll shepherd the note back to the crime lab while I pay a visit to Harker."

"Do you know where he lives?" Theodosia asked.

"Despite our best efforts, his domicile remains elusive to us," Tidwell said. "Therefore, you are going to accompany me to the Stagwood Inn, where Harker is a sometime worker. Then we shall question management until we get the proper answer we need." He pulled himself up to his full height and looked around with half-hooded eyes. "Does anyone have a better idea?"

No one did.

Theodosia felt a tiny thrill as they stepped up to the front desk in the lobby of the Stagwood Inn. Never in her wildest dreams had she believed that Tidwell would allow her to accompany him on an actual police interview. Or maybe he was just humoring her, playing a game of cat and mouse? She'd find out soon enough.

An older man in a tweed jacket with a brass name tag that said D. J. BURTON was manning the front desk tonight. He smiled at them and said, "Did you folks have a reservation?"

"There was none needed, since we are not guests," Tidwell said.

"Oh," Burton said, slightly taken aback. "Then . . . what can I do for you?"

Tidwell pulled out a worn leather case and flipped it open. A gold shield shone brightly under the lights. "We need to speak to your manager," he said.

"Is Mr. Cooper in his office tonight?" Theodosia asked.

"No," Burton said. "He went home. Well, not exactly home—he's in his apartment across the way." Now the man seemed flustered.

"Do you know where that is?" Tidwell asked Theodosia.

"I can probably find it," she said. She glanced at Burton. "What's the room number?"

"Twenty-seven," the desk clerk said. "Across the back patio and then behind the trellis with the jessamine."

"Thank you," Theodosia said.

"Just before you get to the Dumpster."

Tidwell rolled his eyes. "Lovely."

Mitchel Cooper wasn't thrilled about being disturbed. He'd been watching TV and, because it was turned up full volume, Theodosia has a sneaking suspicion it might have been *The Bachelor.*

No matter, Cooper quickly clicked off his guilty pleasure with the remote control as he met them at the door.

Tidwell gave a gruff explanation about needing Jud Harker's address, but made no mention of Timothy's threatening note.

"Didn't someone already give you that information?" Cooper asked. "I was sure they did." When Tidwell didn't answer, he said, "Okay, just a sec. Let me get my shoes on."

Cooper's shoes turned out to be worn leather slippers that slapped loudly all the way across the patio. He led them to the back door, through the kitchen, and to his office underneath the stairway. Then he turned on a light, looked around as if in a daze, and said, "Now, where did I put my personnel book?"

"We really appreciate this," Theodosia said, while Tidwell just stood there like a big, silent statue from Easter Island.

Cooper put on a pair of glasses and studied a row of three-ring binders that sat on a tilting, propped-up shelf. "Mmn." His fingers crawled along the binders. "Here we go." He looked up. "Jud Harker, you said?"

"Correct," Tidwell said.

Cooper thumbed through several dividers and pages. "Let me see, now . . ."

"Either you have it or you do not," Tidwell said impatiently. "You realize, the address of the boardinghouse we were given earlier is an old address. Mr. Harker no longer resides there. We've requested updated information several times and it hasn't been forthcoming."

"You already mentioned that," Cooper replied. He continued paging through his personnel book. "Okay, here it is. Jud Harker." He pushed his glasses up his nose and said, "Four seventy-six Dunbar Street in North Charleston."

"You're sure that's correct?" Tidwell asked.

"Pretty sure," Cooper said.

"Could we trouble you to write down that address for us?" Theodosia asked.

"No problem," Cooper said. He grabbed a piece of notepaper off his desk and scrawled the information, handed it to Theodosia.

She looked at it, noting that Cooper's printing looked nothing like the threatening note Timothy had received. "Thank you," she said.

"I saw what you did there," Tidwell said. They were cruising along in his Crown Victoria, running fast through the darkened city, headed for the address in North Charleston. "You were studying Mitchel Cooper's penmanship to see if it matched up with the note."

"It didn't," Theodosia said.

"No, it didn't."

"Why?" Theodosia asked.

"Why what?"

"Am I here with you?"

"Don't you want to be?" Tidwell asked. "Isn't this what makes your heart go pitty-pat? To be an integral part of the investigation?"

"Yes and no," Theodosia said. "Because too much is happening too fast. It's hard to make heads or tails of all the pieces."

"Kindly enlighten me," Tidwell said. "On all these pieces."

So Theodosia took a deep breath, and from where she was snuggled in the deep cushions of Tidwell's aging Crown Victoria, told him everything. The shouting match and fight between Sissy Lanier and Betty Bates, the rock through her window, the visit to the weapons store, meeting Bob Garver, and then Sissy's claim about the missing Fidelity money.

When Theodosia had finished, and Tidwell still hadn't said a word, she said, "So you see why I'm feeling a bit unsettled."

"Because of all these perceived suspects," Tidwell said. "And the fact that you know too much."

"I didn't set out to," Theodosia said. "I've just been in the right place at the right time." She gave a rueful laugh. "Or maybe the wrong place."

"Either way," Tidwell said, "you have gleaned a few bits of useful information."

"You think so?"

He nodded. "Some of what you've told me is information—and insights—that we might not ordinarily get via regular questioning."

They traveled down Rivers Avenue, past the Charleston International Airport and the Northwoods Mall. Tidwell's police radio was on, and Theodosia half listened to the dispatchers' abbreviated conversations and codes that crackled over the airwaves. It was like being at a large cocktail party surrounded by the excited buzz of conversation. But without a nice bourbon and sour.

Then they twisted and turned down a number of smaller streets until they finally hit Dunbar Street. They cruised down the darkened street until Tidwell slowed in front of number 476. It was a sprawling and dilapidated building that was obviously a rooming house. A battered metal mail receptacle hung next to the front door and had six individual slots.

"Which apartment does Mr. Harker supposedly occupy?" Tidwell asked.

"Number six."

"Upstairs, then."

They walked up the front sidewalk, stepped onto a sagging front porch, and let themselves inside. The smell of cooked potatoes (or maybe it was onions) hung heavy in the air. They crept up a creaking staircase that reminded Theodosia of the back staircase at the Stagwood Inn. When they reached the second floor, however, there was none of the same charm. A narrow hallway extended down the center of the building offering peeled-off wallpaper, worn carpeting, and more cooking odors.

"It's this one," Theodosia said, stopping in front of a door that had a wooden number six nailed to it.

Tidwell pushed past her and knocked on the door. Then they waited. When nobody came to the door, Tidwell knocked again. Harder.

"Maybe he's not home," Theodosia said.

Tidwell grasped the doorknob and shook it. "Mr. Harker," he called out. "Police. Open up."

Still nothing.

"Are you sure this is the correct address?" Tidwell asked.

"It's the one Cooper gave us. Unless Harker moved again."

Tidwell blew out a large glut of air and said, "Wasted trip."

But Theodosia didn't think so. She figured she'd learned enough tonight to nudge another small piece into the puzzle.

18

Even though Theodosia arrived home fairly late, Earl Grey was completely content. Today was one of the days that Mrs. Barry, his dog walker, had stopped by. Mrs. Barry was a retired schoolteacher who'd never met a dog she didn't want to snuggle. Besides coming by to walk and feed Earl Grey, Mrs. Barry also did doggy daycare for a Scottie dog named Mr. Misty and two hyperactive schnauzers named Rock and Roll. She used to walk Tootsie, a poodle from down the block, but Tootsie and her owners moved away. Transferred to Atlanta. The owners, not Tootsie.

"How are you doing?" Theodosia asked Earl Grey. "Everything shipshape and copacetic?"

Earl Grey's ears pricked forward and his tail thumped the floor.

"Did you give Mrs. Barry her check?" Theodosia asked. She glanced over at the dining room table and saw it was gone. "Good, your tuition is paid for another month."

Earl Grey followed Theodosia up to the second floor. Theodosia had done some redesigning and redecorating up here to make it cozy and more personal. She now enjoyed a large bedroom with an en suite bathroom, a small tower room where she'd installed a cozy chair and lamp for reading, and a second bedroom that had been converted into a walk-in closet. Because, for goodness' sake, how could any self-respecting woman jam her entire wardrobe into an old-fashioned three-foot-wide closet? Well, she just couldn't.

"I'm thinking," Theodosia said, "that we should try to fit in a run."

"Rrowr?"

"Yes, right now. I don't mean to burden you, but it's been a long, crazy day and I'm feeling horribly jazzed. What say we try to blow out the carbon, even if it's only for twenty minutes?"

Ten minutes later, the two of them were loping down Meeting Street. Overhead, the sky was blue-black with a few clusters of stars peeping through the clouds. The salt-laced smell of the churning Atlantic hung heavy in the air, intermingled with the fragrant scent of jasmine and jessamine.

Arriving at White Point Garden, that lush park on the very tip of the Peninsula, was always a thrill. Wind gusted in, tossing and bending the trees; ancient cannons loomed up out of the mist; the ocean boomed loudly; and oyster shells littered the narrow, sandy beach. On the opposite shoreline, red and green lights from lighthouses winked reassuringly. The only things missing were the tall ships, which were off for another stop on their six-month-long seafaring adventure.

Theodosia and Earl Grey ran along lightly on the grass, down the entire length of the park. They circled the Victorian bandstand and then ran back again. Not a long run, but a satisfying one. Enough to get a slight but much-needed dopamine hit. They ducked down a short alley that ran past a pattering fountain, came out next to a spectacular fern garden, and then turned down Archdale. They breezed past Timothy's home, which was completely dark now, Timothy being an early-to-bed, early-to-rise kind of guy. Next door at the Stagwood Inn, however, a few lights still burned in the upstairs rooms.

Theodosia couldn't help but glance up at the third floor window. At the—what was it called again? Oh yes, the Treetop Suite—to see if someone was up there. The window was dark, making it look as if the place was unoccupied. Unless someone was sitting up there with the lights turned off, staring down at her. Which was a very spooky thought indeed.

As they jogged down Tradd Street, Theodosia decided to cut down the quaint little alley that ran directly behind the Indigo Tea Shop as well as a dozen other small businesses. It was quiet and protected from the ocean winds, which had started to really kick up. Halfway down the alley, a back door opened and a faint shaft of light fell across her pathway. Then the door slammed shut as a dark, blurry figure emerged.

"Oh!" Theodosia cried as she pulled up short, causing Earl Grey to lurch against her.

There was a metallic tinkling sound—either keys or a chain—and then a pleasant woman's voice said, with a slight quaver to it, "Hello? Who's there?"

"Oh my goodness, it's Alexis," Theodosia blurted out. "You startled me." Her heart was pounding a timpani solo inside her chest.

Alexis James peered at her in the dim light of the alley where an old-fashioned carriage lamp flickered fitfully. "Theodosia?" she said.

"Yes, it's me," Theodosia said. She was relieved to see a friendly face, relieved to realize that she had stopped directly behind Haiku Gallery. "I didn't mean for you to think I was some kind of weird prowler."

"Not a problem," Alexis said, smiling. "I'm happy to see a fellow shopowner." Then she turned her immediate attention to Earl Grey. "Ooh, what a lovely dog we have here. Who is this fine fellow, please?" Alexis was already down on bended knee, accepting a raised paw in her outstretched hand. "And such a proper gentleman to shake hands like that."

"This is Earl Grey," Theodosia said. "Also known as the tea shop dog. He'll shake hands, love you to death, and if you scratch under his chin—or really anywhere on his furry body— he'll give you a great big kiss."

"Well, he's absolutely adorable," Alexis said. "And please don't mind me, because I turn into a mushy-gushy mess whenever I get around animals. Particularly dogs and cats. Although horses make me lose it as well. And any kind of fawn or baby raccoon."

"I'm the same way," Theodosia said. "Love all the critters." And then, as they walked down the alley together, said, "You're working late."

"Yes, well, because of my new business, don't you know?" Alexis said. "This gallery seems to require ten times the amount of time and energy I thought it would. But I guess I don't have to tell you about working long hours."

"I hear you," Theodosia said. "I'm still wondering when I'll finally catch up. And the tea shop's been open for years."

"Wasn't that something today?" Alexis asked. "I mean, at the fashion show?"

"Unbelievable."

"I don't even *know* those women and I was embarrassed for them," Alexis said.

"I felt bad for Delaine," Theodosia said. "Though I'm sure she'll manage to bounce back from it."

They emerged from the alley and stood together under a lamppost. "You're dressed very sporty," Alexis said.

"Running," Theodosia explained.

"Do you and your dog run every night?"

"Almost every night. When the weather cooperates, that is."

Alexis gazed back down her alley. "I know what you mean. When it's foggy or rainy these cobblestones get awfully slippery. Makes me nervous."

"Are you a runner as well?" Theodosia was sensing the possibility of a running partner.

"Me? No, not anymore," Alexis said. "I've got creaky knees from wearing high heels for too many years." She laughed softly. "Now I work out my aggressions in a spin class."

"You enjoy that?" Theodosia asked. She'd heard so much about spin classes and had always wanted to try one.

Alexis grinned. "I love it. Spinning really gets the old heart pumping like crazy. And it's a lot of fun. You're in there with a whole bunch of people, riding as hard as you can . . . it feels very empowering. Like riding in a peloton in the Tour de France. Only with rock music blasting."

"I love it!" Theodosia said.

"You know what? You should try it sometime. I bet you'd be great at spinning. You've probably already built up some terrific endurance."

"Might be fun," Theodosia said, deciding that a workout partner could be just as good as a running partner.

"I've got an idea," Alexis said. "Come with me tomorrow night. They do a late class for working stiffs, nine o'clock, over at Metro Spin Cycle. You know where that is?"

"Over on Cumberland."

"Then it's settled," Alexis said. "We'll meet up at the front door and go in together. I think I even have a coupon for a free class."

"Can't beat that," Theodosia said.

Pete Riley was waiting for her on the street when she got home. He stepped out from the shadow of a magnolia tree and said, "Tell me, do the two of you go running every night?" It was essentially the same question Alexis had just asked.

"Almost every night," Theodosia said. She walked right up to Riley, rose up on tiptoes, and kissed him square on the mouth.

When he'd recovered from his surprise, he grinned and said, "How far do you usually go?"

Theodosia grabbed his hand and led him up the front walk. "Tonight just down to White Point Garden. We maybe managed three miles at best."

"So you were just kind of breezing."

"Something like that." Theodosia stuck her key in the lock and said, "Come on in." She flipped on a light switch and watched as Earl Grey gave Riley a couple of good sniffs and then wandered off, looking disinterested.

"Huh," Riley said. "The story of my life."

"Somehow I doubt that," Theodosia said. Riley was too good-looking, too sure of himself, not to be taken seriously.

Riley reached into his jacket pocket and pulled out a small, colorful gift bag. He handed it to Theodosia.

She lifted an eyebrow. What's this?"

"Just a little something I thought you might like."

"A gift," Theodosia said as she opened the bag slowly and peered in. "Oh, I love this perfume! Thank you." It was a bottle of Maison Margiela REPLICA Tea Escape.

"The scent reminded me of you," Riley said.

"Because tea is one of the actual ingredients, right?" The perfume was a blend of bergamot, green tea, lily of the valley, and jasmine. A tea-drinking Southern girl's fragrance dream.

"Of course."

"Thank you so much, but what's the occasion?" Theodosia asked as they made their way into the kitchen.

"To sweeten the deal?" Riley said.

"That sounds tantalizing. And a bit scary, too."

"Because we have a lot to talk about," Riley said.

"In that case," Theodosia said, "would you care for a bottle of water? Or better yet, a glass of wine?" She opened the refrigerator and stuck her head in. "Chablis or Merlot?"

Riley held up a hand. "Pass."

"You're still on duty?"

"No, I just want to get the full story."

Theodosia grabbed a bottle of water for herself, took a quick glug, and then plopped down at the kitchen table facing Riley. "Long day."

"So, how was your outing with Tidwell?"

"Not very productive, I'm afraid. We got Harker's address okay, then drove all the way over to North Charleston to find out he wasn't home."

"Maybe he was there but he was playing possum."

"Or maybe Harker's slipping down a dark alley somewhere, planning more evil deeds."

"My, we are the suspicious one, aren't we?" Riley said.

"Sometimes it pays to be."

"You still need to bring me up to speed on a few things."

"I suppose if I can unburden myself to Tidwell, I can do the same with you," Theodosia said.

"That's right. So fire when ready."

Theodosia took another sip of water and then proceeded to lay out all the events of the day, same as she'd done for Tidwell. The insults that Sissy Lanier and Betty Bates had hurled at each other, their horrible fight, the rock through her window, meeting Garver at the gun club, and Sissy showing up at the tea shop totally bereft because her Fidelity account was missing a whole bunch of money.

Riley listened, nodded, and, as the stories got wilder, looked slightly horrified. When Theodosia finally ended with Timothy's threatening note, he said, "You certainly did have a full day."

"And I've got the aches, bruises, and a headache to prove it."

Riley reached over, pulled her closer, and kissed her again. "Poor baby," he murmured. "Getting roped in like that."

"The thing is, I didn't *want* to get roped in at first. But now . . ."

"Now you're in it up to your cute little eyeballs."

"I think I am," Theodosia said. "And I have to tell you, if you asked me right now who Lanier's killer is, I'd still put my money on Jud Harker."

"Why is that?" Riley asked.

"Because Harker seems the most unhinged. Trying to stop the weapons show has become—what would you call it? An ideological fight."

"But these other people—Sissy Lanier, Betty Bates, and Bob Garver—there's much more at stake for them," Riley said. "Much more of a financial upside in getting rid of Lanier. And they all profile as somewhat obsessive-compulsive as well."

"In the South we call that eccentric," Theodosia said.

"Except any one of them could be dangerously eccentric," Riley said. "But that's not for you to worry about, because you're not going to be deputized anytime soon."

"Wait, what are you saying?" Theodosia asked.

"That you need to pull back and let law enforcement run the show from here on in," Riley said.

"To be fair, you guys haven't come up with all that much."

"But we will," Riley assured her. "We'll crack this whole thing wide open in another day or two."

"You think?" Theodosia wasn't nearly as optimistic.

"Of course." Riley paused. "Now tell me about this big party Friday night. The Kitty Kat Club."

"You make it sound like a strip club." Theodosia laughed.

"Then what is it again?" Riley asked.

"The Hair Ball. Delaine's fancy dress ball following the big Carolina Cat Show." Theodosia peered at Riley. "You don't really have to go, you know."

"Are you afraid I'll look like something the cat dragged in?" Riley teased.

"That's not it at all. I just don't want you to feel pressure from Delaine."

"That's not who I'm thinking about at the moment." Riley leaned forward and kissed her again.

"Well, okay," Theodosia murmured.

19

Even though Theodosia had tacitly promised Pete Riley that she'd back off from the investigation, she didn't see any harm in attending the private memorial service for Carson Lanier.

So that's exactly where she was this Thursday morning at 10:00 AM. Sitting alongside Drayton and Timothy in the Main Reading Room at the Charleston Library Society.

It was a gorgeous room. Black-and-white marble floors, a skylight overhead that let in a welcome spill of sunlight, plus tall, elegant Palladian windows. Approximately forty chairs had been arranged in a neat semicircle, and every one of them was filled.

Theodosia noted that Betty Bates was present, along with a large contingent of Capital Bank executives. Bob Garver had also shown up, though he was sitting in the back row, toying with his smartphone. Probably trying to kill two birds with one stone; nail down a real estate deal while he shoehorned in a memorial service.

And Tidwell was there, too. Standing in the back of the room, looking like a bull in a china shop. Or maybe a bull in a library.

But Sissy, Lanier's soon-to-be ex-wife, technically his widow now, was a no-show. Which Theodosia didn't find one bit surprising.

"I wish this service would get started," Drayton said under his breath to Theodosia. "I'm worried about leaving Miss Dimple and Jamie in charge."

"They're not in charge," Theodosia whispered back. "Haley is. And she's a pro. She'll make sure morning teatime runs like clockwork."

"And then we've got the Tea Trolley stopping by this afternoon."

"Relax," Theodosia said. "You've got to relax."

As if Drayton's nervousness had seeped out and permeated the atmosphere, a large man suddenly strode up the center aisle and took his place at the podium. He had a shock of white hair, a florid face, and he wore a three-piece, nondescript banker's suit.

"That's Roger Grimley from the bank," Timothy whispered.

"I figured as much," Theodosia said.

Grimley carried a bronze urn in his beefy hands, and he set it down carefully, almost theatrically, on the podium for all to see. Theodosia supposed the contents therein were all that was left of Carson Lanier.

Grimley gave a heartfelt welcome to the group, then gripped the podium with both hands and launched into a masterfully worded testimonial about Carson Lanier. He praised the man's work ethic, his brilliance, and his dedication to community service. Then he moved on to lament Lanier's too-short tenure at Capital Bank.

As Grimley rambled on, Theodosia glanced about the room. Most mourners were staring stolidly ahead, a few women wiped at their eyes with hankies. Tidwell had seemingly disappeared.

Theodosia craned her neck around, looking for him. But Tidwell really was gone. Slipped out like a rat abandoning a sinking ship.

Twenty-five minutes later, Grimley ran out of breath. Red-faced and gasping now, he thanked everyone for coming and urged them to stay for coffee and sweet rolls.

"Sweet rolls," Drayton hissed under his breath. "They're serving industrial-mix sweet rolls when they could have had something civilized like scones."

"Not everyone has your exemplary taste," Theodosia told him. "Or knowledge of artisan scones."

"That's obvious."

But as the mourners rose to leave—or stay for refreshments, as the case might be—Theodosia pushed her way through the crowd and raced after Bob Garver. She buttonholed him just as he was about to step into the hallway.

"Mr. Garver," Theodosia said. "May I have a moment of your time?"

Garver looked up from poking at his cell phone. "Hmm?" Then he seemed to focus more carefully. "You. I remember you."

"I'd like to ask you about . . ."

Garver shoved past her, all businesslike and brusque. "No time," he called over his shoulder. His lips twitched into a sneer. "No interest, either."

"How rude," Theodosia said. It was the second time Garver had brushed her off as if she were an errant mosquito.

"I wanted to talk to him, too," said a voice at her shoulder.

Theodosia turned to find Betty Bates staring at her. Betty didn't exactly have a toothsome, friendly look on her face, but she didn't have murder in her eyes, either. Unless she was cleverly hiding her real intent.

"He's a prime suspect," Theodosia said of the departed Garver.

"And thanks to you, so am I," Betty said. Now she did sound angry and bitter. "I've been forced to answer probing questions directed at me by *two* different detectives. Both pushy, rude detectives, I might add."

"Poor you," Theodosia said. Betty Bates was clearly no blushing little flower. She was hard-shell tough and a real business pro. If she could fight her way up the corporate ladder, she probably possessed a good deal of smarts and cunning. In fact, Theodosia figured it wouldn't be long before Betty was able to bull her way into Lanier's old job. There was a vacancy, after all.

"You think *I* was having an affair with Lanier?" Betty asked. She kept her voice purposely low, but it shook with fury. "You are so off base."

Theodosia met her gaze. "That's not what Sissy Lanier says."

"Sissy Lanier is a nutcase. She wasn't able to hang on to her husband, so now she spews vicious lies wherever she goes."

"Sissy happens to be missing a great deal of money," Theodosia said. "And she's worried that her husband spent it on whoever he was having an affair with."

"Well, it certainly wasn't me," Betty said. "So it has to have been somebody else!"

Miss Dimple's face split into a wide grin when Theodosia and Drayton arrived back at the Indigo Tea Shop.

"There you are," Miss Dimple exclaimed. Then her look turned sorrowful. "How was the service? Haley said you were attending a memorial?"

"It was fine," Drayton said. "But more importantly, how is our tea service going?"

"No problems whatsoever," Miss Dimple said. She was a happy octogenarian who had done their bookkeeping for a number of years. Besides still handling receivables and payables, she also delighted in filling in at the tea shop whenever needed. "And this sweet young fellow you have working here?" Miss Dimple leaned in closer to Drayton. "My advice is to keep him. Jamie's an absolute *treasure*." Plump little Miss Dimple let loose a chuckle that set her entire five-feet-one-inch body into motion, from the tidy bun in her hair and her apple-cheeked face to her dainty size-five feet.

"Indeed," Drayton said. He fingered his polka-dot bow tie and frowned.

"That's high praise coming from you, Miss Dimple," Theodosia said.

"Oh, and a package arrived for Drayton," Miss Dimple said. "I placed it on one of his tea shelves for safekeeping."

Theodosia slipped a black Parisian waiter's apron over her head and tied the strings. "So, what's happening? Where are we at?"

Miss Dimple nodded in the direction of the tea room. "Our customers are just finishing up their morning tea. And Haley was going to share her ideas on luncheon entrées with me."

"Then let's both go into the kitchen and see what she's whipped up," Theodosia said. "While Drayton tries to pull his tea counter back together."

"That's right," Drayton said, slipping behind the front counter. "It's probably a horrible mess."

Miss Dimple's voice floated back to him. "Oh, I don't think so."

*   *   *

"*We've got lots* of good things for lunch," Haley said as Theodosia and Miss Dimple crowded into the small kitchen. "Shrimp salad on a croissant, roast beef and horseradish tea sandwiches, and baked French toast that's just about ready to come out of the oven."

"Baked French toast?" Miss Dimple asked. "What's that?"

"A sinfully rich French toast with lots of cinnamon, sugar, and an inordinate amount of eggs and butter."

"Ooh," Miss Dimple said.

"And what about sweets?" Theodosia asked. "For dessert, that is."

"Got those, too," Haley said. "Red velvet cupcakes and pear scones."

"You've been baking up a storm," Miss Dimple said.

Haley grinned. She had a streak of white flour on her face and looked adorable. "That's good, huh?"

"It's wonderful," Miss Dimple said. "I don't know how you manage all this in such a tiny kitchen."

"It's no big deal," Haley said. "Besides, this is my domain. This is where I get to rule the roost."

"Nobody would ever contest that," Theodosia said.

"In fact," Haley said, "you can start taking luncheon orders as soon as our customers begin to arrive."

"You want to handle that?" Theodosia asked Miss Dimple.

"I'm on it," Miss Dimple said.

Haley slid her hand into an oven mitt. "What are you going to do?" she asked Theodosia.

"I'm going to start working on tomorrow's Plum Blossom Tea," Theodosia said.

"Good," Haley said. "Like Drayton always says, it's never too early to start worrying about tomorrow."

Theodosia sped out into the tea room and grabbed Jamie by the sleeve. "Do you have a minute?"

"I think so," Jamie said. "But let me ditch these dirty dishes first." He disappeared into the kitchen with his plastic bin and was back in two seconds. "What's up?"

"I'd like you to run down the block to Haiku Gallery and pick up a box of Japanese curios."

"Are you gonna use 'em for your tea tomorrow?" Jamie asked.

"That's exactly right," Theodosia said. "Alexis James, the gallery owner, said she'd pull together some decorative items for us, smaller items, that we can display on the tables along with our plum blossom arrangements."

"You want me to go right now?" Jamie sounded excited about the prospect of going to Haiku Gallery.

"That would be the general idea," Theodosia said as Jamie suddenly bolted for the door. "But Jamie," she called after him. "Take care. In all your wild enthusiasm, please don't break anything."

Theodosia cleared two tables, refilled tea, chatted with a few customers, and rang up the purchase of a jar of honey. Then she turned toward the front counter, where Drayton was fussing about. "Were all your tea tins hopelessly messed up like you figured they'd be?"

"Actually, they were surprisingly organized," Drayton said. "We must not have had a very busy morning."

"Miss Dimple told me that every table was filled and some turned over twice."

"Is that so." Drayton reached under the counter and pulled out an elegant pink teapot. "Look what was delivered while we were cooling our heels at the memorial service." He held the oval-shaped teapot in his hands. It had a gold handle, spout, and lid, and the sides were decorated with pink flowers and a small cherub.

Theodosia's eyes lit up with recognition. "That can be only one thing."

"Limoges," Drayton said. "I saw it at Anderson's Antiques last week, and then yesterday I decided I just had to have it. I called them up and told them to send it right over."

"Is it a signed piece?"

Drayton turned the teapot over. "It has the proper Limoges mark on the bottom, but not an actual artist's signature. If it was signed, I'm not sure I could have afforded it."

"Still," Theodosia said, "it's a gorgeous piece."

"Can you believe how deep and true that pink color is? And the delicate shading? It's really quite delicious."

"A collector's item," Theodosia said.

"Now if I could only find a matching sugar bowl. Did you know that during the late eighteenth century, very large, almost outsize sugar bowls were in favor, especially in England and France?"

"Why so supersized?"

"Because sugar cost a small fortune back then, so a large sugar bowl sitting on one's table was a clear sign of wealth."

"Kind of like driving a big honkin' SUV today," Theodosia said.

Just then the front door flew open and Jamie and Alexis came walking in. Both were staggering under the large boxes they held in their arms, with Jamie looking as if he were picking his way along a treacherous mountain path and carrying vials of nitroglycerin.

Theodosia flew around the counter to help them. "Let me take this," she said to Alexis.

Alexis gladly handed over her box to Theodosia. "Thank you. I feel like a pack animal that over-packed," she said with a laugh.

Theodosia set the box on the counter and Jamie slid his box next to it. Drayton peered in, gave a nod of approval, and said, "Loot."

"I tried to give you a diverse assortment," Alexis said. "Some fans, small statues, a few nice pots. All Japanese items that should help accent a fancy table."

"This is just wonderful," Theodosia said as she pulled out a piece of Shino ware. It was a small bowl, milky white with a red ash glaze. "And we promise to take very good care of your treasures."

"I brought you something else," Alexis said with a sly smile. She reached into her handbag and pulled out a copy of *Shooting Star*. "Do you remember when Bill Glass was snapping pictures at Delaine's shop yesterday?"

"Yes, yes," Theodosia said. Then, "Oh good heavens, don't tell me that Glass dared to . . . ?"

But Alexis was already grinning and nodding in the affirmative. "He did dare. The photo's front page above the fold," she said. "You know that old newspaper maxim: If it bleeds, it leads."

Drayton leaned in. "You mean Bill Glass had the gall to actually *print* damaging photos?"

"Take a look," Alex said, holding up her copy of *Shooting Star*. "Three different shots capturing the catfight, all in sharp focus and vivid color."

Theodosia stared at the photos. In the largest one, Sissy was caught with an unflattering snarl on her face and Betty Bates had both fists up, ready to throw a nasty punch. The other two photos were just as bad. Maybe worse. In one shot the two women were sprawled on the floor.

"Let me see that," Drayton said. He snatched the newspaper out of Alexis's hands, scanned the photos, and let his eyes rove down the front page. "Garbage," he spat out.

Alexis's eyes sparkled. "Of course it is. But you're reading it."

Theodosia chuckled. "She's got you there, Drayton."

"Just a glance, just a quick glance," Drayton said brusquely. "The accompanying text is simply a bizarre curiosity."

"We'll give you a pass this time, Drayton," Alexis said. She winked at Theodosia and said, "Are you getting geared up for your first spin class tonight?"

"I'm looking forward to it," Theodosia said as the phone rang. She reached around, grabbed the receiver, and said, "Indigo Tea Shop." She listened a couple of seconds and then cried, "Aunt Libby!" in a delighted voice.

Aunt Libby was one of Theodosia's favorite relatives. She lived at Cane Ridge Plantation out on Rutledge Road with Margaret Rose Reese, her companion and housekeeper. The two of them were quite content at Cane Ridge, feeding the birds, conducting the occasional plantation tour, attending their local church, and enjoying their book club and bridge club.

"Margaret Rose and I are planning to be in town this weekend," Aunt Libby said to Theodosia.

"That's wonderful," Theodosia said. "Then for sure you have to stay with me."

"No, no," Aunt Libby said. "We're planning to stay with cousin Livonia. She's got that enormous house over on King Street, and the poor lady just rattles around in it. She has acres of room."

"Yes, but when was the last time she dusted?" Theodosia asked. Cousin Livonia was a bit of a free spirit. She enjoyed poker, playing the ponies, and smoking an occasional cigar. Housekeeping wasn't just on her back burner—it was relegated to the attic.

"It's probably been a while since she gave that white elephant a good cleaning," Aunt Libby said. "But we don't want to put you out or interfere in any way. After all, we're two old ladies who like to turn in at nine o'clock."

"Then you can at least come to our luncheon tomorrow," Theodosia said. "The tea shop is hosting a Plum Blossom Tea for the Broad Street Garden Club, and I know we have a few seats left."

"That sounds lovely," Aunt Libby said. "But only if it's not too much trouble for you."

"No trouble at all," Theodosia said. She glanced around the tea shop, saw that Miss Dimple was seating two customers and that Drayton had just poured Alexis a cup of tea. "I'm positive you'll be welcome. I think you know Midge Binkley—she's president of the Garden Club now."

"I've known Midge since her husband was in knickers. So it'll be jolly fun to see her again."

"That's just great. I'll see you then." Theodosia hung up the phone and smiled across the counter at Alexis.

"You look happy," Alexis said.

"I am," Theodosia said. "My aunt Libby is coming into town."

"The one who lives out near the Riddle Plantation?"

"That's the one."

"I'd love to meet her sometime. We probably know a few of the same people."

"Then why don't you come to the Plum Blossom Tea tomorrow," Theodosia said. "In fact, I apologize for not inviting you in the first place. Because I know we have a couple of seats left."

"You've got yourself a deal," Alexis said. "I'd love to come."

20

Theodosia sat behind her desk, pushing mounds of paper around. "Things I need to do today," she mumbled to herself. "Number one, find my to-do list."

Or maybe not. Maybe she should kick back and try to go with the flow. Which meant popping out to welcome the ladies who were part of the Tea Trolley today, or else she could . . .

A sharp knock sounded at the back door.

Who's that?

Theodosia crossed her office, unlocked the door, and pulled it open tentatively. And was thankfully greeted by the smiling face of Miss Josette, her favorite sweetgrass basket maker.

"I didn't know you were coming by today," Theodosia said, a smile lighting her face. She was always happy to see Miss Josette. Always delighted to spend some time with a real old-fashioned Southern lady. And a skilled artisan at that.

"I wasn't planning to drop by, either," Miss Josette said in her honeyed drawl. "But then I was in the neighborhood and I figured, why not. Make this my first stop." Miss Josette was an African American woman in her late seventies who could easily pass for early sixties. She had bright, intelligent eyes and smooth skin the color of rich mahogany. Today she wore a rust-colored dress with a tomato-red fringed shawl draped around her shoulders.

But it was the basket Miss Josette held in her hands that caught Theodosia's gaze. It was a classic fruit tray style, shallow and oval shaped, with a large, swooping handle.

"I'll take it," Theodosia said. She knew the basket would be perfect for displaying her T-Bath products. "But I hope you brought along a few more baskets than just that one."

Miss Josette moved aside, revealing four more baskets that were stacked on the back step.

"I want them all," Theodosia said.

Miss Josette waved a hand. "You're too easy. Don't you know you're supposed to let me do my sales pitch? Then you should bargain and play hard to get?"

"No way," Theodosia said. "Because your baskets *are* hard to get."

Sweetgrass baskets were unique to Charleston and the surrounding environs. Elegant and utilitarian, they were woven from long bunches of sweetgrass, pine needles, and bulrush, then bound together by strips from native palmetto trees. Over the years, sweetgrass baskets, crafted predominantly by African American women, had become celebrated pieces of art. A collection of low-country sweetgrass baskets was even on display at the Smithsonian in Washington, D.C.

"Looks like I'm done for the day," Miss Josette said as she and Theodosia moved the baskets into Theodosia's office. "Sold out. And you were my first stop."

"Lucky for me," Theodosia said.

Miss Josette put hands on hips and cocked an eye at her. "Now what am I going to tell my other clients?"

"I don't know, make something up. Tell them there's a severe drought and a shortage of suitable sweetgrass."

"You want me to lie?" Miss Josette said. "You know I'm a church lady. Sing in the choir every Sunday."

"And bless you for it," Theodosia said. "No, don't lie. Just tell them the baskets sold out immediately. And, by the way, you should raise your prices. I mean, just *look* at these baskets."

Besides the fruit tray basket, Miss Josette had brought along a bread basket, a pedestal basket, and a nifty figure-eight basket.

"Uh-huh, I've seen them."

"You're a truly gifted artist," Theodosia said.

"Thank you."

Theodosia slipped behind her desk and pulled out her checkbook. She started to write a check and then stopped. "Let me ask you something. Is your nephew, um . . ." She'd temporarily lost his name.

"Dexter," Miss Josette said.

"That's right, Dexter. Is he still doing grant writing for his nonprofit organization?"

"Are you serious?" Miss Josette said. "Sometimes I think that's all he does. Dex used to be executive director for the Heartsong Kids Club, now he's got two assistants who handle administration and programming while he practically functions as a full-time fund-raiser."

"Does he ever apply for grants from the city?"

Miss Josette bobbed her head. "I think so."

"Do you think Dexter would have time to talk to me? To answer a couple of questions?"

"I'm sure he would," Miss Josette said. She dug in her handbag and pulled out a creamy-colored business card with cartoon kids' faces on it. "Here, this is Dexter's card. Go ahead and give him a ring."

Theodosia wrote out a check to Miss Josette and walked her out to her car. Then she hurried back inside and called Dexter at Heartsong Kids Club, the nonprofit rec center that he'd founded a few years ago.

Dexter was delighted to hear from Theodosia and listened carefully when she asked about obtaining grants from the City of Charleston.

"I've gotten two small grants from them," Dexter told her. "And they were a dream to work with. Easier, in fact, than some of the large private foundations that award grants. They can be real sticklers. But if you've got questions about funding, you really should talk to Ginny Marchand. She heads the MOECD over there and pretty much controls the purse strings. You tell Ginny that I said to call her. She's a real nice lady."

"Thank you," Theodosia said. "I'll give her a ring."

She hung up the phone just as a burst of laughter drifted in from the tea room.

Sounds like they're having fun.

Theodosia peeked out the door and saw two dozen women swarming through the tea shop. All were dressed to the nines in pastel-colored suits and fancy dresses and had arrived on what was really a regular old jitney, but which today was dubbed the Tea Trolley. That is, the clever organizer drove her guests around to three different tea stops on what was billed as a Tea Trolley Tour. First up was the Charleston Tea Plantation out on Wadmalaw Island. That was a short walking tour with a cream tea following. Then they'd dropped by the Lady Good-wood Inn for a relaxing lunch in the Garden Room. The final stop was the Indigo Tea Shop for what Drayton was calling a dessert tea. He and Haley had come up with a wonderful menu that included pear scones, peaches and cream layer cake, sorbet, and vanilla black tea.

Okay. So that tea was humming right along. Now it was time to call the City of Charleston.

It took Theodosia three tries, but she finally got connected to Ginny Marchand, the director at the MOECD, the Mayor's Office of Economic and Community Development. Once Theodosia introduced herself and established that Dexter had told her to call, she confessed that she wasn't quite sure what the MOECD was all about.

"It's fairly straightforward," Ginny explained. "We award grants that deal with urban renewal, historic preservation, housing rehabilitation, and neighborhood development."

"Housing rehabilitation," Theodosia told her. "That's what I'm most interested in."

"You have a property you're looking to rehab?" Ginny asked.

"Actually, I'm interested in some single homes that an acquaintance of mine is working on. A fellow named Bob Garver? He's rehabbing a number of single houses over on Beaufain Street. I think Detective Pete Riley might have called to ask about him, too."

There was a long silence and then Ginny said, "Yes, that's correct. Detective Riley did call about that very same thing."

"I'm kind of following up," Theodosia said.

Ginny sighed. "Well, it's all public record, so I can tell you that our office did indeed award a rather substantial grant to Mr. Garver. Though it wasn't exactly free money."

"How do you mean?"

"The first twenty thousand was a free and clear grant. The balance of the money was loaned to him at an extremely low-interest rate. That money is expected to be repaid."

Theodosia took a chance. "On the whole, how is Garver doing?"

"Not all that well, I'm afraid." Then, "Do you people know something I don't know?"

"I don't mean to be cryptic about this," Theodosia said, "but we're trying to figure out if Garver is a legitimate developer or a really clever crook."

"Oh dear. And he did have such excellent references from his banker."

Who's now deceased, Theodosia thought. *With his murder still unsolved.* "So there have been problems?"

"Not with the loan repayment," Ginny said. "Because that money's not due yet. But Mr. Garver has been remiss with his reports. He's supposed to keep us informed every step of the way . . . architectural plans, timetable, approved contractor list, that sort of thing."

"And he's not doing it?"

"Not yet, anyway," Ginny said. "But I remain hopeful."

"Then so do I," Theodosia said. She thanked Ginny for her candid answers and hung up the phone.

That conversation didn't exactly answer any burning questions. So now what?

Theodosia decided she could throw together some gift baskets while she mulled over the Bob Garver conversation. She knew the baskets would get snapped up at the garden club's Plum Blossom Tea tomorrow. But five minutes after she started, Drayton stuck his head in her office.

"Busy?" he asked. Then he took a quick look at the limp and rather lackluster bow Theodosia had just tied. "No, I see you're not."

"Just because my bow artistry isn't up to snuff . . ."

"What are we going to do about plum blossoms for tomorrow?" Drayton asked.

"I already called Floradora. They promised to deliver a dozen or so branches first thing tomorrow."

"Good."

Theodosia lifted her brows. "Something else?"

"I was hoping we could leave early and pop into the Heritage Society."

"Okay." Theodosia stood up so fast her chair made a *spronging* sound and practically tipped over backward.

"Just like that? You're ready to go?"

"I think we have a few things to talk to Timothy about, don't you?"

Drayton sighed. "I'm afraid we do."

The Great Hall at the Heritage Society was quiet this time of day. The workmen and curators had all apparently finished their chores and gone home. Probably because the staging of the Rare Weapons Show was 99 percent complete.

"This looks wonderful," Drayton said as they stood in the hallway and gazed through the double doors.

"Probably just needs some last-minute touches," Theodosia said. Only a few shards of light came through the clerestory windows, and the lights in the Great Hall had been dimmed so that just a few pinpoint spotlights bounced off the glass display cases. That small bit of light showed off the gleaming weapons inside the cases, creating a sort of kaleidoscopic effect that made the weapons appear somewhat sinister.

"Let's have a look, shall we?" Drayton said.

They stepped into the room, their footsteps echoing hollowly as they approached the first case.

"Look here," Drayton said, pressing forward eagerly. "A set of antique dueling pistols."

"From what era?" Theodosia asked.

Drayton put on his tortoiseshell reading glasses and bent forward to study the small printed placard that sat at the front of the case. "Let's see, now, looks like these are from 1800."

"The Aaron Burr era."

"Approximately, yes." Drayton straightened back up and tapped the case. "But these are British made. Simmons of London. Burr and Hamilton wouldn't have used this sort of pistol."

"Still," Theodosia said, shivering as they moved on to the next case. There was something otherworldly about being in this cavernous room, surrounded by all manner of antique weapons. As though each weapon might have a bloody tale to tell.

"Here's a pistol that was reputedly used by Francis Marion," Drayton said. Marion, best known as the Swamp Fox, had confounded the British during the American Revolution with his hit-and-run guerilla tactics. It was said that General Cornwallis had practically pulled his hair out over the wily Swamp Fox's maneuvers.

Theodosia leaned forward and gazed into the case. The pistol was forged black metal with a wooden handle, technically a muzzleloader. Next to it sat a small pile of black gunpowder, a few lead balls, and bits of paper that looked almost like parchment. The gun required old-fashioned do-it-yourself ammunition, wherein the shooter grabbed a pinch of powder and a lead ball in a fold of paper, and then inserted the hastily folded packet directly behind the hammer of his gun.

"Oops, be careful," Drayton warned as the case rattled slightly. "This hasn't been locked up tight yet. They must still be working on the exhibit."

Theodosia glanced around the room at the flintlocks, Kentucky rifles, derringers, Springfield Trapdoor rifles, knives, swords, and crossbows that were on display. They were interesting, yes, but more than a little unsettling.

"We should go see Timothy," she said, anxious to get out of there.

Timothy was sitting at his desk, turning a small bronze bust of Thomas Jefferson in his hands.

"I was wondering when you two would show up," he said when he saw them hovering in his doorway. "Come in, come in."

Theodosia and Drayton stepped into his office and took seats in the burnished leather and hobnail chairs that faced Timothy's desk.

Drayton inclined his head toward the bronze bust. "American?"

"French," Timothy said. "Circa 1860. There's a small chip in the marble base, so it's headed to our conservation department."

"We just took a quick peek at the Rare Weapons Show," Theodosia said.

"The displays are almost ready for our big opening," Timothy said. "But you didn't come here to talk about the show, did you?"

"No," Theodosia said. "We wanted to bring you up to speed on a few things."

"Good."

Theodosia proceeded to lay out all the background information that she deemed relevant; the insults that Sissy Lanier and Betty Bates had hurled at each other, their horrible fight at Delaine's shop, and the rock tossed through her window. She told Timothy about Bob Garver's crossbow preference and run-

ning into him at the Brittlebush Gun and Bow Club. She mentioned Sissy showing up at the tea shop bereft because her
Fidelity account had been raided, visiting Jud Harker's apartment last night with Tidwell, and her call to the City of Charleston concerning Bob Garver's grant money and loan.

"We didn't want to muddy the waters last night by telling
you about some of these bizarre developments," Theodosia said.
"Because the threatening note you received clearly took prece-
dence. But, as you can see, there's been an undercurrent of
strange happenings. Events that may or may not be related to
Carson Lanier's murder."

"Let me get this straight," Timothy said slowly. "You're telling me that your list of suspects so far includes Betty Bates,
Carson's ex-wife Sissy, Jud Harker, and this Bob Garver person."

"That's correct," Theodosia said.

"But no one from my guest list."

"Not yet, anyway," Drayton said.

Timothy leaned back in his chair. "Well, you've certainly
outdone yourselves. And I had no idea that Carson was disliked
by so many people." He waved a hand. "Do you have any feeling
for one suspect over another?"

"Not really," Theodosia said. "They're all just potential suspects in our book." She threw a hasty glance at Drayton who
said, "We're still sorting things out."

"I see," Timothy said. He touched a finger to his cheek and
said, "You realize, Betty Bates, unless she's convicted of first-
degree murder, will probably end up serving on our board of
directors."

"That might be unfortunate," Theodosia said.

"I understand she's been campaigning," Timothy said. "So
she might have garnered enough sympathetic votes from among
our current board members."

"She doesn't have mine," Drayton said.

Timothy smiled. "No, I daresay not yours."

"How is everything here at the Heritage Society?" Theodosia asked him. "Especially in regard to the threat you received last night. No strange incidents? Jud Harker hasn't shown up where he's not wanted?"

"I haven't laid eyes on anyone who doesn't work here or belong here," Timothy said. "And we've made it a point to tighten security."

"You hired more guards?" Drayton asked.

Timothy bobbed his head. "Four more."

"That should do it," Drayton said.

"I have another question," Theodosia said. "You told us that Carson Lanier had donated a number of weapons that will be featured in your show."

"That's right," Timothy said.

"Do you have a list of those weapons?"

Timothy bent his head like an inquisitive magpie. "Probably. Why do you ask?"

"This might be awfully far-fetched," Theodosia said. "But is it possible that the pistol crossbow and quarrels used to kill Lanier were actually stolen from here?"

Timothy leaned back in his chair, a shocked expression on his face. "That would imply that someone from the Heritage Society was involved."

"We can't rule that out," Theodosia said. She thought of the current board of directors that Drayton said was too often feuding. Did they comprise a plausible suspect pool? She supposed they might. Which meant she was probably back to square one.

But Timothy was looking worried. "Let's talk to the curator and get you that list."

*   *   *

Theodosia dropped Drayton off at his house and then, instead of heading home, turned down Broad Street. She cruised along through late-afternoon traffic, turned right on Franklin, and drove past the Old Jail. Then, as purple twilight morphed into blue-black dusk, she turned down Beaufain Street.

It wasn't difficult to find the Charleston single homes that Bob Garver planned to renovate. There was a large sign at the corner of the block that said HISTORIC RENOVATIONS BY ROBERT T. GARVER. The letters were red against a white background with lots of curlicues and flourishes on the type.

It was a lovely neighborhood, Theodosia decided as she pulled over to the curb. The entire block that stretched ahead of her was populated by classic Charleston single homes, all built in a unique style. That is, the homes were narrow, some no more than twenty feet across, but built very, very deep. Most of the homes were two and three stories, with side piazzas that were also two stories tall. Theodosia also noted that, on this particular block, the Charleston single homes were of mixed styles that included Federal, Greek Revival, and Victorian.

Climbing out of her Jeep, Theodosia walked slowly up the sidewalk. Only one of the homes looked occupied, with lights burning in a first floor back room, though it didn't appear that restoration work had been started on any one of them.

But they were fanciful and uniquely Charleston, well suited to catching the breezes that blew in from the harbor and allowing them to flow the entire length of the house. That kind of natural air-conditioning was important considering Charleston's industrial-strength heat and humidity.

From deep within her hobo bag, Theodosia's cell phone chimed. She dug it out and said, "Hello?" thinking it might be

Pete Riley calling with some sort of update. Who knows—maybe he'd even apprehended Lanier's killer.

But when Theodosia answered, it wasn't Riley at all. Haley was on the line barking out a series of choked gasps. She sounded frantic.

"Theodosia!" Haley cried. "Something awful has happened!"

Theodosia clutched her phone tighter, imagining a grease fire in the kitchen and Haley injured. Or a rock hurled through their *front* window.

"What is it?" Theodosia asked. "Tell me what's wrong."

"It's Jamie!" Haley cried. Her teeth were chattering and she sounded as if she was barely hanging on.

"What happened to Jamie?" Theodosia asked. "Slow down, whatever it is I'm sure we can fix it."

"Jamie got hit by a car in the back alley," Haley managed to stutter out. "And the ambulance guys were pretty sure his leg was broken." She let out an anguished sob. "Theo, it was a hit-and-run!"

21

Theodosia's heels rang out like castanets as she pushed through the door into the ER and ran down the hospital corridor. She'd managed to call Pete Riley as she drove headlong toward Mercy Medical, quickly relating what she knew about Jamie's accident so far. Riley was suitably alarmed and promised to be at the hospital within ten minutes.

Now Theodosia practically flung herself up against the desk at the nurse's station and said, "Jamie Weston. He was just brought in here by ambulance. Where can I find him?"

An efficient-looking African American nurse with a name tag that read SHEREE CRAIG came around the desk and crooked a finger. "Come this way," she said. "I'll show you where he is."

Theodosia followed Nurse Craig to a part of the ER that had a half dozen beds set up in a large, white antiseptic-looking room. Two of the beds were completely surrounded by flowing white curtains.

"Haley?" Theodosia called out. "Are you in here?" The curtains in front of her billowed and puffed and then were suddenly ripped open. Haley's head popped out of the curtained bay.

"We're right here," Haley said.

"Thank you," Theodosia said to Nurse Craig.

The nurse nodded. "Call if you need me." She looked at Jamie, who was lying on a narrow bed, looking pasty white and pained as Haley went back to clutching his hand. "For anything."

"Thank you again," Theodosia said. Then she aimed a concerned look at Haley and Jamie and said, "What happened? Tell me everything."

"He was taking out the trash," Haley said.

"And some jackhole drove right into me," Jamie said. "Clipped my left leg."

"I heard this loud crash," Haley said. "And then Jamie let out this horrible strangled cry."

"I was pretty sure my leg was busted from the get-go," Jamie said. "'Cause it started hurting right away."

"Where was Drayton during all of this?" Theodosia asked.

"Home," Haley said. "He'd already left. We were just finishing up."

"So it really was a hit-and-run?" Theodosia asked. Her mind was going a million miles an hour, revved up and suddenly bothered by all sorts of nagging suspicions.

"Oh yeah," Jamie said. "I don't know if the guy even saw me. At least, he never slowed down."

"A guy," Theodosia repeated. "Was it a man? Did you actually see the driver of the vehicle?"

Jamie shook his head. "Not really. It all happened so fast."

Theodosia wondered if it had been a hit-and-run, versus . . . an intentional hit?

"Are you in a lot of pain?" Theodosia asked Jamie.

"It's pretty much killing me!" Jamie cried. "My leg is *broken.* Just look at it!" He flipped back part of the blanket to show her. "It's knocked all catywampus!"

Theodosia didn't think Jamie's leg looked horribly mangled or anything, but it was pink and terribly swollen. "Oh, Jamie," she said. She hated seeing him in such distress. Hated that someone had raced their car down her back alley and been so callous. Or maybe the suspicion that was expanding by leaps and bounds inside her brain was correct—that someone had taken deliberate aim to make a carefully calculated hit. Either way, another couple of inches and Jamie might have been killed.

"Jamie's already had an X-ray," Haley said. "And the radiologist called it a simple fracture of his tibia. There's no surgery required, thank goodness, but we have to wait for an orthopedist to come and set it."

"I hope I don't have to wait too long," Jamie moaned.

"I hope you don't, either," Theodosia said. She felt awful. And she was starting to convince herself that Jamie getting injured in her alley was all her fault. If Jamie hadn't been working at the Indigo Tea Shop . . . If he hadn't stayed late. If only she'd been there!

The other thing that loomed in Theodosia's consciousness was . . . maybe someone had been after *her*. After all, she'd already had a rock lobbed through her window, and it felt as if someone had been dogging her footsteps in Dueler's Alley the other night.

Is someone trying to stop me from investigating? That possibility suddenly felt very real.

"Theodosia. Theodosia Browning," a voice called out.

Theodosia whirled around and ripped the curtains apart. Seconds later, Detective Pete Riley was gripping her shoulder protectively while his eyes roved over the injured Jamie.

"Everybody okay here?" Riley asked. "Holding on?" He looked like he was ready to pull out his pistol and do serious guard duty.

"We're okay, but Jamie's in tough shape," Theodosia said.

"We're waiting for the orthopedist," Haley said.

Riley stepped over to Jamie's bedside. "Tell me what happened," he said in a soft voice.

"It's kind of hard to say," Jamie gulped. "I was jamming two bags of trash in the Dumpster and this dark car came flying down the alley. I heard tires squealing, and before I knew it— bam! It hit me and I went flying."

"I heard the noise," Haley said. "It was awful."

"When I came to," Jamie continued in a shaky voice, "Haley was standing over me, crying and yelling my name. Then she ran into the tea shop and phoned for an ambulance."

"Did you see the driver's face?" Riley asked.

Jamie shook his head. "No."

"Do you remember the make and model of the car?"

"Dark," Jamie said. "Black or maybe dark blue." He grimaced. "Sorry I can't come up with more."

"You're doing just fine," Riley said. "You're still in shock, so a faulty memory is to be expected. There's a good chance you'll be able to remember a few more details as time goes by."

"I hope he will," Haley said, pounding a fist into the palm of her hand. "Because you gotta get this guy!"

"We will," Riley said. "I promise."

"Hey," a friendly voice called out. "Everybody look this way for a second, okay?"

They collectively turned in the direction of the voice, wondering what was going on, only to find themselves facing a camera lens.

"Smile," Bill Glass said. There was a faint click and a bloom of bright light. "Good. But let me take another shot for insurance."

"No way," Theodosia cried, throwing up a hand to block his view.

"What are you doing here?" Riley asked. His face was an angry thundercloud.

"Just getting a snap," Glass said, trying to sound innocent. But he wore a slightly sheepish grin.

"How did you even know we were here?" Theodosia asked.

"Heard it on my police scanner," Glass said.

"You're lucky I don't confiscate that thing," Riley said. "Rip it right out of your dashboard."

"Come on," Glass argued. "Have some faith, detective, I'm gonna make you look good. Like a real hero."

"Mr. Jamie Weston?" a loud, authoritative voice called out as the curtains billowed and parted once again.

They all turned to look, even Bill Glass, at a tall man in green scrubs who was holding a chart and peering in at them. He had curly gray hair, wire-rim glasses, and a large nose. A doctor, no doubt. Probably the orthopedist.

"That's me," Jamie said, lifting a hand. "My leg is broken."

"Excellent diagnosis," the doctor said. "That's what it says on your chart, too."

"Are you the orthopedist?" Jamie asked.

"Last time I looked I was." He crossed to Jamie's bed and extended his hand. "I'm Dr. Peterson. Nice to meet you."

"You're going to fix my leg?" Jamie asked.

"If that's what you want," Dr. Peterson said.

"Will it hurt?"

Dr. Peterson shook his head. "Maybe a pinch at best. Tell you what, we'll fill you up with good drugs and you won't feel a thing."

"Drugs?" Jamie said. "Good ones?" He sounded interested.

"Maybe not *that* good," Dr. Peterson said. "But we'll make sure you're comfortable anyway."

"Dr. Peterson," Glass said. "Can I get a shot of you? Can you move slightly closer to the kid's bed?"

"I don't think so," Dr. Peterson said.

"Get out of here," Riley snarled.

A few minutes later, Dr. Peterson kicked all of them out. And Haley, Theodosia, and Riley found themselves clumped together in the busy hallway. Dazed-looking people limped past them, the walking wounded who'd been in car crashes, taken headers down porch steps, and had their flesh nipped by paring knives and sharp fishing hooks. The wounded intermingled with efficient-looking hospital personnel.

"What should we do now?" Theodosia asked.

"Nothing to do," Riley said. "Just go home, I guess. I'll drop by again in the morning. Maybe Jamie will be able to remember a few more details by then."

"I should stay here with Haley," Theodosia said.

"No," Haley said. "You heard what the doctor said. They're going to set Jamie's leg and give him a knockout pill. He probably won't wake up again until tomorrow morning. There's nothing you can do here."

"Be here for you?" Theodosia said.

Haley shook her head. "If I need you, I'll give a holler."

Theodosia arrived home, feeling tense and a little out of sorts. She fed Earl Grey, let him out into the backyard, and then called Drayton to give him the bad news.

Drayton was beyond shocked. "Jamie? *Our* Jamie? Hit by a car? Who could have done this?" he sputtered.

"Jamie didn't see the driver, but he said it was a dark car," Theodosia said. "Blue or black."

"A dark car in a dark alley. That's not exactly a stellar ID job."

"I'm only telling you what Jamie told me," Theodosia said.

"I know, I know, but it's very upsetting. I mean, the driver broke his leg!"

"Tell me about it. You should have seen Jamie's face as he tried to bite back the pain."

"Now I feel even worse, since I'm the one who asked him to take out the trash. Oh, Theo, I should have been there," Drayton said. "I should have stayed later."

"You couldn't have known," Theodosia said. "None of us could."

Drayton was silent for a moment, and then he said, "But maybe we should have been a lot more careful."

"What are you getting at, Drayton?" Theodosia figured Drayton was circling toward the same conclusion she'd been tossing around, but she wanted to hear it from him.

"Do you think this might be related to the Lanier murder?" Drayton asked.

"Drayton . . ." Now Theodosia hesitated. "I think it almost has to be. Only I still can't figure out who on earth is trying to stop us."

"The killer, maybe? I mean . . . did the driver of that car think it was you out there in the alley? Or me?"

Theodosia took a deep breath. "I think that's a very real possibility."

"That means we're all in danger," Drayton said. He sounded both scared and flummoxed. "What do you think we should do?"

"We need to put our heads together and figure this out," Theodosia said. "But for the time being, like right now . . . we need to watch our backs."

After Theodosia hung up—once again warning Drayton to take care and lock his doors—she gulped down a small carton of yogurt and then changed into her workout clothes. She figured her bike shorts and black nylon running jacket with the red stripe down the arms would be perfect.

And even though her heart wasn't in it, she had promised to meet Alexis at Metro Spin Cycle tonight. And she didn't want to let down her friend.

Located on Cumberland, in an old storefront, Metro Spin Cycle was sandwiched between Fenwick's Eatery and the Millbrook Art Gallery. As Theodosia waited on the sidewalk, a number of cyclists walked by her. They were all geared up in Lycra and nylon bike shorts and sweatshirts, looking anxious to jump on a bike and pump away to some hot tunes.

She wished she felt as enthusiastic as they looked. But the notion that someone—Lanier's killer?—might be out to destroy her loomed like a dark specter. Who could it be? she wondered. Bob Garver or Sissy Lanier? Possibly Jud Harker, who seemed to be keeping an awfully low profile, or even Betty Bates? Whoever it was, they were dangerous beyond belief. They'd killed once and they'd probably do it again to protect themselves.

Theodosia didn't relish any kind of rendezvous with this crazed bogeyman. Especially since they were more than capable of shooting a silent, deadly arrow.

Theodosia shifted from one foot to the other. The night sky was low and dark as clouds swirled overhead and the weather grew progressively cooler. She stared down the block into darkness that was faintly lit by only a few orange gas lamps, watching for any sign of Alexis. She saw no one. Turning around to peer in the front window of Metro Spin Cycle, she saw, through a partially open door, several people already warming up on their stationary bikes. Then music suddenly blared, driving and loud, with an almost eighties heavy metal edge to it.

Where is Alexis?

Five minutes later, Theodosia was still waiting. The music was pouring out of the building in waves now, the backbeat practically rattling the front windows, the instructor's voice pumped up and booming, urging everyone to stand up and pedal faster. To yearn for the burn.

Figuring that Alexis had forgotten all about her, Theodosia was about to give up and go home when she heard a faint cry. A discordant note, riding high on the wind. She twisted her head left, saw nothing, then scanned right. From far down the block she saw a small, lone figure lift a hand and wave at her.

Finally.

Theodosia waved back. Well, no harm done, she decided. If they joined the class ten minutes late, that was ten minutes knocked off a killer bike ride, right?

But wait—Alexis was still coming toward her, and she was limping slightly. Managing a kind of stutter step.

Was something wrong? Had something happened?

Theodosia frowned as she stepped out to meet her friend.

"Theodosia," Alexis gasped as she drew closer. Her voice was shrill and ragged, tears dribbled down her cheeks. Not only that, Alexis's clothes were in complete disarray, and one side of her face was all smudged.

"Oh my goodness, what happened?" Theodosia cried.

Alexis stumbled up to Theodosia and practically collapsed in her arms.

"Somebody tried to grab me," Alexis cried. Her chin quivered and more tears spilled down her cheeks. "They lunged out of the shadows and tried to hurt me!"

22

"You poor thing," Theodosia said. Alexis was shivering like a Chihuahua left out in a snowstorm. "But *are* you hurt? *Did* they physically injure you?"

Alexis shook her head as she swiped at her nose with the back of her hand. "I fought back like crazy and punched him," she said. "Pummeled him, really. Then I fell down on the sidewalk and scraped my arm, but I managed to kick at him and get away."

"Where did this happen, exactly?"

"Um . . ." Alexis struggled to catch her breath between hiccups. "About two blocks back. I was just bopping along, looking forward to our class. And then this guy . . ."

"Was it a guy?" Theodosia asked urgently. "You're sure of that?"

Alexis nodded. "I think so. But it was really dark. Whoever it was popped out of the bushes where that little pocket park is. Next to Kingston Lane Antiques."

"Okay."

"Anyway, I was so scared I didn't really look all that carefully. My throat closed up tight, so all I could do was make these stupid squeaky screams, but I was flailing away like crazy, trying to make every blow count. When I finally started running, I headed in this direction because I didn't know what else to do. I felt so scared and confused . . . I *still* do. And I knew I was supposed to meet you here."

"Did you get any kind of look at him?" *Or her?*

Alexis shook her head. "Not really. It was so dark and shadowy, and whoever it was wore a big coat with the collar turned way up."

"Who do you think it could have been?" Theodosia asked.

"I don't know!" Alexis wailed. She was gripping her injured arm as tears rolled down her cheeks.

"Just calm down and try to think."

"I'm trying," Alexis said. "I really am."

Theodosia backed off. "Okay, honey, I know you are. We'll let it go for now."

Theodosia put an arm around Alexis and led her inside Metro Spin Cycle. She sat her down in a blue plastic tub chair in the small lobby. "Just sit still for a minute," Theodosia said. "Let me get you something to drink." Theodosia went to a vending machine, fumbled two dollars in, and grabbed a sports drink when it tumbled out. She carried it back to Alexis and handed it to her.

"Here, drink this," Theodosia said.

Alexis shook her head. "I'd rather not."

"It's a sports drink with sugar in it. It'll help knock back the adrenaline that's zapping through your veins. Make you feel better. Calmer."

"Okay." Alexis gave a jittery nod. "Thanks."

Alexis took a couple of gulps, then had another small sip.

Little by little, she started to calm down. At least she stopped shaking.

Theodosia's brain was on another tilt-a-whirl ride. What was going on? First Jamie and now Alexis. Was she to blame? Had someone thought that Alexis was her walking down the street? Maybe so. They were both dressed in similar sport clothes. Dear Lord, did that mean that someone had been spying on her these past few days?

"Tha-thank you," Alexis said. She was still gulping down her drink, but she seemed calmer. More like herself.

"I'm so sorry this happened to you," Theodosia said. She pulled her phone from her bag and said, "I'm going to call the police. I hope you don't mind."

Wide-eyed, Alexis stared at her. "Okay," she whispered. "I suppose that's best."

So Theodosia got back on the phone and called Detective Pete Riley.

"Are you serious?" he said when she got him on the line. "Another assault? You're like a danger magnet, you know that?"

"Don't put the blame on me," Theodosia said. "It's this guy. Whoever this guy is."

"And you're where?"

Theodosia gave Riley the address for Metro Spin Cycle.

"Okay, I'm sending a unit over there right away. Tell them everything you just told me. In fact, have your friend tell them as much as she can remember. I'd come myself, but something else just popped."

"Something to do with Jud Harker or Bob Garver?" Theodosia asked.

"No, I'm afraid not."

"Okay," Theodosia said. "I'll keep a lookout for that unit. And thank you. Thank you for being there."

"Of course," he said, and then clicked off.

"My friend, Detective Riley, is sending a patrol car over," Theodosia said to Alexis. "We'll have to give a report."

"Sure," Alexis said. Then, "Is Detective Riley the cute guy you brought to my gallery the other night?"

"That's the one."

"Must be nice to know someone well-connected in law enforcement. Must make you feel safe, I guess."

"Sometimes," Theodosia said.

Five minutes later a black-and-white squad car rolled to a stop and two uniformed officers got out. Theodosia met them at the door and thanked them for coming. Then they all gathered around Alexis.

Alexis went through her story again. And Theodosia was happy to see that she was able to fill in a few more details this time around. The officers were very solicitous, questioning her gently, then writing their initial report. When they'd scratched out their notes, they had Alexis read them over and then sign the report for them.

"We'd be happy to give you a ride home, ma'am," one of the officers offered.

"That's okay," Theodosia said. "I'm parked right here, I can take her home."

"Thank you," Alexis whispered.

They waved good-bye as the police car rolled away, then Theodosia turned to Alexis and said, "I have to tell you something."

Alexis's brows puckered together. "What? Why do you have a funny look on your face? Is something wrong?"

"You remember that fellow Jamie, who works at my tea shop?"

"The kid who came to pick up the statues and fans and things," Alexis said. "For your Plum Blossom Tea."

"That's right."

So Theodosia took a deep breath and spilled the beans about Jamie getting mowed down by a car in the alley and ending up in the ER.

"And that just happened tonight?" Alexis looked terrified.

"A couple of hours ago."

"Theo, you're not serious!" Alexis was beyond shocked.

"I'm afraid I am."

"What's going on? Am I in danger, too?"

"I'm sorry, but I don't know. At least I don't *think* so."

Alexis put a hand to her neck and touched it carefully, as if she expected to feel a hangman's noose drop at any moment. "Maybe I shouldn't go home tonight. Maybe I should, I don't know, go to a hotel or something."

"Just lock your doors and I'm sure you'll be fine," Theodosia said.

"But your friend, Detective Riley, he's on top of this? I mean, Jamie's accident and my assault?" Alexis took a couple of deep gulps. "I can't believe I'm even using that word. Assault." She shook her head, looking slightly dazed. "But why would . . . ?"

"I don't know, exactly," Theodosia said. "But it could all be tied to Carson Lanier's murder."

Alexis continued to stare at her, almost in disbelief. "The guy who got shot on the roof the other night?"

"That's right."

"How is it tied in? *Why* is it tied in?"

"I've been doing a favor for Timothy Neville," Theodosia said. "Some investigating. On the side." She tried to make it sound peripheral at best.

"And you think the killer knows about this? That you've been . . . what? Poking around? Is that why strange things are happening?"

"Could be," Theodosia said.

Alexis opened her mouth to say something, then closed it again as a frightened look came across her face.

"What?" Theodosia asked.

"Um. Somebody came into my shop today," Alexis said. "They looked around, but didn't buy anything. I didn't think much of it at the time because I was on the phone, talking to a customer in Savannah. But the person who came in acted kind of hinky."

"Can you describe him?"

"Well, he wasn't very well-dressed, for one thing. I think he . . ." She touched a finger to her forehead. "I think he might have been wearing a denim jacket. But not a new one, kind of old and weather-beaten."

"Like a workman might wear?"

"Kind of."

"Do you think it was the same person who came after you tonight?"

"I don't know. I don't think so, but I could be wrong."

Theodosia wondered if it could have been Bob Garver or Jud Harker. And if so, why would either one of them want to stop at Haiku Gallery? On the other hand, Jud Harker had been floating around in the wind for a few days. And Harker seemed perpetually angry. So it could have been him, even if the police hadn't been able to pin anything on him yet.

"Come on," Theodosia said in what she hoped was a calm, even voice. "Let's get you home."

Alexis grabbed her arm. "Please, Theo, promise me that when I walk into my home tonight I'll be safe."

"I promise," Theodosia said. But her words felt hollow. She couldn't be sure *anyone* would be completely safe until the killer—whoever he or she was—was apprehended.

"And you'll call your friend, Detective Riley? Tell him that it would be so great if the police could kind of keep an eye on my house and my shop?"

"Of course, I'll ask him," said Theodosia. "And I'm sure he'll be happy to extend a little extra protection. After all, he's been working on this case for several days now. It's a tangle, but I'm confident he'll get it sorted out."

Because if he doesn't, I'll have to figure it out myself.

When Theodosia arrived back home, she walked in without turning on any lights, still distracted and ruminating about everything that had happened tonight. Someone had strummed the outer edges of a spiderweb, but just who was at the center of that web?

Theodosia passed through her dining room, trailing a hand over the backs of her cane chairs, then walked into the kitchen, where Earl Grey was napping on his dog bed. Standing at the back door, she gazed out the small window into the darkness, wondering if Jud Harker was out there and making plans to come after her. She tilted her head back and looked skyward, where dark clouds scudded across a tiny sliver of moon.

Dark of the moon.

Theodosia stared at the turbulent sky for a moment, then went to her phone and dialed Drayton at home. When he picked up she said, "I'm thinking of doing something illegal and I want you to talk me out of it."

"What are you thinking of doing?"

"Breaking into Jud Harker's apartment."

A few moments of silence spun out, then Drayton said, "How soon can you pick me up?"

23

Theodosia remembered the address from her sojourn with Tidwell last night. But that didn't mean she knew how to get there.

She and Drayton drove through North Charleston down dark twisty-turny streets, spun around Park Circle, and then down North Rhett. Somewhere along the line she made a wrong turn and ended up in a cul-de-sac where some kind of sewer pipe excavation was happening.

"Are you sure you know where you're going?" Drayton asked as their headlights flashed against a yellow dozer that sat hunkered in the street.

"Pretty sure," Theodosia said. She negotiated a sharp K-turn and headed back to North Rhett, which was a sort of main drag. From there she drove on pure instinct.

Yes, I remember seeing Froggie's Pizza on that corner; no I do not recall passing The Washtub Laundromat. But, Holy Hannah, I think Camden might be where we turned last night.

Theodosia jerked the steering wheel and squealed around the corner, causing Drayton to reach out and latch onto the dashboard with a death grip.

"Careful," he said. "We don't want to get arrested before we get arrested."

"We're not going to get arrested," Theodosia said.

"No? Ah, well, I suppose your relationship with Detective Riley gives you brownie points."

"Actually, it probably doesn't."

They rolled past a bowling alley, a small market, and an old fire station that had been turned into a microbrewery.

"Tell me more about your friend Alexis James getting attacked."

"All I know is what I already told you," Theodosia said.

"I hope the poor woman is okay, no residual damage. And I do find it terribly suspicious coming directly on the heels of Jamie's accident."

"That was no accident," Theodosia said, her voice practically cracking with emotion.

"You feel responsible," Drayton said.

Theodosia nodded in the darkness of the car and clenched her jaw. "Yes, of course I do. I think if we hadn't started poking around in this Carson Lanier business, we probably wouldn't have been targeted."

"That's what you think?" Drayton asked.

"The car hitting Jamie, the guy who jumped out at Alexis—that could have been intended for me," Theodosia said.

"Or perhaps it was pure coincidence."

"I don't believe in coincidences," Theodosia said. "Especially when they start piling up one on top of another." She saw the outline of the old house up ahead and maneuvered her Jeep to the curb. She put it in park and they sat there, the engine slowly purring. "This is it," Theodosia said.

Drayton leaned forward and peered out the front window. "The neighborhood looks awfully desolate."

"Just working class."

"Could maybe use some of that rehab money."

"Fat chance of that." Theodosia lifted her hands off the wheel and shut off the ignition. "Well, are you coming with me?"

"What have I got to lose?" Drayton said. "Except my stellar record as a law-abiding citizen."

They walked up the front sidewalk to the rooming house. The sidewalk was pitted and crazed with cracks; the front porch listed toward the street, as if it were about to fall off, but in slow motion.

"This place looks like it's coming apart at the seams," Drayton whispered.

"Pity it was chopped up into apartments," Theodosia said. "Because this old house does have good bones." She noticed that lights shone from first floor windows, but there were only a couple lights coming from the second floor.

"But even bones crumble eventually," Drayton said.

Theodosia pulled open the front door and they stepped into the small entryway. The same yellow sixty-watt bulb dangled from a single wire while ancient linoleum crackled underfoot. Tonight the odor of fried fish was heavy in the air.

"Whew, the aroma of this evening's dinner is certainly heavier than the pan-roasted salmon at Poogan's Porch," Drayton snorted, referring to one of Charleston's favorite restaurants.

"Come on, Harker's place is upstairs."

They climbed the staircase with its threadbare carpet and walked down the dim hallway heading for apartment six. Music blared from behind a door at the front of the building, but the rear of the building was quiet.

Theodosia knocked on Harker's door. She gave it a few moments for the knock to register, then called out, "Anybody home?"

There was no reply.

"Try again," Drayton said. "Maybe Harker's fast asleep. Like we should be."

Theodosia knocked again. They were met with dead silence.

"What do you think?" Drayton asked. "I say he's probably not home." He brushed the back of his hand against his cheek. "This fellow Harker has a real talent for making himself scarce, doesn't he? He's like a regular boo-haunt or something."

"That's what worries me."

"So what now?"

"Considering everything that's happened tonight, I'd sure like to get inside his apartment and look around."

"Now that we're here, I don't know if that's a wise idea." Drayton glanced around. "Plus, there could be cameras."

"In this rattrap? Hardly."

"Breaking and entering is still illegal," Drayton said.

"Then why didn't you talk me out of it when I first called?" Theodosia asked. "I told you I was thinking about doing something illegal."

Drayton pursed his lips. "You make a good point." He glanced over his shoulder to make sure no one was watching, then grasped the doorknob and rattled the door. "This feels like a flimsy lock. You can tell by the way the door shakes in its frame. There's clearly no deadlock, just a latch on the doorknob."

"Too bad we don't have a bump key."

Drayton raised an eyebrow. "Where on earth did you learn about that?"

"Never mind," Theodosia said. "What if we pick the lock?"

"I'm afraid that particular skill isn't in my repertoire."

Theodosia dug in her handbag and pulled out a plastic credit card.

"Don't tell me that really works," Drayton said.

"I've opened doors once or twice this way," Theodosia said. She slid her credit card into the narrow slot between the doorframe and the door. Then she angled her card slightly and seesawed it back and forth. "Sometimes it works, sometimes it doesn't."

"Be careful," Drayton said. "Don't ruin your card. You don't want to have to explain breaking and entering to the folks at Visa."

"I'm guessing they've heard it all before."

Theodosia continued to work the card back and forth, trying to keep a deft touch.

"I don't believe this door can be jimmied," Drayton said.

"I think . . ." Theodosia stopped midsentence.

"Hmm?" Drayton said.

The door swung open.

"Sweet Fanny Adams, you did it," Drayton said in a slightly admiring whisper.

"Finessing the lock was the easy part," Theodosia said. "Now we have to go in and look around."

"Would that be classified as a felony or a misdemeanor?"

"You don't have a police record," Theodosia said. "Which means you'd only be a first-time offender . . . so why worry about it?" She sounded blasé but was actually a little nervous as she slid through the doorway and disappeared into the dark apartment. Then, "Are you coming?"

"Oh my . . . I . . . yes, I suppose I am," Drayton mumbled as he glanced around one more time and then slunk in after her.

Jud Harker's apartment was tiny and cramped and smelled like burned frozen pizza and Marlboro cigarettes. In fact, it wasn't much of an apartment at all, really just two rooms. A combination living room/bedroom area along with a small bathroom.

"No kitchen," Drayton said. There was a small night-light next to the bed, so they were able to make out dim shapes and angles.

"But he's got a hot plate and toaster oven," Theodosia said as she ghosted past him. She reached into the bathroom and flipped on a switch. There was an immediate spill of light into the rest of the apartment.

"Do you think that's wise?" Drayton asked.

Theodosia shrugged. "Probably not. But it makes looking easier."

"What are we looking for?"

"I'm not sure."

Theodosia poked through a dresser drawer, coming up with folded jeans and T-shirts, and then a smaller drawer that held a broken watch, a pile of loose change, a bunch of keys, and a keepsake ticket to a NASCAR race. Nothing earth-shattering, just guy stuff.

"Not much in his closet, either," Drayton said.

"Did you look on the top shelf, especially way in the back? And down on the floor?"

"Yes."

"And?"

"Still nothing. At least, I don't see any hidden compartments or loose boards."

Theodosia pawed through an old TV console and found the usual jumble of cords, plugs, and wires.

"Harker doesn't seem to have much of anything," Drayton said. "He's a bit of an ascetic when it comes to possessions." He threw Theodosia a nervous glance. "We should go."

"Getting cold feet?"

"You know me. Warm heart, cold feet."

"Give me one more second." Theodosia got down on her

hands and knees and peered under the bed. It was a low bed with a nondescript brown coverlet.

Probably just dust bunnies underneath.

But, no, there was something.

"Something here," Theodosia said.

"What?" Drayton was idling near the door, looking nervous and twitchy, anxious to leave.

Theodosia stuck an arm under the bed, hooked the handle of a battered suitcase, and pulled it out.

Drayton glanced over. "Probably empty."

Theodosia flipped open the two metal latches anyway. Then she lifted the lid. Inside was a worn-looking leather book, what looked like an old scrapbook. She lifted the book out and studied it. The book was constructed of good leather, probably cowhide, but it was showing its age. The whole thing was barely a half inch thick, and the inside pages felt dry and crinkly.

"What is it?" Drayton asked, but he sounded disinterested.

"Some kind of scrapbook, I guess." Theodosia opened the book and turned a few pages. Most were blank, a few had keepsakes tucked between them. A handout for a car rally, a program for a Christmas play, but from many years ago.

It was the fifth page that held the stunner. A newspaper article, old and yellowed, cracked where it had been folded many times. The headline said TRAGEDY IN GREEN POND. Green Pond was a small town located halfway between Charleston and Savannah.

Theodosia bent forward and squinted in the dim light, doing her best to read the story on the faded newsprint.

"Oh no," she breathed.

"What?" Drayton asked.

"This is an old newspaper article from . . . let's see . . . um, from 1986."

"Ancient history."

"Not for Jud Harker," Theodosia said.

Drayton fixed her with a questioning gaze. "What are you talking about?"

"That's the year he accidently shot and killed his ten-year-old brother."

"What a horrible thing to have hanging over your head," Drayton said as they crept down the back stairs. "It's heartbreaking, in fact. Even though the article mentioned that Harker had been absolved of the crime, that it was purely accidental, killing his brother must have scarred him for life."

"No wonder Harker is so vehemently opposed to guns and gun shows," Theodosia said. "If he's carrying around that kind of guilt."

They pushed through the back door and came out in a dark parking lot, just a black rectangle of cracked asphalt with spots for six cars.

"The question remains," Theodosia continued, "did the incident with his brother tip Harker over the edge psychologically or did it make him incredibly vulnerable?"

"I'm not sure what you mean by that," Drayton said.

"If Harker is being held prisoner by his terrible mistake, then maybe he's willing to do whatever's necessary to put an end to guns and gun collecting," Theodosia said.

"You mean Harker still could have shot Carson Lanier?"

"Well, he didn't shoot him with a gun, did he?"

"No, he didn't."

They stopped and stared at the six parking spaces that were delineated with haphazard streaks of white paint. Each spot also had a hand-lettered number. Four cars were parked there, but the number six slot that corresponded to Harker's apartment was empty.

"He has a car," Theodosia said.

"I'm not surprised," Drayton said. "So what are you thinking now?"

"Harker could still be the one who clipped Jamie."

Drayton nodded. "We need to get a look at his car."

24

Friday morning dawned sunny and bright with clear blue skies over Charleston and sunbeams streaming through the leaded pane windows of the Indigo Tea Shop. Quite a lovely contrast, considering all the doom and gloom of last night.

And even though it was fairly early in the morning, not quite nine o'clock, the Indigo Tea Shop was a hive of activity. Haley hadn't arrived yet—she'd just called in and promised to be there in about ten minutes—but Theodosia, Drayton, and Miss Dimple were already in the throes of preparing for their Plum Blossom Tea. Drayton had hung a sign on the front door that said CLOSED FOR PRIVATE PARTY, BUT TAKEOUTS ARE WELCOME, so that took some pressure off them. Takeout, as he defined it, was just tea and scones. Which meant they could concentrate on getting the place shipshape for their garden club luncheon guests.

Theodosia had pulled out a set of Johnson Brothers china with a lovely plum blossom design. She'd found the set at a tag sale over in Mount Pleasant last year and paid a song for it. But the set included lovely cream-colored plates, saucers, and teacups with ribbed rims and painted purple plum blossoms. And since plum was the watchword of the day, the dishes were perfect.

"You know," Drayton said, wiping a teaspoon against a towel, "Mikasa also makes a plum blossom pattern. But their color is much more blue than plum."

"Does everything have to be plum colored?" Miss Dimple asked. She was arranging the plates, cups, and saucers just so on all the tables.

"Not really," Theodosia said.

"Yes, it does," Drayton said at the exact same time.

Miss Dimple blinked and stared at them. "I declare, you two are still all shaken up, aren't you?" They'd told her first off about Jamie getting struck by a car last night, which had pretty much rocked Miss Dimple's world and sent her into endless paroxysms of worry.

"We're still a little unnerved," Theodosia admitted. "But when Haley called a while ago, she said Jamie was doing just fine. No problems at all."

"Jamie's such a sweet boy," Miss Dimple crooned. "So eager to pitch in and help."

"I'm sure he'll be back at the tea shop in no time at all," Drayton said. "Limping around, still trying to decipher a Lung Ching from an Assam."

Miss Dimple looked aghast. "Surely you wouldn't put Jamie to work when he's got a cast on his leg!"

"No," Drayton said. "We'll probably just let him lounge around on cashmere pillows and spoon-feed him foie gras topped with a quail egg."

Miss Dimple waved a hand. "Oh, you." She looked at the

tables and said, "We should probably put out the white linen napkins?"

"That sounds perfectly lovely," Theodosia said. "And add some crystal tumblers for water glasses."

Up at the front counter, Drayton crooked a finger, indicating for Theodosia to join him.

She walked over and leaned forward. "What?" she said.

"Have you called Detective Riley yet?"

Theodosia bit her lip. "No."

"I thought you might want to clue him in on last night's extracurricular activities."

"Why would I want to do that?" Theodosia asked.

"The scrapbook?" Drayton said. "The news clipping about the dead brother? Harker's deep, dark past might be pertinent information."

"Somehow I don't think Charleston PD would be thrilled to learn that we jimmied a door and snuck in where we weren't invited."

"We?" Drayton said. "Last time I looked, you were the one with the mangled Visa card."

"I guess I still haven't decided how to play this."

"But you're giving me your trademark surreptitious look, which tells me you'd prefer last night remain our little secret," Drayton said.

Theodosia tapped the counter with an index finger. "For now I would, yes." She gazed at Drayton, trying to decipher his expression. "What about you? How do you feel about staying mum? I think it might be for the best, but I don't want you to compromise your principles."

"My principles went out the door once I stepped through that apartment door."

"So what exactly are you saying?"

Drayton looked thoughtful. "Perhaps you could pay me off with hush money. Unmarked bills in a paper sack?"

"How about my undying thanks? Will that do?"

"For now, yes. And I shall remain mum for as long as you need me to."

"Thank you, Drayton. You're a true friend."

"More like a partner in crime," he said, returning Theodosia's steadfast gaze. Then he glanced past Theodosia's shoulder and said, "Hey, now." His voice and demeanor were suddenly upbeat. "Look what the tabby cat dragged in."

It was Haley. Her arms were wrapped around two large bags stuffed with groceries and she was struggling under the weight.

"Here, over here," Drayton said, waving a hand.

Haley staggered to the counter and plopped down her bags. Drayton hastily grabbed them before they toppled over and spilled their contents.

"I've been shopping," Haley said. "I had to pick up a few ingredients."

"We see that," Theodosia said. "But first things first, how's Jamie?"

"He's wide-awake and talking on his phone like crazy," Haley said. "Taking selfies of his cast and posting them to his Facebook page. Among his friends, a plaster cast is like a badge of honor."

"That's all very nice and anecdotal," Theodosia said. "But how does Jamie actually *feel*? What's his health prognosis?"

"He's says he's uncomfortable, but not having much pain. And his doctor assured me he's doing great."

"A blessing indeed," Drayton said.

"And wouldn't you know it, Jamie feels bad about missing the Plum Blossom Tea today," Haley said.

"Well, he shouldn't think twice about it," Theodosia said.

"The only thing Jamie should be concerned about is rest and recuperation."

Haley nodded. "That's what I told him."

"When does Jamie get out of the hospital?" Theodosia asked. "Wait, is he going back home or will he be coming here?"

"The hospital will release him tomorrow for sure, maybe even today, depending on what his doctor decides," Haley said. "But he won't be coming here. Too hard for him to make it up the stairs." Haley shook back her long blond hair. "No, I'll drive him over to Aunt LaBelle's place in Goose Creek."

"The one with the bad feet?" Drayton asked.

"She's all better now," Haley said.

Theodosia and Drayton hefted Haley's grocery bags and carried them into the kitchen for her.

"I don't mean to put undue pressure on you," Theodosia said. "But we never did finalize today's menu."

"Oh, that," Haley said.

"Yes, that," Drayton said. "We know you planned for a first course of cream scones with plum preserves, but after that the details were sort of fuzzy."

Haley reached into one of her bags and pulled out a bunch of purple asparagus. "Take a look at this." She grinned. "I thought I'd try to make everything as plum colored and purple as possible."

"So the purple asparagus is for . . . what?" Theodosia asked. It was colorful and probably delicious, but how exactly would Haley prepare it?

"I'm going to make an asparagus and Gruyère cheese tart on puff pastry," Haley said. "It's a great way to eat veggies surrounded by cheesy goodness."

"I love it," Drayton said. "And what of our main entrée?" He looked at Haley, then at Theodosia. "I have to plan my tea offerings. Our ladies will expect a different tea with each course."

"Noted," Haley said. "So I thought we'd go with turkey Waldorf sandwiches on brioche, and then a nice gooey plum crisp for dessert."

"Sounds like the full monty," Drayton said.

"I don't know how you manage it, Haley, but your menu sounds wonderfully inventive," Theodosia said. "Especially since the last twelve hours you have been preoccupied with Jamie."

Haley gave an absent nod. "The good thing is, I'm always thinking. My brain is always whirling away like some kind of gyroscopic gizmo that's in perpetual motion."

"Which is good when you're cooking up ideas, but bad when you want to fall asleep," Theodosia said. She often experienced the same thing herself. It was one of the reasons she jogged at night and sang soothing songs to Earl Grey. To calm herself down and turn off the cares of the day.

"So, what do you need from us?" Drayton asked. He was set to grab a knife and chop away at the asparagus.

Haley gave him a beguiling smile. "Just get out of here and leave me alone."

"You're sure?" Theodosia asked. "You don't want any help?"

"No!"

Drayton raised his hands in surrender. "Okay, Ms. *Hell's Kitchen*, you don't have to tell us twice."

"That's for sure," Theodosia said.

"Which plum tea are you planning to serve?" Theodosia asked once she and Drayton were back at the counter, perusing his floor-to-ceiling shelf of teas.

"Mmn . . ." Drayton's fingers walked across a couple of tins, paused, and then kept going. "I think maybe two different varieties. A plum-flavored Ceylonese black tea and my new house blend of Chinese black tea with bits of plum and quince."

"Is that the one that smells a little like coffee cake?"

"It's quite fragrant, yes."

"And do you have a name for it?"

"I've been calling it Plum Crazy."

"Hah," Theodosia said. "A perfect name considering this past week."

Just then, the bell over the front door did its loud *da-ding*.

"Customers," Drayton said. "I hope they're not disappointed that we're only doing takeout."

But it wasn't a customer at all. It was Detective Burt Tidwell. He marched into the tea shop, glanced around, postured with his heels together like a ballet master, and said, "Where is everyone?"

"Didn't you read the sign?" Drayton asked.

Tidwell shook his head. "What sign?"

"On the front door," Theodosia said. "We're only doing takeout this morning because we're getting ready for a private party."

"Who's the private party?" Tidwell asked. He was like that. Nosy. Maybe it came with the territory of being a hotshot detective, or maybe he just liked to bark out questions and sift through answers.

Theodosia came around the counter. "We're hosting the Broad Street Garden Club for a special Plum Blossom Tea."

Tidwell tilted his head back and sniffed the air suspiciously, like a wolf searching for carrion. "Then where are the plum blossoms?"

"I'm glad you mentioned that," Drayton said. "Hopefully, they're on their way from the florist. Although . . ." He reached for the phone. "I'm going to call Floradora right now and check on our order. It should have been delivered by now."

"Is there something I can help you with?" Theodosia asked Tidwell.

Tidwell peered at her. He was dressed in a tweed sport coat that strained mightily over his bulging form. The pockets sagged and the collar flopped up in back. "The strangest reports have been coming across my desk."

"In your position of authority, I'm sure you deal with unusual problems on a routine basis." Theodosia flashed a warm smile. A smile that said, *Please don't ask me too many questions. Please don't dig too deeply.*

Tidwell smiled back, but with very little warmth. "This week has been stranger than most. Off the charts, in fact."

"How nice and challenging. It must make your work very interesting."

"First came the murder of Mr. Lanier," Tidwell said, unfazed. "Followed by bizarre front-page photos of two contenders for the Women's Wrestling Federation crown."

"You read *Shooting Star?*"

"Wouldn't miss it," Tidwell drawled. "Of course, *you* popped up on my radar as soon as you started dogging that real estate developer, Bob Garver."

Theodosia tried her best not to look guilty.

But Tidwell wasn't finished. "Then you decided that lady bank executive, Betty Bates, was a prime suspect, after which you tangled with Jud Harker, and, of course, Timothy Neville was threatened with bodily harm. To top it all off, your young employee and your shopkeeper friend from down the street were both assaulted last night." He rocked back on his run-down heels, looking smugly satisfied.

"Nobody planned any of that," Theodosia said. "And nobody

saw it coming, either." She fought to maintain her cool. Tidwell wasn't just brusque and maddening, he was scary smart. He knew she'd been investigating, that she was poking her nose where it didn't belong.

"And what is the common denominator?" Tidwell continued. He lifted a hand and pointed a chubby finger at her. "You."

"You think all this happened because of me?"

"I think you've been doing a fine job of fanning the flames."

Theodosia put both hands on her hips and stared at him. "What on earth are you talking about?"

"You've become a magnet, a flash point. A nexus of trouble, so to speak."

"Seriously?" Her voice came out in a squeak, but she fought to get it under control. "No. I don't think so."

"Then tell me," Tidwell said. "What were you up to last night?"

"Last night?" *Does he know I creepy-crawled Harker's apartment? Has someone been tailing me?* "After I left the hospital, I went home." *That much is true. Besides, if he didn't want me investigating Jud Harker, he shouldn't have let me tag along with him two nights ago.*

Tidwell studied her carefully, as if he was trying to divine her thoughts.

"Hmph," he said.

"Where are my manners?" Theodosia said suddenly. "May I offer you a scone?" When faced with Tidwell's onslaught of questions, she'd learned to ply him with sugar. It was his downfall. His kryptonite.

"You're trying to change the subject," Tidwell said in a gruff voice.

"Certainly not," Theodosia said. *Of course I am, is it working?* She lifted the glass top on the pie saver where an assortment of baked goodies was on display, and waved a hand as if she were a show hostess on *The Price Is Right.*

"Let's see, now. We've got cream scones, strawberry muffins, and, oh yes, chocolate tea bread."

"Chocolate tea bread?" were the words that sealed Tidwell's fate.

Gotcha.

"Let me put a slice in a take-out box for you," Theodosia said. "Better yet, I'll make up a nice assortment. And Drayton . . ." She gestured frantically at Drayton. "Could you please fix Detective Tidwell a cup of tea, to go?"

And Tidwell finally did go. Clutching his goodies and his cup of tea, he was carefully, gently, with kid gloves, shown the door. It was all done on the pretext that they had to get ready for the Plum Blossom Tea. Which they actually did, of course.

After placing plum-colored tea lights in frosted glasses, Theodosia set about arranging the Japanese artifacts that Alexis had loaned her. There were elegant silk fans in lacquer holders, geisha dolls in colorful silk kimonos, ceramic koi, enamel vases decorated with cranes, and a pair of fierce-looking bronze dragons. She put all of these items on the tables, then stood back to study her handiwork.

"Your tables look lovely," Miss Dimple said.

"Our tables," Theodosia said.

Miss Dimple wrinkled her brow. "But we're still missing the plum blossoms."

"Oh no, we're not," Drayton said. He suddenly swept into the tea room, carrying a tall vase brimming with purple plum blossoms.

"Oh my goodness," Miss Dimple exclaimed. "What a gorgeous arrangement."

"Fantastic," Theodosia said. "Drayton, I had no idea you were so talented when it came to flower arranging."

"Isn't this technically ikebana?" Miss Dimple asked, brushing a hand against a sweep of blossoms. "At least that's what they call it in Japan when flowers are arranged to correspond with the seasons or a special event."

"You're quite right," Drayton said, placing the plum blossoms on one of the tables and then stepping back to admire them. He'd arranged a number of branches in an artful, almost windswept design, so the plum blossoms looked as if they were being caressed by a gentle breeze.

"Because Drayton is such a skilled bonsai master," Miss Dimple said, "it stands to reason he'd be good at ikebana, too."

"You'll get no argument from me," Theodosia said. She gazed around the tea room, which fairly glowed from all the plum and pink colors they'd incorporated into their décor. "In fact, it looks like we're all set."

"We are," Drayton said. "All I have to do is put the rest of the plum blossoms in vases."

"I'd love to help," Miss Dimple said.

"I would welcome your more-than-capable assistance," Drayton said. He glanced over at Theodosia and waggled his eyebrows.

"And I have a short errand to take care of," Theodosia said, picking up on his prompt.

Drayton nodded. "Yes, I thought you did."

25

It was the perfect time for Theodosia to duck out of the tea shop. They still had a good hour before their guests were scheduled to arrive, and she was itching to get a look at Jud Harker's car. Hopefully, he was hard at work at the Stagwood Inn today. Doing his odd jobs, or plumbing work, or whatever.

Theodosia covered the few blocks in no time at all, then skipped up the steps and entered the lobby. A couple was standing at the front desk, checking out, so she had to wait a few minutes. But when it was her turn, she smiled at the young woman who was manning the desk and said, in a breezy tone, "Hi there, have you seen Jud Harker today?"

The young clerk looked thoughtful for a few seconds, then said, "Maybe, like, twenty minutes ago?"

Good, he's here.

"So he's working here today?"

"I think he's probably around somewhere," the desk clerk said. "I know the kitchen sink hasn't been draining properly."

"I just wanted to drop something off for him," Theodosia

said, trying to sound conversational, as if she and Harker were old buddies. "And, um, I'm guessing his car is parked out back? In the lot?"

The desk clerk bobbed her head. "Should be."

"Great." Theodosia turned away, then turned back as if she'd forgotten something. "Remind me again, will you. Jud drives a . . . ?" She left her question hanging in the air.

"He still has his Mustang," the desk clerk said.

Theodosia cocked a finger at her. "Right. Thanks." Then she was down the back hallway, ducking past Mitchel Cooper's office, and stepping outside.

The parking lot was only half-filled, so it was easy to pick out Harker's Mustang. And Theodosia's heart did an extra beat when she saw the car was black. Well, not shiny black, because it had to be at least fifteen years old. More like faded, oxidized-by-the-sun gray-black.

"Perfect," she said, stepping off the patio and heading across the parking lot. She slipped around a silver Audi, then a white Mercedes. But just as she came around the back end of the Mercedes and was about to bend over and examine the front of Harker's car, Mitchel Cooper came walking out from between two large SUVs.

"Hello there," Cooper called out when he saw her.

Theodosia stopped in her tracks.

"Oh, it's you," Cooper said, recognizing her. Then he looked around the lot and frowned. "Is something wrong?"

Theodosia straightened up fast, as if she'd been touched with a hot wire.

"Uh . . . what?" she said, feeling trapped and stalling for time.

"Is there something you want? Something I can help you with?" Cooper sounded cranky and looked harried. Maybe he was late getting to work or was anticipating a flood of guests

checking in for the weekend. Or maybe he just had his proverbial undies in a twist.

"No, I'm just . . . I was wondering if you had any plum blossoms," Theodosia said. It was the first thing that came to mind.
"I mean, that you could possibly spare?"

"Plum blossoms?" Cooper looked perplexed. "You mean like
from plum *trees?*"

"That's right." The smile felt frozen on Theodosia's face. "I'm
sure you've noticed that all the fruit trees in the neighborhood
are blooming." She couldn't believe he hadn't noticed.

Cooper narrowed his eyes and surveyed the nearby grounds.
"I don't think we have any plum trees."

"That's funny, Drayton was sure he'd seen some here." Theodosia hastened to explain her request. "You see, we're hosting
a special event tea today and we need a few more plum blossoms. For decoration in the tea room."

Cooper was getting bored. "Well, take a cutting from one
of the apple trees, then." He turned away from her and headed
for the back door of the inn. "I doubt anyone will even notice
the difference," he muttered.

Thank goodness he's gone.

Theodosia waited a full minute, just to make sure Cooper
wasn't going to double back. Then she bent down and checked
the front of Harker's car. She ran her hand along the bumper
and the rocker panels. There wasn't any obvious damage, but it
was an older car, so it carried a few dents and dings.

Her findings, Theodosia felt, were inconclusive.

The women from the Broad Street Garden Club swept through
the front door of the Indigo Tea Room as if they were headed
for a meet and greet with George Clooney. But of course Dray-

ton was the one standing there to greet them, wearing his Donegal tweed jacket and Drake's bow tie.

Didn't matter. They cooed greetings to him, squealed when they connected with their friends, exchanged air kisses, and then shrieked with delight as their eyes registered the elegantly decorated tables festooned with boughs of plum blossoms.

Midge Binkley, the president of the garden club, gripped Theodosia with both hands and said, "It's pure perfection, dear. The colors, the décor—it just couldn't be any better."

"This is pure pleasure for us, too," Theodosia said. "We're thrilled you chose us to host your tea."

Midge looked around again and her eyes immediately landed on the round table in the center of the tea room.

"Is that the head table?" Midge asked. She was dressed in a plum-colored skirt suit with a white frilly blouse. A ring with a purple-pink stone glinted from one finger. Clearly, she'd taken the notion of a Plum Blossom Tea to heart.

"It is now," Theodosia said.

"Corinne? Angela?" Midge raised a hand and beckoned two of her friends. "We're right over here."

The rest of the ladies poured in then, bustling around the tables, oohing over the very apropos china pattern, tea lights, Japanese antiques, and, of course, Drayton's plum blossom arrangements. And once the guests started taking their seats, Theodosia and Miss Dimple immediately began filling their teacups with aromatic, fresh-brewed tea.

"We're going to have a full house," Miss Dimple whispered to Theodosia.

"Almost, but not quite," Theodosia said as she continued to pour tea. She was still on the lookout for Alexis James as well as Aunt Libby.

"When should we start serving the scones?"

"Not for another ten minutes," Theodosia said. The garden club ladies were still trickling in and she'd just spotted a familiar face among them. Alexis James.

Theodosia hurried over to greet Alexis. "You poor thing," Theodosia said, giving her a gentle hug. "I was wondering if you'd even make it today. How are you feeling?"

Alexis gave a small shrug. "Sore and achy. About how I expected to feel."

"Drayton's going to brew you a pot of chamomile tea. It's good for relaxing sore muscles and has anti-inflammatory properties."

"Tea can actually soothe aches and pains?" Alexis asked.

Theodosia led Alexis to the small table near the fireplace. "Amazingly, yes," she said. "As well as help with lots of other things. For example, jasmine tea calms the nerves, lemon verbena aids in digestion, and ginseng tea boosts the immune system."

"This is all news to me," Alexis said as she took her seat. "But good news. I guess I'll have to start stocking up on different kinds of tea. Maybe even ask Drayton for some guidance."

"Once you get him started, watch out," Theodosia said.

"So," Alexis said. "How's your young man Jamie doing?"

"Still in the hospital with his leg in a cast."

"That's just awful," Alexis said. "And to think it happened right here. I mean, he wasn't even riding his bike in traffic or doing something equally dangerous."

"No, he was just taking out the trash," Theodosia said.

"And you still believe that whoever was driving the car struck him intentionally."

"I'm afraid so."

"And then I got nailed a couple of hours later." Alexis puffed up her cheeks and blew out a stream of air. "Whew."

Theodosia put a hand on Alexis's shoulder. "Like I mentioned last night, there's a chance both incidents are connected."

Alexis looked immediately flustered. "I know you said that, but why would they be?"

"That's what we're trying to figure out."

"Who's we?"

"I've been working with Detective Pete Riley."

Alexis gazed at her. "Yes, your detective friend." She swallowed hard. "This all feels very frightening. And you're positive the police are investigating? That they're trying to make sense of it all?"

"They're on it," Theodosia said. "So I don't want you to worry about a thing. In fact, I want you to enjoy a lovely luncheon."

Alexis looked around and gave a soft smile. "I see all the Japanese antiques I loaned you are on display."

"And they look fabulous," Theodosia said. "In fact, I've heard more than a few compliments, so I wouldn't be surprised if you made a few sales today."

"Nothing wrong with that," Alexis said.

"I'd better help Drayton with the . . ." Theodosia began. But Alexis grabbed her by the hand.

"Do you have a couple more seconds? I have something I'd like to run by you."

Drayton was making the rounds of the tables, chatting with guests, sprinkling compliments like fairy dust, so Theodosia nodded. She had another minute.

"I've met someone," Alexis said. A shy smile danced across her face. "And he's asked me on a date."

"That's wonderful," Theodosia said.

"I think you know him. It's that publisher, Bill Glass."

"Wait. What?" Theodosia said. Had she heard Alexis right?

"What's wrong?" Alexis said. "You're making kind of a lemon face. You don't like him?"

"I guess I never considered Bill Glass date material," Theodosia said. She didn't have the heart to tell Alexis that she thought Glass was a complete buffoon. Oh, and let's not forget gossipmonger. If Glass didn't have a fat, juicy story to spread all over town, he magically manufactured one.

"The thing is, I really enjoy spending time with highly creative people," Alexis said.

Theodosia smiled. Glass scored major points when it came to creativity and a wild imagination. And for stirring the pot whenever possible. "So you're going to go out with him?"

"Ah, well, we've planned what I guess you could call a couple of working dates. We're attending the Carolina Cat Show tonight and then the big opening at the Heritage Society tomorrow."

"So he'll be busy shooting pictures the whole time." Theodosia didn't see this as much of a date, more like Glass having a free hand to hold his cameras and lenses.

"Which is fine with me," Alexis said. "To be honest, I'm kind of a photo nut myself."

"Then you should go for it. It might be fun." Theodosia had seen stranger pairings than theirs work out in the long run.

Five minutes later, Delaine showed up. And wouldn't you know it, she was already bragging about Dominic and Domino, her two Siamese cats.

"I just *know* my dear, sweet fur babies are going to win big tonight at the Carolina Cat Show!" Delaine enthused. "In fact, I've already cleared a space on my mantel for a nice shiny trophy."

"Then best of luck to Dominic and Domino," Theodosia said as she seated Delaine at a table with three other women. Her cats were sweet tempered and gorgeous, in spite of the fact that Delaine was completely crackers.

"Guess who just showed up," Drayton suddenly whispered in Theodosia's ear.

Theodosia turned around with a smile. "Aunt Libby?"

He nodded.

"Fabulous." Theodosia met her aunt at the front door and swept her up in an enormous bear hug. Aunt Libby was in her eighties, but her silver hair was flawless, her smile warm and gracious, and her posture perfectly erect. She was also wearing a Dior suit that she'd probably bought in 1978 and still looked like a million bucks.

"You made it," Theodosia cried.

"Just barely," Aunt Libby said with a chuckle, looking around. "Looks like you're about ready to start."

"Come. Over here," Theodosia said, hustling her along. "I'm putting you at a private table with my friend Alexis James."

"How lovely," Aunt Libby said, smiling at Alexis as she slipped into the chair across from her.

Theodosia started to make quick introductions, but both Alexis and Aunt Libby shushed her and waved her off.

"We're perfectly capable of getting acquainted on our own," Aunt Libby said.

"That's right." Alexis laughed. "It's much more fun that way."

Theodosia walked to the front of the tea room and rang a tiny bell. With that sweet tinkle hanging in the air, the buzz of conversation instantly stopped and all eyes were turned toward her.

"I'd like to welcome each of you to the Indigo Tea Shop," Theodosia said. "We're thrilled that your garden club selected us for your annual Plum Blossom Tea, and we promise to do our best to make your luncheon perfect in every way."

There was a smatter of light applause and then Theodosia continued.

"Our first course today will consist of cream scones complemented by plum preserves and Devonshire cream. Second course will be a puff pastry tart of asparagus and Gruyère cheese. For your entrée we'll be serving turkey Waldorf tea sandwiches on French brioche. And for dessert we have fresh-baked plum crisp."

Drayton stepped forward to stand beside Theodosia.

"You're already sipping a spiced plum herbal tea as well as our house-blend Chinese black tea with plums and quince. But we have two other teas for your enjoyment as well. We'll be serving a Ceylon silver tips tea to complement your second and third courses. This particular Ceylon tea is pale pink in color and brimming with flavor. To accompany your dessert, I'll be brewing an Assam tea from India's Madoorie Tea Estate. Of course, if you have any special tea requests, kindly let us know and we'll try to oblige."

Midge Binkley raised her hand.

Drayton nodded at her. "Yes, Mrs. Binkley."

"I attended one of your Easter teas last year," Midge said. "And, as I recall, Drayton, you regaled us with a few lines of poetry."

Drayton's eyes sparkled. "I take it you'd like something apropos of your Plum Blossom Tea?"

Midge didn't even have to answer. Two dozen women clapped and nodded. Drayton had a reputation for fine recitation.

"Well then," Drayton said. "Perhaps some Japanese haiku are in order."

"I love it," Alexis called out.

Drayton stood erect as a bandleader, one hand tucked behind his back. "One particular haiku that comes to mind was penned by the famed Japanese poet Bashō."

> *With plum blossom scent,*
> *This sudden sun emerges*
> *Along a mountain trail.*

As his words rang out, clear and vibrant with meaning, he was rewarded with smiles and more applause.

"And one additional short poem to get our luncheon started," Drayton said. "This one was written by Kobayashi Yatarō, who pen name Issa literally means 'one cup of tea'."

> *That nightingale there*
> *Is wiping its muddy claws*
> *On the plum blossoms!*

"Wonderful," Midge declared.

That was the cue for Miss Dimple and Haley to emerge from the kitchen carrying silver trays, each tray laden with small plates that contained a scone, dab of plum preserves, and large puff of Devonshire cream.

"And now, ladies," Theodosia said, "your luncheon is served."

From then on it was smooth sailing. The scones were served, nibbled, and drew high praise. More tea was poured as a soft hum of conversation rose up, interspersed with the gentle *click* of bone china cups against saucers.

When the scone plates were cleared away, with nary a crumb left over, Theodosia and Miss Dimple brought out the asparagus and cheese tarts. These appetizers proved amazingly popular as well, and several guests begged for the recipe.

"It's going well, don't you think?" Drayton asked when Theodosia returned to the counter to grab a fresh pot of tea.

"I think you had them in the palm of your hand with the haiku poems," Theodosia said. "After that we could have served peanut butter and jelly sandwiches and they wouldn't have cared less."

"But *we* would have cared. We have our standards to uphold."

"Absolutely, Drayton."

Ten minutes later, Theodosia helped serve their third course, the turkey Waldorf tea sandwiches. And wouldn't you know it? They were a smash hit as well.

Theodosia circled the tables, chatting, pouring refills, enjoying the contact high she was getting from her guests. With the plum blossoms and antiques, and everyone all dressed up, drinking tea and savoring each course, there was a mannered graciousness at work here.

And just as Theodosia was thinking that the petty cares of the world had been temporarily swept aside and the tea room was engulfed in cozy warmth, it all fell apart.

The front door banged open and Bob Garver burst in. He stood in the entry, looking around, red-faced and puffing hard, like a steam engine that was about to explode. He wore a blue sport coat and khaki slacks, as if he'd just rushed out of a business meeting, but his tie was loosened and his shirt had come partially untucked.

"Where is she?" Garver demanded.

"Excuse me?" Drayton said, frowning from behind the counter.

"Where is she? Where's the woman who sicced the freaking cops on me?" Garver lurched forward another couple of steps, spotted Theodosia standing next to a table with a teapot in her hand and said, "You." It came out as a shrill bark, almost a seething, scathing accusation. He thrust his jaw out, shook a finger at her, and said, "You're the one who's causing me a world of trouble!"

26

Theodosia crossed the tea shop with as much grace and purpose as she could muster, hurrying to meet Garver, hoping to forestall any sort of cataclysmic confrontation.

"Please lower your voice this instant," Theodosia told Garver. Honestly, does everybody and his brother think they can stomp in here and start ranting? First Harker, now Garver. It ends right now!

"Make me," Garver snarled back at her.

Theodosia was suddenly aware that every one of her guests had their heads turned, watching her intently. In fact, she was pretty sure some of the women had twisted their chairs around to gain a better sight line.

Theodosia glanced at Alexis's startled expression and wondered briefly if she recognized Garver in the light of day. Then she brushed past Garver and said, in a terse voice, "Follow me." Only when she was outside on the sidewalk did she turn around to see if Garver had tagged along after her. Thankfully, he had.

"What is it you want?" Theodosia asked him.

Garver's face was a thundercloud as he unleashed his fury upon her. "Did you tell Detective Pete Riley that I ran down some kid with my car? And that a couple hours later I attacked a woman?"

Theodosia took a step back in the wake of his onslaught. She was frightened of this man, but vowed not to show any fear. She would treat him like a barking, snapping dog. A dog that was probably more frightened than menacing. Hopefully.

"*Did* you run my employee down?" Theodosia shot back. "Are *you* the one who attacked my friend Alexis?"

"No!" Garver screamed. Then, "Are you completely out of your mind? You concocted every bit of this ridiculous fairy tale and then had the nerve to send the cops after me!"

"I didn't make anything up—those attacks really happened."

"Maybe so, but I had *nothing* to do with them," Garver said. "Nothing!" He shook his head, spun around in a circle on the sidewalk, then said, "Lady, I don't even *know* those people."

Theodosia wasn't about to give Garver immediate absolution, just because he was apoplectic about his innocence. Just because he'd been questioned by the police and then released.

"Where were you last night?" she asked. "Do you have an alibi? Did you tell Detective Riley where you were?"

Garver stared at her, his mouth working furiously. "Of course I did."

"And your alibi was . . . ?" Theodosia wanted to hear it for herself. Wanted the satisfaction of knowing exactly where Garver had been when Jamie was hit, when Alexis was grabbed.

"Like I told the cops, particularly that Detective Riley, I was at a meeting with three of my contractors."

"And these are witnesses, credible people who'll vouch for you?"

"Absolutely." Garver pulled his mouth into a feral snarl.

"What is it with you, anyway? I mean, who are you and why are you trying to railroad me?"

Theodosia thought about the description Alexis had given her. It had been vague, but to her it had sounded like Garver. So much so that she'd begged Riley to take a careful, serious look at him!

Well, obviously, Riley had.

Now it appeared that Theodosia, helped along by the urging of Betty Bates, had been wrong, had jumped the gun. Garver might be mixed up in crooked real estate financing, but it looked as if he wasn't the person who'd engineered the hit-and-run on Jamie or attacked Alexis.

"What's wrong?" Garver shouted at her. "Cat got your tongue? Are you even remotely sorry that I got jerked around by the cops?"

Theodosia stared at him. "When you act the way you did just now . . . coming into my tea shop and making a ridiculous scene . . . then no. I'm not one bit sorry."

And with that Theodosia turned her back on him and went inside.

But, of course, she knew she owed something to her guests. Not exactly an explanation, but certainly an excuse for the bizarre interruption. But when she stood in the center of the tea room and cleared her throat, hoping she'd be able to find the right words, Drayton stepped in with a silver tray held high.

"Plum crisp," Drayton announced in his hale, hearty, oratorical voice. "Plum crisp is one of the signature desserts that we make from scratch at the Indigo Tea Shop using fresh-picked plums from the nearby Perdeaux Fruit Farm."

There were oohs and aahs and nods of approval.

"Theodosia," Drayton continued in his breezy patter. "Would you please tell our guests about the special topping?"

"We top our plum crisp with a special cinnamon whipped cream," Theodosia said. "We use fresh organic cream and imported Ceylonese cinnamon." She glanced over, saw Haley standing in the doorway, all kitted out in her white chef's jacket and tall mushroom-shaped hat. "In fact, here's our head chef right now. Haley's the one who sourced all the ingredients and prepared your lunches."

"Then, she's the one with the recipes," Midge Binkley said.

As soon as all the desserts were served, Theodosia went over to speak with Alexis.

"The man that just came in," Theodosia said. "That was Bob Garver."

Alexis didn't respond, but her eyes widened slightly and she looked pale.

"Did you recognize him? Because there seemed to be a flicker of something on your face." Had it been recognition? Or fear? Theodosia wasn't sure.

"I . . . I don't know," Alexis stammered. "Like I told you last night, it was dark as pitch and the guy, whoever the jerk was, jumped out of the bushes and grabbed me from behind." She gave a slight shudder. "But I have to say, the man who just stormed in here *looked* very frightening. I'm glad you dealt with him outside."

"So you really couldn't identify your attacker either way?" Theodosia pressed. She knew Garver had been questioned and released, but deep in her heart she still harbored a strong feeling of suspicion.

"Think hard, dear," Aunt Libby said. She was filled with concern for her tablemate. "Take your time."

Alexis shook her head slowly. "Sorry . . . but no. I don't think I've ever seen that man before."

"Okay," Theodosia said. Alexis looked like she was getting upset all over again, so it was time to drop the subject. Theodosia drew a calming breath, looked around, and said, "Aside from Garver's nasty outburst, I'd have to say the tea is going well."

"It's been a rip-roaring success," Aunt Libby said. "And I think your blip of excitement added just the right dash of panache. Showed your guests that you're a woman who's not afraid to take charge."

"You were cool under fire," Alexis said to Theodosia. "I wouldn't have stayed that calm. Heck, you saw me last night. I melted like a faulty nuclear reactor."

Theodosia just smiled. Deep down, she hadn't been particularly calm at all.

By two o'clock, the Plum Blossom Tea was declared a hit and all four courses had been served, consumed, and raved about. But still Theodosia's garden club ladies made no motion to leave. In fact, they were wandering around, exclaiming over the décor, and shopping their little hearts out. They grabbed tins of tea, scone mixes, tea towels, and jars of honey from the shelves in Theodosia's gift area.

"Do you have any more of this Palmetto Peach tea?" a woman asked her.

"That's one of Drayton's house blends," Theodosia said. "So I'm sure we do."

"And what about these T-Bath products?" another woman asked.

So Theodosia gave a quick rundown on her private label T-Bath products that included green tea lotion, ginger and chamomile facial mist, lemon verbena bath oil, and green tea feet treat.

Another guest, Candace Jordan, grabbed a package of seeds off a bottom shelf. "What is this, please?" she asked.

"That's something new to our retail area," Theodosia said. "A hummingbird scatter mix. They're flower seeds you scatter in your garden to grow nectar-producing blooms and blossoms that are particularly attractive to hummingbirds." And it had worked for her, too. She'd scattered some of the mixture in her garden last spring and, a couple of months later, all sorts of ruby-and-emerald-green hummingbirds had flown in to sip delicately from the flowers.

When there was a lull, Aunt Libby slipped into the group and touched Theodosia lightly on the arm. "I'm taking off now, dear," she said. "Thank you for a lovely lunch."

"You're leaving so soon?" Theodosia said. "I was hoping we'd have time for a good gab."

"Perhaps later?"

"I have an idea," Theodosia said. "Why don't you come with me to the Carolina Cat Show tonight?"

"Oh, probably not," Aunt Libby said.

"Then how about the Rare Weapons Show tomorrow night?"

Aunt Libby looked slightly more amenable to this idea.

"A weapons show isn't exactly my cup of tea," Aunt Libby said. "Mind you, I'm not opposed to hunting—or dueling over a lady's honor—but I think I'd just be a burden to you and your . . ." Her eyes sparkled. "You do have a date, don't you?"

Theodosia nodded. "Yes, but . . ."

"Perhaps you'd allow me to escort you," Drayton said, cutting in.

Aunt Libby took a careful look at Drayton. "Is that a serious offer?"

"Absolutely," Drayton said. "And I can guarantee you a highly amusing evening. You're well acquainted with Timothy Neville and . . ."

"Is he still so cranky?" Aunt Libby asked.

Drayton glossed over her question. "Timothy is always under fire where funding is concerned. But I'm sure there'll be lots of other folks in attendance that you know. Heritage Society donors and whatnot."

"I've got half a mind to take you up on your offer," Aunt Libby said.

"Then I consider the matter settled," Drayton said. "You'll come along with us tomorrow night."

"You know," Theodosia said, "there's a fancy black-tie ball afterward. If you'd like, you could . . ."

Aunt Libby smiled even as she shook her head. "The weapons show sounds interesting. Not so much the fancy ball."

"What's wrong?" Drayton asked. "Didn't you pack your dancing shoes?"

Aunt Libby patted his arm. "I haven't for a while, dear."

Midafternoon and Theodosia, Drayton, and Miss Dimple were busy cleaning up. Haley was rattling around in the kitchen, packing up leftovers, putting things right in her personal fiefdom.

"Knock knock," said a voice.

Theodosia glanced toward the front door. She hadn't heard it snick open, hadn't heard anyone come in. But there was Detective Pete Riley looking inquisitive and (she had to admit) awfully cute.

"Are you busy?" Riley asked.

Theodosia set down a tub of dirty dishes and walked over to greet him.

"Not too busy for you," she said, just this side of flirtatious. In his khaki trench coat she thought he looked like a modern-day Columbo. But cuter, much cuter.

Riley looked at the half-cleared tables, the candles guttering in their holders, the plum blossoms just beginning to wilt. "Looks like you had a big shindig here today."

"That's not the half of it. We also had a guest of honor." When Riley just lifted an eyebrow, Theodosia continued. "Bob Garver—the slimy real estate guy, remember?—dropped in to yell at me."

"He was *here*?" Riley looked positively gobsmacked. "But I was just questioning him a couple of hours ago."

"Well, he was here in the flesh and making a terrible fool of himself."

"Why? What did he say?" Riley asked.

Theodosia shrugged. "He blamed me for putting you on his tail. For having him hauled in for questioning."

"Doggone it," Riley said. "I didn't physically *haul* Garver in. I just kind of suggested we talk." He stroked a hand against his chin. "Ah, I should have figured him for a hothead."

"You should see him in action."

"Oh, I saw enough. We didn't just question Garver about his whereabouts last night; we were trying to get a handle on those low-interest loans, too. He got pretty upset when we peppered him with questions."

"Garver claimed he had an alibi for last night," Theodosia said. "That he had nothing to do with Jamie's hit-and-run or the attack on Alexis."

"He was alibied up the wazoo, all right," Riley said. "But when we drilled him about those loans, he wasn't quite so glib."

"So you think something crooked is going on?"

"I'd put money on it. Just not the city's money."

"Say, now," Drayton called to them. "How would you both like to taste a new Japanese tea?"

"Why not," Theodosia said. She felt bushed and the back of her neck was sore. Tension, she figured. She could use a pick-me-up because the day wasn't over yet.

"I'll give it a shot," Riley said.

Drayton walked over to them carrying two small ceramic cups filled to the brim with steaming amber-colored tea. With great care, he handed a cup to Theodosia, and one to Riley.

"These cups don't have any handles," Riley said.

"Esoteric Japanese design," Drayton said over his shoulder.

Theodosia took a sip of tea, swallowed quickly, and said, "I have to tell you something. And it's kind of tricky."

"What now?" Riley asked. He looked as if he was prepared for bad news.

"I've been doing some investigating on my own."

"Well, I knew *that*." Riley relaxed some, took a sip of tea, and wrinkled his nose.

"No," Theodosia said. She didn't really want to tell him about her foray into Harker's apartment, but what she'd discovered was too hot to keep quiet. "I mean I've done some hard-core investigating and I found something very dark in Jud Harker's past."

"The man who's been number one on your suspect list. Is he still?"

"I'm not sure," Theodosia said. "But I did discover a deep, dark secret."

Riley made a rolling motion with his hand. "Come on, spit it out."

"I found out that, a number of years ago, Jud Harker accidently shot his ten-year-old brother." There, she'd gone and dropped the A-bomb.

"Uh—what?" Riley said.

What? He didn't hear me? "I found out that . . ."

Riley made a hasty stopping motion with his free hand. "Whoa. Rewind, please. Um . . . seriously? Harker shot his own brother?"

"That's right."

"How exactly did you find this out?"

"You don't want to know," Theodosia said. She figured his brains would explode in his skull if she came completely clean.

"What is this?" Riley said. "Don't ask, don't tell?"

"Something like that."

"No, you've got to tell me," Riley said. "You can't just dole out heavy-duty information like this in a casual manner."

"Okay. I found a clipping in his scrapbook." Theodosia stopped and offered him a rueful half smile. A look that said, *Yup, I messed with his stuff.*

"In his *what?*" Riley was unsettled, but fought to recover his composure. "You see, since I'm an actual detective, I am detecting the fact that you might have entered Harker's domicile illegally." He peered at her. "Just how far off am I in making this assumption?"

"Not too far," Theodosia admitted.

"You're absolutely positive about this shooting?" Riley asked.

"I read the newspaper clipping from, like, twenty years ago. Harker wasn't charged because his brother's death was ruled an accident." Theodosia was slightly breathless now. She was also weak with relief that Riley wasn't going to strangle her. "You can see how this might be pertinent to the Carson Lanier case."

"Because of Harker's nasty threats and the gun collection, yes," Riley said slowly. "This new information does shade things a bit."

"But which way?" Theodosia asked, trying to read Riley's expression. "That Harker might be innocent, or . . . ?"

"Not necessarily innocent at all," Riley said. "In fact, I'm sufficiently bowled over by this new information that I'm going to pick Harker up for questioning. If we can hold him for twenty-four hours, maybe we can sort a few things out."

"Can you do that? Hold him, I mean."

"My dear, Detective Tidwell has been trying to do exactly that for almost a week. So I'm about to make his fondest wish come true."

"What about Bob Garver?"

"We'll keep an eye on him, too."

"Good. Great. Thank you." *And thank you for not going ballistic.*

"I have one more question," Riley said.

"Yes?"

"What *is* this tea? It tastes like some kind of weird broth you'd feed to horses."

"Barley tea," Drayton called from behind the counter. "Known as *mugicha*. It's a traditional Japanese drink that is, in fact, made from roasted barley. Delicious, no?"

Riley shook his head. "No."

27

First Drayton wanted to stop at the Opera Society to pick up some tickets at the will-call window, then they had to stop by Cousin Livonia's house and drop off some leftover scones and tea sandwiches that Haley had packaged up. So by the time Theodosia and Drayton made it to the Carolina Cat Show in Charleston's massive Gaillard Center, it was late afternoon, almost five o'clock. So they'd missed the early judging.

But just being there was an absolute stitch. Because it was, to put it mildly, cataclysmic. Cats were everywhere. In show rings, in wire crates, cuddled in their fawning owners' arms and, yes, a few of them were running around the enormous auditorium where the show was being held. Free-range cats, Theodosia decided.

"It's amazing how many different breeds there are," Drayton said, as they walked down a narrow aisle between piled-up crates, where cats preened as their owners wielded blow-dryers on fur. "Look at that beauty, a Manx. And there's a Burmese cat and a Russian blue."

"I don't know which ones I like best," Theodosia said. "The elegant, sleek ones or the rapturously furry ones."

"They're all quite lovely," Drayton said. "If I were a judge I'd award them all blue ribbons."

"You see, that's why you're not a judge," Theodosia said. "In fact, you'd probably go out on the street and give blue ribbons to the strays."

"Of course. And I'd feed the little darlings, too."

"Okay, we've got to find Delaine. She made me pinky swear that I'd stop by, so I have to show the flag."

"There she is."

"Where?" Theodosia peered around, but didn't see Delaine anywhere. Which was odd, since she was one of the organizers. Which meant she should be prancing around, shouting out orders to everyone. In other words, being Delaine.

"Next aisle over."

"I still don't see her," Theodosia said.

"You see that slim woman in the red turban?" Drayton said, his lips curling faintly at the corners.

"Oh, good gracious. What *has* she got on her head?"

"*Why are you* wearing that?" Theodosia asked, once they'd finally homed in on Delaine. "Did you singe your hair with your blow-dryer or are you planning to tell people's fortunes?"

"I'm in *disguise*," Delaine hissed. She lifted a hand to touch the red scarf she'd wrapped around her head and pinned in place with a jeweled brooch. "A couple of exhibitors were passing around copies of *Shooting Star* and I was afraid someone would *recognize* me!"

"So what if they do?" Theodosia said.

"No, no, no, I don't want to be associated with those awful pictures in *Shooting Star.* The ones that captured the horrible fight between Betty and Sissy."

"But *you* weren't in the fight, Delaine. As I recall, you weren't anywhere near it."

"Doesn't matter," Delaine said. "The fight took place at my *boutique.* Which means my sterling reputation might be impinged!"

"I see your cats have already won a couple of ribbons," Drayton said, gamely changing the subject. He gestured to a wire crate where a string of blue and purple ribbons hung. Two sleek Siamese cats peeked out at them, their eyes bright with curiosity.

"Oh yes," Delaine said. "Domino just received a purple ribbon and Dominic a blue ribbon. But of course, we're just getting started. There's more judging tonight and then there's best in show tomorrow afternoon."

"Which I'm sure you'll win," Drayton said.

"I'm sure, too," Delaine said. She bobbed her head fast and then had to put a hand up to steady her turban.

Theodosia and Drayton wandered away then, over to one of the rings to watch the judging process. A judge in a three-piece suit walked from crate to crate, then reached in and gently lifted up one of the cats and took it over to a table.

"So many cats," Drayton mused. "Must take a long time to judge."

But Theodosia didn't respond. She'd just seen a familiar face that brought her back to the here and now.

"Sissy Lanier is over there," Theodosia said. "We need to go . . ."

Instead of finishing her sentence Theodosia grabbed Drayton by the arm and dragged him in Sissy's direction.

"Sissy!" Theodosia raised a hand and waved.

Sissy saw Theodosia waving and hurried over to meet her.

"Hi there, hello," Sissy said. "And to Drayton, too." She shook her mane of blond hair. "Looks like the gang's all here."

"Sissy, I've been dying to hear," Theodosia said. "How did the meeting go with the attorney? I haven't talked to you since . . ." Theodosia was going to say *since your meltdown*, but stopped short. No need to bring *that* up.

Sissy brightened even more. "It couldn't have gone better, Theo. Mr. Alston is working with Fidelity to track down my missing money. It turns out there could have been a clerical error on the statement. Isn't that something?"

"So all that drama for nothing," Drayton said.

Sissy pursed her lips. "I wouldn't say that. Because if Delaine hadn't dragged me over to the Indigo Tea Shop, then Theodosia wouldn't have been so kind as to recommend her uncle to assist me." She gave a lopsided smile. "So you see, it was meant to be."

"Kismet," Drayton said.

"Whatever." Sissy shrugged. "So . . ." Her eyes lasered on Theodosia. "I heard a rumor that both Jud Harker and Bob Garver have been questioned." Sissy gave an eager nod. "Wouldn't it be wonderful if Carson's murder was finally solved? Then I could . . . well, at least I'd have some closure."

"It would be a great relief to all of us," Theodosia said.

Sissy glanced around, gave a perfunctory smile, and said, "Oops, gotta go. I'm supposed to hook up with a friend."

"Is Sissy still on your suspect list?" Drayton asked once they were out of earshot.

"Yes, she is," Theodosia said. "I still find her flippant attitude toward her almost ex-husband awfully disconcerting. Plus, she has an almost unholy appetite for money."

They circled back past the judging ring and Drayton said,

"Have we stayed long enough? I think we've seen most every-thing. No need to check out the vendors." Over to the left were two dozen retail booths selling everything from cat food to tiger-striped cat beds to custom-made cat collars.

"I was just wondering . . ." Theodosia said, looking around.

"About?"

"Alexis was supposed to be here on a date with Bill Glass."

Drayton halted in his tracks. "You're not serious."

"About as serious as a heart attack."

"Why on earth would an attractive, cultured woman like Alexis want to go on a date with a . . . a . . ."

"A rude, obnoxious boor?"

"Thank you, Theo, you snatched the words right out of my mouth."

"I don't know," Theodosia said. "Maybe Alexis is lonely. Maybe, through some strange circumstance, she and Glass are right for each other."

"As in opposites attract? Mars and Venus?"

"Mmn . . . something like that."

WAH-HOO!

Theodosia jerked her head around. "What on earth was that awful noise?"

"Some kind of disturbance," Drayton said. "Maybe . . . a fight?"

WAH-HOO!

"There it is again," Theodosia said.

"It came from over near the vendor booths," Drayton said.

Theodosia looked around, noticed that others in the crowd were frowning and glancing around as well. "I hope there's not some kind of problem."

"Amen. We've had enough problems lately."

WHEEEE-OOOOH!

"Good heavens," Drayton said, "it sounds like there's a barn owl loose in here."

"Or maybe it's malfunctioning equipment?" Theodosia said. "The PA system? The HVAC?"

"No." Drayton gripped Theodosia's arm and gave it a little shake. "Look over there."

Theodosia peered through the crowd and saw Bill Glass. He was bent over sharply, almost at a forty-five-degree angle. Three cameras dangled from around his neck as he pressed an enormous hanky to his nose. And sneezed again . . .

HOO-WAH!

Glass's fourth, explosive sneeze echoed off the rafters and practically rattled all the cat crates.

Theodosia pursed her lips. "Bill Glass."

"He must be allergic to all the cat hair that's floating around," Drayton said. "Somebody better toss an antihistamine down that poor man's throat."

"I'm surprised that he's reacting so violently, since most of these cats have been groomed to within an inch of their lives."

Drayton lifted a single eyebrow. "Don't you mean nine lives?"

"Very funny. And look, Alexis is over there with him. Well, actually, she's kind of standing off to one side, watching."

"Does she look like she's having fun?" Drayton asked.

Theodosia wanted to give Alexis the benefit of the doubt. But, in the end, she shook her head. "I wouldn't count on it."

28

Theodosia's good mood over a successful Plum Blossom Tea carried into Saturday as well. Humming to herself, a tune from Adele's newest album, she quickly set the tables, lit candles, and built a small fire in the fireplace. Cheered the place up, as Drayton would say.

Drayton. Theodosia looked over toward the front counter where he was whistling softly as he measured heaping scoops of tea into a pair of Shelley teapots. She decided he was probably looking forward to the Rare Weapons Show tonight. Formal Heritage Society events always put him in a good mood. He was after all, a kind of pomp and circumstance guy.

Theodosia walked over to the counter and said, "You know what?"

Drayton tossed a small tin of tea in the air and caught it. "What?"

"I let this percolate in my brain all night, and now I have a bad feeling about Jud Harker."

Drayton raised an eyebrow. "I thought you figured that Harker's unfortunate past pretty much exonerated him. That he was so traumatized by shooting his brother that he was basically anti-gun."

She shook her head. "I think I changed my mind."

"Why is that?"

"Reason number one," Theodosia said, "because Detective Riley decided to hold Harker for twenty-four hours to sort of sweat him. I figure Riley knows more than I do."

"He certainly has extensive field experience," Drayton said. "I'll grant him that."

"And number two, now that I look back on it, Harker exhibited all kinds of telltale warning signs. He was angry and confrontational. And his apartment had a dismal look about it."

"As if his surroundings reflected a guilty mind?"

"Something like that."

"Then you've got nothing to worry about," Drayton said. "The right man has been apprehended and is being held in custody."

"Which means Timothy won't be threatened again, and the show tonight will go off without a hitch."

"Let's hope so."

"Hey guys," Haley said. "I want you to taste something." She walked up to the counter carrying a small plate of scones. Or were they scones?

"What have you got there?" Drayton asked.

"Griddle scones," Haley said.

"So that was the wonderful aroma emanating from your kitchen," Theodosia said. "I knew you were baking some kind of goodness."

Drayton reached for one of the scones and studied it. "They're darker than usual."

"Because they've been cooked on a griddle rather than baked," Haley said.

"So somewhat nontraditional," Drayton said.

"Actually, griddle scones *were* a tradition until conventional ovens were invented," Haley said. "C'mon, try one. Take a bite."

Drayton took a bite and chewed thoughtfully.

Haley gazed at him. "Well? Whad'ya think? Be honest, now."

"Delicious," Drayton said. "Quirky but flavorful."

"They're from one of my granny's old receipts," Haley said. *Receipt* was the old-timey Southern way of saying "recipe."

"Your griddle scones are delicious," Theodosia said. She'd tried one as well. "Maybe slightly chewier than traditional baked scones."

"That's good, huh?" Haley asked. "Gives it that farm-to-table cachét?"

"Sounds like smart marketing to me," Drayton said. "Did you make enough so we can put them on the menu?"

"Sure did."

"When are you going to pick up Jamie?" Theodosia asked. Today was the day he was being released from the hospital.

"As soon as we close up here," Haley said. "I'll probably get to the hospital around one-thirty. Load up Jamie and all the baskets of flowers and fruit that he's gotten from well-wishers. I'll take him to Aunt LaBelle's and then stay with him for the weekend. Drive back Monday morning."

"You're a treasure, Haley," Theodosia said, just as the phone rang. "Jamie is blessed to have you as his cousin." She reached over, grabbed the phone, and said, "Indigo Tea Shop, how can I help you?"

"You can help by not blowing a gasket," Pete Riley said.

"Why? What happened?" Theodosia asked.

"We had to release Harker."

Theodosia's heart caught in her throat. "So soon? But I thought you were going to hold Harker for most of the day."

"Funny thing about that," Riley said. "His public defender, a particularly zealous fellow by the name of Arthur Pinckney, saw things differently."

"So Harker is out and walking around," Theodosia said. She looked at Drayton, who was watching her closely, and shook her head. Haley had drifted back into the kitchen.

"For all I know, Harker's back at the Stagwood Inn by now," Riley said. "Painting soffits or laying tile or whatever it is he does there."

"But what if he's the killer?" Theodosia tried to keep the rising tide of fear out of her voice, but wasn't very successful. All she could think about was Harker coming back and storming into the Indigo Tea Shop!

"All I can tell you right now is that Detective Tidwell has decided to pursue other angles."

"Wait a minute." Riley's words had thrown her for a loop. "Like what? Who?"

"I can't tell you that."

"Sure, you can," Theodosia said. "In fact, you have to."

"Sorry," was all Riley said.

Theodosia dropped the phone to her chest and thought for a few moments. She put it back up again and said, "Tidwell's put all his money on Bob Garver, hasn't he?"

There was a long pause and then Riley said, "Doggone it."

"I think Tidwell's wrong. In fact, you've got to convince him that he's dead wrong."

"Hey, I *work* for the man. When he says jump, I say 'How high?'"

"Then I'll tell him," Theodosia said.

There was a soft chuckle and Riley said, "Good luck with that."

"They released Harker?" Drayton asked, once Theodosia had hung up the phone.

"Under Tidwell's order," Theodosia said. "And, I guess, the public defender."

"And you think Tidwell's wrong?"

"I do, but . . ."

"But what?"

Theodosia hesitated, then tried to pick her words carefully. "On the other hand, Tidwell's a professional with thirty years of law enforcement under his belt." She shrugged. "I'm just an amateur with an opinion."

"Yes, but you have something Tidwell doesn't have."

"What's that?"

Drayton smiled. "You're blessed with intuition."

They got busy then, welcoming guests, seating them, pouring tea. And, for the next couple of hours, the issue of murder suspects was forgotten. Haley's griddle scones were a hit, of course. Along with her crab salad tea sandwiches and Greek meat loaf.

"You look vexed," Drayton said as he handed a pot of green tea to Theodosia. "That's for table four, by the way. Tell them it needs to steep an additional two minutes."

"I'm still thinking about Tidwell's decision to release Harker," Theodosia said. "Upset about it. I think he made a huge mistake."

"Maybe it's time to let this go," Drayton said. "I know Timothy asked you to step in and help ferret out suspects—and you've certainly done more than your fair share. But you can't carry the weight of the world on your shoulders."

"Is that what I'm doing?"

"You take it all to heart, yes," Drayton said. "And by the way, that tea only needs to steep for one more minute now."

The rest of the morning went by in a whirlwind of customers coming and going, take-out orders being packed up, and a few last-minute to-go orders that were called in by Angie at the Featherbed House B and B. Haley worked like a whirling dervish until one o'clock, at which point Theodosia plucked her apron off her and kicked her out the door. Picking up Jamie was far more important than last-minute sweeping up.

Then, just as the last teapot was being wiped dry, Betty Bates came creeping through the front door of the Indigo Tea Shop.

"Oh no," Theodosia murmured when she saw her. She really didn't want to deal with Betty Bates. The woman had proved herself to be . . . impossible.

"Theodosia," Betty said, clearing her throat. "We need to talk."

Those were not the words Theodosia wanted to hear. She shook her head. "I don't think so, Betty."

"Please." Betty held out both hands in a conciliatory gesture. "Extend me this small courtesy."

"I'm sorry, but the tea shop is closed. Perhaps another time."

But Betty was insistent. She crossed her arms and planted herself, unwilling to be ignored. Reluctantly, Theodosia relinquished her broom and sat down at a table with her.

"What's up?"

"I've been investigating bank records," Betty said.

"Okay." Theodosia was determined to remain noncommittal, no matter what Betty said. She didn't need a repeat performance of Betty grabbing her—or anyone else—in a wrestling headlock.

"It looks as if Carson Lanier made a loan that wasn't exactly aboveboard."

"What are you talking about?" Theodosia asked. "What does

'not aboveboard' mean? That Mr. Lanier made a bank loan that wasn't approved? Wasn't secured?" *And why is that my problem?*

"It means the loan wasn't even recorded on our books," Betty said.

Theodosia shook her head. "I'm still not sure what you're talking about."

"Let me ask you this," Betty said. "Have you ever applied for a loan?"

Theodosia shrugged. "Sure. Car loan, home loan, whatever."

"And you had to fill out about a million papers, right?"

"The paperwork was tedious, yes." *Please let this conversation be over with soon.*

"Well, for this particular loan, the one that Mr. Lanier made about a month ago, there weren't any papers at all."

"You mean the loan was completely off-the-books?" Theodosia asked. "As in, here's the money, but don't tell anybody I gave it to you?"

"I'm afraid that's it exactly." Betty had a sick, nervous expression on her face.

Now Theodosia was interested. Now Betty had her attention.

"What was the amount of this loan?" Theodosia asked.

"As far as I can tell, five million dollars are missing."

"What!" Theodosia shook her head. "That's crazy. You're a *bank*, for crying out loud. You're supposed to be a reputable financial institution. Backed by the FDIC. There's supposed to be a paper trail a mile long."

"And we *are* highly reputable," Betty said, assuming a slightly defensive posture. "It's just that this particular transaction seems to be an anomaly."

Theodosia leaned back in her chair. "Why are you telling me this?"

"Because as far as I can see, you're the only one who's been pursuing the Lanier case with any aggressiveness. And if some-one received a loan of five million dollars and then decided they didn't want to pay it back . . . well . . ." Betty paused, her gaze holding Theodosia's.

"Then it would be worth murdering for. To keep the secret."

"That's what I'm thinking at this point," Betty said. "That's my fear."

"Have you told the police about . . . what would you even call this? A secret loan?"

"I haven't told a soul. Not even told Mr. Grimley or the bank auditors."

"Why not?"

"Because I'm not sure what the missing five million dollars means," Betty said. "Perhaps it was an honest mistake on Mr. Lanier's part."

"And you don't want to get him in trouble." *Or besmirch his reputation.*

Betty's head bobbed. "That's right."

"On the other hand, Lanier could have had a terrible lapse of judgment," Theodosia said. "One that might have gotten him fired. Or earned him ten years in Club Fed."

Betty pursed her lips. "Mr. Lanier's poor judgment, well, that is a possibility. But . . ." She fell silent, seemed to ruminate over her words, and said, "But the police are questioning a man named Jud Harker for Lanier's murder."

"Not anymore, they're not," Theodosia said. "They turned Harker loose this morning."

Betty sat forward in her chair. "So they're looking at another suspect?"

"Yes," Theodosia said slowly.

"Is it a man?"

"It's Bob Garver, the fellow *you* pointed a finger at."

"Garver," Betty breathed.

"We think Garver may have attacked one of my employees two nights ago. And then gone after a friend of mine, the woman who owns Haiku Gallery." *Or did you do it, Betty? You were on my suspect list once before. Maybe you should still be on that list. Maybe you were the one having an affair with Lanier. Maybe you've got Sissy's money as well as the bank's money!*

Betty gazed at Theodosia, as if reading her mind. Then she said in a cool, confidential tone, "You thought I was involved with Lanier, but I wasn't."

"You denied your involvement, but never elaborated on who he was having an affair with," Theodosia said.

"Because I never *knew* who it was. But I know what I saw. And I saw Lanier with someone. At the Peninsula Grill and then again at the Coosaw Creek Country Club."

"Wait a minute, are you implying that Lanier might have given this mystery woman the missing five million dollars?"

"I . . . I don't know."

"This is all very confusing," Theodosia said.

Betty stood up from the table. "I know it is. And I'm sorry for bringing this mess to you. But I needed to talk to someone."

Theodosia got up and walked Betty to the door. "Whatever," she said. "Things are already a tangled mess."

Theodosia shut the door, hung the CLOSED sign, and turned the dead bolt. *There, now we're as secure as Fort Knox and the Batcave put together.* She walked back through the tea room and into her office.

Theodosia still wasn't sure what to make of Betty's visit. Maybe Betty was throwing up a smoke screen in her own defense? Or maybe Carson Lanier had stolen the money from the bank and given it to Sissy? But why would he do that?

To shut her up? To pay her off?

Maybe Sissy had threatened Lanier with something. Or maybe Lanier borrowed the money with every good intention of paying it back. But then he'd been murdered and the money had gone . . . where?

On the other hand, maybe Lanier had absconded with the money and had plans to flee to South America. Disappear into the jungle and live on a banana plantation for the rest of his life. Sip piña coladas and work on his tan.

Then another worry spun through Theodosia's mind. Betty would be at the Rare Weapons Show tonight. Yes, of course she would. The board hadn't voted on accepting her as a member yet, so Betty would no doubt be there, politicking her brains out. And maybe causing trouble?

The honk of a horn in the back alley brought Theodosia out of ruminating mode. She stood up, peered out the newly installed window, and smiled.

"Drayton," Theodosia hollered into the tea room, "Come quick! Haley and Jamie just pulled up out back!"

Drayton came pounding into her office, red-faced and slightly breathless. "They're here now?"

"Stopped by to say hi, I guess."

Drayton ripped open the back door and they both stepped out into bright sunlight that was made even brighter by Haley's smile. She was sitting in the driver's seat of her VW Bug with the window rolled down. Jamie was folded, origami style, into the passenger seat.

"Jamie didn't want to leave town without saying good-bye," Haley said.

A split second later, Jamie's door flew open and a pair of wooden crutches poked out. Then Jamie emerged, pulling himself up carefully. When he saw Drayton coming around the front of the car to greet him, he grinned from ear to ear and cried, "Dude!"

Drayton threw his arms around Jamie and pulled him close. "My dear boy," he said. His voice was thick as he surreptitiously wiped away a tear. "I've been so worried about you."

29

~❦~

Champagne corks popped, a string quartet played a sprightly tune by Vivaldi, and men in tuxedos and women in cocktail dresses wandered among the glass cases at the Rare Weapons Show.

Theodosia was on the arm of Detective Pete Riley, who had told her in no uncertain terms that they weren't about to discuss the Carson Lanier case tonight. Or even breathe a word. Or pass a note in class. Tonight he'd issued a strict moratorium.

And Theodosia had readily agreed. She was ready to let it all go and have a gangbusters good time. After all, how often did a girl get to attend a fancy black-tie party, then rush home, throw on a formal gown, and, just like Cinderella, attend a drop-dead fabulous ball at the ultrafancy Commodore Hotel? Yes, tonight was the night this was all going to happen. And Theodosia was prepared to savor every delirious moment.

"This show is fascinating," Riley said as he leaned over one of the weapons cases. "Look at this Colt Dragoon. It's practically a piece of art."

"You're like a kid in a candy store, detective," Theodosia murmured. "With all these fancy weapons on display." Under her gentle urging, Riley had worn a navy blazer and dark slacks. She thought he looked great, even though he was still wearing thick-soled cop shoes.

"The cool thing is they're *nothing* like the regulation .45-caliber Glocks that we carry," Riley said. "I mean, these pieces are drop-dead gorgeous. And historic." He moved swiftly to another case. "Take a look at this French 20-shot pinfire."

"Having fun?" A woman's voice with a hint of merriment. Standing directly behind Theodosia.

Theodosia turned around to find Alexis James grinning at her. She was wearing a short silver dress with a white wool jacket (possibly Chanel?) and silver stilettos, and she held a small clutch purse along with a wide-angle lens.

"I'm having a great time," Theodosia smiled back at her. She touched Alexis's arm. "How about you? Everything good? Same escort as last night?" Theodosia wondered how that was working out. *If* that was working out.

"Bill and I are having a fabulous time together," Alexis said. "Do you know he used to work at the *Herald* in Rock Hill? He actually has a lot of serious journalistic experience."

"Good to know," Theodosia said. She wasn't about to touch Glass's press credentials with a ten-foot pole. Or do anything to dissuade Alexis of his charms. (Which still weren't obvious to her.)

"Honey. Hey, doll." Bill Glass was calling to Alexis, snapping his fingers to get her attention.

"Oops, gotta go," Alexis said. "Bill asked me to help him sweet-talk some of the society types into posing for him. Says it helps sell magazines." Alexis toddled off on her high heels, waving. "See you later, have fun."

"I think I might be having more fun than you are," Theodosia said under her breath. Then she turned to look for Riley and ended up running smack-dab into Drayton and Aunt Libby.

"There you are," Aunt Libby said, leaning forward to kiss Theodosia on both cheeks. She wore a short pink tunic dress and had a rose-colored pashmina draped around her shoulders. "We were wondering if you were here yet."

"Mmn, we got here maybe ten minutes ago," Theodosia said. Then she glanced at Drayton. He was wearing his Brioni tux with a bright red cummerbund and matching bow tie, and smiling ear to ear. No, not just smiling—he was looking positively beatific. "Pray tell, Drayton, why do you suddenly look like the cat who swallowed the canary?" Theodosia asked.

"Theo, I am absolutely dancing on cloud nine," Drayton said. "Capering on tiptoes."

"Tell her," Aunt Libby urged.

"Tell me what?" Theodosia asked. Had something big happened? Did it pertain to the Carson Lanier case, which she was sworn not to mention? But no, it seemed Drayton had other news.

"I just received the most fortuitous call," Drayton said. "From *Southern Interiors Magazine.* They want to photograph some of the rooms in my home for their September issue."

"Drayton!" Theodosia squealed. "That's fabulous news."

"Isn't it?" Aunt Libby said.

"You'll be famous," Theodosia said. Drayton lived in a 175-year-old home that had once been occupied by a well-known Civil War doctor.

Drayton shook his head. "Oh no. My home might enjoy the notoriety, but not I."

"But the editors are surely going to want a shot of you," Theodosia said. "After all, the interior restoration you masterminded is exquisite. The heart pine flooring you refinished, all the searching you did in antique shops to find just the right brass fittings. And remember when you discovered that cache of old cobblestones at a stone yard out by Goose Creek? You picked through that enormous pile, one by one, looking for the perfect salt-and-pepper pavers for your patio."

"Well, perhaps I could pose for a single photo," Drayton said. "Maybe in front of the French marble fireplace?"

"With your pipe and your velvet slippers," Aunt Libby joked.

"And Honey Bee," Drayton said. Honey Bee was his dog, a Cavalier King Charles who was the love of his life.

"Are you glad you came tonight?" Theodosia asked Aunt Libby.

Aunt Libby nodded. "I am. I've already run into several old friends. It's fun to catch up on people's lives."

Drayton surveyed the crowd. "Mmn, lots of antique dealers here as well as donors."

"There's Murrell Chasen from Chasen's," Theodosia said.

"And Tod Graham from Cornerstone Antiques," Drayton added. "But that's to be expected. A lot of the antique weapons here are on loan, so the dealers might want to make offers to the owners."

Two seconds later, Timothy Neville was coming toward them, cutting through the crowd like a well-heeled, bespoke-dressed shark.

"Well, well," Timothy said, greeting Aunt Libby, "I haven't seen you in ages. Welcome to the Heritage Society." He bent forward to kiss her on the cheek and Aunt Libby let him.

"I'm quite enjoying your show," Aunt Libby said.

"It's turned out to be a splendid show," Drayton said, extending a hand to Timothy. "You really pulled it off."

"You've also drawn quite a crowd," Theodosia said. Now that the Great Hall was filled with women in cocktail dresses and men in black tie, the display of weapons seemed a lot less disconcerting.

"And did you take a look at the special cases we built?" Timothy asked. "Like museum-quality shadow boxes. Or glass cases that a fine jewelry store might employ. Cases that slide out to reveal prized wares."

"They're lovely," Theodosia said. She hadn't really given the cases a second glance.

Then Timothy was off to glad-hand more guests as the three of them wandered among the exhibits.

"Where is your date?" Aunt Libby asked Theodosia.

"He's around here somewhere," Theodosia said. Riley had wandered off, mesmerized by all the weapons. Then again, he was a police officer.

"I will get a chance to meet him, won't I?"

"Count on it."

After ten minutes of scoping out the show and exchanging pleasantries with other guests, Drayton suggested they help themselves to some refreshments.

"How refreshing are these refreshments?" Aunt Libby asked.

"I know they've got a champagne bar set up," Drayton said.

"Mmn," Aunt Libby said.

Theodosia grinned. "You're a girl after my own heart."

Turned out the champagne bar also served wine and fruit juices. Along with small cheese plates and crostini. So after grabbing drinks and a plate for sharing, they sat down, the three of them, at a table for four.

"I know he'll be along *sometime*," Theodosia said. She was scanning the crowd, looking for Riley, fretting a bit. But she still didn't see him.

Aunt Libby took a sip of champagne and said, "So, tell me about this crazy investigation you're involved in."

"Wait a minute," Theodosia said. "Who told you I was involved in an investigation?"

Aunt Libby smiled. "Drayton did."

Theodosia nodded at Drayton. "Thank you very much for that."

"Don't be so hard on him," Aunt Libby said. "Drayton only has your best interests at heart. And besides." She looked properly contrite. "I pried."

"Your aunt is a very skilled interrogator," Drayton said.

"Don't I know it," Theodosia said. She glanced around again and saw Betty Bates ghosting by. Betty was talking earnestly to a tall man with silver-gray hair. Politicking, she supposed.

EEEEEYOWWW!

The scream rang out, so loud and plaintive that it made the hairs on the back of Theodosia's neck stand up. Then she rose out of her chair. "What was that?" It had sounded like the death knell of some horrible beast.

YOWWWWWW!

There it was again! Echoing off the walls, seeming to circle around and around as it lifted and then died. But this time it sounded more like a woman's scream, high and piercing, as if she feared for her life.

All around them people stirred, looking this way and that, buzzing excitedly, trying to figure out where the horrible screams were coming from.

Theodosia and Drayton peered over the heads of guests, but saw only a huge scuffle going on. Oh no! Three security guards were attempting to tackle someone!

But who could it be?

30

Anxious to see what was going on, Theodosia and Drayton pushed their way through the curious, muttering crowd.

"Do you see anything?" Theodosia asked. After a few steps in, it felt like she was being carried along on a tide of bodies. Then the man next to her lurched into her so hard she was thrown against Drayton's shoulder.

Drayton helped steady her. "Easy, easy. No, I still can't see a thing."

They pushed their way deeper into the crowd of well-heeled, cosmopolitan Charlestonites who, at this very moment, looked like a mass of wild, shoving fans at a WrestleMania event.

"Oh no," Drayton cried out. He'd been carried almost to the front of the pack. "It's Jud Harker."

Theodosia ducked low and wormed her way through the mash of people, only to see three security guards quickly wrestle Jud Harker to the floor.

"I didn't *do* anything!" Harker screamed as he went down hard. "I was only *looking.*"

Under three sets of experienced hands, Harker was hastily subdued. One of the security guards snapped a harsh warning at him, and then Harker was hauled to his feet like a stuffed turkey, and quickly dragged out of the gallery.

"Make way, make way," one of the security guards shouted. He was tall and burly with brush-cut hair like an ex-linebacker.

"What happened?" Theodosia asked the dark-haired woman standing next to her.

The woman shook her head. "I don't know. Somebody screamed and then security rushed in and grabbed some guy wearing a ratty hoodie." She shrugged, disinterested now. "They hauled him away."

But Theodosia had heard that scream loud and clear. And she was fairly sure it hadn't been Jud Harker warbling his lungs out. But who had it been?

When Theodosia connected with Drayton a few seconds later, she said, "Somebody screamed, but it wasn't Harker. I think it was a woman. In fact, I'm sure of it."

Drayton shook his head. "Maybe Harker frightened someone. Maybe he said or did something strange."

"And then she screamed?" Theodosia said.

"Whoever it was, the poor woman probably doesn't want to admit to it. She probably feels embarrassed at having overreacted."

"I don't know," Theodosia said. Something felt fishy. Like maybe Harker had been set up? Or maybe not. At any rate, he'd been wrestled to the ground and then unceremoniously hauled away. She plucked at Drayton's sleeve. "I feel like we should follow up on this."

They walked out of the Great Hall and looked up and down the hallway. Saw nothing.

"The security team must have already called the police," Drayton said. "And then hauled Harker outside?"

"That fast?" Theodosia said. She held up a hand and stilled Drayton, so they could listen carefully.

A high-pitched voice was babbling excitedly in an office at the far end of the hallway.

"Harker's still here," Theodosia said.

"They must have put him in one of the conference rooms," Drayton said as they tiptoed down the hallway.

They paused and stopped outside a room marked J. CLAYTON MEETING ROOM and listened carefully. Harker was in there, all right, talking a mile a minute, being questioned by the three men from the security detail as well as Detective Pete Riley. Theodosia would recognize Riley's voice anywhere.

"What's Harker saying?" Drayton whispered.

Theodosia squeezed her eyes shut, the better to hear. "He's saying he wasn't the one who screamed. But he's so rattled and scared that most of his words are incoherent."

Then one of the security guys started yelling, and it sounded like Harker began to sniffle.

They listened for another couple of minutes until Detective Riley came speedballing out of the room and practically collided with them.

"What!" Riley said when he saw Theodosia and Drayton. "What are you doing here?"

"What's going on?" Theodosia asked.

Riley just shook his head.

Theodosia held up both hands in surrender. "I know, I know, we're not supposed to be listening in, we're not even supposed to talk about this. But come on, I have to know what's going on. I mean, Harker was knocked to the ground practically right in front of us."

Riley looked sufficiently mollified. "Well, don't hold your breath, but it looks like we might have our man."

"What are you talking about?" Theodosia asked. "Wait, you mean Harker is good for Carson Lanier's murder?"

"Harker's jabbering about all sorts of things," Riley said. "How some woman shoved him and then started yelling. Frankly, I think Harker's the one who did the shoving."

"So what happens now?"

"I just called the boss," Riley said.

"Tidwell," Theodosia said. Yes, he would be involved.

Riley nodded. "Tidwell wants us to transport Harker downtown."

"Thank goodness," Drayton said.

"And interrogate him?" Theodosia asked.

"We'll see," Riley said. "Harker's in kind of bad shape. Confused, babbling like crazy. We might have to do a psych hold on him."

"At least he's off the streets for now," Theodosia said.

"That's right."

Theodosia let loose a shaky breath. For the first time in almost a week she felt that she could rest easy because Jud Harker would be in custody for sure. But was he guilty of killing Lanier?

That single thought gave her pause.

"Come on," Drayton said to Theodosia. "Let's get back to your Aunt Libby. We kind of ran out on her."

"Are you coming?" Theodosia asked Riley.

He nodded. "Give me a couple minutes."

Aunt Libby demanded to hear the full story when they returned to their table. So Drayton and Theodosia laid it all out for her. From Carson Lanier getting shot with the quarrel almost a week ago, to all the suspects they'd been wondering about—Jud Harker, Betty Bates, Bob Garver, even Sissy Lanier.

"But you haven't solved the mystery," Aunt Libby said. She didn't sound accusatory, she sounded interested.

"Maybe it is solved," Theodosia said. "Maybe the killer was Jud Harker."

Aunt Libby shook her head. "No, it isn't him."

"Why would you say that?" Drayton asked.

"It just isn't," Aunt Libby said. "Your man Harker sounds angry and misguided. But that business you mentioned about him accidentally shooting his brother . . . it completely rules him out."

"Interesting," Theodosia said. Aunt Libby's words had given her pause, because Aunt Libby was an awfully smart cookie. "That would mean we're still nowhere."

"You'll figure it out," Aunt Libby said. "You always do." She smiled serenely and took a sip of her champagne, tilted her head back and watched the guests float by.

Theodosia watched, too, finding herself falling into a kind of reverie. Like watching a well-dressed human merry-go-round. "There's Alexis," she said, as Alexis and Bill Glass walked past. Glass was dipping and dodging, snapping photos like crazy while Alexis seemed content to be his assistant.

"Alexis was telling me all about her new Haiku Gallery when we had tea yesterday," Aunt Libby said.

"Did Alexis mention that she obtained a good bit of her merchandise from a fellow that you're probably familiar with?" Theodosia asked. "An antique dealer named Riddle who was in the process of unloading his inventory? I guess he wanted to retire, so he had a huge going-out-of-business sale."

Libby shook her head. "George Riddle didn't close his shop—he was murdered."

Theodosia frowned. "Excuse me?" Had she heard her aunt correctly?

"Oh, it was an awful, brutal thing," Aunt Libby said. "George was shot point-blank with some kind of small-caliber weapon. And they never did catch his killer. The police are still working the case as far as I know. His nephew, David, who inherited the shop, was completely distraught by the crime. Cried his eyes out at the funeral and then afterward at the cemetery by St. Stephen's. In fact, David was so upset about his uncle George's murder that he sold everything in the shop for pennies on the dollar."

Theodosia touched a hand to Aunt Libby's arm. "When did all this happen?"

Aunt Libby thought for a moment. "It hasn't been that long. Perhaps three or four months?"

Theodosia was getting a strange feeling. As if every nerve ending in her body had been pulled tight and was starting to strum. "And they never figured out who did it? Who killed George Riddle?"

Aunt Libby shook her head. "No."

Theodosia's thoughts careened one way and then another, like an out-of-control gyroscope. Alexis had told her one story; Aunt Libby had just given her a completely different version. Which one was correct?

Or maybe, parts of both stories were correct. Sure, that had to be it.

Still, the murder of George Riddle bothered her, gnawed at her.

Theodosia glanced over, saw Alexis throw back her head and laugh, amused by something Bill Glass had just said to her.

And as she watched Alexis, looking so happy and carefree, a couple pieces of the puzzle seemed to nudge grudgingly into place.

Alexis had obviously come into a good deal of money. Enough to buy—or negotiate—a whole lot of Japanese art.

A lot of money. Who was missing a lot of money?

Sissy Lanier was. And Carson Lanier had taken money from his own bank. So maybe . . .

"Excuse me," Theodosia said. She stood up abruptly, walked away from the table, and pulled out her phone. It took her a few minutes to find Sissy's number, but then she had Sissy on the line.

"Sissy," Theodosia said. "Did you ever find out what happened to your Fidelity account?"

"I did," Sissy said. She sounded happy, practically gleeful. "It was a clerical error after all. Everything's just fine even though Fidelity is eating crow like mad."

"That's wonderful," Theodosia said, with very little enthusiasm.

"Theo," Sissy said. "You caught me getting ready. Are you coming to the Fur Ball tonight? I know Delaine said you were going to . . ."

But Theodosia had already hung up. Because another dark thought suddenly rumbled through her head and then burst like cannon fire.

Could Alexis be the mystery woman that Lanier had been dating? Had he taken funds from the bank and given them to her? Had Carson Lanier been that besotted?

And there was another question to be answered.

Had Alexis murdered George Riddle so she could buy his inventory on the cheap?

And along the way, as Haiku Gallery took shape, had Lanier grown suspicious of Alexis? Had he started wondering about her newly purchased inventory and started to ask questions? Too many questions? Had he realized she had no intention of ever paying the money back?

One thought rapidly led to another, like dominos suddenly collapsing in a line.

If Alexis was the mystery woman, then . . . had she murdered her mystery man?

Theodosia glanced around, searching for Alexis. There was no sign of her or Glass. Maybe they had . . .

Theodosia's eyes continued to rove across the crowd, but still didn't see them. She started to feel woozy. Maybe if she went back to the table and talked this out with Drayton.

Theodosia walked back to the refreshment area and blinked. Drayton wasn't sitting at their table anymore. Neither was Aunt Libby.

Theodosia's eyes scoured the entire room, looking for Drayton and Aunt Libby. Feeling a sense of panic, she pushed her way through the crowd, glancing left and then right. Finally, Theodosia caught the top of Drayton's head bobbing in the crowd. But when she drew closer, she saw that Drayton and Aunt Libby were talking to Alexis.

A chill ran down Theodosia's spine.

Oh no.

She had to get Drayton and Aunt Libby away from Alexis, just in case. And she had to find Detective Riley. Immediately.

Theodosia rushed over to Drayton and Aunt Libby, hoping to pull them away. But Drayton—wouldn't you know it?—was smack-dab in the middle of telling his story about *Southern Interiors Magazine* wanting to photograph his home.

"Did you hear the news about Drayton's photo shoot?" Alexis asked as Theodosia joined their group. "Isn't it exciting?"

"It's wonderful," Theodosia said in a voice devoid of emotion. All she could think about was getting Drayton and Aunt Libby to safety.

Alexis rocked back on her heels. "I would think you'd be

more excited than that," she said. She stared at Theodosia, an odd gleam in her eyes.

"I'm sorry, but we have to leave," Theodosia said. She grabbed Aunt Libby by the arm and pulled her close. "We have to go now. Something's come up."

Alexis continued to stare at Theodosia. "Theodosia's a cool one, aren't you?" she said. "Always busy, always on the move."

Theodosia tried to swallow the lump that had lodged in her throat. Maybe she should confront Alexis. On the other hand, maybe she was completely off base about her.

"Alexis," Theodosia said, "when I asked where you obtained your inventory, you gave me a lovely story about a retiring antique dealer."

"George Riddle," Alexis said, nodding.

"But I just learned from Aunt Libby that Riddle didn't retire at all. He was murdered."

Alexis's brows pinched together in a look of concern. "Oh no. And this happened recently?"

"A couple of months ago," Theodosia said.

"Really? I hadn't heard," Alexis said.

Bill Glass was suddenly at Alexis's side. "Gimme that other lens, will you, doll?" Then he caught sight of all the serious faces. "What's wrong? You all look like your best friend just died."

"I'm just trying to clear something up," Theodosia said. "No need for you to get involved."

"Clear what up?" Glass asked. Now he sounded almost belligerent.

"I think Theodosia might have some very misguided ideas about me," Alexis purred.

"Is that so?" Glass put a protective arm around Alexis and glowered at Theodosia. "Then maybe it's best you mind your own business."

"You're right," Theodosia said. This whole encounter was escalating faster than she could control it. Better to just leave and sort things out later.

But Aunt Libby had a puzzled look on her face. "What's wrong?" she asked Theodosia.

"I was just trying to get the story straight," Theodosia said. "But it doesn't matter."

Alexis smirked. "That's right, it doesn't matter because there is no story." She tightened her grip on the lens she held in her hand.

"No," Theodosia said, her temper flaring, her anger suddenly getting the better of her. "I think there is. In fact, why don't we ask Detective Riley to come over and join us. Then you can proclaim your innocence before he arrests you."

"Say, now," Glass said.

Alexis handed the lens to Glass, then slipped her hand into her black evening bag. Slick as melted butter, she pulled out a gun.

"Don't . . ." Theodosia began. But Alexis was already moving quickly, sneaky as a weasel in a henhouse. She wrenched one arm around Aunt Libby's throat, pulled her backward, and put the gun to the side of her head.

"What are you doing?" Bill Glass gasped. They were standing in a tight group, the five of them. Nobody else could see what was happening!

Theodosia was terrified. Time seemed to slow to a sickening crawl as she glanced around, looking for help. Where was Riley? Where were the security guards? Nobody was in sight.

"Just back away slowly," Alexis said through gritted teeth. "Don't anybody make a fuss, just keep your mouths shut."

Theodosia took a step back and found herself flat up against the case that held the muzzleloader pistol. She glanced to her left, saw the determined look on Drayton's face, as if he was about to make a preemptive move and try to wrench the gun away from Alexis.

"You," Alexis said to Drayton. "Whatever you're thinking, don't."

Drayton touched a hand to his bow tie. "Whaaat?" he said, sounding confused and hollow.

"What's going on?" Glass asked again. His mental faculties weren't exactly clicking along. He was way slow to the party.

"Shut up, just shut up!" Alexis told him.

Glass looked stunned, like he'd just been forced to swallow a bug. "Alexis? Sweetheart?"

Theodosia put her hands behind her and took a deep breath. Was the case still unlocked? If it was, then maybe she could . . . what? Grab the gun?

Please, dear Lord, let the case be unlocked.

Carefully, she touched the cool glass of the case and felt around until she hit smooth wood. She pressed on the edge of the case and felt rather than heard a slight ping. Did that mean the hinge had sprung open?

Alexis curled a lip. "I'm going to walk out of here, and I'm taking the old lady with me."

"Please," Drayton reasoned. "Everything's negotiable. I know we can work something out."

Reaching in, Theodosia grabbed a small twist of parchment paper and then swept it sideways, picking up a lead ball and a smidgeon of gunpowder.

"You! Tea lady," Alexis suddenly hissed. "What are you doing there? What do you have in your hand?"

Almost shyly, Theodosia brought her hands around to the front. "Just a tea bag," she said, opening one hand slowly so Alexis could see the small fold of parchment paper with the black powder inside. "Just tea."

"You're such a goody-goody," Alexis sneered. "Always thinking about tea. The modern world could rush right past you and you wouldn't even know it."

"Just let Aunt Libby go," Drayton implored. "Please, no one needs to get hurt." He took a step forward, but Alexis shifted her aim and waggled the gun in his direction.

"Nobody takes another step," Alexis said. "Don't be stupid, don't try to get cute. I'm walking out of here right now. Any one of you makes a wrong move, I shoot. Then I take somebody else hostage." She shrugged. "Up to you. Your call."

"I beg you," Drayton said again.

Theodosia was only half listening as Drayton tried to reason with Alexis. Instead, she was totally focused on snaking her hand back into the display case.

Drayton tried again, making an impassioned appeal to take him as a hostage and not Aunt Libby.

All the while, Theodosia's hand crawled into the display case, slowly, oh so slowly as she tried not to move a muscle or betray her actions with any kind of facial tic. When Theodosia's fingers finally touched the cold metal handle of the pistol, she breathed a tentative sigh of relief and slipped her index finger through the trigger guard. Then she slowly pulled the pistol forward. With both hands still behind her, she worked the powder pellet into the breech of the gun.

Please let this work, please let this work, was the only mantra that spun inside Theodosia's head. Because if her gun misfired . . . or Alexis fired first . . .

Theodosia drew a breath and cocked the trigger. "You killed Carson Lanier," she said to Alexis in an ice-cold voice. "You swindled him out of five million dollars."

"Shut up," Alexis snapped. "What if I did? I've had enough of your eternal snooping." She tightened her grip on Aunt Libby. "Come on, Miss Libby. I'm leaving and you're coming with me."

Aunt Libby threw a terrified glance at Theodosia.

Theodosia met her aunt's eyes with steely conviction.

"Enough talk," Alexis spat out. She jerked Aunt Libby sharply, upsetting her balance and causing her to stumble. Terrified, Aunt Libby grabbed Alexis's arm to keep from falling.

For a split second, the muzzle of Alexis's gun dipped away from Aunt Libby's head.

It was all the time Theodosia needed.

Center of mass was the phrase that streaked like lightning through Theodosia's frantic brain as she snapped her pistol up sure and fast. Find center of mass and aim slightly right. Wound Alexis, disarm her, but don't kill her. And for heaven's sake, don't hit Aunt Libby.

In that same split second, as everything hung in the balance, Theodosia brought her other hand around to grasp the pistol tightly. It was now or never. Time to roll the dice and hope she didn't come up with snake eyes. She had one shot and it had to be perfect. Her aim had to be true and she couldn't dare flinch.

At the very last millisecond, Alexis caught a flash of Theodosia's hands snapping together, gripping the pistol, and taking aim. She barely had time to blink, to think what to do or adjust her own aim . . .

Theodosia squeezed the trigger.

BOOM!

31

~❧~

The noise was deafening, reverberating and throbbing throughout the entire Great Hall. Glass cases rattled, people screamed. Fearing stray bullets or even a terrorist attack, many guests flung themselves down on the floor and covered their heads.

The pistol, which was heavy and clunky to begin with, bucked hard in Theodosia's hands and threw off a galaxy of hot white sparks. Her inner ear registered a concussion of noise that rendered her practically deaf; the right side of her face absorbed a slight blowback of gunpowder, like a fine silk mist. The smell of sulfur burned strong in her nose.

Two seconds later, Theodosia blinked rapidly as she peered through a haze of smoke. Had her shot hit its mark? She wasn't sure.

Alexis was still standing there, staring at her. Her mouth had dropped open, her eyes were steely bright like a pair of silver nickels.

What do I do now? was Theodosia's first, panicked thought.

Then a red spot suddenly bloomed on Alexis's white wool jacket. Like poppies on a dead soldier's grave. The spot grew larger.

Alexis looked down at her jacket. "You . . ." she stammered. The horror of what had just happened slowly registered on her face. "You . . ."

"You shot her," was Drayton's whisper, hot in Theodosia's ear. "Good work."

Then everything happened at once. People screamed, Alexis dropped her gun, Aunt Libby wriggled free.

One second later, Pete Riley was there, talking softly to Theodosia, telling her it was over, trying to pry the pistol out of her frozen hands.

Bill Glass didn't know what to do, so he started taking pictures, his strobe going *boom, boom, boom,* flashing as brilliantly as that first bomb at Trinity Site.

Alexis, still standing, and then slowly crumpling to the floor like the melting witch in *The Wizard of Oz,* finally thought to scream. "Help me, I'm shot! She shot me!"

Theodosia didn't much care. She turned her back on Alexis, grabbed for Aunt Libby, and swept her into her arms. Aunt Libby stared at Theodosia, searching her niece's face, first looking stunned, and then grateful.

"You saved me," Aunt Libby whispered.

"Yes," Theodosia murmured. "Of course." She would have given her life for her. Pressing Aunt Libby's head against her shoulder, she hugged her tight. Her aunt's shoulders felt frail and narrow in her grasp. But she was alive and well.

"You daring girl," Aunt Libby whispered. "So brave, just like your father."

That was the one thing that finally brought hot tears to Theodosia's eyes. Her dad, Aunt Libby's brother, had been dead a dozen years or more, but was always in her heart. Maybe even watching over her.

32

They say it isn't over until the fat lady sings. Or, in this case, a fat detective—Detective Burt Tidwell, to be exact—who showed up to declare the evening over.

Alexis had been taken away in an ambulance some ten minutes earlier, though Bill Glass had opted not to ride along with her. He seemed content to remain at the Heritage Society and annoy everyone by snapping pictures. When an officer asked him to quit it, he wandered around looking sad and discombobulated.

Names of guests were quickly recorded by a bevy of uniformed officers. The police would request formal witness statements at a later date.

Timothy rounded up his board of directors for a hasty meeting. They took a vote and decided to table the election of any new board members for the time being.

And Theodosia—well, Theodosia seemed to be at the center of the swirling maelstrom.

Betty Bates was the first to approach her. She sidled up to

Theodosia and sneered, "Thanks to you I probably won't be elected to the board of directors." She hurled her words at Theodosia as if they were an accusation of treason.

"Say, now," Tidwell said, cutting in to what was essentially a verbal attack. "You get away from her." He made a shooing motion with his hands. "Officer Lowry?" He lowered a furry eyebrow at a uniformed officer who stood directly at his elbow. "Kindly remove this person from our presence."

"You can't do . . ." Betty began to burble a protest. But to no avail. The officer was bigger, stronger, and carried a gun.

"It was Aunt Libby who cracked the case," Theodosia said to Tidwell. "Alexis was never on our radar at all." She shook her head as Tidwell gazed sympathetically at her. "We thought it might be Sissy Lanier . . ."

"No, never her," Tidwell said. "Lady didn't have the guts for killing."

"Or Jud Harker," Theodosia continued.

"Harker's only crime was being a lost soul," Tidwell said, sounding almost philosophical.

"Or Bob Garver," Theodosia said, rounding out her list.

Tidwell snapped an index finger at her. "Now, that fellow is in serious trouble. We're not just talking felony here, we could be looking at multiple counts of fraud and breaking federal statutes." He sounded almost gleeful as he rocked back on his heels and clasped his hands across his belly. "But not murder, though you were certainly on him for it like a foul stench on a skunk." He stopped abruptly, aware that Theodosia might not be appreciating his particular brand of humor. "Miss Browning?" he said. "Are you feeling all right?" Tidwell had gone from rapturous gloating to solicitous concern.

Theodosia shook her head. "Not really. I'm feeling a little shaky."

Tidwell raised a hand and made a twirling motion.

Detective Pete Riley was there in a heartbeat.

"Our Miss Browning is not feeling well," Tidwell said. "Perhaps you could attend to her properly and then see that she is escorted home?"

"Of course," Riley said. He put an arm around Theodosia and led her to one of the tables in the now-deserted bar area. His hands were gentle, as if he were caring for a precious Dresden doll. When they were both seated, Riley reached across the table and took both of Theodosia's hands in his. "Are you okay?"

"No," Theodosia said. Then, "Well, I will be. I think I just need to catch my breath."

"Lots of excitement tonight. Probably too much." Riley looked worried. As if he were about to call another ambulance.

Theodosia met his gaze. "Are you disappointed in me?" she asked. She hoped he wasn't. She hoped he wouldn't go all law enforcement on her and lecture her on taking foolish risks. Or discharging firearms in public. And she really hoped he wasn't going to tell her they were finished. That tonight had been the final straw.

"No!" Riley said. "I'm not disappointed in you at all. I'm actually quite . . . impressed."

"You mean because I had the guts to actually shoot someone?"

"I was thinking more about your aim." Now a faint smile played across Riley's handsome face. "I think I might put you up as a ringer in our next interdepartmental shooting match."

Theodosia offered a smile of her own. "I did get some practice in tonight."

They sat there in companionable silence then, watching everything wind down around them, seeing all the guests ushered out.

"What about this black-tie cat ball?" Riley finally asked her.

Theodosia nodded. "You mean the Hair Ball? Over at the Commodore Hotel?"

"Right," Riley said. "Should I take you home and then get changed into that monkey suit I rented? Do you still want to go?"

Theodosia peered at him carefully. "Do *you* want to go?"

"Not really," Riley said almost sheepishly. "Black tie isn't exactly my style, and that suit wasn't engineered for comfort."

"You know what?" Theodosia said. "I have a better idea." She stood up, walked over to the bar, and grabbed an unopened bottle of champagne. Good French champagne. She came back and set it on the table. "Compliments of Timothy and the Heritage Society."

"I like how you think," Riley said with a grin. "Your house, kick back with a bottle of champagne in front of the fireplace . . . what else do you need?"

Theodosia smiled. "I can probably think of something."

A Winter Night

BY SUNG DYNASTY POET TU HSIAO-SHAN

One winter night
A friend dropped in.
We drank not wine but tea.
The kettle hissed,
The charcoal glowed,
A bright moon shone outside.
The moon itself
Was nothing special—
But, ah, the plum-tree blossom!

Haley's Plum Crazy Plum Crisp

12 plums, pitted and chopped
1 cup sugar, divided
1 cup sifted flour
1½ tsp. baking powder
1 tsp. salt
1 beaten egg
½ cup melted butter

PREHEAT oven to 350 degrees. Grease an 8-inch-by-8-inch baking dish. Spread plums into the baking dish and sprinkle with ¼ cup sugar. In a bowl, mix together ¾ cup sugar, flour, baking powder, and salt. Combine with beaten egg and spoon mixture over plums. Drizzle batter with melted butter. Bake in oven until topping is golden brown, about 40 minutes. Serve with cream, whipped cream, or cinnamon whipped cream. Serves 4 to 6.

Cinnamon Whipped Cream

> 2 cups heavy cream
> ¼ cup sugar
> 1½ tsp. ground cinnamon
> ½ tsp. vanilla extract

BEAT heavy cream on high speed in well-chilled bowl. Slowly add sugar, cinnamon, and vanilla extract. Continue beating until stiff peaks form. Serve on your favorite dessert; store any extra in refrigerator.

Turkey Waldorf Tea Sandwiches

> ½ cup mayonnaise
> 1½ cups diced, cooked turkey
> ½ cup dried cranberries
> ½ cup chopped, toasted pecans
> 1 apple, diced
> ¼ cup chopped onion
> Butter
> 6 slices bread

IN medium bowl, combine all ingredients, adding a small amount of extra mayonnaise if needed. Butter 6 slices of bread. Top 3 of the slices with the turkey mixture, then place the remaining three slices on top. Cut off crusts, slice sandwich diagonally into quarters. Yields 12 small tea sandwiches.

Sinfully Chocolate Tea Bread

¼ cup butter

⅔ cup sugar

1 egg, beaten

2 cups sifted cake flour

1 tsp. baking soda

½ tsp. salt

⅓ cup powdered cocoa, unsweetened

1 cup buttermilk

¾ cup chopped walnuts

CREAM together butter, sugar, and egg. Gently stir in cake flour, baking soda, salt, powdered cocoa, buttermilk, and walnuts. When ingredients are well mixed, pour into a greased loaf pan. Bake at 350 degrees for 1 hour, or until silver knife comes out clean. Yields 1 large loaf.

Baked French Toast

1 stick butter

1 cup brown sugar

12 slices bread

5 eggs

1½ cup milk

Cinnamon

MAKE ahead in the evening: Melt butter and pour into a 9-inch-by-12-inch pan. Mix in brown sugar. Lay bread in pan,

2 slices deep. Beat together eggs and milk. Pour mixture over bread and sprinkle with cinnamon to taste. Cover overnight. In the morning, bake uncovered at 350 degrees for 45 minutes. Serve for breakfast. Yields 4 to 6 servings.

Greek Meatloaf

1 lb. ground turkey
½ cup crumbled feta cheese
1 cup fresh spinach, chopped
1 egg
¼ cup bread crumbs
Garlic powder
Oregano
Salt and pepper

PREHEAT oven to 325 degrees. In large bowl, mix together turkey, feta cheese, chopped spinach, egg, and bread crumbs. Add garlic powder, oregano, and salt and pepper to taste. Place gently in large loaf pan. Bake for approximately 45 minutes. Slice and serve with a salad for dinner. Yields 4 to 6 servings.

Apple-Yogurt Chicken Bake

4 unpeeled tart apples, chopped
1 cup plain yogurt
4 medium chicken breasts
2 oranges

PREHEAT oven to 350 degrees. Spread chopped apples in the bottom of a lightly oiled casserole dish. Pour yogurt over the apples and stir lightly to combine. Place the chicken breasts over the apple-yogurt mixture. Cut unpeeled oranges into thin slices and place atop chicken for flavor and to keep it from drying out. Bake for 1 hour. Remove orange slices before serving. Yields 4 servings.

Old-Fashioned Griddle Scones

2 cups flour
1 tsp. baking soda
½ tsp. cream of tartar
1 Tbsp. sugar
¼ tsp. salt
¼ cup butter, chilled and cut into pieces
1¼ cups buttermilk
1 large egg, beaten

IN a large bowl, combine flour, baking soda, cream of tartar, sugar, and salt. Using a knife or pastry blender, cut in butter until mixture is coarse and crumbly. Add buttermilk and beaten egg and mix lightly until mixture forms a soft dough. (If you need to add a little more buttermilk, that's okay.) Grease a griddle or fry pan and bring to medium heat. Drop heaping tablespoons of dough to create 3 or 4 scones. Using the back of a spoon, press each one gently to flatten. Cook scones until golden brown, then flip to grill the other side. Scones are cooked when they are golden brown on both sides and center is firm to the touch. Remove from heat and cook the rest of the scones.

Serve warm with Devonshire cream or butter and jam. Yields 8 scones.

Drayton's Easy-Peasy Devonshire Cream

    1 pkg. cream cheese (3 oz.)
    1 Tbsp. sugar
    1 pinch salt
    1 cup heavy cream

IN medium bowl, cream together cream cheese, sugar, and salt. Beat in cream until stiff peaks form. Chill until serving. Perfect for topping your fresh-baked scones!

Asparagus and Gruyère Cheese Tart

    1 sheet frozen puff pastry
    2 cups Gruyère cheese, shredded
    1½ lbs. medium-sized asparagus
    1 Tbsp. olive oil
    Salt and pepper

PREHEAT oven to 400 degrees. On a floured work surface, roll the puff pastry into a 16-inch-by-10-inch rectangle. Trim any uneven edges and place pastry on a lightly greased baking sheet. Using a sharp knife, lightly score pastry dough 1 inch in from the edges to form a rectangle. Using a fork, pierce the dough inside the markings at half-inch intervals. Bake dough until golden brown, about 15 minutes. Sprinkle Gruyère cheese on baked pastry shell. Trim the bottoms of the asparagus spears to fit crosswise inside the tart shell. Arrange asparagus in a single layer over the Gruyère, alternating tips and ends. Brush with olive oil, season with salt and pepper. Bake until spears are tender, about 20 to 25 minutes. Serves 4 to 6 as a side dish.

TEA TIME TIPS FROM
Laura Childs

Artist's Tea

Channel the artists of eighteenth-century Paris who'd gather in the afternoon for a leisurely tea. Stack art and photography books in the middle of your table and create a centerpiece using paintbrushes, ferns, and flowers. Color copies of famous artworks make wonderful place mats. Be sure to use your art pottery or a fun array of mix-and-match china. Parmesan-rosemary scones are a lovely first course, followed by shrimp risotto and pear cheesecake bites for dessert. Serve a Ceylon black tea with your meal and a crème brûlée–flavored black tea with your dessert.

Tea Exchange

Have you heard of the famed tea auctions in Amsterdam? Well, this is a simplified mini version. Invite your friends to tea and ask them to bring a tin of their very favorite tea. Then have a good supply of muslin tea sacks or paper tea bags available so guests can exchange their favorite teas with each other. Then sit down for a simple but lovely cream tea. Serve cranberry or chocolate chip scones with clotted cream, a small chicken salad tea sandwich, and peanut butter bars for dessert. And enjoy the aromas from all those fresh-brewed teas!

French Tea

After a stroll through the Louvre or shopping at Galeries Lafayette, a French tea is in order. This can be served casually in front of a fireplace or at an elegant table. Polish all your best silver and put out your fine china—this is the time to let it sparkle. Fresh flowers are a must, as are white candles and sugar crystals in your sugar bowl. Édith Piaf on the sound system will set the mood for your first course of raspberry scones with crème fraîche. Crab salad on brioche is a delicious second course, and madeleines or an opera cake is perfect for dessert. If you can't get to Mariage Frères in Paris for their gourmet tea, simply order from mariagefreres.com.

Tea Totalers Tea

Because caffeinated tea isn't everyone's cup of tea, why not have a Tea Totalers Tea? This is your chance to explore a riot of herbal teas and floral infusions. Think lemon verbena, catnip, chamomile, ginger, chrysanthemum, and even lavender. In keeping with the herbal and floral theme, serve cranberry-orange scones with clotted cream, herbed cream cheese on dark bread, and hazelnut-spice bars. Pretty up your tea table with your best china and a bouquet of flowers and give everyone a packet of seeds as a party favor.

Winter White Tea

When the earth is iced in soothing white, let your tea table reflect this as well. Start with a crisp linen tablecloth and small crystal vases filled with white tea roses. White candles and pure white china are also an elegant addition. Serve cream scones with Devonshire cream, salmon and roasted red pepper tea sandwiches, and mushroom tartlets. For dessert, spice cookies dusted with powdered sugar or white chocolate cake. You'll want to serve a white tea such as a white peony tea, a silver needle tea, or even a Formosan oolong with a slight peach flavor.

Fairy Tea

Let your imagination soar with a magical Fairy Tea theme, always a delight for children as well as adults. Decorate your table with a strip of bright green moss and scatter it with leaves, acorns, and silk butterflies that you source from a craft store. For a floral centerpiece, use snapdragons, daylilies, or other fanciful flowers. Hang white twinkle lights overhead and use as many pink and green dishes as you can round up. Begin your tea with cream scones, strawberry jam, and Devonshire cream. Ham and cheese quiche makes a delicious main course, and red velvet cupcakes are a perfect dessert. If you're inviting children to your Fairy Tea, be sure to serve strawberry juice in teacups and PB and J tea sandwiches. If you have a supply of gossamer wings for your real-life fairies, so much the better. And remember, fairies were a particular favorite of the Victorians!

> *When the first baby laughed for the first time, its laugh broke into a thousand pieces, and they all went skipping about, and that was the beginning of fairies.*
>
> —*JAMES M. BARRIE*

TEA RESOURCES

TEA MAGAZINES AND PUBLICATIONS

TeaTime—A luscious magazine profiling tea and tea lore. Filled with glossy photos and wonderful recipes. (teatimemagazine.com)

Southern Lady—From the publishers of *TeaTime*, with a focus on people and places in the South as well as wonderful teatime recipes. (southernladymagazine.com)

The Tea House Times—Go to theteahousetimes.com for subscription information and dozens of links to tea shops, purveyors of tea, gift shops, and tea events. Visit the Laura Childs guest blog!

Victoria—Articles and pictorials on homes, home design, gardens, and tea. (victoriamag.com)

Texas Tea & Travel—Highlighting Texas and other Southern tea rooms, tea events, and fun travel. (teaintexas.com)

Fresh Cup Magazine—For tea and coffee professionals. (freshcup.com)

Tea & Coffee—Trade journal for the tea and coffee industry. (teaandcoffee.net)

Bruce Richardson—This author has written several definitive books on tea. (elmwoodinn.com /tea-books)

Jane Pettigrew—This author has written thirteen books on the varied aspects of tea and its history and culture. (janepettigrew.com /books)

A Tea Reader—by Katrina Avila Munichiello, an anthology of tea stories and reflections.

AMERICAN TEA PLANTATIONS

Charleston Tea Plantation—The oldest and largest tea plantation in the United States. Order their fine black tea or schedule a visit at bigelowtea.com.

Table Rock Tea Company—This Pickens, South Carolina, plantation is growing premium whole-leaf tea. Target production date is 2018. (tablerocktea.com)

Fairhope Tea Plantation—Tea plantation in Fairhope, Alabama.

The Great Mississippi Tea Company—Up-and-coming Mississippi tea farm about ready to go into production. (greatmsteacompany.com)

Sakuma Brothers Farm—This tea garden just outside Burlington, Washington, has been growing white and green tea for almost twenty years. (sakumamarket.com)

Big Island Tea—Organic artisan tea from Hawaii. (bigislandtea.com)

Mauna Kea Tea—Organic green and oolong tea from Hawaii's Big Island. (maunakeatea.com)

Onomea Tea—Nine-acre tea estate near Hilo, Hawaii. (onotea.com)

TEA WEBSITES AND INTERESTING BLOGS

Teamap.com—Directory of hundreds of tea shops in the United States and Canada.

Afternoontea.co.uk—Guide to tea rooms in the UK.

Cookingwithideas.typepad.com—Recipes and book reviews for the Bibliochef.

Seedrack.com—Order *Camellia sinensis* seeds and grow your own tea!

RTbookreviews.com—Wonderful romance and mystery book review site.

Adelightsomelife.com—Tea, gardening, and cottage crafts.

Jennybakes.com—Fabulous recipes from a real make-it-from-scratch baker.

Cozyupwithkathy.blogspot.com—Cozy mystery reviews.

Southernwritersmagazine.com—Inspiration, writing advice, and author interviews of Southern writers.

Thedailytea.com—Formerly *Tea Magazine*, this online publication is filled with tea news, recipes, inspiration, and tea travel.

Allteapots.com—Teapots from around the world.

Fireflyspirits.com—South Carolina purveyors of sweet tea vodka, raspberry tea vodka, peach tea vodka, and more. Just visiting this website is a trip in itself!

Teasquared.blogspot.com—Fun, well-written blog about tea, tea shops, and tea musings.

Blog.bernideens.com—Bernideen's teatime blog about tea, baking, decorating, and gardening.

Possibili-teas.net—Tea consultants with a terrific monthly newsletter.

Relevanttealeaf.blogspot.com—All about tea.

Stephcupoftea.blogspot.com—Blog on tea, food, and inspiration.

Teawithfriends.blogspot.com—Lovely blog on tea, friendship, and tea accoutrements.

Bellaonline.com/site/tea—Features and forums on tea.

Napkinfoldingguide.com—Photo illustrations of twenty-seven different (and sometimes elaborate) napkin folds.

Worldteaexpo.com—This premier business-to-business trade show features more than three hundred tea suppliers, vendors, and tea innovators.

Fatcatscones.com—Frozen, ready-to-bake scones.

Kingarthurflour.com—One of the best flours for baking. This is what many professional pastry chefs use.

Teagw.com—Visit this website and click on Products to find dreamy tea pillows filled with jasmine, rose, lavender, and green tea.

Californiateahouse.com—Order Machu's Blend, a special herbal tea for dogs that promotes healthy skin, lowers stress, and aids digestion.

Vintageteaworks.com—This company offers six unique wine-flavored tea blends that celebrate wine and respect the tea.

Downtonabbeycooks.com—A *Downton Abbey* blog with news and recipes. You can also order their book *Abbey Cooks.*

Auntannie.com—Crafting site that will teach you how to make your own petal envelopes, pillow boxes, gift bags, etc.

Victorianhousescones.com—Scone, biscuit, and cookie mixes for both retail and wholesale orders. Plus baking and scone making tips.

Englishteastore.com—Buy a jar of English Double Devon Cream here as well as British foods and candies.

Stickyfingersbakeries.com—Scone mixes and English curds.

Teasipperssociety.com—Join this international tea community of tea sippers, growers, and educators. A terrific newsletter!

Teabox.com—Wonderful international webzine about all aspects of tea.

Serendipitea.com—They sell an organic tea named Plum Crazy. Also check out their recipe for Plum Crazy Punch.

PURVEYORS OF FINE TEA

Adagio.com
Harney.com
Stashtea.com
Serendipitea.com
Bingleysteas.com
Marktwendell.com
Globalteamart.com
Republicoftea.com
Teazaanti.com
Bigelowtea.com
Celestialseasonings.com
Goldenmoontea.com
Uptontea.com
Svtea.com (Simpson & Vail)
Gracetea.com

VISITING CHARLESTON

Charleston.com—Travel and hotel guide.

Charlestoncvb.com—The official Charleston convention and visitor bureau.

Charlestontour.wordpress.com—Private tours of homes and gardens, some including lunch or tea.

Charlestonplace.com—Charleston Place Hotel serves an excellent afternoon tea, Thursday through Saturday, 1 to 3 PM.

Culinarytoursofcharleston.com—Sample specialties from Charleston's local eateries, markets, and bakeries.

Poogansporch.com—This restored Victorian house serves traditional lowcountry cuisine. Be sure to ask about Poogan!

Preservationsociety.org—Hosts Charleston's annual Fall Candlelight Tour.

Palmettocarriage.com—Horse-drawn carriage rides.

Charlestonharbortours.com—Boat tours and harbor cruises.

Ghostwalk.net—Stroll into Charleston's haunted history. Ask them about the "original" Theodosia!

Charlestontours.net—Ghost tours plus tours of plantations and historic homes.

Follybeach.com—Official guide to Folly Beach activities, hotels, rentals, restaurants, and events.

KEEP READING FOR A PREVIEW OF
LAURA CHILDS'S NEXT
SCRAPBOOKING MYSTERY . . .

Glitter Bomb

AVAILABLE SOON FROM
BERKLEY PRIME CRIME!

"Lookit!" Ava cried. "There's your butthead of an ex-husband riding up there on the King Neptune float."

Carmela Bertrand stood on tiptoes and turned ice chip-blue eyes toward the enormous, glittering Mardi Gras float that was steamrolling toward them. Sure enough, there he was, grinning from ear to ear as he and two dozen krewe members tossed strands of golden beads into the hands of a screaming, frenzied crowd.

"Shamus," Carmela said, his name dripping from her lips like honeyed poison. Any follow-up comment was completely drowned out as fifty brass horns blared a collective note and lithe dancers twirling flaming candelabras high-stepped their way down Royal Street. It was Tuesday night, a full week before Fat Tuesday, and most of New Orleans was already caught in the manic grip of Mardi Gras. The city was cranked up, ready to rock, and Carmela Bertrand and her BFF Ava Gruiex were smack dab in the center of the maelstrom. Dressed for action in tight jeans, tighter T-shirts, and multiple strands of colored beads looped around their necks, they clutched geaux cups frothing with Abita beer.

"Wouldn't you know it, Shamus is riding the very first float in the Pluvius Parade," Carmela shouted to Ava above the raucous noise of the crowd. She tipped her head and pushed back loose strands of her shaggy blond bob as she took in the spectacle. A dozen marching bands had already tromped past them, along with clanking knights on horseback, a clown contingent, and a flotilla of exotic convertibles that carried smiling, waving, Pluvius krewe royalty wearing gaudy, bedazzled crowns and capes of white faux fur. Enough white faux fur to decorate a Santa's village for decades to come.

"Gotta grab some of those gold beads," Ava said as she grabbed Carmela's arm and pulled her closer to the curb, closer to the action. "Throw me somethin' mister," she shouted out. Ava was tall and stacked, with a saturnine face and masses of dark curly hair. Men either loved Ava or were frightened to death by her. She was vivacious bordering on brash and oozed raw sex appeal.

Carmela would've scoffed at the notion that she was sexy, too. But her appeal was in her quiet, contained, almost mischievous persona. She was smart as a whip, driven to be a successful businesswoman (though her scrapbook shop was small and humble by most standards), and she could hold her own with men. Carmela wasn't adverse to tossing back a bourbon and branch while hashing out politics and smoking an occasional cigar.

"What's the parade theme this year?" Ava asked.

"Spirits of the Sea," Carmela said. "The theme's always supposed to be a deep dark secret until they start rolling, but you know Shamus . . . can't keep a secret."

Shamus, Carmela's ex, was an indolent Southern boy who, when he wasn't out drinking or chasing younger women, worked at his family's Crescent City Bank. Work being a very loose and haphazard description for what Shamus actually accomplished.

"Spirits," Ava said. "I guess that explains why King Neptune is hoisting that ginormous jug of wine."

The float was built to represent an ancient sea going galleon complete with billowing sails, three decks piled one on top of another, and a carved, barely decent mermaid figure on the prow. Pluvius krewe members hung off every railing and crossbeam, tossing beads and waving at the crowd. Fifty-one weeks of the year, these men were business moguls and staid society leaders. Their walk-in closets probably held a pair of Berluti shoes to match every one of their Zegna, Burberry, and Armani suits. Tonight, however, they were all robed in white satin and wore white, expressionless masks.

On the very top deck of the float, a rotund King Neptune figure was firmly ensconced on his golden throne. His gigantic motorized head lolled back and forth, his mouth gaped open, and his eyes fluttered and blazed yellow. Every few seconds, a surge of golden glitter pumped out of his trident and shot high into the dark night sky.

"What's old King Neptune made out of?" Ava asked Carmela. "You're the crafty one, the resident scrapbook lady. Does it look like papier-mâché?"

"I think Jekyl repurposed an old King Arthur figure from three years ago," Carmela said. "Reworked the face, added the trident, and draped that necklace of fish and shells around him." Jekyl Hardy was a well-known float builder and one of Carmela's dearest friends.

"Whatever he did it's impressive," Ava said as the float rolled ever closer to them. "It even looks as if Neptune's tipping that big jug forward to offer us a nice splash of vino." She suddenly pinched Carmela's arm. "Wait, is something wrong? It almost looks like the float is tipping *over.*"

Carmela blinked as the enormous float slowly listed to one side and an obnoxious screeching sound, like steel wheels grinding against hot coals, pierced the air. Krewe members grasped for handholds on their now-unsteady perch as the float began to shimmy and shake.

Had the float blown a tire? Or worse? Carmela decided it had to be worse because the float was suddenly pogoing up and down, jouncing and bouncing its krewe like mad. Then the entire float began to shiver and shudder from stem to stern. Its tall mast with billowing sails trembled violently.

"Dear Lord," Ava said as people all around them began to cry out in alarm.

A mounted police officer tried to make his way toward the malfunctioning float, his horse's hooves clattering harshly against pavement. But the horse, sensing imminent danger, snorted and reared up in protest, wildly pawing the air. The officer leaned forward, tugging the reins, trying to get his horse under control as the float continued to sway side to side, each motion more drastic and violent than the last.

"That float's about to crash and burn," Carmela yelled as the crowd began to back away. She glanced at the front of the float where Shamus and a few other krewe members were hanging on for dear life. And no wonder, the float seemed to have lost all control over its direction. It was headed directly into a throng of onlookers, rolling like some deadly Trojan Horse as it listed badly, a ruptured ocean liner about to sink.

"Get back, get back!" Ava yelped. And the frightened crowd did jump back. Sort of.

But not all the way. Because watching the big float pitch and shiver was strangely and dangerously hypnotic, like watching a train wreck. And how often did you see a big-assed Mardi Gras float completely out of control? Well . . . never.

But the show had just begun.

Just as the prow of the Neptune float hit the curb and bounced hard, a deep and ominous rumbling sounded from deep within, as if some horrible monster was about to make an appearance.

"That thing's going to blow," Carmela shouted as she tried desperately to pull a hypnotized Ava out of harm's way.

The sound built in terrifying waves, rolling across the crowd, almost taking people's breath away as it rattled shop windows and neon bar signs with all the ferocity of an F-6 tornado. When the explosion finally came it was enormous, a deafening blast that was enough to call out the dead.

Carmela literally felt her jaw drop as she stared at the very top of the float. King Neptune's head was spinning violently like a child's top. Then, with a *whomp* that resonated deep within the pit of her stomach, Neptune's head blew off and a shimmering fountain of glitter spewed forth into the velvety dark night sky. It flew up, up, up, until the sky was ablaze with what looked like a million points of light. When the glitter had reached its ultimate trajectory, it began to sift downwards, landing softly on the heads of the crowd.

The float let loose a final gut-wrenching belch and shiver, so violent it catapulted krewe members off their perches. Some somersaulted down harmlessly to lower decks, but a few were tossed off the float only to land—splat—on the pavement!

"Somebody call 911!" Carmela cried out. She knew men were injured and in desperate need of help.

"We just called," a man behind her yelled. "Ambulance is on its way."

"Is Shamus . . . ?" Carmela's eyes searched the float for him. Had he been shaken off, too? She felt her stomach wobble as she gazed at the men lying in the street. *Oh dear Lord, are they hurt badly? Please don't let anyone be dead,* she prayed.

But wait. Men were slowly picking themselves up. They were groaning, but they were alive. Thank goodness.

Then a pile of white satin stirred and Carmela recognized Shamus. Without thinking, she rushed over and threw her arms around him.

"Are you all right?" Carmela cried. Ava was right there next to her, helping pull Shamus to his feet.

"Whuh hoppen?" Shamus stammered. He had a wonky look on his face and his eyes didn't quite focus.

"Your float crashed," Ava told him.

"No," Shamus said in a loud pronouncement, as if he'd just been told the earth was flat. Then, "It crashed, really?" His left eye wandered to the far left, hesitated, then seemed to pop back.

"Are you okay?" Carmela asked. "Anything broken?"

"You don't look so good, buddy," Ava said. "Your eyes have gone all googly."

Shamus took one step on wobbly legs and said, "I don't feel so good."

"Well, don't toss your cookies on me," Carmela said. She glanced around, deciding they'd all been incredibly lucky. Yes, the float was ruined, but it could have been so much worse. Nobody in the crowd seemed to be hurt . . .

Then she saw one man, still crumpled on the ground, who hadn't moved an inch. "Oh no," Carmela said, her voice catching in her throat. "We need to . . ."

Shamus limped over to the man who was still lying on the pavement, looking like a fallen ghost in his bunched-up white robes, his body twisted in a most unnatural way. "Hey," he said, kneeling down, putting a hand on the man's shoulder. "Hey guy."

"Maybe you shouldn't try to move him," Carmela said. Now she and Ava had gathered around the fallen man as well. "Maybe we should wait for the EMT's. Let them bring in a back board or something."

"The least we could do is wipe that gold glitter off the back of his head," Ava said, trying to be helpful.

Carmela bent closer and stared at the man as the screams of multiple sirens rose above the din of the crowd. Something didn't look right to her. And as Shamus gently brushed glitter from the man, his features slowly came into focus.

"That's not the back of his head," Carmela cried. "The glitter's all over his face! Quick, we have to clear an airway before he smothers."

"I'm on it," Shamus said.

With gold glitter still clinging to every square inch of the man's face, Carmela thought he looked as if he were wearing a solid gold mask, like some kind of ancient Persian king.

"Is he breathing?" Carmela asked Shamus as he scrubbed feverishly.

Ava shook her mane of dark hair, prompting another miniature waterfall of glitter. "Not if he inhaled a nose-full of this stuff," she drawled.